# Oshun
## PUBLISHING

**Oshun**
PUBLISHING

Oshun Publishing Company, Inc.
7715 Crittenden Street
Box 377
Philadelphia, PA 19118

Printed in the United States of America

First Edition: January 2009

10  9  8  7  6  5  4  3  2  1

ISBN-13: 978-0-9676028-6-8
ISBN-10: 0-9676028-6-6

Cover design by Candacek – www.candann.com
Cover photography design by La Pizzazz Productions - www.lapizzazz.com
Cover photo by Muata Mobely
Cover models, Rhadia Ramseur, Ronald Chavous, Jazmine

# IF LOVING TWO

# IS WRONG...

## KIM BEVERLY

# DEDICATION

*This book is dedicated to the memories of my sister,* **Kelly Beverly** *and both sets of grandparents,* **The Beverly's** and the **Flemings:**

Your influences are what inspire me to keep pursuing my dreams and thoughts of all of you serve as my motivation!

# ACKNOWLEDGEMENTS

I must first give all praises and honor to GOD for bestowing the gift to write upon me, a wretched and lowly servant

Secondly, praise goes to Jesus Christ, my personal saviour, who without HIM, I would be lost!

Now, to everyone else:

I must thank my parents, Jerry and Charlene Beverly! You have been so supportive of me throughout my pursuit of my dreams. Thank you for your encouragement and allowing me to do me even when it didn't jive with your dreams! I love you dearly, Mom and Dad!

To my sisters: Stacie and Sharleen, (hey, I didn't call you Buttons, smile) Unbeknownst to you, you two serve as inspiration and motivation for me also! I'm determined to be the big sister that you can count on and that you deserve. Love you two...Yeah, I said it!

To Frankie: Mere words cannot express the feelings of love I have for you or the inspiration that you've been, not only to me, but anyone who's heard you sing or had the pleasure of your company. I admire the man you are and aspire to have at least one third of the impact that you have on folks! Simply, A-MAZE-ING!

To my nieces: Kelhi and Madison, Aunt Kim loves you both dearly and will always try to keep a positive foundation for you in this crazy, mixed up world!

To 4gurlzproductionz: Pam, Robin and Willa: Thank you all for helping my dream come to fruition and taking each step with me along the way. I see big things in our future!

To Karen E. Quinones Miller: What can I say Karen? We went from "no, I won't read your manuscript, (Tee Hee) to this! I must say, you have provided invaluable guidance, support and even more importantly, friendship! You a true example of paying it forward!

To my entire extended family: You know who you are, you're just too numerous to mention. Think back to Dorney Park when you had to buy tickets to ride. Those were simple, happy and loving times. I wish those sentiments for you now! Stay strong, dare to continue to pursue your dreams and encourage the younger generation to do the same!

To my many friends: Now, you *know* I'm not gonna play the name game! I'm sure somewhere from around the way, to elementary, to Girl's High, Florida A&M, Penn State and my numerous jobs and exploits; you've provided some fodder for my creativity. If not in this book, don't worry, it's coming!

Lastly, but definitely not least, to you, the reader: I want to thank you, sincerely, for choosing my book out of all the other capable authors vying for your attention. I can only hope that this is the beginning of a beautiful relationship between you and me!

To anyone that I've missed: It is *definitely* an omission of the mind, not the heart!

# If Loving Two is Wrong . . .

## Chapter One

The rain was really coming down outside my bathroom window as I watched with nervous anticipation for the cab to pull up. I told Mark I would pick him up from the airport when he called, making the surprising announcement that he was here in town. "Hi stranger," the distantly familiar voice had come over the line, barely recognizable with all of the background noise.

"Who is this?" I had huffed, slightly annoyed by the bad connection in conjunction with the balancing act I was trying to perform. I was attempting to hold the phone between my shoulder and ear while blowing on my freshly painted fingernails.

"Guess," the muffled voice replied. I had never been one for phone games, add the possibility of smudging my golden honey nail polish, which was already in short supply, and it was on. I quickly informed the caller that I was about to hang up.

"Hold on Sunshine, when'd you get so short on patience?" the voice laughed.

"Mark?" I shrieked, excited yet shocked to hear from this blast from the past. It had to be Mark. No one else called me Sunshine, the nickname he gave me because he said I had such a radiant smile, but secretly; I knew it was because I was so light complected. The kids used to pretend they were shielding their eyes whenever I came around. With that simple nickname, Mark made all their teasing a little easier to bear. I loved Mark.

"Sunshine, are you still there?" he asked nervously, fearing we had lost our connection.

"Yes, Mark I'm here," I stammered. "When?... Why?... Where?..." I didn't know what to say.

"Let's see," he chuckled. "When? I just got here. Why? I'm on business. And lastly, where? I'm at the airport.

1

**Kim Beverly**

I thought about you the whole trip. I wanted to surprise you, that's why I didn't call ahead of time. But when I got here, I was hoping it didn't backfire on me. I'm glad your number was listed and I am so glad you're home. Is it okay if I come by to see you?"

"Of course it is, I'll come and get you. What terminal are you at?" I asked, squinting as I tried to picture the airport layout in my mind.

"It's too messy outside, I'll just catch a cab. What's the address?" he asked.

You wouldn't have to ask if you had kept in touch.

"It's no problem," I said, with forced gaiety. "I only live about a half hour away."

"No, he insisted. "I'll take the cab, besides, it'll give me some time to think about everything I want to ask you." Suddenly the cab ride sounded like a good idea. I could use the time to think about just what I could and couldn't tell Mark. In all the excitement, I had forgotten about reality.

"Okay, Mark," I relented and gave him the address. "Just tell that cab driver he better be careful because he's carrying precious cargo."

"That's my Sunshine," he said. "I can't wait to see you, be there soon."

At the sound of the click, my mind went into overdrive. How did I feel about him coming here, how did I feel about him, why was he coming straight from the airport to see me? See me? Oh my gosh, look at me. I'd better get myself together, I thought. I didn't want him to walk into and back out of my life on the same day. Or did I? Things could become quite complicated.

No sooner than I hung up with Mark, the phone rang again. I thought he was calling back.

"Did you forget the address?" I asked, saucily.

"What?" a familiar voice answered.

Damn, I need caller ID.

"Sorry, I thought you were someone else," I said, nervously.

"Obviously," came the taut reply. "And just who might that be?"

2

# If Loving Two is Wrong . . .

"An old friend of mine just got into town and they're coming by to see me," I hedged.

"Do I know this friend?" Irritation was seeping into their tone.

"No, you've never met them," I answered coyly.

"What's with all the pronouns, Kayla? Does this friend have a name and a gender?"

I really didn't need this right now. Mark would be arriving in a few minutes and I was sitting there looking like a plucked chicken, engaged in a game of verbal combat.

"Well..." the caller continued, sounding more agitated by the minute.

"I'm sorry, I forgot the question," I stalled for time.

"Oh, so you want to play games, huh? I'm coming over. I'll just have to check out this friend for myself." And with that, the line just went dead. I started to have a panic attack, but realized I didn't have enough time. I ran upstairs, took a shower and quickly styled my closely cropped, jet-black hair. It seemed as if it was taking me forever to get ready because I kept pausing, thinking I heard someone at the door, only to realize it was my heart pounding. I was filled with anxiety at the thought of Mark coming over and the scene that could develop.

Why did Chloe have to call now? And I knew the threat of her coming over was very real. Just as I was putting on my charcoal-black eyeliner, I heard a car pull up from outside my bathroom window. I looked at the clock radio on my bathroom counter; it was eleven a.m., exactly thirty-five minutes since she had called. I held my breath as I peeked through the curtain. Only then did I let out a sigh of relief as I watched Mark hand the cab driver a few bills and wave off the change. It was hard to discern his features since it was overcast outside and the rain was still pouring down in buckets. But there it was, that walk. Mark had a way of walking that made you lick your lips in anticipation. He had a swagger that I likened to Denzel. If nothing else turned me on about Denzel Washington, that walk did. And I was convinced he got it from Mark. I mean his stride was so confident, with a slight dip to it. Not thuggish, but smooth. As I headed down the steps, I heard the bell. I gave myself one last look in the body length mirror by the door; decided I was presentable, cute even, and reached for the knob. With one last sigh, I quickly jerked the door open. Standing in front of me was a black Adonis, the handsomest man I'd ever seen in my life. All of a sudden he was MY MARK! Secretly and silently I did my Fred Sanford imitation. I was having THE BIG ONE!! Only it wasn't just my heart that was filled with throbbing pressure. I must have stared for a while because Mark was looking at me strangely, as if waiting for me to answer a question he'd just asked.

"I'm sorry, Mark, did you say something?" I asked, shaking off the cobwebs.

"I was just asking if you'd mind me coming in out of the rain," he replied, smiling.

"Get in here," I laughed, pulling him not only into my house, but also into my arms. I couldn't believe the sudden rush I was getting from seeing Mark again.

# If Loving Two is Wrong . . .

## Chapter Two

Mark Fountaine used to live on my block. He was five years older than me and I'd had a crush on him since I was in the fourth grade. He was my brother Tony's best friend, but he never treated me like an annoying little sister my brother did. He always took time to ask me if I was okay, how things were at school and most importantly; he often supplied the funds when the ice cream man came around. To me, Mark was an all-around good guy. I vowed that someday I would marry him.

I don't know how I managed to get through grade school watching Mark flirt with the girls in the neighborhood, not to mention the occasional stray that would come from other neighborhoods and knock on his door. I often would tell Mark that he didn't have to waste his time and good looks on those girls, because what he needed was right here, and I would point to myself. And the great thing about Mark was, he wouldn't laugh at me like all the other older kids, including my lame-ass brother. He would just smile and say, "When you get a little older, Sunshine, but by then, you probably won't want anything to do with me. All the guys will be fighting for your attention and you won't give me a second thought." Deep inside I knew Mark was wrong; I would always want him. But I never got a chance to tell him because Tony would always mug me in the face and tell me to go play with the rest of the kids. But somehow jacks and tag or even doing cheers, which I loved, and would shake my butt extra hard when Mark was watching, didn't seem as exciting if he wasn't around. And so, this little childhood admiration continued until I was a teenager. Then it became teenage admiration. As my thirteenth birthday approached I was filled with excitement, thinking: 'I'm catching up to Mark. Now we both had the word teen in our ages, I know he'll think of me differently now.'

Finally August 13th arrived – my birthday, and I just knew this was going to be a turning point in my life.

I could smell a cake baking, and I knew my mother was making my favorite, chocolate cake with butter crème frosting. I had already peeked in my parent's closet and saw at least six wrapped packages with bows and all. If they knew what I knew, they could've saved their money and time on the wrapping; it just meant it would take longer to get to the nitty-gritty. And Mom always used a lot of tape, so that just when you thought you were through, there was always five or six more pieces of invisible tape somewhere.

For a while, I just laid in bed thinking about all the things being thirteen meant. I could stay up until ten o'clock on a school night instead of nine. It would be my last year of junior high, and most importantly, Mom said we could go shopping for my first bra when I turned thirteen. She said something about a training bra and burst out laughing when I asked her why would my breast need training and exactly how would a bra go about doing it. Oh, I almost forgot, the bra wasn't the most important thing. What was I thinking? The very most important thing was; I would finally be old enough for Mark, or at least I thought.

I dressed so carefully that day, knowing that although it was my day, I wanted to look special for Mark. I had put on a pair of suede jeans that I had convinced my grandfather I absolutely had to have or I would die. Grandpop was so easy. Once he even let me back the car out of the driveway because I said all of the other kids' Grandpops' let them. And when I backed over the two big tin trash cans, smashing them with a loud crunch, and then over Grandmom's fresh flowerbed; he didn't even yell. But Grandmom sure did. She even asked him if he had lost his everlasting mind. Grandpop just waved her off and smiled. I saw that as a good sign. And when I told him that I was glad he had an everlasting mind because a lot of my friends' grandparents had that old-timers disease or whatever you call it, and their minds were gone, he laughed so loud I thought the police would come for sure. Then he took me to get some ice cream, after we went to Home Depot and got two more big tin trashcans, then to Axelrod & Bennett on Chelten Avenue for flowers for Grandmom.

I had matched the black suede jeans, which my mother had never let me wear because she said they were too grown for a twelve-year-old, with my favorite green silk shirt. My green suede Bass shoes topped off the outfit like nobody's business. I found it hard to leave the mirror, until I looked at my head. My hair was a big mass of confusion that spanned out like a peacock's feathers. I had begged my mother to let me cut it a few times, but she always said no. I decided I wasn't even going to try to tangle with that mess.

Although I hated to think about it, I had to do it. Tears welled up in my eyes at the thought of it, but I knew my debut into womanhood and to Mark depended on it. So I balled up my fists, clenched my teeth and headed down the hallway. When I got to the stairs, I descended them slowly, as if in a death march. I almost turned back twice. As I reached the bottom, the aroma of fresh brewed coffee bombarded my nostrils; I could see my mother in the kitchen pouring herself a cup. She was wearing the once bright red robe, now dingy and faded, that I had bought her for Christmas two years ago. She said it was still her favorite. I tried to find my voice to ask my mom the dreaded question that was bubbling just beneath the surface, but nothing came out. I cleared my throat and just blurted it out.

"Mom, will you hot comb my hair?"

There, I had done it; the words just floated out and reverberated around the kitchen. It was too late to grab them back.

"Is that my birthday girl?" my mother asked without turning around. "Sure I will ba..." she stopped mid-sentence as she faced me. "Girl, if you don't get upstairs and take those hot clothes off... Here it is ninety degrees outside and you're dressing like it's the middle of January."

"But Ma," I started.

"But Ma, nothing" she interrupted. "Go on upstairs and look on my bed, I got a little outfit for you the other day. And there's no need for you to look nowhere else. Everything you need is on the bed. I mean it Kayla, I know how nosy you are," she said, pointing her finger at me.

In spite of myself, I had to laugh. Mom looked a sight in her slightly askew robe; hands on her hips and seven or eight strategically placed rollers in her chemically altered blonde hair. The color was a result of an experiment gone wrong. Mom had decided not to give her hard-earned money to her lifelong hairdresser for something she could do just as well herself. The result was hair the color of corn silk. It was a startling contrast to her milk chocolate skin. Although she would never admit to messing up, everybody knew that she was just waiting for the day that her hairdresser said it was safe to dye again, professionally.

I was beginning to sweat a little, so I didn't protest too much about changing. But I really did want to wear that outfit.

"Now come here and give me a hug, birthday girl," my mother said in a loving tone. I folded myself into her arms and squeezed, hoping she could feel how much I loved her. As she hugged me back, she lifted one hand to my head.

"Girl, look at this mop," she laughed. Then she went to fish the hot comb out of the utility drawer in the kitchen that held all the odds and ends. I couldn't find any humor in the situation. Whenever Mama hot combed and curled my hair; I swore I suffered form third degree burns all over my head. Each time I yelled, "Ouch," Mama would say, 'It must be from the heat'. But I know she knew good and well that she was touching my scalp with those hot things!

For my birthday dinner Mama made fried chicken, mashed potatoes and gravy, greens and biscuits. All my favorite things were there, except for Mark. My aunts, uncles, and cousins had come over throughout the day to wish me happy birthday and bring presents. Each time the doorbell rung, I would pose prettily in front of the door, hoping Mark was on the other side. Considering I had four aunts, three uncles, and well over twenty cousins, I did quite a lot of posing. By dinnertime, I was finding it very hard to hide my disappointment. When it was time for me to open my presents and I was neatly peeling off all of the tape and folding the wrapping paper before opening each gift, my mother had had enough.

"Kayla, what is your problem? You've been moping around here all day and by the time you finish opening those gifts, it'll be Christmas and we won't have to get you anything else."

"Yeah, Princess," my dad added, "You usually tear through presents like a tornado."

I could always count on dad to jump on Mom's bandwagon.

"Oh she's just mad because her boyfriend, Mark, didn't show up," Tony chimed in.

"What?" mama screeched, "Boyfriend?"

"Isn't Mark your age?" Daddy asked Tony, once again riding on that bandwagon.

"Aw come on, Mark's not thinking about Kay," Tony said, not believing Mom and Dad were even considering the possibility of Mark wanting to date me.

"She's been following him around like a love sick puppy dog for years. He just never wanted to hurt her feelings because she's just a kid."

This was all too much for me. I had just gotten my first period two weeks ago, amidst much fanfare from my mother and grandmother, which to my everlasting shame, led to "the talk". Secondly, it was my birthday and Mark wasn't here. And now, Tony and my parents were discussing my love life in front of everyone. I had to escape.

"Shut up, Tony," I shrieked. "I'm not a kid, I'm a woman now!" And with that, I raced up the stairs, went straight to my room and commenced to cry.

## Chapter Three

And that was the story I recounted to Mark, as he looked at me with amusement dancing in his sexy, dark brown eyes. Although we had discussed all of this before, each revisit was like a freshly dealt blow.

"You really shouldn't be smiling, Mark, that was a very traumatic experience for me," I admonished. But I found it hard to even pretend to be mad at him. He smelled so good, wearing polo cologne. It had always been his signature fragrance. Whenever anyone wore that scent, I always thought of Mark, who was now watching me with a childlike grin. I loved the way his eyes crinkled around the edges and the dimples in each cheek made deep indentations when he smiled.

"I'm sorry, baby," he chuckled. "I just felt like I was transported back in time as you were telling me those things. It just felt so good I couldn't help but smile. You were so cute back then, following me all around and looking at me with those pretty, big, brown eyes. I didn't have the heart to tell you then that you were way too young for me."

"That's alright, you didn't have to," I said, rolling my eyes. "Tony, let me know every opportunity he got. But," I said with an exaggerated pause, "do you have the heart to tell me that now?"

With that, I gave him one of my best seductive looks, at least I'd hoped it was seductive, turned on my heels and proceeded to the kitchen to get some glasses. I wanted that thought to simmer in his mind for a little while. And it didn't hurt that I gave him a full back view as I exited because, Baby got back.

"Would you like something..."I paused for dramatic effect, "...to drink?" I finished smoothly, over my shoulder.

"Do you have any wine?" he asked.

# If Loving Two is Wrong . . .

"Zinfandel," I hollered back, "will that do?" I asked, saucily.

"For now," he answered.

Now, I was the one left wondering if his reply had a double meaning; but I decided to stop this verbal spy mission. I didn't want too much to be revealed, at least not yet. I had too many variables to consider before soliciting romantic intentions from Mark.

"So," I said, switching gears, "Uncle Sam was more appealing to you than a thirteen year-old's birthday party, huh?"

"Actually," Mark said, his face growing serious, "When Tony told me what happened; I was quite upset. You know I would've never done anything to hurt your feelings intentionally. I had actually left for basic training the night before your birthday. My recruiter called and said I needed to leave that night instead of the day after your party. When I called to say my good-byes, you were sleep. I emphatically told Tony to tell you I said goodbye and that I was very sorry that I had to miss your party."

"Well," I said, suddenly feeling the pains of that thirteen year-old little girl fifteen years ago; "that child psychological killer didn't tell me any of that. He said you told him you didn't have time for no kiddy party and you had more important things to worry about, like fighting for our country." With each word, I rocked my head back and forth with fake attitude.

"Girl, your brother always did have a way of irritating you," he grinned. "He loved to tease you. I used to tell him it wasn't good to constantly make fun of your emotions. But you know Tony. He'd just say, 'Aw, she'll be alright.' But he really does love you. He'd brag about you all the time. When you were a cheerleader for the Rec Center football team, we would sneak around and watch you. Tony would always say, 'Look at her with her fresh behind. But she's the best one, ain't she, Mark?' When you won MVP for the girls' basketball team, he bragged all week. When you went on your prom, he wanted to follow you and your date all night, just in case he had to break up the guy for making any moves on you."

I knew I was watching Mark with wide-eyed and open-mouthed wonder. This was actually the first time I had ever heard that Tony had thought of me as anything but a brat back then. I mean, I had always wanted his approval, but never seemed to get it. As I got further into my teens we grew closer. I wondered if my good-looking girlfriends had anything to do with it. It was safe to say that we developed a pretty good relationship since then. We could talk about almost anything. Looking back, maybe that was the problem. Tony just didn't know how to relate to a little sister, other than trying to boss her around.

"How is Tony anyway?" Mark asked, interrupting my train of thought. "It feels like I haven't talked to him in years. It's a shame too. We were so close," he reminisced.

"Oh, he's doing great. He's been an investment banker at Capital General for the last few years. He loves taking chances with other people's money."

"Yeah, tell me about it. All the crap games he promised he couldn't lose, but somehow did. With my money, might I add? But it's refreshing to know he's settled into something. He didn't know what he wanted to do after high school."

"Well, actually, there was never a question about after high school. Mom and Dad were emphatic about college for both of us. Tony bounced around a little after he graduated, but I think he's found a home at Capital General."

"I see he has the job front covered. What about the romance department? Is he still a Casanova?" Mark asked, chuckling. I found myself enchanted by his boyish grin and pearly white teeth, but I was determined to exercise control.

"You know a leopard can't change his spots. But he does seem to be serious about this girl named Keilani. She seems real nice," I said, trying to appear cavalier about this whole exchange with Mark.

"Will wonders never cease?" Mark joked, apparently ignoring my attitude. "Well, what about you?" he continued, catching me off-guard.

"What about me?" I stalled.

"Are you seeing someone?" he asked with furrowed brows. My mind was scrambling for the right words.

"I'm sort of in a transitional phase right now," was all I could manage.

"What does that mean?" he pushed.

This is on the verge of harassment. Only because I wasn't prepared to answer his questions.

"Well..." Mark said, waiting for an answer.

(Ding Dong)

"Saved by the bell," I laughed, appearing more confident than I felt.

"The question will still be waiting for you when your company leaves," Mark assured me.

I reached for the doorknob and held my breath, expecting the worst. I was prepared to beg Chloe not to make a scene. But relief washed all over my body as I was met by one of the most beautiful sights imaginable at that particular moment.

"Tony!" I screeched. "I'm so glad to see you."

My brother just stood there with his nose wrinkled up and looked at me as if I was growing another head right in front of his face.

"Who are you and what have you done with my sister?" he asked as he stepped in from the rain. Before I could speak, he saw Mark, and almost knocked me down in his rush to hug him.

"Hey, man, how have you been? What are you doing here? When did you get in?" Tony asked, not waiting for any answers. Then he turned to me.

"Why didn't you tell me Mark was coming?" he asked accusingly. "Oh, I see," he continued as if he was suddenly on to something. "You wanted to keep him to yourself. You never did get over that childhood crush, huh?"

I felt the curse words rising to the surface. Mark must

have sensed it because he rushed to Tony's rescue.

"Hey, man, why don't you fill me in on what's been happening with you?" Mark said as he wrapped his arms around Tony's shoulders. Then Tony led Mark into the dining room, where I kept a fully stocked bar.

"Remember Stacie Allen?" I could hear Tony saying as they reached the dining room.

"Yeah she was a real looker," Mark answered.

And so the reminiscing had begun. I was about to join them when I noticed headlights in the driveway. I watched her park and couldn't help but think that her BMW fit her image perfectly: black, sleek, well built, and upwardly mobile. Chloe Lane was definitely a person who knew what she wanted and had no qualms about going after it; and that included people.

## Chapter Four

As I watched Chloe park and then exit her vehicle, umbrella in hand; I couldn't help but remember the sense of foreboding I had when I woke up that morning, but had dismissed as being silly. I realized I was right on point as I watched Chloe ascend the driveway, amidst the driving rain, with a look of sheer determination on her face. I felt as if my stomach was tied in knots and I could hear my heart pounding in my ears as Chloe reached the door. I tried to hurry and open it before she rang the bell. I didn't want to attract Tony and Mark's attention before I had a chance to talk with her. But I was too late, the bell's chimes brought Tony and Mark's loud talking to a halt. Chloe's face was a mask of irate confusion when I opened the door to let her in. She obviously thought I was up to something sneaky. As she stepped past me, into the house; I could feel a slight chill coming from her. I closed the door and turned to face her. Newsy and newsier had heard the bell and raced to the living room to see who it was.

"Chloe," Tony boomed, as he grabbed her in a bear hug and began kissing her all over her face, an act he'd been doing for months and knew how much she hated it. It was a mock hate because she almost always burst out in laughter, but not this time. Chloe simply shrugged Tony off with a sharp, "Will you stop it," clearly annoyed. Always the optimist, Tony brushed off Chloe's mood with a smile.

"Wow, what's got your panties in a bunch, sis?" Calling her "sis" was another habit he'd adopted months ago.

"And what in the world," he continued, "conspired to bring us all over here to see Kayla on such a gruesome day? Hey, maybe that's the coincidence, we saw it was a gruesome day and we immediately thought about Kayla."

There was a brief pause as he scanned our faces with a look indicating he expected us to finish his thought. "Because," another slight pause, "Kayla's gruesome." Tony began laughing as if he had just told the best joke in the world. It was obviously a male thing because it wasn't long before Mark was snickering, too. Frowning, I looked at Chloe to see her reaction and she was as stone-faced as when she first arrived. Yeah, it was definitely a man thing. Chloe and I could only watch as the two imbeciles erupted into one fit of laughter after another, over something so incredibly unfunny. It became apparent to me that it was beyond what Tony had just said. They were sharing something private. Coming down from his laugh high, Mark caught a glimpse of my face.

"I'm sorry, Kayla," Mark managed to get out between snorts, "But you just don't understand." Holding his stomach as if in pain, Tony struggled to regain his composure and hush Mark at the same time.

"Mark, come on brother, you can't spill the beans. That was costa nostros," Tony said in his best Italian accent, which was really bad.

"Aw, Tony, I have to tell her, she's beginning to look pissed and I may want to marry her one day, " he said half jokingly. At that point, I snuck, a peek at Chloe, who appeared to be seething. I had yet to introduce her and I don't think her entrance went as planned, whatever it was. But truthfully, I wasn't in a rush to find out.

"Kayla," Mark interrupted my private thought, "remember your girlfriend, Ruthie?"

Ruthie was my best friend from kindergarten through high school. We lost contact once we went to different colleges.

"Yes," I said in response to Mark's question. "But what does Ruthie have to do with y'all's little laugh fest?"

"Well," Mark began, fighting off another fit of laughter. "I always thought you were an adorable young lady, even when you went through that nappy-haired, braces and acne stage." Tony couldn't help it; he erupted again. That same mental picture that cracked them up, made me

16

cringe. That was definitely a rough period in my life.

"But on the other hand," Mark continued, "Your friend, Ruthie, was a gawky, clumsy, little girl with buck teeth. Tony always referred to you two as the gruesome twosome."

So that was their dumb punch line. Although I didn't think it was funny, personally; I could see how two silly guys like Mark and Tony could laugh for hours on such a memory.

Abruptly, Mark turned his attention to Chloe, as if noticing for the first time that she was even in the room.

"I'm sorry for my rudeness," he apologized. "But I haven't seen these two in almost two years and I've missed them dearly. He looked at me as he finished his sentence.

"I'm sorry," I stuttered, taken aback by the intensity of Mark's stare and the way it was affecting me.

"I'm the hostess, which makes me the rude one. Mark, this is Chloe," I said turning towards Chloe, "Chloe this..."

"I can make my own introduction," Chloe interrupted icily. The chill I had felt when she entered the house had turned into a full-fledged frost as Mark and Tony watched Chloe with folded arms and puzzled looks on their faces. My look was more of an expression of sheer terror as I nervously wrung my hands. I was petrified of her next words.

## Chapter Five

"So, you're the infamous Mark Fountaine," Chloe said with a sly smile and a hint of arrogance. "I'm Chloe Lane," she continued, extending her hand in Mark's direction.

"I don't know about the infamous part, but I definitely am Mark Fountaine," he laughed, gently shaking Chloe's well-manicured hand.

"It's just that I had heard so much about you, but I was beginning to think that you were just a figment of Kayla's imagination."

Under the guise of being charming, Chloe was spitting pure venom. She knew I had been very hurt by Mark's absence in the past, and was putting him on the spot for an explanation.

"Yeah, I know it's been a while since Kayla and I have talked," Mark sighed.

"Try almost almost eight months," I interjected bitterly, recalling the many nights I had cried myself to sleep. I didn't remember who had stopped calling first, but I did remember saying to myself that I refused to chase a man that didn't want to be caught. There had been a few periodic phone calls and postcards, but even that, had ended before I met Chloe. Mark seemed genuinely surprised by the acidity in my tone. It took me by surprise also, because I had been so happy with Chloe.

"Well, the last few months have been so hectic," Mark said, looking at Chloe, but directing his words to me. "This is the first real break that I've had. For almost the whole first year and a half since I left, I was commuting back and forth from the states to London, Africa, Hong Kong, Japan; you name it, I've been there. You got the postcards I sent, didn't you, Kayla?" he asked, turning his gaze toward me.

"I received a few," I pouted. I found myself trying to fight off the hurt feelings that threatened to envelop me. I was thinking about all the hopes, dreams and plans that I had made for Mark, and me, that simply faded over the past few months. As I focused on his handsome face, I wondered what effect his visit would have on Chloe, him, and me, before it was over.

"The last six months, I've been establishing the business and setting up residence in Chicago," Mark announced. He was looking me squarely in the eyes, as if willing this last disclosure to have an effect on me. Realizing the meaning behind his statement. I mean, business is booming. Have you seen the commercial about the new Japanese vehicle where the man is using 'Enthusiastic Car Cleaner' to keep it shiny and brand new looking?" Mark asked, practically beaming, looking at each of us expectantly.

"Uh, duh," I said sarcastically. "It only comes on every five minutes.

"Well that marketing concept was developed by my company. Not only did we come up with the commercial, but we also developed the concept of marrying two different business in one commercial. This way, they share the advertising costs and aren't competing in the same market!" Mark's beautiful brown eyes were lit up with excitement. Chloe reacted.

"Sounds interesting, Mark," she said, with no real enthusiasm. "When are you going back?"
Mark had a bewildered look on his face, sensing animosity from Chloe, but not knowing why.

"Well, that depends," he answered slowly, never taking his eyes off me.

"On what," Chloe wanted to know, asking the question that I was afraid to know the answer to.

"On how long it takes me to convince Kayla to marry me and move to Chicago." We all reacted.

I let out the gulp that was heard around the world. Tony did a medley of wedding songs. Mark came over and hugged me, tightly. And Chloe stood stock-still and glared a hole into the back of Mark's head.

Still in shock, I asked if anyone wanted a drink. I brushed over Mark's implied proposal without comment.

"Hell yeah, I need a drink," Tony laughed. "If this knucklehead is going to be my brother-in-law, I'm gonna need a continuous IV filled with Jack Daniels. Stat!"

I let out a nervous laugh, silently willing Tony to shut up. He was making an awkward moment unbearable. Sensing my embarrassment, Mark changed the subject.

"Kayla and I can discuss that later. Why don't you tell me some more about all those girls you dated before Keilani."

"Well, you know," Tony said, doing his J.J. from 'Good Times' impression. "We'll get into all of that later. I want to hear more about this advertising agency you have. It sounds major.

"Major is an understatement," I could hear Mark saying as they disappeared into the dining room to talk and have drinks. I approached Chloe, who had a look of hurt, surprise, bewilderment and anger, all combined.

"Thank you," I said softly.

"For what?" she asked sharply.

"For showing such restraint. I had no idea that Mark was coming to town until just before you called earlier; and I definitely didn't know that he was going to imply that we get married."

"Well, you know now. How do you feel about that," she asked, her eyes narrowing to mere slits.

"About what?" I asked, dumbly, stalling for time. Chloe folded her arms across her chest and sucked her teeth. She was hip to all of my stalling tactics. To tell the truth, I wasn't sure how I felt. I always thought that if and when this moment came, I would know how to react, that I was on solid ground with Chloe. But when I was actually confronted with the situation, I was torn.

"Kayla, I asked you a simple question. At least I thought it was simple. But I guess the fact that you're wrestling with it so hard should tell me something," she said in an accusatory tone.

"I'm sorry, Chloe, this whole thing has taken me by

surprise. One minute I'm wondering how you and I are going to spend the day, then, the next minute, Mark's in my living room, talking as if nothing has changed between him and me," I said, exasperated.

"Has anything changed, Kayla? I mean, as far as your feelings for him are concerned?"

"No, I mean, yes. Oh I don't know what I mean. I think I need a minute to catch my breath."

"The fact that you are so indecisive and flustered, is telling me more than I want to know," Chloe said, softly.

"Chloe, don't talk like that. I just need a little time to think and put things in perspective," I said, pleadingly.

"I know, Kayla, and that's what makes it sad," she said dejectedly, as she headed toward the door.

"Where are you going?" I asked, raising my voice, feeling panicky inside. Although I could feel the inner turmoil that was brewing from seeing Mark again, I knew I wasn't ready to let go of Chloe, not that easily.

"We both have a lot to digest, Kayla. And me being here, watching you interact with Mark, knowing his intentions..." she paused for a moment. "Let's just say, it wouldn't be a good idea."

I knew she was right. It wouldn't be fair to ask her to sit by quietly, while Mark unknowingly sliced into her heart with each remark pertaining to "us".

"You're right," I sighed. "But I'm going to call you as soon as he leaves."

"I'll be waiting," she whispered softly in my ear, as she hugged me goodbye.

I watched her as she strode purposely to her car. Nothing in her mannerisms indicated how she was feeling inside. Once in the driver's seat, she flung her hair behind her shoulders, reached into her glove compartment, put on her shades and sped out of the driveway. The rain that had poured earlier had stopped. A brilliant sun had replaced it. As I closed the door, I was hoping that my situation would become as clear as the weather had.

"Where's Chloe," Tony asked as he and Mark

21

returned to the living room.

"She wasn't feeling well," I covered.

"Maybe that explains her sour attitude. I was beginning to think it was me," Mark said. My eyes widened at the thought of how close he was to the truth.

"Naw, man. I don't know what was wrong with Chloe, today. Usually, she's so live. But you know how women can get once in awhile," Tony said, winking at Mark who looked totally confused.

"Maybe I should have said once every month," Tony clarified, looking at Mark as if he was the dumbest thing in the world.

"Ooh," Mark said, finally catching on. "Yeah, that would account for her mood. My mom used to be a trip. It was so bad, my dad used to take us out for a few hours each day until she was over it. And you don't even want to know about those women in the military."

"I can imagine," Tony cut in. "They're already bossy to begin with, they've got to be, in order to ever think about joining the Army. Add some cramps to that..." he ended, shaking his head.

"Hello, I am in the room," I interrupted.

"And what," Tony asked, smartly. "Don't tell me you got it too."

"No, I don't got it, too," I said, exasperated. "And I didn't say that Chloe had it either."

"You didn't have to, her attitude said it all," Tony laughed. I decided to let it go. It was an easy explanation for Chloe's mood, and I didn't feel like debating the finer points of a woman's monthly surge of estrogen with these two morons.

"So, are you going to stay with your parents," I asked Mark.

"Why can't he stay here with you," Tony butted in. "I mean, he already has his bags and everything."

I was fit to be tied and it must have showed because the glimmer of hope that I had saw on Mark's face quickly disappeared. I closed my mouth, which had popped open on it's own accord, and tried to recover from Tony's outburst.

# If Loving Two is Wrong . . .

"I'm sure Mark's family is anxious to spend time with him," I said, smiling through clenched teeth. Silently, I vowed to kill Tony at the earliest possible moment. I knew Mark had caught my reaction to Tony's suggestion. I felt bad, but there was no way that I could invite him to stay with me. Mark, being the sensitive, thoughtful guy that I've always known him to be, bowed out gracefully.

"My mom would have a horse if she knew I was in town and wasn't staying at home," he said, smiling. I knew what he was doing and it just reinforced why I had fallen in love with him in the first place, so long ago. He was always putting the feeling of others before his own; that was why he let me off the hook, easy.

"But I'm sure I'll be seeing quite a lot of Kayla anyway," he said, with conviction.

"Let's order a couple of pizzas and talk," Tony suggested.

"Yeah, I want to hear more about this company that took you away from me for so long," I said, glaring at Mark.

"Oh Kayla, we've already talked about that. Mark might even throw a few investment dollars my way," Tony said, winking at Mark.

"What's that got to do with me knowing?" I asked, rolling my eyes at Tony.

"It means, catch up on your own time. Right now I want to find out how much this old man remembers."

"Don't worry, Kayla. I'm going to fill you in completely," Mark said, seductively.

"Oh, please wait until I leave before y'all start talking nasty, eh" Tony said in a whiny voice, reminiscent of Archie Bunker. Mark and I burst out laughing. Then Tony and Mark compared notes on old girlfriends and some of the silly antics they used to engage in. Eventually, it got around to how they had to protect me.

"At first, it was from those bullying Russell sisters who used to live down the street," Tony laughed.

"But when they tried to get some of those old cat-faced girls at school to jump you, we knew we had to take

23

action."

"Yeah," Mark said, loudly, excited by the memory. "We knew it was time to teach you how to fight."

"But we didn't know that we were creating a monster," Tony added. "You started challenging everybody. Some of those girls took it to you the first couple of times, remember."

"Yeah, I remember," I sighed, not amused by the story so far.

"Remember that time you came running and screaming to me and Tony with your halter top in your hands?" Mark asked, howling with laughter. Tony spit out the beer he was drinking, almost choking on the memory. In spite of myself, I had to laugh, too.

"Yeah," Tony took over the story as if he and Mark were a tag team. "You were hysterical, running to us with your little raisins exposed.

"Uh huh, I remember." Now I was getting loud as I visualized the scene. "Those damn Russell sisters cornered me after school. They held me, while Latoya Rider pulled off my halter-top. I was screaming bloody murder. When they saw you and Mark coming up the street, they threw the top toward y'all, like it was a rock or something, and then took off running!"

"Girl, you were a sight. Your ponytails were all over your head and one of your front teeth was already missing," Mark laughed, warming even more to the story.

"Damn," was all I could say at the thought of that embarrassing moment over fifteen years ago. I also recalled Mark giving me his t-shirt because my top had been stretched way out of shape. But before I could relate that part of the story, Tony burst in.

"On top of all that embarrassment, you got a beating. Mom told you not to wear that top, but you always thought you were so grown anyway."

"Shut up," I said, rolling my eyes and punching him playfully in his stomach.

"How about when you got that beating for eating that candy bar?" I laughed, emphasizing the word candy.

# If Loving Two is Wrong . . .

"That wasn't no damn candy bar, Tony announced. "That was ex-lax!"

"Well, Mom told you that you couldn't have it, but you were so grown," I ended, turning his words back on him. "Yeah, but I shouldn't have gotten a beating," Tony sulked. "Having the runs all day was punishment enough. Where was that child abuse number when I needed it."

"Punishment enough?" Mark chimed in, boy, you must've been watching too much 'Brady Bunch'. Ain't no way your mama was gonna let you get off without a beating. She had to wash your stinky draws and sheets. You should feel lucky that you're able to come outside to this very day!" We all laughed in agreement. Mark seemed to find these stories very amusing, mostly because they were at Tony's and my expense.

"I don't know why you're laughing, man," Tony said, noticing Mark's extra loud laughter. "I can remember a certain person calling my mom all hysterical, asking if he could come live with us."

"Oh yeah," I said, almost screaming, recalling the incident. "We knew it had to be something major! It was Christmas Eve and we had already seen all the boxes under the tree with your name on it."

Mark had stopped laughing. He could remember the incident with total recall.

"Aw, man," he sighed. "I thought my dad was going to kill me sure 'nuff."

"That was some crazy stunt you pulled, man." Tony had started laughing again. "What were you thinking?"

"I don't know! You know kids do some dumb things. That's a prerequisite for being a kid."

"But Mark, you painted your grandmother's face like a clown," I said, chidingly.

"A spooky clown at that," Tony added. Now, Tony and I had become the tag team, and I took over the story,

"Your grandmother was in the hospital on Christmas Eve, recovering from a stroke. You knew your mom and dad were on their way back from the airport with your aunt and

25

uncle, and you still did that?" I said, in awe.

"I know," Mark shook his head as if he still couldn't believe the incident himself "She was watching me the whole time. How was I supposed to know that she didn't want me to do it? She didn't say anything."

"She had a stroke, dummy!" Tony and I yelled in unison.

"Boy, I thought my pop would never stop beating me. Then, when Grandma regained the use of her arm again, she gave it to me too. But hers didn't really hurt," Mark laughed.

"That's because Ma Ma didn't want to hurt you. She was laughing, herself. But your dad wore you out. You couldn't even ride your new bike with us for a whole week,' I snickered.

"But I'll tell you one thing," Mark said, "if you could've seen the look on my family's face when they walked into that hospital room," he paused for dramatic effect. "Priceless. It was almost worth that booty whooping. I got a good laugh out before the crying started," he said, rubbing his behind jokingly. Tony and I lost it. It turned into an all out laughfest. Then, I noticed the time. It was almost midnight, ten hours since Chloe had left.

"Alright guys, it's time to call it a night," I said. I was wondering if Chloe was still awaiting my call and what she must be thinking by now.

"Wow," Mark said. "Time does fly when you're having fun. I better get movin'. It's bad enough that my parents didn't know that I was coming. If I just waltz in any later, I might get shot."

"You're dad don't have no B-B gun anymore," Tony said, seriously. "He went out and got himself a 38. He showed it to me last year when I helped him with his financial portfolio."

"What?" Mark asked in amazement.

"Yeah man, your dad has a few good investments with me," Tony beamed, proudly.

"No dummy, I'm talking about the gun. Why'd he get that?"

# If Loving Two is Wrong . . .

"There were a few break-ins around the way last year. Everybody was getting nervous. My dad even bought a gun, but Mom's made him lock it up so tight, a guy could've stole the whole house before Pop's could get it out," Tony laughed. "But they caught the guy, some knucklehead from out of town. Turns out, he was dating one of those dumb Russell girls and had used her to case the neighborhood. Everybody chilled out after that. The vigilante furor is over."

"I'm glad to hear it," Mark said. "Well, I'm gonna get going. Tony, I'm going to catch up with you; we definitely have some talking to do. As for you," he paused and turned towards me, "I'll see you tomorrow."

"Okay," I said, hugging him around the waist. I was beginning to feel guilty because it felt so good to have my arms around him.

"Girl, you just don't know how good it feels to finally be back here again, to see you again," he said, shaking his head as he walked toward the door.

"I'm glad you feel that way," I said, non-committedly. He stepped out the door; his hand was lingering on the doorknob and he was looking at me with raised eyebrows, like he was expecting something to happen.

"Uh, uh," I said, rolling my eyes. "You must've forgot that you took a cab. Besides, you better not leave out of here without taking pita with you." I was attempting to divert the effect of Mark's piercing gaze.

"Pita?" he repeated, confused.

"Yeah, that's short for pain in the ass," I said as I pushed Tony in Mark's direction.

"Aw, that's cold," Tony said, grabbing his coat.

"C'mon here, pita, drop me off," Mark laughed.

"Okay, man. Sis, I'll talk to you later," Tony said, as he hugged me, then stepped out of the doorway. I shut the door behind him, fighting off the urge to stare at Mark until he reached the car. Shakily, I sat down on the couch in the living room and silently waited for the sound of the car to exit the driveway. Only then did I allow myself the luxury of exhaling. I decided to fix a drink and steady my nerves before calling Chloe. I wanted to get my thoughts together before the grilling began. As soon as I took the first sip of my Screwdriver, the phone rang. Intuitively, I knew it was Chloe. I took a deep breath before I picked up the receiver.

"Hello," I answered.

"Did you plan on calling me tonight?" came the taut reply.

"Yeah, I'm sorry. Tony and Mark just left."

"I guess I don't have to wonder where I fit in when it comes to importance," she said, matter-of-factly.

"Chloe please," I groaned pleading for some degree of understanding. My mind and emotions were in utter turmoil. I imagined that Chloe's were, too.

"I'm sorry," she said quietly. Her voice no longer reflected anger, but more of a hint of resignation.

"I don't mean to take it out on you. I know it's not easy for you either. But I feel helpless."

"What do you mean?" I asked.

"It's as if major decisions can be made that will affect my life drastically, and I have no say in the matter," she continued speaking softly. Her tone let me know that she was speaking from hurt, rather than anger.

"What do you mean you have no say? I would never shut you out like that."

"Maybe not intentionally, but face it, Kayla; I have no choice but to sit by, idly, while you and Mark play out this little soap opera. No one, but us, knows about our illicit relationship, which makes it impossible for me to vent my feelings without your family finding out."

Her voice was beginning to rise. I knew how much she disliked keeping our relationship a secret. Before meeting me, Chloe was openly gay. It wasn't that she wanted to shout her sexual orientation from the rooftops, but she did want to be able to express her emotions, freely; like Tony did with Keilani. They held hands, said those little cute things and occasionally kissed. All of which my parents thought were so precious. The only comments Chloe and I got were questions about when we were going to find a man that would treat us the way Tony treats Keilani. At that moment I had an overwhelming need to see Chloe and comfort her.

"Are you going to bed anytime soon?" I asked.

"I doubt it," she answered, despondently. "I don't think I'll be able to sleep."

"Would it be okay if I came over?" I asked, hopefully.

"Would you?" she responded, her tone brightening just a little.

"I'm on my way out the door, see you in a few minutes."

"Okay," she answered.

My mind traveled through a maelstrom of emotions as I absentmindedly drove the route, which I knew like the back of my hand, to Chloe's apartment. I played and replayed the day's events over and over in my head. Then my mind wondered back to when we met and all the drama that followed. I was meeting Jackie, an old college friend, for lunch. She was a secretary at a law firm down the street from the drug store where I worked as a pharmacist. We usually had lunch at least twice a week at Mokas, a little bistro at Thirty-fifth and Lancaster that served Mediterranean food and a mean Chicken Caesar salad. Well, on this particular day, Jackie brought one of the lawyers who she worked for, to lunch with her.

"Hey Kayla, what's up? I want you to meet Chloe Lane; she's one of the bosses I usually complain to you about. She decided to continue to exert her authority over me through lunch," Jackie laughed, waving her long, bright red acrylic nails in the air.

"Knock it off, Jackie," Chloe rolled her eyes, jokingly. "You know first impressions are lasting ones," she said, looking at me through lowered lashes. I was a little perplexed by her expression, but shook it off. "And we wouldn't want your friend Kayla, here, thinking I'm some kind of tyrant," she continued, extending her hand in my direction. "Nice to finally meet you, Kayla. I've heard so much about you."

"Likewise," I said as I shook her slender hand. I noticed she had manicured nails with French tips. Her nails were a natural length, nowhere near the talons that Jackie sported.

"I'm almost afraid to ask," Chloe stated, glaring at Jackie.

"Don't worry, it's all been good," I assured her.

"Well, if we're finished with the 'What Did Jackie Say Show,' do you both think we can order now? I mean, lunch is only an hour." Jackie said, rolling her eyes and motioning for the waiter. She was still sporting an exaggerated frown on her silky red #5 lips. I was just contemplating how blemish free Jackie was able to keep her toffee colored skin, when the waiter arrived. We each ordered Chicken Caesar salads and iced teas.

For the next 45 minutes we enjoyed lunch and casual conversation that bounced from diets to work and inevitably to men.

"Chile, I'm just getting Lonnie to the point where I can stand to be around him for more than two days out the week," Jackie said, dramatically fluttering extended black eyelashes, courtesy of Cover Girl.

"Girl, what are you talking about," I jumped in.

"You've been with Lonnie for over two years now," I offered while emptying my fifth packet of sugar into my unsweetened tea.

"That's how long it takes to break 'em in and mold them," Jackie dead- panned.

"Girl, you're crazy," Chloe laughed. "Well, what about you," she asked, looking straight at me. "Do you have a significant other in your life?"

"No," I answered. "I've been dating on and off since college, but no one has stuck to me yet."

"Can't no man stick to you, Kayla," Jackie chimed in, "You've got that 'If you ain't Mark, step off', repellant emanating from your ass."

"That's not true," I countered. "What about Kevin, I really liked him."

"Yeah, I'll give you that," Jackie relented. "That

lasted all of about two months."

"Why, what happened?" Chloe asked, extremely interested as she stabbed a piece of seasoned chicken with her fork.

"Oh, I don't know, that was so long ago," I answered, dismissively.

"If I remember correctly," Jackie interjected, "He couldn't take you continuously calling him Mark," she said matter-of-factly as she shook her fourth sugar packet.

"Jackie, I'm gonna hurt you, girl. That was an innocent mistake," I said defensively. I masked my discomfort with the subject by taking a sip of tea. I purposely avoided mentioning Mark. That was still a soft spot for me

"Oh, no, baby," Jackie insisted; 'one or two times might be an innocent mistake, but continuously," she paused for dramatic effect, "now that's just downright ugly."

"Wow, this Mark must be an incredible man," Chloe said with a smile. (you keep using the word interjected. Please watch that. And I don't think it fits here anyway.) "What happened that you're not together now?"

So I told her the whole story of how I had been in love with Mark since childhood and how he had went into the service and would come home occasionally. When he did, he would always visit Tony and I made sure he got an eyeful of me, because I was developing quite nicely. When I was twenty-four and finishing Pharmacy School, Mark had come home for an extended visit. By then, he had been out of the service for almost two years and was trying to develop his own marketing firm.

"He had finally asked me out on an official date," I recounted to Chloe.

Jackie, who had heard the story many times already, sighed loudly and looked quite bored as she picked through her salad.

"Anyway," I said loudly, rolling my eyes at Jackie, "I was so excited. After asking him twenty times and confirming it wasn't a joke, I immediately ran to my dorm

31

and told my mother."

"And so, Mark and I went on our date that next night and subsequent nights for almost two years; in between his trips back and forth from Chicago and everywhere else he tried to make business connections."

"Then what happened?" Chloe interrupted smirked, leaning in close, as if I was telling the greatest story in the world. She emptied a packet of Sweet and Low into her tea and stirred.

"Well, Mark informed me that he had received some good leads and needed to be in Chicago where he had some investors lined up."

"So he just dropped you like that?" Chloe seemed to be telling me more than asking me. "That's a typical man move," she continued with a smirk.

"No, it wasn't like that," I said, quickly jumping to Mark's defense. "We had a long talk over a nice intimate dinner. He explained it was something he had to do if he was going to be independent and have his own business. I thought of our time apart as an investment in our future."

"How long has it been since you've seen him?" she asked, taking a sip of tea and frowning.

"A little over a year," I relented embarrassingly.

"I rest my case," Chloe slapped the table with her hand, indicating she'd made her point.

"I may not have seen him in over a year, but we did keep in constant contact up to a few months ago," I said, defensively. "Then the telephone calls and postcards just dwindled off," I said, softly.

"I hate to break up this little hen clucking," Jackie sulked, "but some of us are accountable for our time."

I silently thanked big-mouthed Jackie for getting me out of the hot seat.

"Well, y'all have a nice day at work," I teased. "I'm only doing half a day today."

"Oh yeah," Jackie exclaimed, sucking her teeth. "If I had known that, I would've left a half hour ago, as much attention as y'all paid me. C'mon Chloe," she huffed, acting like she was truly mad.

# If Loving Two is Wrong . . .

"Count me out, too," Chloe grinned. "I'm not going back to work today either."

"Oh, I see," Jackie snorted. "I guess the key to taking off whenever I want is to own my own business, or have an extremely generous boss," she cooed, fluttering her Cover Girl's at Chloe.

"I don't care if you take off," Chloe said slyly. "But Robert and Maurice might have a problem with it."

"I must've lost my mind taking a job as a secretary for three lawyers. Well, I better get going. Both Robert and Maurice have appointments scheduled for this afternoon." Jackie sulked.

"Don't forget to type those letters on my desk and send them out, they're on the Butler case and they're very important," Chloe added to Jackie's burdens.

"Don't forget my raise," Jackie shouted over her shoulder as she left, leaving a trail of White Diamonds in her wake.

"She always did have to have the last word," I laughed nervously, suddenly very aware that I was alone with the Mark basher.

"Well I guess I'd better get going," I added hastily, gathering my belongings together.

"Do you have to run so quickly," Chloe asked. Can't you join me for a cup of coffee? I see you didn't like the tea either," she grinned, pointing at my glass, which was still full.

"Sure," I said uneasily. "But only if we agree not to talk about Mark."

"It's a deal," she replied.

So, our introduction to each other continued for another hour. Chloe told me she was the youngest of two boys and three girls and the only one to graduate from college. Her family was extremely proud of her and their expectations were very high. She finished law school a year earlier than anticipated and was recruited by many top law firms. She worked for Kleinman and Ross, a very prestigious law firm

33

in New York for two years. There she learned how to do research, how to read people, and fine-tuned her case presentation. She started out researching the small nuisance cases and fast-tracked her way to representing some of the most influential people and corporations in the country. Amidst many tears and pleas from her bosses and co-workers, she decided to move back to Philadelphia and open her own firm.

"Wow, Chloe," I said, genuinely impressed. "You've made some major accomplishments. You should be very proud of yourself."

"I am," she said wistfully, like something was missing. "Unfortunately, to be successful, sometimes you have to make sacrifices. For me, it was a social life."

"How ironic," I said.

"What do you mean?" she asked.

"Well, when I told you about Mark leaving to try to make a success of himself, you were so negative. It seems to me that you, of all people, should understand."

"I thought you said we weren't to discuss Mark," she said accusingly.

"You're right," I laughed. "But you stepped right into that one."

"Touche," she grinned.

"You must have had a few boyfriends," I said incredulously, "I mean, you're gorgeous."

I was not exaggerating. Chloe was 5'7", about 130lbs, with long black hair that reached the middle of her back. She was caramel complexioned with hazel green eyes and a wide sensuous mouth. She had a sexy way of licking her lips, which she seemed to do subconsciously. As she excused herself to go to the ladies room, I found myself checking out her measurements. She had nice full breasts, which I determined were about a 38C. Her torso tapered into a 26" waistline that drifted back out into curvy hips. Chloe wasn't muscular, but well toned. I could only imagine that her legs, hidden by her crisply pleated, navy blue, linen pants, were as perfectly matched to her body as the rest of her. And from the rear, you couldn't help but notice her firm behind.

# If Loving Two is Wrong . . .

As if snapping out of a trance, I turned my head quickly and looked out the window. I was suddenly embarrassed at the way I was scrutinizing this woman. "Now where were we?" she was asking as she returned to her chair.

"I was asking you about your love life," I said without missing a beat. "I'm sure there are many men out there willing to take you off the market."

"To tell the truth, Kayla, I wouldn't know. I've always been kind of introverted when it came to men," she said, sipping her coffee.

"What?" I exclaimed, genuinely surprised. "If anything, I would think you would intimidate them."

"Well my parents were kind of strict, not allowing us girls to date until our senior year in high school. And since my two older sisters got pregnant before they were twenty, they were extremely strict on me in the boy department. So, by the time I got to the dating age, the boys around my way had already labeled me a tease and no longer bothered."

"Well, that's one big difference between guys around your way and my way. In my neighborhood, they would have pursued you well into the 23$^{rd}$ century. And they wouldn't have cared if you had one eye, one arm, and a wooden leg," I assured her.

"That just proves my 'men are dogs' theory," she said matter-of-factly. "But anyway," she continued quickly, before I could debate, "in college, I was determined to finish in the top one percent of my class, so I put myself on a strict diet of study, study, and more study."

"But all work and no play makes Chloe a dull girl," I chimed in.

"I dated a few guys," she said, "But they always demanded more time than I could give. So they never lasted very long. Besides, all work and no play might make Chloe a dull girl, but a very successful woman. Now, if I meet that right person, I can concentrate on them without worrying about the consequences."

"Oh, I see," was all I could respond with.

"Like today," she said staring into my eyes, "I had work to do, but I was enjoying your company so much I decided to stay here with you."

She continued to watch me, gauging my reaction to what she had just said. Now I'm not slow by any means, but I was more than a little perplexed by her mannerisms.

"So," she said, continuing as if that little awkward moment had never taken place, "here I am, 29 years old and haven't mastered the concept of male manipulation."

"That's not exactly how I would define a relationship," I said, "but I'll save that debate for our next meeting."

"Well, at least I know I haven't scared you off, since you did say our next meeting," she stated as she motioned to the waiter for the check. It was only then, as we looked at the bill, that we realized Jackie had left without paying.

"That girl is always stiffing me," Chloe laughed. "But paying for her lunch is the least I can do, since she introduced me to such an interesting person. Put your money away, this one's on me."

"Are you sure?" I asked as I stuffed my money back into my purse.

"Positive," she purred. "Well, I hope to hear from you soon," Chloe said as she pulled a business card from her purse and wrote her home and pager number on the back. I followed suit and gave her my numbers.

"By the way, Kayla," she continued as she gathered her things preparing to leave. "I hope it won't make too much of a difference to you," she continued, easing from her chair and standing, "but I'm gay." And with that, she winked her eye and sashayed out of the restaurant.

My mouth hit the floor.

## Chapter Six

"Did you know she was like that?" I asked Jackie, whom I called as soon as I got in the house.

# If Loving Two is Wrong . . .

"Like what?" Jackie asked stupidly.

"Gay," I whispered in a conspiratorial tone, as if Chloe were in the room with me.

"Yeah, but so what? Did she make a move on you or something? Come on, Kayla, dish the dirt, girl, dish the dirt," she urged.

"No," I said guardedly. "Well, I don't know. How should I know when a woman is making a move on me? I've never been in that kind of predicament before. How come you never told me about her?"

"I thought I did," she rushed. "Girl, did she ask you on a date? Did she try to touch your butt? What?" Jackie demanded to know.

"No, she didn't do any of that, never mind, it's probably just my imagination. Forget I even said anything," I said, rubbing the arm of my gray leather sofa.

"Forget it? Oooh No!" Jackie howled. "I don't know if I can do that, girl, but I tell you what. If I were you, I'd get with her. That girl got bank, you hear me? Mucho dinero, plenty of pesos, in other words, lots of loot."

"Jackie you're crazy, girl" I laughed.

"Call me what you want," she said seriously. "But I know a good opportunity when I see it."

"Yeah, like the way you took off at lunch time without paying your share of the bill?" I asked jokingly.

"She paid it, didn't she? And she probably told you I always stick her like that, didn't she?"

"Yeah," I admitted.

"See," Jackie declared, as if proud of this accomplishment, "I told you I know a good thing when I see it."

"But that's taking advantage, Jackie," I admonished.

"Girl, please," she returned. "You think that girl did all those years of college, taking up law, mind you, and is getting conned out of lunch a few times by me. You're the crazy one."

"I see your point," I laughed, realizing how silly I sounded.

"Besides," Jackie went on, "what can it hurt to spend some time with Chloe? She can't get you pregnant, she's beautiful, nice, and has loads of money. Kayla, you're in a win/win situation."

"You're forgetting one thing," I reminded Jackie.

"What's that?" she asked.

"Chloe is Chloe, not Clyde or Joey. She's a woman."

"Minor detail," Jackie said. "Minor detail. But you need to seriously consider the possibility."

"Why?" I asked.

"Why not?" she countered.

"I never even entertained the thought of having a relationship with a woman," I responded indignantly.

Of course, I never considered those childhood crushes on my female teachers as lesbian tendencies. In all the books I read, that was a natural phenomenon.

"There are a lot of things we don't consider until we're confronted with it," Jackie said.

"Since when did you become such a wealth of knowledge?" I asked.

"Kayla, just because I decided to become a secretary with a B.S in business, doesn't mean I'm stupid. It's just a means to an end. The money I'm making now is fantastic, the money I save on lunch is great, thanks to Chloe," she laughed. "But seriously, I plan to open a secretarial school and pool. I'll charge tuition to train them and then arrange jobs for them and make a commission from their employers. I'm making a lot of contacts now through the firms, corporations and influential people I meet because of this job. Pretty soon, I'll be able to decide not to go back to work after lunch on a whim too."

"Wow, Jackie, that's a great plan you have. But if Chloe's sooo great, how come you never got with her?" I asked as my other line beeped.

"Girl, you know I'm strictly dickly," she laughed. "Get your other line, but don't forget about what I said.

Besides, Chloe ain't never asked me." And she quickly hung up.
Before I even had a chance to digest our conversation, I had clicked over to the other line.
"Hello," I answered.
"Hi, Kayla." I knew instantly it was Chloe.
"Hi, Chloe," I tried to sound casual, but for some reason, my heart was pounding.
"You recognized my voice, huh? That's a good sign. I hope I'm not catching you at a bad time," she said. I could tell she was smiling, by her singsong tone. "I was just thinking about you and the conversation we had and I got the urge to call you. I didn't freak you out too bad did I?"
"Oh, no," I said, trying to sound convincing. "You just caught me a little off guard."
"I bet," she laughed. "But I just believe in getting the awful truth out of the way early."
"I can't deny, I was surprised," I admitted. "But it's no tragedy."
"I'm glad you feel that way Kayla because I would really like to get to know you better, but I wouldn't want you to feel uncomfortable."
"I'd like to think I'm a little more open-minded than that. But you do understand that I'm not gay. Don't you?"
"If you say it's so, then I believe it," she answered slyly. "But I don't want my sexual orientation to be the focal point of our friendship. I admit, I do think you're very attractive, but I have many attractive friends and I'm not trying to sleep with them, Kayla."
"I'm sorry, I don't mean to sound paranoid. It's just that I've never had to deal with anyone coming out to me before. As a matter of fact, I don't think I have any gay friends."
"Well, that may or may not be true," Chloe said. "But what I'm interested in is getting to know you, as a friend."
"I'd like that," I answered sincerely.

"Well, why put off until tomorrow what you can do today, I always say," she began hesitantly. "If you don't have any plans, maybe we can meet later for a few drinks," she ended hopefully.

"Sure. What did you have in mind?"

"Well, there's a little bar downtown I usually go to. Right off of Pecan, before you get to Broad, it's on a little street, I never remember the name of the street, but you can't miss it. Just go down Pecan, past 13<sup>th</sup> and turn on that little street. The bar is right there."

"I'm sure I can find it," I assured her. "What time did you have in mind?"

"How about seven?"

"Sounds good," I answered.

"Or I could pick you up?" she offered.

"Oh, no," I said. I always make sure I keep an escape route open. "That's too much trouble to pick me up and bring me back. I'll meet you there at seven."

"Ok," Chloe said. "I look forward to seeing you again." Then we both hung up.

Now I found myself engaged in a little game of devil's advocate. Kayla, what are you getting yourself into? I asked myself. But at the same time, I was filled with an adventurous curiosity.

"Remember… curiosity killed the cat," I reminded myself aloud. "One life down, eight more to go," I countered. Then I went upstairs to get ready.

All the way to the bar I kept having imaginary scenarios, and they all started with Chloe making a move on me and me storming out of the bar. I saw the little street she was talking about just ahead. I made the turn and just like Chloe, I didn't bother to get the name. I found the place easily enough. As I reached for the door, I was hoping she was sitting where I could easily find her. I hated walking into a place alone and having to search through all the faces looking at me to find who I'm looking for. Sure enough, she was sitting at the front of the bar and smiled when she saw me.

"Have any trouble finding it?" she asked.

# If Loving Two is Wrong . . .

"No," I replied, "it was easy, just like you said. As a matter of fact, I didn't even bother to get the name of that street either. I just turned."

"I told you," Chloe laughed.

"What do you drink?" she asked.

"I'll have a Fuzzy Navel," I told the bartender. As I turned back to Chloe, I couldn't help but notice how pretty she looked with her hair pulled back in a ponytail and light make-up. She was wearing jeans and a pretty green t-shirt that really brought out the color of her eyes. Once again I was embarrassed by my thoughts. I mean, yeah, I recognize when a woman is attractive, but now I was analyzing this woman from head to toe. What is going on?

After my third drink, I suddenly became very aware of my surroundings.

"Chloe," I whispered.

"What?" she said as she leaned in to hear what I was saying.

"Have you noticed that there are no men in here?" I asked, as if letting her in on a big secret.

She just sat back and laughed aloud. "That's because it's a gay bar."

"Oh, no wonder we've been paying for all our drinks." I gulped down what was left in my glass.

"I'm sorry you didn't know, Kayla. If you're uncomfortable, we can leave," she said apologetically.

"Oh, no, it's okay," I stammered. "I guess I was so engrossed in our conversation that I didn't recognize."

But suddenly, knowing I was in a gay bar, made me very self-conscious. I wanted to scream, I'm not gay, but I was determined to be sophisticated about this.

"I guess it might've happened one day anyway," I said stupidly.

"What might?" Chloe asked, looking puzzled.

"I don't know," I hesitated. "Maybe I would've eventually gone to a gay bar."

"Oh yeah," Chloe smiled.

"I mean, just to see what it's like," I added hastily.

"Kayla, it's no big deal. Look around."

I began by looking out the corner of my eye. When I realized I wasn't able to see much with my peripheral vision, I slowly began to turn my head. What I noticed was several couples and groups of women scattered around the bar and at tables, engrossed in their own conversations.

"They're not even thinking about me," I said almost absentmindedly. "But how can that be, they're gay," I said, turning to Chloe. "I'm reasonably attractive, aren't I?" I asked on the verge of feeling offended.

"Yes, you're very attractive," Chloe answered.

"But now you're assuming that everyone in here is gay. You're not, right?"

"Right," I answered slowly, eyeing Chloe suspiciously. I was beginning to feel as if I was being set up for something, but wasn't sure exactly what.

"Besides," Chloe said innocently, "gay women don't just fall over every woman they see simply because they're women. I mean, we do have qualities and traits that we're attracted to in others, just like straight people."

This conversation was beginning to blow my mind. I went from having a routine lunch with Jackie, to sitting in a gay bar with a beautiful gay woman discussing lesbian dating habits. And I was actually enjoying spending time with Chloe, but I was also beginning to feel that I might be getting in over my head.

"Would you like to check out the dance floor?" Chloe asked, snapping me out of my thoughts.

"What?" I asked, so sure I didn't hear what I thought I heard.

"Do you want to dance?" she asked again, reconfirming my worst fears.

"I don't think I'm ready to be that liberated yet," I answered.

"There's nothing to it," Chloe said easily, "it's just women dancing to music."

"With other women," I added.

"Yes, with other women."

# If Loving Two is Wrong . . .

"You do know that's not something black women do, don't you?" I asked.

"Traditionally, no," she laughed, "but it's something us gay black women do all the time."

"Why do I bother arguing with a lawyer?" I sighed, exasperated.

"My point exactly," she responded as she grabbed my hand and led me upstairs, where couples and groups of women sparsely covered the dance floor.

There were two or three rebels doing their own thing in front of the mirrors surrounding the dance area. I almost laughed out loud at some of the women. They seemed to be lost in their own dance mode, as if each were listening to their own personal music instead of the rhythmic house music that was pumping out of the large speakers at the edge of the floor. Some were fast, some were slow, and many were just way off beat.

"These sure aren't no soul-train dancers up in here," I laughed.

"Well, why don't you show them how it's done," she said as she tried to nudge me onto the dance floor.

I had only come upstairs to be nosey, not to join in.

"Girl, you must've bumped your head on a brick, hard too, if you think I'm going out there to dance," I chortled, twisting my shoulders out of her reach.

"Why?" she asked, laughing.

"What if I see someone I know," I asked, doing a quick scan of the room.

"So what?" she answered. "They're in here too, so what can they say? You'll be even." She looked at me as if she had just made a convincing argument, but I quickly assured her that she hadn't.

Chloe went and got us another drink. Now I was really beginning to feel the effect of the four drinks I already had. Before I knew it, Chloe had maneuvered me on to the dance floor.

What the hell, it's no big deal.

So we danced to Chubb Rock's 'Treat 'Em Right'. A

little old, but I can still really jam on this. Another good song came on so we stayed on the floor. In spite of myself, I was actually having a really good time.

All of a sudden, Marvin Gaye's 'Let's Get It On' came on. THE LOVE SONG OF ALL TIME. I did some mean grinding at parties with some of my old boyfriends to that song. I surveyed the dance floor and saw the women getting closer to each other and embracing. THEY'RE SLOW DRAGGING! I screamed in my mind. I mean, actually looking like they're in love, some of them. I was about to say something about this to Chloe, but as I faced her, she was looking at me questioningly, as if she wanted to ask me to dance on this song. With Her! Time out! This was definitely my cue to leave.

"Girl, look at the time," I said aloud. "I better get going. I have to get up early tomorrow."

"Yeah, me too," she said, sounding a little disappointed, but trying not to let it show.

Outside the bar, Chloe grabbed my hands and squeezed. "I really enjoyed spending time with you, Kayla. I hope we can go out again sometime."

"Most definitely," I answered. "I really had a good time too."

Chloe leaned over and kissed me on the cheek, then we both went to our cars.

All the way home I recounted the evening. Why wasn't I repulsed by what I had just encountered? But what did I really see? Women were sitting, talking, and dancing with each other. What's so repulsive about that? 'Kayla', I thought to myself, 'you're just trying to justify why you're not feeling as turned off by the whole gay bar thing as you thought you would be, or should be'. Knowing how deep these conversations with myself could get, I decided to drop it for now. Besides, all I did was go out to a bar, which happened to be gay, with a new friend, who happened to be gay and had a good gay time. I wasn't going to make a habit of it. Was I?

# If Loving Two is Wrong . . .

## Chapter Seven

W eeks went by and Chloe and I had been spending more and more time with each other. We went to movies, plays, dinner, and yes, dancing. Sometimes we went to gay clubs and other times to straight clubs. I was still dating occasionally, but found I preferred spending time with Chloe. It was just something about having someone around who loved shopping as much as I did, seemed genuinely interested in my different moods, shared my sense of humor and didn't look at me expectantly when we sat around relaxing after she had just treated me to dinner and a movie. Don't get me wrong; I still had cravings for male companionship. I enjoyed being able to take walks at Penn's Landing, a meeting spot down by the river, where folks do artsy things, while holding hands with my mate. I liked being able to kiss or show other forms of affection in public without feeling out of place. Not that I was a big stickler for that sort of thing anyway, but it was an option that I didn't feel women who dated women had. Sure, there were the bold ones who were that satisfied and comfortable with their life choice that they didn't care what John Q Public thought. But even that wasn't something that I saw too often.

"Excuse me, Miss, but is my prescription ready?" a voice said, catching my attention. Lately at work I had been doing a lot of daydreaming about my friendship with Chloe.

"Oh, I'm sorry," I said, suddenly focusing on this dark chocolate man with the deepest, most melodic voice I'd ever heard.

"That's okay, you seemed as if you were miles away from here," he smiled, revealing perfect white teeth and a dimple in his left cheek. I almost had an instant orgasm.

"It's just been one of those kind of weeks," I responded, trying to sound casual. "When did you drop your prescription off?"

"Around 11:30 or so, a man was here and I gave it to him. He told me to come back around 2pm," he answered.

"Okay," I said. "That must've been when I was on my break. What's your name?"

"Sands," he answered, "Barry Sands."

I just stared at him a moment, thinking 'That's right, his voice reminds me of Barry White.' I was also trying to think of more questions to ask him so I could keep him there, talking. He misunderstood my stare.

"No, I'm not the famous football player, his name is Barry Sanders," he said, stressing the E-R-S on the end.

"I know that," I said indignantly, knowing I was lying. I had no idea who Barry Sanders was.

"Oh yeah?" he laughed, as if reading my mind, "Who does he play for?"

"Do you want to play Jeopardy or would you rather I get your medicine?" I smirked, trying to weasel my way out of his question.

"Well, I do need my medicine, but I also wouldn't mind playing Jeopardy," pause, "with you. The home version," he added with a sly wink.

Now we're getting somewhere.

"I take it that's a statement, since it wasn't in the form of a question," I said coyly, as I headed to the back for his prescription. He just laughed, a deep smooth laugh that sent a tingle up my spine. After finding his name in the basket of prescriptions, I checked to find out what his prescriptions was for. Hmm, Azithromicin, allergy medicine. Nothing serious. It wouldn't do to go out with cute and crazy!

"I like the way your mind works," he said upon my return "Well here's a question for you. Do you think that I could take you out to dinner tonight?"

"Sure," I answered a little too quickly, I thought after it had already slipped out.

If he noticed the anxiousness in my voice, he graciously overlooked it and simply said, "Great."

"What time should I pick you up?" he asked, smiling that gorgeous smile.

"How about seven o'clock?"

"Sounds good, but I think I put the cart before the horse,"

"What do you mean?" I asked, puzzled.

"Here I am asking you out without knowing any particulars."

"Like what?"

"Like your name, where you live, and if you're currently seeing someone."

"Yeah, I can see where that information might come in handy," I laughed. "Kayla Thomas," I announced, extending my hand.

"It's my extreme pleasure, Ms. Thomas, I assume."

He took hold of my hand, which I had offered for a handshake and pressed his warm soft lips to the back of it. From anyone else, I would've rolled my eyes and thought, 'How corny,' but from him, it seemed like the perfect gesture. On it's own accord; my mind began to devilishly think of other places I wouldn't mind feeling those lips. As I regained my senses, both physically and mentally, I suggested that we just meet at the restaurant.

"Why?" Barry asked. "Is there something at your house you don't want me to see?"

"Yes, my address," I answered honestly.

Now Barry looked totally perplexed.

"What do you think I am, some type of serial killer or something?" He took a step back and screwed up his nose as if I had just pulled a gun on him.

"Not by the looks of you, but a girl has to be careful nowadays," I answered. "Don't be offended; just try to understand my point of view."

"I do," he said, "But it's a damn shame when times have gotten so bad that a man can't come to a woman's house and pick her up for a date."

"I agree," I said apologetically. "But it's just a sign of the times. These days, going out on a date is a calculated risk, especially a first date."

# If Loving Two is Wrong . . .

"Well," Barry sighed, "I guess I'd better quit while I'm ahead. Next thing I know, we'll be meeting at the McDonald's drive-thru and eating in the parking lot."

"Don't be so dramatic," I laughed.

"Do you like Jazz?" he asked.

"I love it," I answered, mesmerized by his hazel-green eyes. Did I mention his beautiful eyes? Well, if I didn't they were the most sensual looking eyes ever. Especially with his smooth chocolate skin and wavy, jet-black hair. And if that isn't enough, there's the piece de resistance, a neatly trimmed moustache and goatee. I'm talking good hair, chile. No nappy-haired beard and all that jazz.

Jazz? Oh yeah, that's where we were. I mean, I like jazz alright, but I would've said I loved crack if he'd asked me with that voice, those eyes, and those good looks all working against me.

"How about Zanzibar Blue? Have you ever been there?" he asked, looking so innocent, totally oblivious to my thoughts.

"No, but I've heard of it. I've always said I was going to try it," I cooed.

"Well, why put off until tomorrow, what you can do today?" Barry asked. Immediately, a feeling of dé ja vu washed over me. This unexpected meeting, the instant attraction, those hazel-green eyes and now, that statement: it had all happened before. Suddenly, a vision of Chloe popped into my mind. Were we supposed to be doing something together tonight? Well, if we were, I'm sure she'll understand.

"How true," I said, returning to my conversation with Barry. "So, I'll meet you there at seven thirty, okay?"

"Great," Barry said, "I look forward to it."

My eyes followed him down the aisle to the exit. He had a very muscular upper body, not too big; but it showed nicely in the form fitting, silk t-shirt he was wearing. His torso tapered down to a small waist, which was tucked snugly into a very well worn pair of jeans. Very nice butt.

**Kim Beverly**

Subconsciously, I glanced at the circular mirror mounted near the ceiling at the front of the pharmacy. At that very moment, our eyes met. Had he been watching me watching him the whole time? I felt the redness creeping into my cheeks as I watched him smile devilishly into the mirror, wink and leave the store. For the rest of the day, I was on cloud nine, because at seven thirty, I would be having a date with an angel.

All the way home it was if my mind and my car were one entity, both racing along at eighty miles per hour, zigzagging across the divided highway. I was very excited by the thought of seeing Barry that night, but at the same time, I was apprehensive about telling Chloe. I mean, no clear lines had been established between Chloe and me. True, I had been seeing her almost exclusively for the past few months and she did seem to be very comfortable with that arrangement, but nothing sexual had ever occurred between us. Besides, I still considered myself very much heterosexual. It was just that there had been no interesting prospects in the past few months and I was content with shopping, going to the movies, dinner, and so on with Chloe.

As soon as I walked through the door, I was greeted by the constant blinking of the message indicator on my answering machine. The first message was from my mother. 'Why haven't you called? I've been worried sick. Your brother calls me everyday, why can't you? Do you have a boyfriend yet? I'm ready for some grandkids,' and so on, and so on. Same old story every time. Mental note... call Mom... sometime. The second message was from Chloe.

'Hey, Kayla, I knew you wouldn't be home, but I'm heading out for a minute. Just wanted to remind you that we're supposed to be checking out that new Oprah Winfrey movie, Beloved, tonight. Call me on my cellular and let me know if you want to eat first. That way we can meet in town before the movie. Okay, hon, gotta go, but I'm really looking forward to tonight. See ya.'

Damn, she did nothing but talk about that movie for weeks, ever since the first previews. How could I had forgotten? All of a sudden, an image of Barry drifted into my mind. Oh yeah, and if my mind wasn't a strong enough reminder, my body reconfirmed it by becoming wet.

"Well, she's just gonna have to understand," I said with more conviction than I felt. Then I stumbled on the first two steps as I headed to my room to search for something to wear.

---

"Kayla, how could you," Chloe pouted, more of an accusation than a question.

"You knew I had been looking forward to this for weeks. And now you let a perfect stranger mess up our plans. Why can't you change your date until tomorrow night?"

"Why can't we just change our plans until tomorrow night?" I countered. "Besides, I don't have his number. We're just going to meet at the place at seven thirty."

"Kayla, the man was getting a prescription filled. He had to put his phone number on file. So all you have to do is call your job and get it."

Damn Chloe and her analytical mind.

"Chloe, the same movie will be playing tomorrow," I said matter-of-factly.

"You know what, Kayla? You're right," she said with a sudden calmness that caught me by surprise. "Go out and have a good time. Call me tomorrow and let me know how things went."

"Why the sudden change of ..." (click) The line went dead. The hussy hung up on me. I dialed her number, but the answering machine came on. She'll get over it. I hung up without leaving a message.

Two hours, four outfits, three hairstyles, and two make-up applications later, I was headed to meet Barry. Although I was excited by the thought of seeing him again, my last conversation with Chloe kept gnawing at my conscience. I began to feel guilty about choosing Barry over her, but as soon as I saw his beautiful frame unfolding from his cream colored Corvette, all thoughts of Chloe disappeared.

I smiled as I watched him check his watch and begin to scan the area. Finally, his eyes caught mine and his beautiful face exploded into a radiant smile that took my breath away. We waved simultaneously and met at the restaurant door. Barry hugged me, and pressed his soft, moist lips to my cheek.

"Hello, Ms. Thomas. You've just made me a very happy man," he said as he took a long appreciative look at me in my short black spaghetti-strapped dress and black pumps. My hair, which I had finally cut, without my mother's approval, was tapered in the back and on the sides. The top was full and wavy, quite sexy, if I must say so myself. Black Onyx earrings and bangles were my only accessories. Add a touch of subtle make-up – I prefer the natural look – a splash of Amarige and I was looking like a date. I agreed with the adage, 'A little goes a long way.'

I could only imagine what other people were thinking as they watched Barry and me enter the restaurant. I knew we had that superstar aura. Barry had on well-tailored, brown pants, another snug, brown body shirt, and a dark tan blazer. He wore a pair of soft suede brown shoes. On one wrist he had a diamond tennis bracelet; on the other, was a stylish gold watch. As he reached out to take my hand, I noticed his nails were manicured. He wore one gold, diamond-encrusted ring on his forth finger. It wasn't a wedding ring, but it was impressive. He grabbed my hand. I loved the feeling of his strong fingers taking charge of mine. The maitre d' showed us to our table and Barry insisted that he be the one to seat me. This was the kind of thing that I had been missing; the subtle gestures men made that made a woman feel like a lady. I sighed with contentment as the waiter brought us two menus.

"Wow, Kayla," Barry said in that smooth sexy voice. "I thought you looked good in that white coat at the pharmacy. But this," he said, spreading his hands in my direction, "is to the tenth power."

"Oh, Barry, don't stop," I sighed jokingly. "But seriously, you look great," I said, staring straight into his eyes.

"Well, if you play your cards right," he paused for a moment. "This could be all yours," he said gesturing towards himself. I smiled, looking for a hint that he was joking, but he looked quite serious. A warning light came on in my head, which I quickly turned off.

'Of course he's playing,' I said silently, trying to convince myself. And so the night progressed smoothly as we dined on lobster fettuccini and steamed, mixed vegetables. Barry exhibited great taste in wine as he picked a fabulous white wine that accented the meal perfectly. There was a great band playing that night and we danced to some of the most romantic jazz I'd heard in a long time. The lead singer traversed between Billie Holiday, Mary Wilson, and even a little Sarah Vaughn with such ease, I wondered why she wasn't already a household name.

It was almost nine-thirty and I wasn't ready to end the dream date, so when Barry suggested a nightcap at his place, I had graciously accepted.

"Too bad you drove," Barry said. I was expecting him to say something romantic, like we could've taken a ride along East River Drive, parked, had a bottle of wine, and listened to love songs on the radio. But no, instead he said, "Then maybe we could've drove deep in the woods and knocked boots in my Corvette. That would've been a blast."

My heart began to sink. It seemed as if my Prince Charming had turned into an ugly toad, right in front of my eyes.

"But that's okay," he continued, "It'll be better at my place anyway. I have a king-size bed and plenty of rubbers. You're about to find out why my nickname is Duracell."

"Are you serious," I asked incredulously.

"Oh yeah, I got that name in college," he answered, obviously having no understanding of a rhetorical question. Suddenly I felt an enormous need to get out of the nightmare that was this date.

"You know, Barry, on second thought, maybe I

should just go home. I feel a headache coming on."

"Oh, Kayla, don't disappoint me. We had a wonderful night. I bought you a nice dinner; showed you a good time and I just want to end it right. Besides, it's a well known fact that good sex can cure a headache."

Wow, this guy is too much! "I don't know Barry," I started.

"Kayla," he interrupted, "There are a lot of women who would love to be in your shoes right now, to be out with a good- looking, successful man, who's not afraid to spend money to show a woman a good time, come on. Don't blow it."

"You know what, Barry? You're right," I said slowly.

"Now you're talking," he smiled. "I'll wait for you to get your car, then you can follow me."

"Okay," I answered. I went to my car and pulled up behind Barry's. As he gunned his engine to show the power of his Corvette and took off with a screech, I did the same, made a u-turn and headed in the opposite direction.

All the way home, I kept imagining Chloe's reaction when I told her about my date. I braced myself for the 'I told you so's' and the 'You would've had a better time with me's'. As soon as I got in the house, I checked for the blinking red light on the answering machine. There was none. I was so sure that Chloe would've called at least a half dozen times to see if I was home and how things went.

She probably went to bed early, since we didn't go out, I rationalized. It never dawned on me that she could have gone out without me. And it never even entered my psyche that she would've gone out with someone else. Thus, I went to bed smiling, satisfied with the notion that Chloe didn't call me because she went to bed early since I was not available.

# If Loving Two is Wrong . . .

## Chapter Eight

I woke up to the sound of pouring rain. I eyed the alarm clock with disbelief. It was almost noon. I hardly ever slept until twelve on a Saturday unless something physically or mentally stressed me out the night before. Then I remembered him. Barry Sanders, Sands, or whatever the hell his name was. How could I have ever gone out with him? Then my mind formed a mental picture of him. Oh yeah, but that just proved that a handsome face was a waste on an ugly disposition. I was getting a headache thinking about last night.

As I shuddered, trying to shake off the effects of our date, I glanced at the answering machine. Hmm, no calls. I looked back at the clock to double check that it was actually noon. Yep, it was now ten after and still, no Chloe. Maybe she was a little angrier than I had anticipated. Well, I'll just call her, apologize, tell her how horrible the date was and invite her out to breakfast. That should break the ice and soothe hurt feelings, I reckoned. After the third ring, I was about to hang up. Suddenly, I heard the sound of someone picking up.

"Hello," a man's voice came over the line. I was taken aback. "Hello? Is anyone there?" the voice came over a second time.

"I-I'm sorry," I responded when I was finally able to find my voice. "Is Chloe there?"

I was hoping that I had dialed the wrong number.

"Chloe's not here," he answered, confirming my worst fears. Since I didn't go out with Chloe last night, she decided to turn straight and spent the night with the first man she saw. Damn, what have I done?

"I'm sorry, but who am I speaking to?" I asked, not sure if I wanted to know the truth.

"I'm her brother, David," he answered. Relief flooded through my entire body.

55

"Hi, David," I said cheerfully. "I've heard a lot about you. My name is Kayla and I was supposed to meet Chloe last night but something came up, I was just calling to check on her."

"Oh, hi Kayla, I've heard a lot about you, too. I decided to surprise Chloe last night by flying in from Vegas, but when I got here, she was on her way out. I haven't even really had a chance to speak with her. But when she comes in, I'll tell her you called," he said, oblivious to the distress he was causing me. In the background I could hear a door opening, then the sound of laughter. Definitely female voices, I decided as I pushed the phone's earpiece damn near into my ear, straining to hear.

"Chloe, I'm definitely going to have to see it again. The theater was so noisy, I think we missed half the dialogue." That was a voice I had never heard before. I thought I knew most of Chloe's female friends.

"I know," Chloe agreed. "But if you had read the book, like I did, you would have had an easier time following the movie." Chloe was using that teasing tone that I had become accustomed to. What the hell was going on here? And who is that woman she's with?

"Hold on a sec," her brother was saying, "Here she comes now."

"Shh," I said impulsively, still trying to hear. I could hear Chloe inviting the girl in. But just as she was saying her name, Chloe's big-mouthed brother had started talking.

"I wish I could," the honey-voiced hussy was saying. "But I have a few errands to run. I'll call you when I get in."

"Excuse me," David said with a hint of irritation, obviously a delayed reaction to my hushing him.

"I'm sorry," I replied, trying to hide my annoyance. "That wasn't directed at you." I crossed my fingers for that blatant lie.

"No problem," he said with some degree of skepticism. I could hear the door closing in the background.

"Bye," David said just before the door shut.

So he knew the bitch too, huh. Well just how long

had Chloe been talking to this girl?

"Chloe, this is for you," he said handing her the phone.

"Hello," she answered cheerfully. Now that she was actually on the phone, I wasn't sure what to say, especially after what I had just heard. On the one hand, I was fuming.

How dare she go see Beloved without me, with another woman no less. And to top it all off, she stayed out the whole night. But on the other hand, what right did I have to get mad? I had gone out and did my own thing, at Chloe's expense for that matter. Plus, Chloe and I were just friends. I had no claims or exclusive rights to her time.

So if I knew all of this, why did I feel angry and jealous by what had transpired?

"Hello, is anyone here?" she asked for the second time. "David, there's no one there. Did they say who they were?" I heard her asking as she was lowering the receiver from her ear.

"It was your friend, Kayla, I told her you were coming. I guess she got impatient." That was the last thing I heard before the click.

Damn, why'd I give him my name? I waited by the phone for an hour to see if Chloe would call me. She didn't. Determined not to let the situation get the best of me, I decided to go to the video store, rent some movies, get some popcorn, and settle in alone for the first night since our meeting, that I would have no interaction with Chloe.

## Chapter Nine

Two weeks had passed by and Chloe and I had not spoken.

"Girl, what did you do to Chloe?" Jackie asked at one of our lunch meetings.

"What do you mean?" I asked, anxious to find out how Chloe was coping without me.

"Kayla, for the last week or so, she's been a real bitch. Staying at work late and piling up work on my desk with little nasty grams attached. Snapping out over the smallest things. And the coup d' grace, she hasn't paid for my lunch at all in the last two weeks. Now I don't know what the hell you did, but you better fix it."

"Really," I laughed, happy to hear how our separation was making Chloe grumpy. That meant that she must miss me.

"It ain't funny girl," Jackie said, rolling her eyes.

"It's getting to the point where I'm gonna have to start brown baggin' it. Now you know!"

"Oh, stop exaggerating," I said smacking her hand playfully.

"Seriously though," Jackie began, "She is miserable. We've never seen Chloe act like this. She's usually the upbeat one of the three. Even those two miserable men are starting to complain."

"Well, what do you want me to do?" I asked.

"I don't know," she said exasperated. "What ever you did to get her like that, undo it. Do the opposite."

"Get real, Jackie," I said half jokingly. "What makes you think that I can control Chloe's moods?"

"Well, all I know is, Chloe's mood change seemed to mysteriously happen around the same time you told me that you and her had a difference of opinion."

I never told Jackie the whole story behind me and

# If Loving Two is Wrong . . .

Chloe's falling out. Mainly because I felt that it was my fault. Maybe it was time for me to break the ice. I decided to extend the olive branch. Besides, truth be known; I was kind of miserable without Chloe. Her absence left a big void in my life.

"I'll talk to her," I said to Jackie. "But I don't know if it'll do any good."

"Well, it sure can't hurt," Jackie insisted. "Oh, girl, look at the time. I got three minutes to get back and I dare not be even one minute late. I'm telling you, Kayla," Jackie said as she stood and hurriedly put on her pink suede coat.

"Chloe has been a real bear lately. I don't even have time to wait for the check. You pay it this time and I'll get it next time. Love ya." She blew a kiss and rushed out the door before I could even get a sound out.

"That girl," was all I could say as I shook my head, laughing.

For the rest of the workday and all the way home, I did nothing but think about what I was going to say to Chloe. I wondered if I should I invite her to dinner and apologize over a nice home-cooked meal, or, apologize and then invite her out to dinner. That way, if she agreed to go to dinner, at least I'd know that she was somewhat accepting of my apology. On the other hand, if she accepted the apology, but declined dinner, she wasn't exactly ready to restore our friendship. Then again, I could just stop by and apologize in person. I quickly discarded that idea. What if during my surprise visit, I was the one surprised. I saw two weeks earlier how easily Chloe could bounce back.

When I entered the house, it was as if the answering machine was beckoning for my attention. Although I wished it deep down, I dared not hope that there would be a message from Chloe. It would just be too disappointing for me to listen to the three indicated messages, expecting to hear Chloe's voice telling me how much she missed me, and she hadn't even called. So, with false bravado, I pressed the button that held my heart at bay.

"Ms. Thomas, this is Dr. Sutton's office calling to

remind you about your dentist appointment on Monday. There's no need to call back if you plan to come, however..." I angrily fast-forwarded, mad at the receptionist for not being Chloe. The second message was breathing, but no words. I wondered if that was Chloe. Oh, this was agonizing. I felt my chest closing up as I held my breath and waited for the next message. Just as the message was about to play, the phone rang, automatically shutting off the machine.

"Hello," I said anxiously, desperately hoping it was Chloe.

"Hi, Baby," the familiar voice said, quickly dousing my hopes.

"Hi, Mom," I answered, trying not to sound disappointed, but failing miserably.

"Well, you don't have to sound so happy to hear from me," she said sarcastically.

"I'm sorry. It's just that I had a rough day and I just stepped in the house," I answered, only partly telling the truth.

"Oh, I'm sorry you had a bad day, baby. I was just calling to see if you could take me to Bingo tonight. Your father has a meeting to go to at five-thirty and he won't be back in time."

Great, just what I need, I thought.

"Hold on, Kayla, my other line is clicking."

Damn, I was definitely not in the mood. I had already decided that I would go home, fix myself a nice dinner, run a hot bath, enjoy a soothing drink and watch the two movies I had rented. Oh, well, I guess I might as well get myself ready to pick her up. As I was resigning myself to my fate, my mother clicked back over.

"Never mind, Kayla, you don't have to take me," she said jovially, so sure that I was going to in the first place.

"Are you sure?" I asked, instantly angry with myself for leaving an opening.

"Yeah, Baby. That was Miss Esther. She's driving tonight, so I can ride with her. Thanks anyway."

# If Loving Two is Wrong . . .

"Okay, Mom," I answered, relieved.

"Okay, baby, but before I go, I'll just tell you that your brother is doing fine. He calls me almost everyday, unlike my other child, who acts like she can't call her mama."

"Oh, Mom," I groaned, not wanting to hear the familiar tirade.

"Don't worry, Kayla," she continued. "I don't have time to get into it. I have to cook dinner for your father before I leave. I guess you're lucky, not having to worry about that, not having a man and all. I guess I'll just have to depend on Tony for my grandchildren. Oh, well. I have to go, baby. Talk to you later."

She hung up before I could respond, even though I doubt I would've tried. It was better to let her have the last word, especially on that subject.

As I was about to head to the kitchen to start dinner, I noticed the blinking light on the answering machine. Oh yeah, I had one more message. Once again I felt the blood rushing to my head as I pressed the button, prepared for the worst, but secretly hoping to hear Chloe's voice.

'Hi, Kayla,' the feminine voice began, 'this is Jackie. Just calling to remind you to call Chloe.' As I exhaled, I had to smile. The jig was up. Chloe hadn't called and I experienced all that anxiety for nothing. I was too mentally exhausted to call Chloe now. Perhaps after I ate and took my bath, I would be relaxed enough to call. I went to the kitchen, took out a nice steak, that I had marinated the night before and decided to have a broccoli and cheese baked potato with it. Quick, easy and delicious. I placed a few small bottles of Verdi in the freezer to chill. Now, all that was left was to run my steamy hot bubble bath and relax. As I started up the stairs, I could hear the vibrating sound of my beeper. I looked down to watch it dance noisily across the table, bounce off the answering machine and come to rest nervously against the telephone. I'm not going to check it; I lied to myself as I descended the stairs.

Voicemail, hmm. It better not be Carl calling to ask

61

me to fill in for Henry again tomorrow. This would make the third Saturday in a row that Henry had called out for some reason or another.

Carl had started paging me after I told him I didn't get a few of his messages because my answering machine had jammed, lying of course. So, I reluctantly dialed my voice mail, punched in my code and waited for Carl's droning voice.

"Hi, Kayla, I tried to catch you at work, but they said you had already left. Give me a call when you get this message."

It was Chloe! My heart and pulse were racing as I elatedly dialed her number.

"Hello," a silky voice answered, but it wasn't Chloe. I felt a mixture of disappointment and anger welling up inside of me. Chloe had set me up to see for myself just how well she was doing without me.

"Hello?" the sugary-voiced hussy repeated. I was about to hang up, and then decided, what the hell, I might as well get it over with.

"Hello, may I speak to Chloe?"

"Who," she asked sweetly. Oh, this bitch was about to get on my last nerve. I wanted to say, you know, Chloe, the woman who's giving me an anxiety attack and you happen to be sleeping with. But instead I simply repeated, "Chloe."

"I'm sorry, you have the wrong number," the sweet paragon of loveliness answered.

"I'm sorry for disturbing you," I said with as much sincerity as I could muster. Silently, I apologized for all the bad things I had just thought about her.

"No problem," she continued, sweet as apple pie. I hung up feeling as though I had just spoken with an angel. In all my excitement, I had dialed the wrong number. I decided to calm down and take some time to regroup before I attempted to call her again. I had to get my game plan ready. I was determined not to appear anxious. She must never know how much I missed her or how badly I wanted to talk to her. I took several deep breaths, and then carefully dialed her number. After three agonizing rings, I heard the click of the receiver being picked up.

"Hello?" It was her; I'd know her voice anywhere.

"Hey, Chloe, it's Kayla," I blurted out. So much for rule number one, be calm, cool, and collected.

"Hi, Kayla. I had called you at home earlier, but your answering machine came on. I didn't leave a message because I figured I'd catch you at work. But when I called there, you had left already, so I paged you. You can be really elusive you know?"

I was just so happy to be speaking to her that I didn't hear half of what she said. I was thinking, if I had known that was her breathing on my answering machine, I would have saved it. Boy, I'm really getting ridiculous.

"Actually, I was going to call you," I blurted out again. Careful, stick to the game plan, I reminded myself. Don't appear anxious.

"Oh, really," she said mockingly.

"Seriously," I said. "I couldn't take it anymore. I've been miserable not talking to you. I know I was wrong to choose to go out with that jerk, Barry, when you and I had plans. There's no excuse for what I did. I know it hurt your feelings and I'm so sorry."

I must have rambled on for another minute or so before Chloe finally stopped me.

"Kayla, slow down," she laughed.

Well, now that my game plan was blown to hell, I figured I might as well be completely honest. "I'm sorry, I've just missed you so much. I guess I just took your friendship for granted."

"Yeah, I was pretty steamed," she said. "You acted as though this man was your last chance for happiness."

"Girl, you just don't know. It turned out to be the date from hell."

"What happened?" she asked, surprised.

"He turned out to be nothing more than a poorly trained, well-dressed ape, that could drive." I recounted the whole date to her and when I got to the part where he

63

suggested we have sex, Chloe was silent in stunned disbelief.

"Wow, this guy is an asshole," she exclaimed.

"More like a whole ass," I countered.

"You didn't go, did you?" she asked incredulously

"Hell no," I responded. "I acted like I was going to follow him. Then I made a u-turn and came home."

"Damn, he's' so self-indulgent, he probably didn't even realize you weren't there until he got home."

"Maybe not even then," I answered. "He probably got home and was relieved I wasn't there. That way he could make love to his own beautiful, egotistical self." Chloe had to laugh at that.

"But you're not off the hook," she added. Although her tone was light, I could still hear the hurt in it.

"I know," I sighed. "I was wrong, but you delivered a little heart dart yourself."

"What do you mean?" she asked innocently.

"I called you the day after my date. Your brother answered the phone," I began.

"Oh yeah, I remember that," she interrupted. "Why'd you hang up?"

"Because I heard when you came home from your date with that female. I was angry and upset that you went to the movies to see Beloved with her instead of me."

"Well," Chloe began, but this time I interrupted.

"I know, I know. I've got a lot of nerve, but that's how I felt."

"Is that why you didn't call me back?" she asked.

"Yes," I admitted. "I heard your brother tell you that it was me on the other line, but when you took the phone, I just didn't say anything. After you hung up, I thought you would call me back, but you didn't."

"Damn right," Chloe snorted. "I was very hurt and I have my pride too, girl."

"I know," I said, "I'm so sorry." I was beginning to sound like a broken record.

"So what's happening with you and that girl?" I asked, not sure if I really wanted to know.

"What girl," she asked, as if she really didn't know who I was talking about.

"The one you were so giddy with that day. The one who you took to see the movie we were supposed to see," I said, feeling the anger and jealousy all over again.

"Oh, her," she chuckled, as if dismissing the whole concept. "Well, if you would've had the balls to speak up that day you would've found out that was my cousin, Crystal."

"Oh," I said dumbfounded. Once again I silently apologized for saying hateful things about an innocent bystander.

"And we went to a Black Women In Film Festival. The feature of the day was The Color Purple by Alice Walker, not Beloved by Toni Morrison," she said, making an obvious point.

"Oh, I assumed when you talked about having read the book, you were talking about Beloved," I countered.

Chloe was not going to make this easy, but I didn't care. After hearing that was her cousin, I was on cloud nine. I had a sudden urge to see Chloe right away.

"Why don't you come by," I asked, desperately hoping she'd say yes.

"Well I have a few things that I need to do but how about we meet for breakfast tomorrow?" I was disappointed, but managed to say, okay.

"Oh, and Kayla," she said suddenly.

"Yes," I answered.

"Plan on spending the whole day with me. We have a lot of catching up to do."

"Okay," I said elatedly.

Once we hung up, I bounced up the stairs singing Alyson Williams' 'Just Call My Name.' It was only after I settled into my peach scented bubble bath that I allowed myself the luxury of daydreaming about a fun-filled tomorrow, now that my best friend was talking to me again.

## Chapter Ten

I woke up on a high note. Birds were chirping and the sun was playing peek-a-boo with the clouds, hinting of a bright, warm beautiful day. I reached over and turned the radio on to aid me in my getting up process. The booming voice of the DJ roused me from my warm covers and I headed to the bathroom to get washed.

Frankie Beverly's 'Love Is The Key' was playing on the radio and I was thinking, Sho' you right, as I brushed my teeth in rhythm with the uptempo tune. What a difference a day could make. Everyday for the past two weeks, I had been getting up and following the same routine, dragging. But that day, I was moving like someone had stuck a stick of dynamite in the crack of my ass, and I was happy about it. Of course, I knew the underlying reason, but I was not quite ready to attribute all of that happiness to reuniting with Chloe. I mean, what would that be saying about me and my dependence on her?

"It's going to be a beautiful day," the DJ's voice broke through my consciousness.

"Bright and sunny with a high of eighty degrees. Right now it's sixty-eight out there, so get up and get out of the house!" I had to smile at his enthusiasm as I headed toward the closet to find something to wear. Since it was double play Tuesday, another Frankie Beverly and Maze tune floated from the radio. 'Joy and pain, like sunshine and rain', the lyrics wafted from the bathroom to my room.

"You got that right, Frankie, love is just like that," I said, snapping my fingers to the beat.
R-ring

"The moment I've been waiting for," I said aloud. "Good morning, heartache," I sang playfully into the receiver.

# If Loving Two is Wrong . . .

"Well, good morning to you too, nuisance," my mother's agitated voice snapped back at me.

"Oh, Mom, I'm sorry, I thought you were somebody else," I added, hastily.

"Well now," she began. "That should teach you to answer the phone with some common sense. You should at least know who you're insulting before you do it. Now who's giving my baby such heartache?"

"No one, Mom, I was just being playful."

"Anyone in particular that I should know about?" she picked.

"No," I sighed. "What's up?"

"Your father decided to barbecue today. Tony's coming by with a date; I was calling to see if you'd like to join us. You know, the whole family together. It would be nice for a change."

"Sorry, Mom, but I already have plans for the day," I said as gently as I could.

"Oh, Kayla, we hardly ever get together like this and it's such a beautiful day. Why don't you just call whoever you've made plans with and..." just then my other line beeped.

"Hold that thought, Mom, I have to get the other line." I clicked over before she could object.

"Hey, lifesaver," I answered. Once again putting my intuition on the line.

"Wow, what a greeting, what did I do to deserve it?" Chloe responded.

"Mom's on the other line," I answered.

"Say no more, do you want me to call you back?"

"Hang up and die," was my response "Hold on a second."

"Mom, I'll call you back, okay?"

"Okay, Kayla," she said resignedly.

"What's up?" I asked, returning to Chloe.

"Is everything okay with your mom?"

"She and my Dad are cooking out today and my presence has been requested," I said, exasperated.

"Kayla, I think it's sweet how your parents always want you around. I miss my family dinners and barbecues," Chloe lamented.

"Yeah, that's because you're so far from home and don't get the constant inquiries and nagging," I laughed.

"But seriously, I do appreciate my mom, but sometimes I feel smothered. Like I'm not truly in charge of my own actions. Like today, I already had plans, but I feel guilty telling my mom no."

"Well, Kayla, if you want to go to your mom's today, I understand," Chloe said sympathetically.

"No, Chloe," I said adamantly. "I've made plans to spend the day with you and that's that. If my mom doesn't want to do something, she doesn't do it. She's just going to have to learn to accept the word, no, from me."

"Okay, Miss Grown," Chloe laughed, "How about a little breakfast this morning?"

"Good, I've been wanting some pancakes all week."

"Okay," Chloe answered. "It's nine o'clock now. How about we meet at the IHOP on the Boulevard at ten."

"See you then," I said, and we hung up. I decided to put on my white tennis dress with the blue stripe down the side. It stopped just above the knee. I chose my white cloth Nike sneakers with ankle socks. The effect was sporty cute. Who you dressing so cute for?

"Shut up," I said, aloud, refusing to admit that I wanted to look cute for Chloe. A little light make-up and I was out of the house by nine-thirty.

I reached the restaurant before Chloe, so I decided to get the table before the line got long. Knowing Chloe's taste and punctual nature, I took the initiative and ordered coffee and breakfast for both of us. At two minutes to ten, Chloe strolled through the doors. She looked gorgeous as usual. I had just gotten used to being comfortable with the idea of looking at her appreciatively before we stopped talking to each other; now, that feeling of embarrassment was creeping up on me again.

Chloe spotted me and walked towards me, smiling. She was wearing tan slacks, and an off the shoulder, salmon colored knit shirt that really showed off her cleavage. She had on a choker, which matched the color of her shirt, matching earrings and a pair of tan sling-back sandals. Her hair was pulled back into a ponytail and she wore a light coating of make-up, which I never thought she needed. Casual, yet sophisticated.

The consummate lawyer.

I smiled as she approached the table.

"Are you just going to sit there?" she asked, breaking my concentration.

"Huh?" I said dumbly.

"Get up and give me a hug," she demanded.

I stood and wrapped my arms around her. I inhaled deeply, taking in the scent of her familiar Cool Water perfume. I hadn't realized how much I missed it until that moment. The embrace felt so good that I didn't want to let go; it seemed as if she shared my sentiment. Finally, she broke the embrace with a kiss on the cheek.

"We've been acting so juvenile," she announced. "It's really good to see you. It almost feels like the first time we met."

"Yeah, it does," I agreed. We skipped over 'the I'm sorries' and 'you did me wrongs' and started catching up on what had been happening with each other.

"Nothing exciting to report," I said stoically, "I've just been working and going home."

"I've been kind of busy," Chloe said excitedly. "I've acquired three new clients and won big settlements for two other ones." She had that familiar twinkle in her eye as she talked about her work. I had missed that, too.

For the next hour and a half we talked and laughed, basking in the joy of being in each other's company again. I was so mesmerized with being back with my friend that I hardly remembered tasting the pancakes I had wanted so badly.

We decided to go into town and stroll through downtown Philadelphia, better known as Center City. It's the hub of the city, consisting of different clothing, electronic, and specialty shops and the main shopping mall, known as 'The Gallery'. There is also a plethora of restaurants, record stores, street vendors, arcades, and movie theaters. For culturalists, there's the Art Museum on the Parkway or the African American Cultural Museum on Seventh and Arch Streets. For the romantic history buff, you can take a horse drawn carriage ride through historical Philadelphia. You'll see the Betsy Ross House, home of the original U.S. flag maker, and a small street of cobblestone, reminiscent of how narrow streets used to be before automobiles, when horses were the main mode of transportation. South Street is also a popular hangout, especially for teens and young adults who enjoy trendy clothing stores and artsy folks. When the sun sets, the older crowds gather at the indoor and outdoor jazz café's or stroll hand in hand enjoying the sights and sounds that South Street offers. You could dip into a bar at anytime and experience a live band or stop at the comedy club and witness up and coming comedians honing their skills on the dream-laden stairs to Hollywood. Then there's Penn's Landing, an area by the river that's bustling with a mecca of activities during the day, from musical acts to mimes. At night, lovers enjoy the moonlit starry setting, watching boats sail across the river and cuddling against the breeze generated by the water. It can never be said that there's nothing to do in Philly.

As Chloe and I strolled down Walnut Street, we passed a movie theater; the marquee had the word 'Beloved' emblazoned in bold black letters. Chloe and I just looked at each other and laughed. Without saying a word, she grabbed my arm and we headed toward the ticket booth. A little over two hours later, we emerged from the theater, both unsure of what we had just witnessed. Although Chloe had read the book, we both decided we should see it again. As we headed down Tenth Street towards the Gallery, there was a ringing sound coming from Chloe's pocketbook. I watched as Chloe took the phone from her bag and put it to her ear.

"Hello," she answered. "I see, well, give me forty-five minutes."

## If Loving Two is Wrong . . .

My heart sank. I knew our reunion was about to end.

"I'm sorry, Kayla," Chloe said turning to me. "That was the answering service. Something very important has come up and I have to take care of it."

"I understand," I said, trying to sound as if I really meant it.

"Look, why don't you go ahead to your mother's house for the barbecue. Your family will be happy to see you and I'll call you as soon as I'm finished at the office."

"Yeah, right," I answered with a pout, "you know you'll be gone all day."

"No I won't, Kayla," she said, "I promise I'll call you in a few hours."

## Chapter Eleven

All the way to my parent's house; I lamented on how much I missed Chloe already after seeing her for only a few hours. I drove into my parents' driveway and was surprised by the level of noise and loud music I heard emanating from the backyard. I eased down the walkway and peeked curiously through the gate. I could see my dad with his chef's hat on, tending to the grill and laughing loudly, as if he had just heard the funniest joke in the world: a trait he got from Grandpop, I'm sure. Mom was placing another bowl of what looked like macaroni salad on the table. The yard was full of kids running and skipping. The adults were doing the bop to the oldies blaring out of the speakers placed strategically around the patio. I knew Uncle Peanut had to be behind turntables number one and two. He used to be called Peanut Butter because he was so smooth; at least that's what he says. My mom said it was because he was, and still is, so nutty. But anyway, whenever the family gets together, he always settles himself behind the stereo system and mixes the oldies with a little hip-hop. He always travels with his own collection of tapes and cd's. 'You never know when a funky occasion may arise, and old Peanut is called on to get funkdafied'. Unfortunately, that was one of his favorite sayings. I eased on in the gate, marveling at the sight of cousins, uncles and aunts that I hadn't seen since last summer. I braced myself for the kiss and hug fest as I made my way towards my mom.

"Kayla!" I'd been spotted.

"Hey, Mom."

"I thought you were too busy to make it," she said, hands on her hips.

"That's not what I said, Mom. I said I already had plans. But they were interrupted, so I came over."

# If Loving Two is Wrong . . .

"Well, La Di Da," she said sarcastically.

"You didn't tell me it was going to be a blow out like this," I said, ignoring her sarcasm.

"Well initially it wasn't planned to be this big. But I told Peanut and he told Jesse and who knows who Jesse told. But in any event, word got around and everyone called to see what he or she should bring. I'm glad you came. Everyone was asking for you and I didn't know what to tell them."

I could feel my eyes going to the top of my head.

"I mean, a family cookout and you didn't want to show up," she continued without missing a beat.

"I'm glad I came, Mom," I said earnestly. "Where's Tony?"

"He's out here somewhere. Oh, and he brought the loveliest young lady with him, Kayla. I haven't had time to talk to her yet, but she seems so nice."

I tried to break camp before the inevitable, but I was too slow. "How come you didn't bring someone, Kayla?"

"I told you, Mom, I didn't know I was going to stop by," I answered, hoping in vain that she would let that answer suffice.

"I'm sure you were with someone, how come you didn't bring them by?"

"I was with my friend, Chloe,"

"Well how come you didn't invite her?"

"She's a lawyer, and she had some important business come up, so she had to go to the office."

"Oh," mom answered, "Well whatever happened to that nice young man you brought here the other day?" Man, she can be like a dog on a bone. Just won't let it go.

"Mom," I sighed, "that was over three months ago, and Rick and I don't even see each other anymore."

"Well, why not Kayla? He was such a nice guy and what was it he did again?" she paused, acting as if she really didn't know. Then suddenly, "that's right," she crowed, snapping her fingers. "He was a doctor wasn't he? An

73

orthopedic surgeon if I remember correctly."

I had to laugh in spite of myself. For the life of me, I couldn't understand how the Oscar committee could miss nominating my mother for best actress.

"Yes, Mom, you're right. He is a surgeon, but he didn't just cut up in the operating room, he cut up everywhere. Rick was so pompous. He felt just being with him was such a privilege that I should drop everything and be at his beck and call."

"Oh, Kayla, he couldn't have been that bad."

"Trust me, yes he was."

"Well, what about…"

"Mom," I interrupted, "I just want to be here and enjoy myself like everyone else. You're about to run me out of here with the third degree."

"Oh, girl, get on outta my face. I'm just trying to find out what's going on with you; that's all. You never offer any information."

Suddenly, at that moment my mother looked very fragile. Although she was far from old at fifty-seven, I could see the changes of time on her from when I was that nappy-headed girl of thirteen, begging her to let me wear suede in the dead of summer.

"You know what, Mom," I said, feeling very sentimental, "You're right. I don't spend enough time with you."

Don't do it Kayla, my subconscious was screaming at me. But that hopeful look in my Mom's face just pushed me over the edge.

"How about we get together one day next week for lunch."

"Oh, Kayla, I'd love that," Mom answered, smiling so affectatiously, I found myself with a big ol' Kool Aid smile on my face.

"I'm gonna call you first thing Monday morning and lock down a date because I know you'll act like you forgot. Well I'm going back in the kitchen to see what's going on in there. You go ahead and mingle."

As I watched my mom retreat into the house, I could

feel my humongous smile dissipate. It reminded me of a cartoon where the character has a plastered on smile that literally begins to crack. What the hell did I just do, I was thinking as the last visage of a smile fell from my lips. Feeling quite victimized, I decided to stalk some prey of my own.

Now, the first rule of a good stalker is to know your prey, so I zeroed in on the table that held the ambrosia. The long picnic table was covered with the traditional red and white-checkered cloth and held big tins of fried, barbecued and baked chicken, barbecue ribs, various salads, and rolls. Collard greens and green beans were in foil pans on burners and, of course, there were the traditional hot dogs, sausages, burgers, and baked beans. There were two large trashcans full of crabs, I know that was Uncle Peanut's contribution. He's a crab enthusiast, and believe you me, he'll try to eat each and every last one of them. Two other trashcans were filled with sodas and juices for the kids. A fully stocked bar was set up outside for adult pleasures. I found it incredible that such an impromptu gathering could yield so much food, drink and people. But then again, the Thomas' were notorious for liking to get their groove and, especially, their eat on. And there he was, just as I knew he would be, my target. Sticking out like a sore thumb, climbing over the kids to get to the different platters, was my brother, Tony.

"Hi, there, suck up," I said sidling up to him.

"Hey Kayla," he grinned turning to face me, actually acting as if he was happy to see me. "Suck up?" he asked with raised eyebrows.

"Yes, suck up," I said, nodding my head on each syllable. "All I hear is Tony is coming by to see me, Tony calls me everyday, Tony is seeing a nice young lady, Tony, Tony, Tony," I whined doing my best Jan Brady impression.

"Aw, come on, girl," he laughed, "You know Mom exaggerates. I call her maybe twice a week and I stop by occasionally. It's just more occasionally than you."

What could I say? I was guilty. Suddenly I was feeling very defeated. I had come to Tony expecting to ridicule him in some form or fashion, but instead, he avoided my shots and adeptly fired back a few of his own. He had succeeded in making me feel like a lousy daughter. And to add insult to injury, I had roped myself into a lunch date with Mom. Wait a minute. Maybe that was my problem. Attitude. Maybe if I approached the idea of spending time with Mom more positively, the experience might be more pleasant. Doubtful, but I'd give it a try. So, armed with a new plan and outlook; I set forth to enjoy myself at my family cookout.

"Kayla!" I turned to see my dad behind me with a fresh batch of ribs.

"Hi, Dad," I returned. "Nice spread you put on here."

"How about that," he said jovially, "And so unexpected."

Just then, Mom came over with a pot of corn on the cob. Here we were, the whole immediate family, together within the rest of the family. It would've made a nice Norman Rockwell painting.

"So, Kayla, have you met Tony's lady friend?" Mom asked.

Here we go. I guess this is as good a time as any to practice that new attitude.

"As a matter of fact, I haven't," I answered more cheerily than I would've under normal circumstances. Ooh, I was actually doing it. Thinking positively.

"Neither have we," Mom said, giving Tony the evil eye.

"Where is she Tony," I asked pleasantly, warming up to my new concept.

"Over there," he said, pointing to a woman seated under the canopy. She looked quite uncomfortable, surrounded by the seven or eight little aliens that seemed intent on invading her space. If that wasn't enough, my sixteen-year-old cousins, Vance and Lance, Peanut's twins, were ogling her like fresh new meat. But the coup de grace was Aunt Ernie, short for Ernestine. She was my great aunt and she had a face that made Esther from Sanford and Son look like Halle Berry. And right now her bulging eyes were glaring at the poor young woman who did nothing more than accompany Tony to the cookout. See, Aunt Ernie had fashioned herself as the family matchmaker, and right about now, she was none too happy with Tony's choice. She couldn't understand for the life of her and those were her own words, why Tony didn't like Sissy Mae, the niece of one of Aunt Ernie's good friends. Sissy Mae was from the backwoods of King Queen County, VA. Now, I'm not saying that King Queen County doesn't have it's share of beautiful women, I'm quite sure it does. But Sissy Mae was not one of them. Besides being seven years older than Tony, Sissy Mae's most prized possessions were the four teeth that seemed to be renting space in her mouth. And their lease was almost up. It had been nearly three years since Tony told Aunt Ernie that he wasn't interested in her girlfriend's niece. But each time she saw Tony with a woman, she acted as if it were a freshly dealt blow.

"Hey, K" Tony called to his friend. She turned toward Tony with an expression that seemed to be screaming for help.

"Come here a minute, baby, and meet my family."

"Baby," I whispered mockingly. Tony nudged me with his elbow. It may have been my imagination, but it appeared as if his girlfriend bounded over to us like a wild deer sprung from a trap. Tony began the introductions.

"Keilani, this is my mother, Toni, my father, Gerald, and my sister, Kayla. And this," he said placing his arms around her, "is Keilani. Keilani Thomas."

"Oh Lord, Gerald," Mom wailed dramatically, turning toward my father, "they done got married and didn't tell us a thing. Bring me a chair baby, I feel like I'm going to faint."

"Oh Mom, calm down," Tony said, embarrassed. "We didn't get married. Thomas is Keilani's family name too."

"Oh, chile, don't' scare mama like that. I almost dropped dead," she said, fanning herself with her hand.

Poor Keilani, I thought, as I looked at her. She wore an expression that flashed, "mortified" like a beacon.

"Keilani, relax," I said, breaking the ice. "Those comments were not meant as a personal attack on you."

"Oh, no, baby," Mom interrupted. "I'm sorry if I hurt your feelings. I think you're a lovely girl. It's just when I heard him say your name like that, like he was making some real big announcement," she paused to place her hands on her hip and glare at Tony. "I thought he was trying to tell us that y'all eloped or something."

"Aw, come on, Mom," Tony laughed. "You know I wouldn't do anything like that to you. I mean, with your bad heart and high blood pressure and whatever else flares up whenever we do something you don't' like." We all had to laugh at that, even Keilani.

"Aw, boy, shut up," Mom laughed, playfully hitting Tony and rolling her eyes.

"Come here, Keilani," my mother, said extending her hand to the woman. "Let me get a good look at you." Somewhat embarrassed, but less mortified, she took my mother's hand and walked toward her.

It was easy to see why Tony chose Keilani; she was beautiful. She was about 5'8", 145 lbs with long jet-black hair and beautiful, slightly slanted gray eyes. Her honey brown skin was flawless. She was very exotic looking and her manner was sophisticated yet warm and approachable. Like I said, it was easy to see why Tony liked her, but what in the world did she see in him? I looked over at Tony. He is kind of cute, I acknowledged grudgingly. He was 6'2", 235 lbs, all muscle, had curly, black hair and brown eyes that seemed to lighten when you looked directly in them. He also had a smile that could just melt your heart away. Right now, he was looking like a proud father showing off his adorable little girl.

"You're such a beautiful girl, Keilani," Mom was saying. "And your name, I know it's Hawaiian. Are you from there?"

"Actually, I was born and raised in Philadelphia. But my mother is a native of Hawaii," Keilani answered.

"How about your father?" Mom asked, getting deep down nosy. But I must admit that I wanted to know the answers too.

"Well, my dad," Keilani continued, "is half African American and French Canadian."

"Hmm," Mom said raising her hand to her chin as if considering something very heavy. "Maybe I should've married someone half Hawaiian and French Canadian, I got the African American part covered. Then, maybe I could've had some good looking children," she laughed.

"Hey," Tony, Dad, and I chimed in unison.

"Just joking babies, I know I have some beautiful children and a husband that's better looking than Billy Dee and cooler than Calvin Lockhart in their prime."

"Who?" I said jokingly. Looking at my mother and father, I felt very proud of my family. My father was still good looking at fifty-nine. Not very tall, dad was about 5'7", 245 lbs, light skinned with curly black hair and a jovial manner that made him adorable. Mom was a little more serious, heck, a lot more serious. But mom was very giving, warm hearted and very sensitive. Always ready to lend a helping hand and willing to go out of her way, especially when it came to family. When she was happy, you were happy. And when mom was happy, you knew it. Two of the deepest dimples popped out on either side of her cheeks, caused by a smile big enough to make Nipsey Russell jealous. And her eyes gave off a twinkle. It wasn't uncommon for her and Dad to be mistaken for brother and sister; they'd been married for almost forty years.

"Why didn't you bring a date, Kayla?" Tony blurted out of the blue. The effect was as if he was screaming, but he was actually speaking in a normal tone. Nonetheless, it messed up my little Kodak moment.

"Oh, no, don't tell me," he continued, ignoring my obvious glare. "You're still waiting for Mark? You haven't gotten over that crush, have you?"

Although I knew he was joking, Tony struck the same chord in me that he struck on my thirteenth birthday. The only difference was, now I really was a woman. I couldn't just stomp up the stairs to my bedroom anymore. In one brief moment, Tony had destroyed the closeness it had taken us over fifteen years to build. Yeah, I knew I was being dramatic, but since I had been hanging out with Chloe, I hadn't really thought much about Mark. Now, when Tony brought up his name; a whole flood of memories came rushing back and it was kind of painful. I had loved Mark with all my heart and those feelings weren't gone; they had just been tucked safely away in a compartment in my heart. My facial expression must've indicated what I was feeling because Tony immediately began apologizing.

"Kayla, I'm sorry," he said sincerely. "I didn't realize Mark was still a soft spot for you."

"Girl, I know you don't call yourself waiting for Mark," Mom interrupted. All of a sudden, it seemed as if everything was moving in slow motion. I could see my dad pretending to ask Mom a serious question, but I knew it was just an attempt to derail my mom's inevitable barrage. I saw Tony and Keilani watching me as if I was the most pitiful sight they'd ever seen. I turned and looked around the yard at my aunts and uncles and cousins with their boyfriends and girlfriends. It appeared as if they were all looking and laughing at me, pitiful Kayla, the only woman in the world without a boyfriend or husband. I began to feel like Carrie, a character in a movie who was a social outcast. Most of the other high school students ridiculed her, and on prom night, they humiliated her so bad, she set the gym on fire with her telekinetic powers, extinguishing everyone in sight. I was just about to do the same to the barbecue when my pager began to vibrate, catching my attention and saving everyone. I slowly checked my pager; there was Chloe's phone number. Suddenly everything sped up to real time. Mom, dad, Tony, and Keilani were still watching me, but everyone else was busy doing their own thing.

"Kayla, are you alright, honey," Dad asked, his face and voice filled with concern.

"Oh, yes, Daddy, I'm fine," I said, regaining my composure. I shuddered, feeling as if I had really just acted out a scene from that movie.

"Excuse me, everyone," I said, "but I have to use the

phone," and I disappeared into the house, leaving them watching my departure with bewilderment. I strode purposely toward the phone to call Chloe. Right now, she was the next best thing to Calgon.

"Speak to me, " she said, answering on the second ring.

"Hey, Chloe, it's me."

"I know, baby," she answered, instantly sending a chill up my spine. "How's the barbecue?"

"Quite a spread," I answered distractedly. 'I know, baby' kept reverberating in my head. She had called me baby. I kept thinking how it sounded so nice and natural.

"Kayla, did you hear me?" Chloe asked, sounding as if she had repeated herself a few times.

Snapping out of it, I managed to say, "Huh, what were you saying?"

"Girl, where is your head at?" Chloe asked.
If only you knew, but instead I said, "I must've been day dreaming."

"Okay, baby, well snap out of it."
She had said it again! Boy, I was really tripping, but this time I managed to stay with the conversation.

"I had asked you if you could meet me at my apartment in about an hour," she continued.

An hour, why not now, but I simply said, "Okay."

"Alright, see you then, bye," and she hung up. I desperately pressed my ear to the phone,
hoping to hear one last baby, but it never came. I looked at the phone as if it had somehow captured the words and hid them deep within its electronic mechanisms. I shook the phone jokingly, as if the words I wanted to hear would magically fall out.

"Kayla, get a grip girl," I said to myself, laughingly. Bounding from the house, I literally skipped back over to the little circle I had left dejectedly only two minutes ago. I was almost bubbly when I announced that I had to leave.

"Are you sure you're okay dear?" Mom asked slowly, a puzzled look on her face. And judging from the rest of the group's facial expressions, they were all wondering the same thing.

"I'm fine, really," I said almost laughing, leaving them even further confused about my change of emotions. Satisfied that they had no idea what was going on with me, I gave Mom, Dad, and Tony a kiss on the cheek and shook Keilani's hand. Then I headed to my car. I could hear Mom's voice in the background.

"I wonder who that page was from. It sure changed her attitude." I was dreading our lunch date next week already. As I backed my car out of the driveway, I turned the radio on. There was an oldies song playing that literally made me put on my brakes. 'Too busy Thinking About My Baby' by the Temptations. I recalled a long time ago, at one of my parent's get-togethers, Uncle Peanut played that song. Right then and there I adopted it as my theme song for Mark. Humming, I continued out of the driveway, my mind on Mark. Why did Tony have to bring him up? It had been months since I last heard from him and I had finally gotten over my insecurity complex. Now I began to wonder all over again. Why did he stop calling me, coming to see me, wanting me? All of these questions I had pondered endlessly, crying myself to sleep nightly. Just when I was able to go weeks without thinking of him, this had to happen. Memories began to flood my mind and tears welled up in my eyes as I drove almost blindly and definitely distractedly towards my destination. Destination? Just then I thought of Chloe. She had been a bright spot that shined at just the right time. She was the part of the equation that made losing Mark a less bitter pill to swallow. Now my mind began to traverse between Mark and Chloe. Absentmindedly, I pulled up in front of Chloe's building. I didn't remember stopping for any lights or making any turns. Man, my head was really doing a number on me. Mr. Williams, the elderly doorman greeted me at the entrance. Chloe had already notified the staff that I was allowed access, even in her absence. I had a key to her apartment, but only used it when necessary. If she was home, I always knocked or rang the bell instead of just letting myself in. I took the elevator to the third floor. As I approached her condo, I was questioning my feelings for either of them. I reached for her doorbell, trying to shake the cobwebs from my mind. I didn't want to burden or upset her with my impending emotional breakdown.

"Come in, it's open," I heard Chloe call out, breaking through my mental fog. As I turned the knob, I was determined to put on my best face.

I definitely was not prepared for what greeted me when I entered Chloe's apartment. The lights were off, but the rooms were illuminated by candlelight. White and rose colored candles, in beautiful gold-rimmed crystal holders, were strategically set about the room, creating a smoky, yet mystical glow. Two rows of white candles started at the door and made a pathway atop the maroon colored carpet to the downstairs bathroom. Second only to the beautiful sight, was the magnificent aroma of the jasmine, daffodil, and berry scents emanating from the combination of candles. Rose petals had been sprinkled in the lined walkway.

What the hell? I knew Chloe was expecting me, or was she? I began to feel confused. I checked my beeper again; yeah it was Chloe who had paged me almost an hour before. What is going on?

"Kayla, close the door and follow the lighted path," I heard Chloe's voice wafting softly from the bathroom area, answering most of my questions within that one sentence. I hadn't realized that I was still standing in the doorway. I stepped in, closed the door and slowly made through the candlelit living room towards her voice. As I neared the bathroom, Chloe's voice softly spoke out again.

"Stop right there, Kayla. Remove all of your clothing."

"What?" I began in protest, but was interrupted by Chloe.

"Kayla, do you trust me?" she asked.

"Of course," I said slowly, "But..."

"No buts," Chloe interrupted again, "if you trust me, just do as I say."

83

**Kim Beverly**

I stood stock still for a moment, contemplating what I was in store for. At that moment I realized that we were reaching a turning point in our friendship and how I proceeded from that moment on, would forever change the course of our relationship. I took a deep breath and then exhaled. Slowly, I began to unbutton my shirt. My heart was beating so strongly that I could hear and feel the pounding in my ears. I was so preoccupied with my thoughts that I barely noticed when the stereo magically came to life. The romantic stylings of Gerald Albright saturated the room and I found myself getting lost in the mood as I unfastened my jeans. As if in a trance and totally oblivious to my nakedness; I bent over to pick up my clothing. Once again, Chloe's faceless voice broke through my reverie.

"Kayla, leave the clothes where they are and walk towards my voice." Obeying her command, I entered the pale pink and white bathroom, which was also lit by the wonderful fragrant candles. As I focused, I could see the bathtub was filled with bubbles. A steel tray table was set up next to the tub with a bottle of chilled champagne on ice and a small plate of cheese and grapes. A bowl of giant strawberries topped with whipped cream also occupied the tray. On another tray were two very fluffy towels that lay atop a terry cloth robe that looked as if it would surround your body in luxury.

"Step into the tub, Kayla, and acclimate yourself to the water," I could hear Chloe saying from behind the bathroom door that led into the adjoining bedroom that I used when I spent the night. Gingerly, I stepped into the tub. The water was delicious. Just hot enough to envelop you into its depths, but warm enough not to scald. As I eased into the bath, subconsciously, I let out a sigh as a testament of how wonderful the bubbly, strawberry scented water smelled and felt. It also felt as if years of tension were melting from my body.

"Open your eyes, Kayla," I heard Chloe say softly, barely above a whisper.

I was so taken by the ambiance; I was unaware that my eyes had been closed. When I opened them, Chloe was

# If Loving Two is Wrong . . .

kneeling beside me with her arms resting on the side of the tub. She was wearing a robe identical to the one on the tray. Her hair smelled freshly washed and was cascading down her shoulders in curly ringlets. She was staring deeply into my eyes and her appetizingly naked lips were slightly parted. Her tongue moved slowly across them creating a natural lip-gloss. Once again, I was acutely aware of how beautiful she was devoid of all make-up. I parted my lips, prepared to break the magical silence, but Chloe softly placed her index finger across my lips, hushing any utterances I was about to make.

"Shh, Kayla, don't say anything." Her voice was a soft, sweet whisper. At that moment, she had my full, undivided attention.

"Now you know I would never do anything to hurt you, don't you?" she was staring intensely into my eyes. Her finger was still resting softly yet insistently across my lips, so I slowly nodded yes.

"Good," she continued, "Just relax and allow yourself to be pampered. Allow me to show you how special you are and how much you mean to me, okay."

Although she had removed her fingers, I was unsure if it was okay to speak and I definitely did not want to disrupt this mood. So, once again, I nodded my compliance. Chloe stood and slowly parted her robe, unveiling her nakedness. She continued to stare pointedly into my eyes, as if gauging my reaction. As the last of the fabric left her manicured fingers and the robe dwindled softly to the floor, I stared, mesmerized. Almost instantly, I felt self-conscious and embarrassed by my reaction. I began to look away when Chloe stopped me with her voice.

"Wow, Kayla," she laughed gently, "don't be ashamed to look. The human body is a wonderful phenomenon; it was meant to be revered and explored."

At that moment, I was flustered, yet curiously excited by this latest turn of events. Silently, I inched my way toward the front of the tub as Chloe had motioned. I could feel her entering the tub. She settled behind me with such aplomb; I

Kim Beverly

instantly as well as jealously wondered how many had shared such a moment before me. But as I felt her well-toned, slightly muscular legs slide along my thighs, all thoughts of anything other than what was happening at the moment quickly evaporated. Once in the tub, Chloe leaned forward and I could feel her breasts against my back as her arms encircled me from behind. A whole wave of emotions was swirling within my heart and mind. Chloe was seducing me! Countless times I had envisioned this moment, unsure if it would ever happen. Now that it was taking place, I was unsure how to feel. This was a woman touching me sensuously, erotically, and preparing, I assumed, to make love to me. I could envision the clichéd angel and devil on my shoulders, "Don't do it, Kayla" the angel implored.

"Shut up," the devil said snappishly, jabbing his pitchfork in the angel's direction.

"There's nothing wrong with you exploring your feelings," the devil said to me. "Besides, don't you really care for this girl," he continued, raising his sinister eyebrows.

"Yes, I do," I said sheepishly, looking at the angel. The devil began to go in for the kill.

"Where, in your book of directions," he said sarcastically to the angel, "does it say it is an unforgivable sin for a woman to have uncontrollable feelings about another woman." The angel appeared to be contemplating his answer, and just when he was about to speak, Chloe's voice intruded into my consciousness, bouncing them both from my shoulders.

"Relax, Kayla, you're so tense," she was saying as she softly began to caress my shoulders. I had been unaware of how uptight I was until I relaxed and released my tensions to her capable fingers. With a tell-tale sigh, I surrendered, easing myself back into Chloe's bosom. In turn, she rested her back against the rear of the tub. For a while, we both lay still and silent, luxuriating in the warmth of the moment. Finally, Chloe reached over and poured us a glass of the bubbly.

"To a wonderful friendship," Chloe began, as I

86

twisted my face toward her. "That will endure eternally, regardless of what may occur tonight, tomorrow night, ever or never. And a bond so strong that even we can't break it."

I raised my glass in tribute to her touching toast. And for the next forty-five minutes, we drank champagne and Chloe fed us the grapes, cheese and strawberries with whipped cream. Few words were said, both of us together, interacting, yet separately lost in our own private thoughts. I was thinking how in my wildest dreams, I never would've imagined myself in this type of erotic setting with a woman, yet there I was. A sea of conflicting emotions was storming its way through my mind; but the serenity of the moment, mixed with the soothing music and Chloe's gentleness, had a calming effect. I felt as though I was in the middle of a torrential downpour, where the temperature was warm and I was standing barefoot in the street. The heavy raindrops were cascading down my body, drenching me, yet at the same time, embracing me. I knew the metaphor was dramatic, but it seemed to fit. I was feeling overwhelmed by what was happening, but at the same time, I was curiously content and at ease. Chloe exited the tub before me, instructing me to remain in the bath for a moment. She meticulously dried herself with one of the fluffy towels from the tray, making each movement equivalent to an erotic striptease. Once dry, she wrapped herself in the towel and disappeared momentarily into the bedroom. When she reappeared, she was wearing a short, sheer, black teddy with a matching robe. She looked spectacular. Amazingly, my first thoughts were of an egotistical nature. How many men, I wondered, would kill to be in my position right now? Yet, here I am, a woman, and she'd rather be here with me.

"Stand up, baby," Chloe said softly.

Dazedly, I did as she said. She reached for the towel on the tray and methodically dried me off from head to toe. Afterwards, she put the robe on me and then led me toward the bedroom. As I followed Chloe, the effect of the champagne was putting an ethereal glow on the entire situation. It seemed almost unreal, but I knew all too well that it was. Following the same motif as the living room and bathroom, the usually bright, pale pink bedroom was also dark, except for a few aromatic candles. The top half of the maroon bedcovers on the large, cherry wood four-poster bed was pulled back and a corner turned down. There was a tiger print sleeping mask placed on one of the fluffy pillows with matching pink pillowcases. Chloe sat me on the edge of the bed, where the corner was turned down, then went over to the night table, where there were two glasses of champagne. She offered me one, which I declined. I was still feeling the effects of what we had already drank in the tub. I didn't want to get drunk and use it as an excuse later on. I wanted to experience and remember every nuance of the evening clearly. It was as if Chloe was reading my mind because she smiled knowingly, set the glasses down, and sat beside me. Then she cradled my face in the palms of her hands and stared intently into my eyes.

"I'm not sure how you feel, Kayla, but I've building up to this moment for quite some time," she said, searching my brown eyes with her hazel ones.

"That two-week separation just punctuated it. I know I acted pretty cavalier about the whole thing, but I felt like I was dying inside, not talking to you or seeing you. And although this has been my chosen lifestyle for a while, the depths of my feelings for you took me aback, which has brought us to this moment." She let out a deep sigh before continuing.

"Now, Kayla, I know we're both adults and I'm pretty sure you're no stranger to making love, and neither am I," she added with a wink. "But I know for you, this is an entirely different situation. So, I want to make perfectly sure that you're okay with what's happening here tonight," she said sincerely.

She had a pleading look on her face as if willing me to say everything was okay. I took a hold of her hands and gently squeezed, giving her all of the assurance she needed. Chloe leaned forward and kissed me softly on the forehead.

"Kayla, I want this to be a beautiful and memorable experience for you, with no regrets," she said softly, yet full

## If Loving Two is Wrong . . .

of emotion. Finding it hard to speak, I simply nodded. Chloe reached past me and took the blindfold from the pillow. The simple brush of her body against mine, mixed with the fresh berry scents that lingered from the bath, were enough to send a tingle up my spine. I was now a bundle of nerves. Anticipation, mixed with excitement and a little fear of the unknown. Chloe was now placing the mask gently over my eyes. I knew she felt this would make it a little easier on me, not actually having to watch everything that was happening. She was right. I was already beginning to feel anxious. I could feel Chloe rising from the bed and as her scent passed by me, I knew she was walking away from me. Now that I was blindfolded, my other senses seemed to spring to life, making me keenly aware and sensitive to my surroundings. Suddenly, the sounds of "Adore" by Prince, before he became "The Artist Formerly Known As," softly saturated the room. I loved that song and it definitely help set the mood. Once again, Chloe was in front of me.

"Stand up, baby," she commanded and I obeyed. She unbelted the robe and pulled it from me. I could only imagine that at this moment she was looking at my naked body from head to toe. I was really grateful for the blindfold at that moment.

"Kayla, you're so beautiful," she said in a whisper. I could sense her closing the gap between us as she wrapped her arms around me in a full body hug. On its own accord, my body began to tingle as she caressed my back and ran her fingers through my hair. Then she did it. She placed her hands on either side of my face. I could feel, as well as smell, her minty breath as she neared my face. I tried to anticipate the moment of touchdown, but she still caught me off guard as her moist, warm lips pressed against mine. I know it sounds corny, but rockets literally exploded in my head. I was totally unprepared for my reaction and in spite of myself; I could feel myself becoming moist in my lower region.

"Wow," was all I could say as the kiss ended. It was simple, it was sweet, but it was also bombastic. I could feel

Chloe smiling as she directed me toward the center of the bed.

"Lay on your stomach," she said softly, and once again I complied. She left the bed and I could hear a drawer opening and closing. My mind began playing tricks on me as to what she could be taking from the drawer. I couldn't resist the urge to ask her what she was doing.

"Trust me, Kayla," was all she said as she returned to the bed and straddled my legs. My spider senses were really tingling now as I heard the "pop" of a tube or bottle being opened, then that familiar squirting sound. It took everything in me not to rip the mask from my face and find out what she was up to.

"Relax, Kayla," she repeated as I began to nervously rock back and forth. I tried, but was only soothed when I felt her soft, warm, slippery hands caressing my back.

Aah, a massage. Deftly, she ran her fingers across my back and over my shoulders, easing any and all tensions that I was feeling. Just as I was totally relaxed, she began to massage my lower back, dangerously close to my butt. But by now, I was so into my own groove, that I didn't care what she did. Now, Luther Vandross was singing, 'If Only For One Night'. Flower and berry scents were dancing in my nose and Chloe was massaging my body with the skill of a professional masseuse. So, when she finally did run her hands sensuously, yet firmly across my behind, then moved down to my legs, it seemed to be the most natural progression in the world. I didn't even raise an eyebrow beneath the mask. Chloe ended by massaging my feet, which was an incredible feeling. I had never realized how relaxing, sensual and soothing a foot massage could be.

"Roll over, Kayla," she said, taking me by surprise. Yet I did so without thinking. I had stopped concentrating on my nakedness long ago. I was totally consumed by the scents, sounds, and touching that was taking place. Now, R Kelly's, "Seems Like You're Ready," was playing, as Chloe began to apply her skills to the front of my body. This time she started at my toes and worked her way up my legs. As she got close to my private island, things began to come back into focus for me again. Sensing this, Chloe whispered, "Relax, baby," and totally skipped that area. Somewhat embarrassed, I became keenly aware of the moisture welling between my legs. Chloe was now massaging my shoulders, neck, and forehead. Once again, easing my tensions. So, when she began caressing my breast, I knew the tide had turned from massage to seduction. AND I WAS READY! When Chloe leaned forward and kissed me softly on the lips, it was my turn to surprise her and myself with a response that combined passion with a sense of urgency of my own. Wow, I guess the combination of ambiance and Chloe had really worked me up. Chloe was now straddling my legs and I could feel her warm breath descending upon my breast. The sound of the tape changing sides caught my attention and I was actually anxious to hear what was going to play next. So far, the music had done so much to help set the mood. Just as her warm mouth claimed its prize, the O'Jays, 'Stairway To Heaven', emanated from the speakers. I totally surrendered. I had no more strength or will to protest anything. I had resigned myself to giving into the moment. I began to run my fingers through Chloe's silky hair as her tongue swirled around my nipple, stirring emotions deep within me. Chloe took her time, as she made sure to give each of my breast an equal amount of attention. While her mouth was busy, her hands weren't idle. She was caressing my thighs ensuring that my lower half didn't feel left out. I couldn't believe the tingling I was feeling between my legs from the sensation of her tongue, lips, and mouth working on my nipples. My mind was naughtily imagining the way those same motions would feel at the place where her hand was now sliding in, and out, and across my wetness. I moaned at the thought and feel of it. Chloe was now kissing a slow agonizing trail down my stomach, stopping momentarily at my belly button. My mind and my body were now screaming for her to hasten her journey and reach the destination we were both yearning for. Then there was another music change. I began to wonder if Chloe had choreographed her lovemaking. I took a quick second from the intensity of the moment to chuckle. Once again, there was the sound of the former Prince. 'When Two Are In Love', was the next selection. Just as I was about to hum the first verse, I FELT IT! Chloe had worked her way through my trimmed garden and began to explore my natural flower. She gently peeled back the petals and went in close to take in the natural scents and textures. Gently, she licked all around the area that was begging for her attentions. I began to gyrate my hips, hoping to direct her to the place where I wanted her to be, but she seemed to have an agenda of her own and deftly avoided my attempts. 'The speed of their hips move faster than a runaway train,' Prince's song was saying, and I could relate, because Chloe was working me up to an absolute frenzy. She would gently touch my pulsating button, then quickly move elsewhere. My heart was racing and my breath was labored as I thought I couldn't possibly take another minute of this maddening teasing. Suddenly, I tore off the mask, grabbed Chloe's head and literally placed her where I needed her to be. This time it was her turn to acquiesce. Gently, she took my nerve center between her teeth and slowly, achingly built me to the point of erupting. As I moaned her name, she set forth a full assault. Like an orchestra building to a crescendo, she started slow and then hastened the pace until I was almost delirious. That's when it happened. I saw firecrackers, heard bells, and felt the euphoria of reaching my climax. I could literally feel my floodgates opening as I eased back onto the pillow attempting to bring myself down from the explosion that had just taken place. Chloe stayed where she was and continued to please me gently in an effort to calm me. But once again, she had built my sensations up to a point, like ascending the hill of a roller coaster. My heart was pounding with anticipation of reaching the peak, then descending and doing loops only to reach the top again. As I arched my back in sweet release, I echoed Chloe's name again and again. Only when I assured her that I couldn't possibly take a moment more, did she rise form her position to lie beside me. She could only smile as she watched me continue to try to catch my breath. I could feel her move as if to get up.

# If Loving Two is Wrong . . .

"Where are you going?" I asked breathlessly, still reeling from the way this woman had made me feel.

"To the bathroom to freshen up," she answered. I rolled over on my side, placing my leg over hers to keep her from moving. Propped up on my elbow, I just watched Chloe with a whirlwind of emotions flowing through me.

"What's up," she asked, a look of concern clouding her face.

"Nothing, why," I asked; suddenly realizing I was staring.

"Well," she began, "first of all, you trap me with your gargantuan thigh, and then, you stare at me as if you're seeing me for the first time."

"I'm sorry," I said as I began rubbing her face and hair with my free hand. "But in a sense, it is as if I'm seeing you for the first time. I mean, I don't know if there's a protocol for what just transpired, but I would think that a person would have to care a hell of a lot for someone, to do the things you've done for me tonight."

"Well I," Chloe began.

"Shh," I said, this time I placed my fingers over her lips, "Let me finish."

Chloe nodded to show her compliance.

"I'm not only talking about what just occurred, I'm talking about the entire day. I was so happy to see you, so much so that I began to question myself about my feelings. When your office paged you, I was so disappointed, but I didn't want you to know. All the time that I was at my parent's barbecue, I was thinking about you." I omitted the mini-breakdown I had on my way to her apartment.

"But when I got here, Chloe," I paused for a second, reliving the moment. "Damn, I was shocked. Believe it or not, my first thought was that you were expecting someone else, and I was instantly mortified. But when you called out to me, I was relieved at first, then nervously anxious. Girl, you really had me going through it."

Chloe couldn't help but to chuckle.

"I have a confession to make," she said smiling.

93

"My office didn't call me," she said slyly. "I had Jackie call me."

"Why?" I asked, confused.

"So I could come home and set up for this evening."

"Oh," I said, faking annoyance. "You were that sure of yourself, huh?"

"No, I wasn't," she answered, suddenly growing serious, "But if there was any chance of this happening, I wanted to make sure it would be perfect."

"Chloe, lighten up," I said in response to her impassioned reaction. "Everything was perfect, perfect beyond my wildest imagination."

"Really," she asked skeptically.

"Really," I responded, sealing it with a kiss. Chloe was watching me closely, a sly sneer on her face.

"Why are you looking at me like that," I asked. But before she could answer, it dawned on me. "Oh, I get it, you were expecting a different reaction."

"What do you mean," she smiled with false innocence.

"You know what I mean," I said playfully. "You were watching me to see if I would cringe once I realized I kissed you after you had just made love to me."

"You got me," Chloe laughed. "I was shocked when you kissed me, first of all. But I truly expected a reaction to you encountering your taste and scent."

"Chloe," I smiled, "you're the first woman who has ever made love to me like that, but not the first person. I am definitely not a stranger to my own," I paused, searching for a word. "Essence," I finally came up with.

"That's definitely a different way of putting it," Chloe laughed. "Essence, huh."

"Yeah, I think that's appropriate," I smiled. With great effort, I raised my leg, releasing Chloe from her imprisonment.

"Thank you warden," she laughed. I smiled, thinking how in tune she was with my silent thought. I watched both appreciatively and proudly, as she swayed provocatively towards the bathroom. I laid back with my arms folded

# If Loving Two is Wrong . . .

behind my head and sighed as I replayed the last couple of hours in my mind. Now, reality was beginning to set in.

I had actually allowed a woman to make love to me. On top of that, I actually enjoyed it. What did this mean? Was I gay? Oh boy, I wasn't ready to answer these questions just yet. This was getting deep.

I How come we didn't just let the intrigue continue? That way, I could always hide behind the fact that I had never made love to a woman. Technically, I still hadn't made love to a woman, but that was just a matter of semantics. In all ways, except one, I had played as much an integral part in what happened as Chloe. Hmm, Chloe.

I began to picture her in my mind. She sure is beautiful. And sensuous. And sexy. AND, she made me feel like as much of a woman as any man I had ever made love with. This is all so confusing. How am I supposed to feel? Embarrassed, or ashamed that I have these truly incredible feelings for a woman? Proud, because a woman as beautiful on the inside, as she is on the outside, has truly incredible feelings for me? I heard the water in the shower running and I decided to swap all of these deep questions for an impulsive gesture. I grabbed the bottle of champagne from the nightstand, burst through the bathroom door, and joined Chloe for an incredible round two.

## Chapter Twelve

I awoke to a wonderful aroma and unfamiliar surroundings. Then I remembered I spent the night at Chloe's. After the shower last night, we came upstairs to Chloe's black and gray room. It was a direct contrast to the pastel colors of the bedroom downstairs. In the ten months that we'd known each other, I'd never slept in her room. Sure, I'd been in it, but I'd always slept in the bedroom downstairs. My mind began to wander to last night, but before the little angel and devil could get comfortable on my shoulders, I jumped up and followed my senses downstairs to the kitchen, where Chloe was pouring a cup of coffee. I loved the layout of Chloe's condo. The doorway opened to a spacious living room where a cream-colored leather couch and matching loveseats dominated the center of the room. There was a large screen television on the wall facing the couch. On the opposite wall was an electric fireplace. A spiral staircase wove its way from the living room to the upstairs where Chloe's bed and bathroom were. There was also spare room, which she used as her home office. Outside her bedroom was a balcony that overlooked the Delaware River. Back downstairs, to the right of the living room, was a short hallway that led into the dining room. Chloe had a very formal dining area with a heavy cherry wood table that could easily seat ten and a matching breakfront. The table was always set with expensive chinaware and crystal. Directly behind the dining room was the pristine kitchen with its cream colored fixtures. A large chef's workspace dominated the center of the kitchen and counter with four stools marked the entrance. She had every major and minor appliance known to man. But I had to admit that she put it all to good use. Beyond the kitchen and dining room was the guest bed and bathroom as well as a furnished den, complete with a fireplace.

# If Loving Two is Wrong . . .

"Morning babe, how'd you sleep?" she asked with a wicked grin.

"As if you don't know," I answered, trying to sound as casual and confident as she did.

"Wow," I said, looking at the spread of bacon, eggs, croissants, home fries, fresh orange juice and coffee.

"Did you get any sleep?"

"Some," she said. "But then I was awakened by your snoring. So... after watching you sleep so soundly for about a half hour, I decided you deserved a nice breakfast."

"Aw that's so sweet," I responded' "but what did I do to deserve it?"

"I don't know," she laughed, "but you were snoring sooo loud, I figured you must've worked up a sweat somewhere," she said with a wink. Just at that moment, there was a loud cracking noise, like gunfire. Chloe and I stood stock-still. I was wondering if I looked as funny as Chloe at that moment, because she looked terrified, eyes bulging and mouth all frowned up. A second later, the rain could be heard cascading down the roof and onto the windows. We both sagged with relief and laughter.

"Wow, Mother Nature must have her eyes on us," Chloe smiled.

"Why do you say that?" I asked, puzzled.

"After an incredible night like last night, she backs it up with a beautiful rainy Sunday. Now if that ain't some powerful match-making in the works, I don't know what is." It was the first mention of last night and a feeling of uneasiness washed over me. I wanted so badly to be able to discuss it in the same cavalier, matter-of-fact way that Chloe did, but I couldn't. Chloe acted as if it was just the most natural thing in the world, but I was still having a little head trauma about the whole thing.

"Are you alright Kayla?" Chloe asked, obviously reading my thoughts through my facial expressions.

"Oh yeah, I'm fine," I answered a little too quickly.

"Kayla, you don't have to pretend for me." Chloe said earnestly.

97

"No, seriously, I'm okay," I answered, trying to shake off the distant edge I was adopting. I knew Chloe had done nothing wrong, but for some reason, I resented her for placing me in this state of confusion. It was so much easier to cope with our relationship before we crossed the line. I had felt secure in my heterosexuality, since there had been no intimate contact. But now, I was forced to deal with the reality that I might not be a full, red-blooded heterosexual. Now, what am I? Gay? Bisexual? I'm going to kill Jackie. She was the instigator of all this. If only Chloe were a man. This would be so much easier, a beautiful situation in fact. Boy, this really has me tripping. I know I'm a sensible person; therefore, I should be able to analyze and rationalize this whole ordeal and place things into proper perspective.

I let out a deep sigh and looked at Chloe, who was studying me intently. Almost instantly, I felt embarrassed and ashamed. I realized I had been so completely lost in my own thoughts and my emotional turmoil was probably exposed through my facial expressions, as usual. Chloe's face showed a combination of sadness, disappointment and hurt.

"Kayla," Chloe began, "I'm sorry. I can see now that I made a colossal error in judgment. I can only hope that you won't resent me for it and we can salvage our friendship."

The hurt was evident in Chloe's voice and I felt like such a bitch for making her feel that way. On the other hand, I couldn't help the way I was feeling. I didn't want to feel this way. But I knew that I was going to have to allow myself to go through this thought process in order to sort things out. However, I decided that I had to make Chloe understand that she didn't do anything wrong and that I wasn't angry with her. Hell, I wasn't even angry with myself, truthfully. I was just trying to find a way to cope with the idea that I had found someone who truly made me happy in every way. And that someone was a WOMAN. I walked over to Chloe, who looked so vulnerable at the moment and wrapped her in my arms.

"Baby, I'm sorry for making you feel guilty about caring for me. I know your feelings are genuine."

# If Loving Two is Wrong . . .

"I don't just care for you," Chloe sobbed, "I love you." (Pause) "I'm in love with you."

"I love you, too, sweetie," I said, impulsively. Intuitively, I stopped short of saying I was "in love" with her. Truthfully, I didn't know if I was or not. That was not a phrase I uttered freely. As a matter of fact, I didn't know if I'd ever said it before. I knew I felt it before, with Mark. Now, I became the strong one, as I held Chloe at arm's length and stared into her eyes.

"Chloe, what occurred between us last night was a beautiful experience based on genuine emotions, and I definitely don't want either of us to have any regrets. But you have to realize, this has been a way of life that you adopted willingly, a long time ago. It's all new to me and it goes against everything that I've thought and felt for almost twenty-nine years. Perhaps it should be as simple as realizing that I love spending time with you and I love the way you make me feel, but there's more to it than that."

"I know," she said softly.

"But what you don't know, is that I'm trying to find a way to accept this and move on with you. Not a way to get over it and move on without you."

Chloe cocked her head to one side as she contemplated what I had just said. Suddenly, she burst into a radiant smile. It was as if the clouds had parted and revealed a silver lining.

"Well, I'm not going to push it," Chloe said. "Just know that I'm here for you in any capacity that you need me." Once again she knew exactly what to say.

"Well, right now," I paused briefly to kiss her on the cheek, "I need you to help me demolish some of this food."

"My pleasure," she smiled and we laughed as we both reached for the same croissant.

The next few months went by in a whirlwind and I became more and more comfortable with the intimate moments Chloe and I spent together. However, I still wasn't quite ready to wear that "exclusive" or "gay" moniker. Chloe was great; she never pushed the issue. Things ran pretty smoothly. Sure, we had our occasional disagreements, but it was never anything major. I was truly amazed at how compatible we were.

My parents and Tony had adopted Chloe into the family almost immediately. If there was any speculation about the closeness of our relationship, it was never brought to our attention. Of course, Mom would occasionally ask whatever happened to some old boyfriend of mine; but she wouldn't harp on it like she used to. And for the life of her, as she put it, she couldn't understand how someone as pretty as Chloe, didn't have a different man for each day of the week, like she did in her day.

"I had to beat them off with a stick." she quipped. And she had the nerve to look as if she was serious. "I just got tired of juggling them and decided your father deserved to have someone like me in his life," she ended with a wistful sigh. I began to clap. Chloe and my mother looked at me questioningly.

"And the Oscar for best dramatic actress in a true life series goes to... "And we all burst into laughter.

Chloe and I had settled into a comfortable routine of seeing each other on a daily basis, nightly too. We just let it happen. No ultimatums, demands or labels, and that's the way I liked it. I didn't think I could've dealt with our "relationship" under any other terms. I felt a certain comfort level in considering us as two friends, who legitimately cared about each other and expressed those feeling, opposed to being labeled as 'lovers'. Although they may have been the same things, somehow the first definition didn't seem to place emphasis on sex, like the word 'lovers' did. I decided to go with whatever justified things in my mind.

A loud crashing sound, followed by the jolt of a sudden impact, jarred me into consciousness. As I unbuckled my seatbelt, my mind was racing. Did I travel through a stop sign or a red light? I had been so preoccupied by my thoughts, I couldn't recall paying attention to any traffic devices, or even to the other cars. As I exited my vehicle, a tall, brown skin man, with gentle eyes approached me.

"I'm so sorry, are you okay," he asked, talking

quickly. His voice was filled with concern.

"I, I think so." I was stunned by the whole situation. I was mentally alert enough to know that his apology meant that I didn't' cause the accident. On its own accord, my body sighed with relief.

"I don't know what happened," he continued, excitedly. "I must have fallen asleep. I've been working two jobs and going to school part-time. I'm wearing myself out. This is a real wake-up call. I'm going to have to let something go." I imagined that he was rambling from nervous tension. I waited for him to calm down, and then I checked out my car. His front bumper had caught the tail end of my rear bumper. The sound of the impact was worse than the actual damage. I had a small scrape on my bumper that truthfully, I didn't know if it had been there before or not. The man, who was wearing the kind of uniform worn by most auto mechanics, was reaching into his wallet for his license.

"Here, let me give you this," he said, extending the card toward me. "I'll go to my car and get my insurance information."

I was just thinking about how cute and sincere he seemed when I noticed the name sewn on the right breast pocket of his uniform.

"Mark," I gasped, reading his name aloud.

"Yes?" he answered slowly, frowning.

"I'm sorry," I apologized while giggling at myself.

"I was just thinking about how much you remind me of someone, then I noticed that you both share the same name."

"Oh," he said, relieved, "You said my name as if you had been looking for me for child support or something," he laughed. "Hey, wait. That's not possible, is it?" he asked, raising his eyebrows with fake concern.

"Oh, no," I said, adding my laughter to his.

"Listen," I said, pushing away the license that he was still extending in my direction. "This little scratch isn't worth the hassle of an insurance claim. Why don't we just call this a little wake-up call for you to get more rest and leave it at that?"

"Are you sure," he asked. His face was a mixture of relief and despair as he realized that he had just opened himself up to a woman's prerogative.

"Don't worry, I'm not going to change my mind," I smiled.

"Oh, so you read minds, huh," he said grinning.

"No, but me know human nature," I said, doing my best Chloe imitation. Chloe was a popular psychic from the islands, whose commercials ran on every television station known to man. But the reference instantly made me think of my Chloe. Boy, this whole incident reminded me of my situation. There I was, sailing smoothly along with Chloe, when all of a sudden, BAM, I was blindsided by Mark. I tuned back in, just in time to hear Mark say, "Since we're not going to exchange insurance information, do you think we can exchange phone numbers?" I thought his approach was corny, but cute. However, I had enough on my plate right now and didn't want to add any more confusion.

"You seem like a really nice guy, Mark, believe me. Any other time, I think I would've jumped at the chance to get to know you better. But right now, I'm going through a few changes and need to sort a few things out."

"Maybe I can help," he said with a hint of sincerity.

"Trust me, you don't want to get involved," I said, half-jokingly.

"Are you sure?" he asked.

"Didn't I let you off the hook the last time you asked me if I was sure?" I admonished. "Sometimes when someone cuts you a break, it's best to take it and run," I laughed.

"I hear you sister," he smiled. "At least you can take this," he handed me his business card. "You can come in any time and I'll take care of that dent for you, free of charge."

"Thanks," I said enthusiastically, as I read the card. 'Mark Lyles's Complete Auto Care Service'.

"Mark Lyles, is that you?"

"Yes it is," he beamed.

"Then that would make you the owner, huh," I continued, sufficiently impressed.

"Yes it would," he said proudly.

"So, are you going to work on my car personally, or will you get one of your employees to do it," I asked teasingly.

"Oh, I'll handle you personally," he answered with a touch of flirtation in his voice.

I was tempted to flirt back, but thought better of it.

"Okay Mark, I'll give you a call and see when it will be convenient to bring my car in," I responded in a more business-like tone. It was time to bring this little meeting to an end before I waded too far into the deep end of the pool. Taking my cue, Mark straightened up from his relaxed stance.

" Sure, just call and we'll set you up." We shook hands and went about our business. He would definitely be a keeper, if I weren't already involved, I thought briefly. But you are, came the sobering self-reply. And the thing was, I had two wonderful people vying for my attentions. This should be a wonderful, dreamy predicament, but it was more like a nightmare. How do you choose between someone you've loved since childhood and someone you've know for a short time, but have grown to love almost as much? I was still pondering this as I knocked softly on Chloe's door. There was no answer and after a few minutes, I used my key to enter her apartment. There were no lights on and my eyes took a moment to adjust. As things began to come into focus, I could make out a form seated on the couch; it was Chloe. Her legs were curled under her and she had a glass of wine in her hand, staring silently ahead.

"Why are you sitting here in the dark?" I asked, concerned.

"It matches my mood," she said, somberly.

Silently, I walked over and lit the jasmine scented candle that was on top of the entertainment center by the television. Next, I pushed the power button on the stereo and tuned into WDAS for the slow jams. I poured myself a glass of wine and settled next to Chloe on the cushion. Without saying a word, I gently pulled her back to me and we nestled on the couch. For half an hour, neither of us spoke. Absent-mindedly, I caressed her neck and shoulders. Soothing love songs wafted softly through the apartment, but fell on deaf ears. We were each absorbed in our own private thoughts. Ironically, we later learned that we were both thinking of the other. I closed my eyes as I thought about the day's events and how it could affect our relationship. As I was reflecting on my feelings for her, I must've fallen asleep. When I opened my eyes, I Chloe was huddled on the opposite side of the couch, staring at me, intensely.

"I'm sorry I fell asleep, babe," I yawned. "It just felt so good and comfortable holding you in my arms."

Chloe remained silent. Her eyes were glistening with the threat of tears.

"What's the matter, honey," I asked, although I felt I already knew.

"I'm sorry," she sniffed, fighting for control. "I don't mean to be depressing, but I just feel so threatened by Mark's presence. I know I might lose you," she sobbed softly.

"Chloe," I sighed, preparing to say something condescending, but the truth of the matter was; I was overwhelmed by my own feelings of confusion. I couldn't believe the effect that seeing Mark again, after almost two years, was having on my life.

"No, Kayla," Chloe said abruptly, halting any attempt of mine to pacify her. "I saw how Mark was looking at you."

"That's him," I defended, weakly.

"No, Kayla, it wasn't just him. Both of you were watching each other as if you couldn't believe that you were together again. The chemistry between you two was almost tangible. As competitive as I am, I truly felt, at that moment, that I was out of my league. I don't think there's any way that I can compete for your affections where Mark is concerned."

"Chloe," I moaned, reaching out and grabbing her

hands, "this isn't a competition. I love you. Why are you being so quick to push me into Mark's arms?"

"Trust me Kayla," she said, seriously, "the last thing I want to do, is lose you to Mark, to anyone, for that matter. But if there's one thing that I am, it's a realist. Mark has held a place deep in your heart for many years. Those feelings just don't go away that easily."

"Maybe not, but neither does the type of relationship that you and I have built." I knew I believed what I was saying, but I also knew that Chloe had some valid points. I could feel the familiar tightening in my chest that usually occurred when I was dealing with something stressful. I didn't want to deal with this right now. I wanted to hold Chloe close, shut my eyes tightly and when I opened them, everything would be just like it was before Mark's return.

## Chapter Thirteen

I awoke to the aroma of bacon and fresh brewing coffee. As usual, Chloe got up before me and started breakfast. It was no coincidence that I always made it downstairs just in time to say, 'you should've woke me up so I could've helped you'. And she'd always respond, 'yeah, right. Go on and take your shower. When you're done, everything will be ready'. It was our Sunday ritual and it was so matter-of-fact that I hadn't really scrutinized it before. Why, all of a sudden, did it seem so important today? As I looked around Chloe's room, I began to feel very sentimental about everything. She had a collage hanging on her wall. It was made up of various pictures that we had taken at different places. There was one of us dressed up as western bandits from the eighteen hundreds that we took at Wildwood and a strip of photos that we took in one of those two dollar booths downtown, making silly gestures and faces behind each other's back. But the one picture that I focused on most was the one Chloe insisted we take at a professional photography studio. She had the picture blown up and framed. A large print hung over her headboard and smaller ones, with different poses, adorned her dresser. In the photos, I was sitting on a stool, with my hands on my lap, looking very demure in my cream-colored pants set. Chloe was standing behind me, but slightly to the side, with her hands on my shoulders. She looked so pretty in her powder blue pants suit and cream shirt. She had worn her hair down and straight. That look really became her. I remembered that we went out to a club the same night that we had taken the pictures and had a really good time. There were a lot of good-looking men who asked us to dance and offered us drinks. For the most part, it was all good-natured fun. But when a few of the guys got a little carried away with their flirting, with me or her, Chloe would give me a hug or a kiss on the cheek, and state clearly that she and I were 'together'. That stopped a few guys in their tracks, but it seemed to encourage the die-hards even more. The old, 'every man's fantasy' was hard at work. That was one of the few times that I didn't mind her disclosing the nature of our relationship. Half of them didn't believe it and I wasn't the least bit interested in the ones that did. All at once, a feeling of sadness overcame me. I realized that I was reminiscing as if something was going to change. The reality of my situation snuck up on me. Yesterday had really happened. It was no dream. Mark really was back in town and he really did say he wanted to marry me.

"Kayla," I heard Chloe calling my name.

"Yes," I hollered back.

"Come on, breakfast is ready."

"Okay," I said, realizing that this was the first time; in I don't know how long, that she actually had to call me down for breakfast.

"Do I have time for a shower?" I called out.

"If you want ice-cold food, you do," she answered, edgily.

"Okay, be right down." I rushed to the bathroom to wash my face and hands before heading downstairs.

"Wow, everything looks great," I said, eyeballing the spread of waffles, fluffy, cheese eggs, bacon, coffee and fresh strawberries with whipped cream.

"Rough night?" she asked, sarcastically.

Instinctively, I knew the fact that she had to call me for breakfast wasn't lost on her.

"Kinda. How'd you guess?" I responded gibly, inappropriately playing along with her little melodrama.

"Did you realize that this is the first time, in a long time, that I had to call you down for breakfast?" A hint of iciness had crept into her voice.

"Is it?" I asked with feigned innocence.

"Now is not the time to be cute, Kayla" she said, seriously.

"I'm sorry," I responded, hanging my head low, like

107

a child that had just been scolded.

"Mark's presence is already starting to affect our relationship," she said, flatly.

"How?" I asked, even though I knew she was right.

"Small things that seemed so insignificant before, suddenly seem huge."

"Like what?" I pushed.

Narrowing her eyes, Chloe looked at me, and if looks could kill...

"I know you know what I mean, Kayla, but I'll humor you anyway. The fact that I had to call you for breakfast is one. I can't remember ever having to do that before. And last night, you fell asleep while you were holding me.

"You can't say that I've never done that before," I interrupted.

"Not in the setting that we had. Romantic music, low lights and wine, that usually leads to lovemaking," she said with sadness.

"You were upset," I responded, slightly exasperated. "How was I supposed to know that you would want to make love?"

"That's just it, Kayla. We've always been so in tune with each other's emotions. Any other time when I needed comforting, you've been so gentle and indulgent with me, but this time..." she paused as if hurt feelings were halting her speech.

"What," I urged softly. Although I knew she was right; I wanted to hear her take on the situation.

"This time, you held me in silence and then drifted off to sleep." A tear began to well in Chloe's eye. I'd hardly ever seen her cry, so I knew this was affecting her deeply.

"Then, when we went to bed," she continued, "you just rolled to your side of the bed and went right back to sleep." She began to sob a little now. I didn't know what to do. If I tried to comfort her, would she feel like I was being condescending because of what she had said about last night? But, if I didn't, would she see that as being cold and indifferent? I was feeling confused about everything. It was

## If Loving Two is Wrong . . .

as if all of my emotions were closing in on me at once.

"Look Chloe, I have a lot on my mind, too," I was beginning to feel defensive, but decided to change my tone. "I did come to comfort you," I continued, softening my voice. "But knowing that I was the cause of your pain, I simply didn't know what to say, so I just held you. It had been such a long day, Chloe. I didn't get here until almost two o'clock in the morning. The dim setting, the love music, mixed with the wine and the intensity of the day..." I paused, letting that little vignette sink in. "I guess I just drifted off to sleep. I'm sorry, my actions weren't meant to hurt you. I just wanted to be with you last night."

"Forgive me, Kayla. Everything just seems to have a double meaning. Your coming over didn't mean that you wanted to see me; it meant that you found some spare time to grace me with your presence. You falling asleep didn't mean you were tired; it meant that you were indifferent to my feelings. And my having to call you for breakfast, didn't mean that you overslept; it meant that you were so overwhelmed with thoughts of Mark, you couldn't bear to wake yourself. And as I'm saying this, I'm realizing that I'm losing it," she said with a hint of a smile.

"No you're not, baby. We're just both under a lot of strain," I said, soothingly.

"Well, let's see if we can strain ourselves to eat some of this food," Chloe said, grinning.

"I think I can handle that," I answered with a grin of my own. After breakfast, we shared cleanup duty. I washed and she dried.

"So, what's your plans for today?" she asked, casually.

"I don't have any," I answered.

"Mm, hmm," she murmured, twisting her mouth into a half frown.

"What's that all about?" I asked.

"Are you going to see Mark today?"

"We hadn't really discussed it," I answered, honestly.

"What do you mean really discussed it?" she asked suspiciously.

"As he was leaving, he did say he would see me today, but that wasn't a definite plan."

"Sounds pretty definite to me," Chloe said as she dried the last dish and placed it in the cabinet.

"Don't start Chloe," I said with a frown.

"I'm just talking to you," she said, defensively.

"Do you have plans for us today?" I asked.

"Oh, no, sweetness, I have a couple of cases that I need to prepare for this week," she answered, easily.

"Well, I can stay and keep you company," I offered. I just wanted to be with her.

"I have to go to the office," she responded.

"But it's Sunday," I said, realizing that I was whining, slightly.

"You know when you're a superstar lawyer like myself, you can't keep conventional hours," she said with a wink as she headed upstairs.

I poured myself another cup of coffee and sat at the kitchen counter to think things over. I didn't know if I was being overly sensitive, but I sensed that Chloe was changing. Sunday was the day that we reserved for each other. If there was going to be a change in plans, we usually discussed it, beforehand. I could remember only four times, in the last year, that she worked on a Sunday. And each of those times, she knew by the prior Friday that she would be working. Switching gears, I wondered if I would see Mark today. Probably so, I reasoned. I didn't have anything else on my calendar. The very thought of encountering him again brought a pang to my stomach. I knew that in a very short time, I was going to have to make a decision that would hurt somebody's feelings and alter my life, completely. If I stayed with Chloe, I would always wonder about how it would've been with Mark. After all, I had spent a lifetime loving him. But, if I went with Mark, I would always lament about hurting Chloe and wonder how things would've been between us over the years. I mean, until now, being with Chloe had been close to paradise. Sure, we had our few tense moments, but we worked through them with flying colors. An answer should be obvious, but it wasn't. I didn't know how long Chloe had been watching me before making her presence known by clearing her throat; but, from the furrow of her brow, it must've been awhile.

"You look as if you have a dilemma," she said, all too knowingly.

"No, just wondering what to do today," I said half-truthfully.

"Oh, I'm sure you'll find something," she responded, trying to look innocent.

I decided not to call her on her implied meaning. That would only open up a can of worms that I wasn't ready to deal with.

"Since I don't know how long I'll be at the office, I'll page you when I'm done and see what you're up to."

I looked at her for a hint of sarcasm, but there was none. Still, I had a feeling that her words had a double meaning.

"Okay," I said airily, "but if you don't think you'll be that long, I'll wait around."

"Oh, I already know that I'm going to be a few hours at least," she said, convincingly.

I was getting the distinct feeling that Chloe was pushing me away, just as I was trying to maintain a strong grip.

## Chapter Fourteen

As I drove home, my thoughts were filled with Chloe. Even sweat pants, an oversized jersey and a slight scowl, she was still beautiful. I inhaled deeply, still carrying the scent of her perfume from the hug I gave her before I left her apartment. Our good-bye was so polite that it felt eerie. Oh Chloe, what's happening to us? As I turned my key in the lock, I heard the phone ringing. Hoping it was Chloe calling to say that she had changed her mind and wanted to spend the day with me; I hurried into the house without bothering to shut the door.

"Hello," I answered, breathlessly.

"Hey girl, I was about to hang up," Mark's voice boomed through the line. I felt a twinge of guilt about being disappointed that it was him instead of Chloe.

"Hi Mark," I said with forced gaiety.

"I've been calling you all morning," he said I quickly glanced at my answering machine, which indicated that I had five messages.

"So, what's up?"

"I called this morning to see if you wanted to go to breakfast, but now it's almost lunch time," he said, enthusiastically. At the mere mention of food, I patted my stomach, which was still full from the hearty breakfast that Chloe had fixed. Thinking of Chloe, I felt a tweak of resentment toward Mark. If he hadn't come back with his quick explanations for his absence, and looking so good, I wouldn't be in this emotionally nerve-wracking predicament. And the tricky part was, Mark had no idea how much confusion he was causing.

"I'm not hungry," I said, a tad icier than I meant to.

"Did someone wake up on the wrong side of the bed this morning?" he asked, responding to my tone.

"I'm sorry, Mark. I just have a few things on my

mind," I said, softly.

"Anything I can do to help," he asked sympathetically, his voice filled with concern.

'Yeah,' I thought to myself. Turn back the hands of time and: 1. never leave, 2. never have come back, or 3. come back with a wife and kids. All of those options ended with an absolute, not much room for change. But instead, I answered, "No, this is something that I'll have to handle on my own."

"Well, I'd like to see you today," he said, brightly. "How about a movie? That might take your mind off your troubles, a least for a little while."

"That's my Mark, er, I mean, that's always been you, Mark," I attempted to recover from my slip of the tongue. "Always trying to make someone feel better."

"I'm still your Mark," he answered, responding to my correction.

"So, what did you want to see," I asked, opting not to respond to his comment.

"I don't know what's out," he answered. "Let's just go to the King of Prussia Mall. They used to have a really nice theater from what I remember. They have about seven or eight different theaters, don't they?"

"I think so," I answered slowly, still not convinced that I wanted to go.

"Well, let's just see what happening there, then we can grab something to eat afterwards."

"Okay," I sighed, resignedly.

"Pick you up at one," he said.

"I'll be ready," I responded.

"I can't wait to see you, girl," he said, huskily before he hung up.

I have two hours to mentally prepare for my date with Mark. I headed upstairs to get ready. What a change, there was a time when there wouldn't have been the slightest hesitation

At one o'clock sharp, I heard a car pulling into the driveway. I knew Mark would come in to get me because he was too much of a gentleman to ever blow his horn for a lady. But I didn't want to chance the awkwardness of us being in the house alone, so I rushed out to meet him.

"You look great," he said, eyeing my baby blue sundress. "You know that's my favorite color, girl" he said with a wink.

"After all this time, I had forgot," I responded, rolling my eyes, playfully. Actually, I did remember. I had decided that just because I was upset with him for his disappearing act, didn't mean I couldn't look cute for our date.

"You look awright," I said, sassily. But truthfully, he looked damn good in his crisp tan chinos and short-sleeved white Polo shirt that showed off his biceps and muscular chest. 'Down girl', I thought to myself as I eased into the front seat of a baby blue Lincoln Continental. "Nice car," I commented aloud.

"It's alright, I guess. It's a rental. The Benz is my kinda car, but they didn't have any," he offered before shutting the passenger door.

"Well La di da," I said as we backed out of the driveway.

We never made it to the mall. Instead, we opted to go to South Street. We strolled around Penn's Landing, then sat awhile and watched the boats and various people taking in the sights.

"So tell me more about your business," I said, leaning back into his broad chest.

"Kayla, it's unbelievable," he said hugging me tightly from behind and kissing the top of my head. "When I was in the service, I became best friends with this guy named Troy Waters. He was my roommate in the barracks and we used to talk about our dreams for the future all the time. We both wanted to have a family and start a successful business. Troy already had a degree in business management and I had always wanted to be in advertising. Every time I saw a commercial, I'd always think that I could created something better." Mark's voice was filled with such exuberance; I had to turn to face him. He looked like a little boy who had just received his first bicycle. For a moment, I just stared at him, feeling all warm and fuzzy.

"Go on," I said, turning back around and leaning on him once again. I was beginning to feel overwhelmed by my feelings and I didn't want that to happen.

"Well, Troy and I figured we would have to come up with something big and different in order to excell in the advertising business. So I suggested combining large named companies in commercials. We had never seen it done and figured if we could break that concept in, we would be on easy street. While we were in the service, we started taking advantage of having so many people of such diverse backgrounds at our fingertips. A lot of people had families that owned businesses. Japanese, Chinese, French, African, you name it, we made a contact. So when we got out, we both traveled around trying to develop those contacts into business propositions."

"Yeah, I remember," I said, dryly.

Mark ignored my attitude and continued. "When we finally had enough potential clientele that had signed letters of intent, the banks agreed to conditional financing and the rest is history."

"Did Troy have a girlfriend that was left in the dark, too," I asked without turning around.

"Kayla," Mark said softly as he turned me towards him. "It was never my intention for you to be in the dark. Maybe I should've done things differently, but I had no idea that you were back here questioning our relationship." The sincerity in his eyes almost melted my heart. Once again, I had to turn away.

"Well you're here now," I said, changing gears. I didn't want to have this discussion right now. I had just left Chloe this morning and feeling crazy about that and this conversation was just complicating things for me.

"Come on," I said, standing and grabbing his hands, pulling him up.

Back on South Street, we found a restaurant, ate and had a few drinks. Afterwards, we caught a comedy show. It had been a full day. Now, it was eleven o'clock and we were heading home. I had a wonderful time, just like before he left. But he did leave, and during his absence, I had met a wonderful person. As we pulled into the driveway, I realized that it was the first time I had thought of Chloe in hours.

"Penny for your thoughts," Mark was saying as he pulled to a stop behind my jet black Jetta.

"I was just thinking how nice a day it's been. It felt just like old times," I said sincerely. I could feel a tear threatening to fall.

"Well don't cry, sweetheart. We'll have many more days like this, even better ones," he said, sounding like a doting dad talking to his little girl. I didn't know how to respond. Part of me wished I could just pick up where we left off and live happily ever after. But the other part of me knew that things were far from being that simple. It was only after Mark gave me a goodnight kiss on the cheek and I was heading up the walkway, that I realized Chloe hadn't beeped me all day. That was just enough of a little heart dart to put a damper on an otherwise wonderful day. Maybe she called, I reasoned as I was opening the door. But the answering machine held the same five messages that were there this morning. I had never checked them because I had assumed that they were all from Mark, since he said that he had been trying to reach me all morning. I pressed the play button, then headed to the kitchen for a glass of White Zinfandel. The first call was from my mother, reminding me that she was still alive and that it would be nice to hear from me from time to time. I had to smile. I had just talked to my mom the day before, for an hour and a half as a matter of fact. The next three calls were from Mark. They ranged from telling me to wake up, to playfully demanding to know my whereabouts. I laughed aloud at his joking demeanor. The last call was from Chloe. She had called from her cell phone earlier today.

"Hey Kayla, I know you just left, but I'm feeling kind of crazy about how we're relating to each other. When you get in, give me a call on my cell. Maybe we can meet downtown and do something, okay? Well, I love you and

## If Loving Two is Wrong . . .

I'm looking forward to your call."

"Oh shit," I muttered as I rushed from the kitchen to replay the message and check the time. She had called at ten fifteen, exactly ten minutes after I left her. Now it was after midnight. My ass was grass and Chloe was going to be the lawnmower. Trying to please two people was getting old, fast. I sat on the sofa with my wine and contemplated calling her. Maybe I'll just wait until morning, I reasoned, knowing full well that I was chickening out. The phone rang, startling me. I just stared at it for a moment like it was some kind of foreign object. Once again, I berated myself for not getting caller ID.

"I'm gonna order that, first thing in the morning," I said aloud.

"H-hello," I stuttered.

"Hey, sorry to call so late, but I just wanted to let you know that I made it home safely."

"Oh, Mark, it's you," I sighed with relief.

"Who else did you think it would be at this time of night? You're not two-timing me, are you?" he asked, half jokingly.

"Two-timing?" I repeated, faking an attitude. "Wouldn't you and I need to be together in order for me to two-time you?" As the words were leaving my mouth, I knew I was treading into dangerous waters, but I couldn't help myself.

"Oh, we're going to be together," he said confidently. "Today just felt so right, don't you think?"

Just then, the other line beeped.

"Saved by the bell," I laughed. "That's my other line." But deep down inside, I felt dread. I knew it had to be Chloe. This was a worst-case scenario, being on the phone with Mark and Chloe beeping in. Maybe Mark would let me off the hook and decide to hang up.

"I'll hold," he said, quickly dousing that hope.

"Besides, I want to know who's calling you this time of night." I contemplated not clicking over, but quickly decided that would be wrong. My allegiance was still with

117

Chloe, wasn't it? I took a deep breath as I pressed the call-waiting button.

"Hello," I said, acting as if I didn't know who was on the other end.

"Kayla, what's going on?" Chloe asked in a business-like tone.

"What do you mean?" I played dumb.

"Didn't you get my message this morning?" she asked, almost hissing.

"I didn't hear it until just a few minutes ago," I responded.

"What have you been doing all day," she asked in an accusatory tone. That question reminded me that Mark was on the other line.

"Uh, Chloe, could you hold on for a second?" I asked timidly.

"Why?" she responded, suspiciously.

"I have someone on the other line," I answered slowly.

"Who is it? Mark?" she demanded.

"Yes," I answered, truthfully.

"Don't bother clicking over," she said, full of attitude. "I'm hanging up."

"Chloe wait," I begged. But her response was a loud click. I returned to Mark.

"Sorry for taking so long," I apologized.

"How sorry?" he asked jokingly, not knowing that I was in no mood for games.

"Not very," I said, edgily.

"Wow, what a mood change. Who was that who could bring you down so fast," he asked, surprised by my attitude.

"That was Chloe," I sighed.

"What's up with that girl? She seems to always have an attitude." He was obviously becoming frustrated with Chloe's affect on me.

"She's just having a rough time," I defended.

"Well I would sure like to meet the Chloe that you and Tony are always talking about."

# If Loving Two is Wrong . . .

"You did meet her," I answered, falling into his trap.

"No I haven't," he said adamantly. "I've only met that Sybil woman that came to your house yesterday." His comment caught me off guard; I had to laugh.

"Really Mark, Chloe is a good person, she's just going through a little something right now."

"I'll take your word for it," he answered. "Besides, you're my focus right now."

"I had a real nice time today," I said, tap dancing around his words.

"Kayla, how come every time I comment about you and me, you always change the subject? Is there someone else?"

He had done it, asked me straight out. This was my moment of truth.

"No," I lied through my teeth, deciding that I just wasn't ready to let the cat out of the bag about Chloe and me.

"Then what is it? Are you angry about the amount of time it took for me to come back?"

Now this was a question that I didn't have to lie about.

"That's still very unsettling," I answered honestly.

"But Kayla," he was pleading now. "I told you that I was busy the whole time, traveling in and out of the country making business deals. I was working to secure our future."

"But two years, Mark," I sulked. "That's a long time without hardly any contact. How was I supposed to know what you were or weren't up to?"

"Because you know me, Kayla. At least I thought you did. In my last letters and postcards, I did nothing but talk about how things were going to be when I finally got back." His voice was thick with emotion.

"You must've had some kind of companionship during all that time," I said, fishing for something to assuage my guilt.

"As a matter of fact, I did," he answered, nonchalantly.

"Yeah, I figured that," I said, accusingly.

"I had your picture in my wallet, my thoughts of you in my mind and my hopes and dreams for our future in my heart."

I was quiet for a moment, speechless. What do you say to something like that?

"Kayla, are you still there?" he asked.

"I'm here, Mark. You just caught me off guard with that one," I answered softly.

"Can you say the same, Kayla," he asked, his voice begging me to say I could.

"Well, I did go on a date recently," I said, telling a partial truth. I told him about the encounter I had with Barry Sands, the guy I met while I was at work.

"Do you still have his number?" he asked when I was done.

"No, why?"

"So I can call and tell him if I ever catch up to him; I'm going to wring his neck," he said with mock anger.

"Nice mental picture," I laughed. "But I'd much rather leave Mr. Sanders right where he's probably at," I said, bristling with disgust at the thought of Barry.

"And where might that be?" Mark asked.

"Alone, I don't think anybody else could stand to be with him."

"He must've had something about him," Mark said sarcastically. "You went out with him."

"Only long enough to get a whiff of the real him. And boy did he stink," I said seriously. "Can we please stop talking about him?" I pleaded.

"Do, done deal," Mark answered. "Well, I don't know what I'm going to have to do to convince you to be with me. I didn't realize the fragile condition that our relationship was in." There was a touch of hurt in his voice. "But I have to leave this weekend. If I don't convince you by then…" he trailed off without finishing the sentence.

"Then what?" I asked, dripping with attitude.

"Then, I'll just have to keep coming back until I do convince you," he answered, matter-of -factly. "Well look, it's getting late," he said quickly. "We have the whole week to catch up and get things back on track, okay?"

"Okay," I said, dumbly, following his lead.

"Goodnight, Sunshine."

"Goodnight Mark." I returned the phone to its cradle. The name Chloe abruptly popped into my head.

'Oh no you don't,' I warned my conscience, aloud. I forced my mind clear of all thoughts of Mark and Chloe, then headed to the kitchen for another glass of wine before I went to bed.

## Chapter Fifteen

The next day, Chloe adeptly avoided me. I had tried to call her at home and at work. I called her cell phone and I paged her, all to no avail. So, when Mark invited me to dinner, I accepted. He had made reservations aboard a boat on the waterfront. Our table was overlooking the water and we had a magnificent view of the skyline. After a superb meal of flounder stuffed with crabmeat, steamed broccoli, bliss potatoes and drinks; he led me to the dance floor. The combination of the romantic music, the wine and Mark holding me in his strong arms was magical. I felt like Cinderella. More like one of the ugly, wicked stepsisters, my conscience invaded my thoughts. What about Chloe, it continued. I pushed those thoughts from my mind. I didn't want anything to ruin this evening. Mark was looking so good. His olive green suit accentuated his light brown almond skin perfectly. He was wearing black alligator skin shoes and his hair was perfectly tapered. I'm not even going to talk about how wonderful he smelled. The whole scene was making me lightheaded.

"Do you mind if we sit down for awhile?" I asked after our second dance.

"Of course not," he replied as he placed his hand at the small of my back and maneuvered me toward our table. As I sat, I noticed that the moon had replaced the sun, and its light was shimmering prettily across the water. Looking up, I noticed a single star in the sky and immediately closed my eyes. When I opened them, Mark was watching me, grinning.

"Making a wish, huh," he smiled, remembering my ritual since I had been a young girl. I would always tell him that I wished on a lone star, and if my wish came true, he and I would be getting married. He was looking straight into my eyes as if reading my mind. When he reached to grab my hand, I noticed it. A small, blue velvet box had been placed

next to my wineglass. I looked at Mark, flabbergasted.
"Well," he said, noticing my hesitation, "open it, baby." I didn't know what to do. This was the moment, that up until six months ago, I had waited for, all my life. This was so bittersweet.

"Mark, I don't know if I'm ready for this yet," I said, apprehensively. Hurt registered on his face, but his voice was still tender.

"I know it seems sudden because I just got back, but actually, it's not. We've been heading for this moment for a long time," he said passionately.

"I know, Mark," I replied, haltingly. "I've been loving you all my life. You just caught me off guard."

"Well, I'm not going to pressure you," he said softly. "Just hold onto the ring. It'll remind you that you have a man who's deeply in love with you and wants to make you his wife." I started to protest, but Mark grabbed the velvet box and pressed it into my hand.

"I know you've got a lot to contemplate, so how about I take you home and you can get a good night's sleep." I was truly at a loss for words, so I just nodded in agreement. The ride home was quiet except for the love songs that played on the radio. Making love was definitely on my mind, but I knew it was out of the question. That would definitely close the door on Chloe and me. Besides, when we first started dating, Mark had vowed to wait until we were married. Although I had been willing to let him off the hook a few times, he had held fast. And at this very moment, I was thankful for his willpower. Once we arrived at my house, Mark escorted me to the door.

"Goodnight Kayla," he said, embracing me, and then he gave me a short, but passionate, kiss. I almost swooned, but managed to control myself.

"Goodnight Mark," I cooed before disappearing behind the door.

Once inside, I checked my answering machine. There were no messages. I flopped onto the couch, clutching my purse to my chest. I contemplated looking at the ring, but decided against it. Instead, I grabbed the remote and started flipping channels. I needed to find something to take my mind off of today's events. After a few clicks, a program caught my eye. There was a group of people, including cameramen, rushing towards a man and a woman. One of the female members of group confronted the male in the couple. They started arguing. Writing appeared at the bottom of the screen, explaining the confrontation. The woman had hired the group of men that she arrived with, to spy on her boyfriend. They were private detectives. She thought that he was cheating, and they had just proven her right. They had videotapes of his numerous rendezvous and indiscretions. Some of the images were quite graphic. The name of the show was, 'Caught Ya!' I couldn't believe it.

Television is getting out of hand. Then, I thought about my own predicament. What if Chloe had been staking me out? Boy, just the idea made me cringe with embarrassment. "Girl, you're getting paranoid", I laughed out loud, then went upstairs to bed.

The next couple of days went by in a blur. I was a wreck at work. I couldn't concentrate. I had to get Henry to fill all of the prescriptions for fear that I would mess them up. He complained, but did it anyway. I spoke to Mark on the phone, but I had avoided seeing him. I still had not had any contact with Chloe. I had called all her numbers and even stopped by her apartment, all to no avail. I left numerous messages on her machine. When I finally got in touch with Jackie, who had been out of town, she dropped a bombshell on me.

"Girl, Chloe's been gone since Monday. She came in, reassigned her cases and said she wouldn't be back for at least a week.

"How come the secretary didn't tell me that," I asked, annoyed.

"Chile, you know how some of them temps are. They don't give a damn. They know it's only a three-day assignment, so they're not emotionally attached. Now when I start my business, they're going to be professional until the end. I don't care if it's a fifteen-minute assignment. That temp had all the info written down right here. It's even in Chloe's handwriting. Now if she wasn't dumb, I don't know who is. I just hope that she didn't screw up my system."

"Thanks a lot, Jackie," I interrupted. I knew if I didn't stop her, she would go on for the next two hours about the difference between a temp and a full-time employee, like herself.

"Wait a minute," she said suspiciously.

"What?" I asked, instantly regretting giving her an opening.

"If Chloe ain't here," she started, slowly, "and you don't know where she's at..." she trailed off.

I could picture her suddenly narrowing her eyes, focusing on me. "What did you do to her now, Kayla?" she asked, accusingly.

"Nothing Jackie," I groaned, not wanting to get into it with her. "Thanks for your help," I said and hung up before she could get started again. Chloe and I had never disclosed our relationship to Jackie. We both knew that would be like submitting it to the 'Enquirer' and I wasn't ready for that. But she always kept her detective hat on, searching for any sign of weakness, prepared to pounce at a single misstep or slip of the tongue. There were even times when Chloe and I enjoyed her attempts to finagle a confession out of us.

"Chloe, what are you doing?" I wondered aloud.

By Thursday, my family had already heard about Mark's proposal. As soon as I got home from work, the phone was ringing. Wishing it to be Chloe, I rushed to answer it.

"Hello," I said, hopefully.

"Girl, have you lost your mind?" my mother's voice boomed through the telephone line.

"What are you talking about Mom?" I asked, wearily.

"Just when were you planning on telling me about the wedding?" she demanded.

"What wedding?" I asked, innocently.

"You and Mark," she squawked, indicating that she

125

was losing her patience.

"Tony came in here carrying on about Mark being his brother-in-law or some nonsense. I told him that it simply couldn't be true because I'm so sure that I would've been the first person to know," she said accusingly.

I didn't feel like beating around the bush, so I told her the truth.

"Mom, Mark hinted about us getting married when Tony was here last weekend. But he didn't officially ask me until three days ago. I haven't given him an answer yet."

"I should crack your skull like a walnut," she said, huffily. "Every since you were little, all I've ever heard was, 'I'm gonna marry Mark', she said, imitating a younger me.

"Now's your chance. What're you waiting for?"

"Mom, marriage is a big step. Mark just got back into town. I need a little time to think."

"Think about what? The man went away to prepare for your future, now he's back. What is there to think about?"

"Mom, listen at you," I griped.

"What do you mean, listen at me?"

"Do you remember when we had that family barbeque?"

"Yeah," she said, suspiciously.

"You were like, 'I know you don't call yourself still waiting on Mark', remember that," I asked, sassily.

"Girl, that was so long ago. No, I don't remember that." She said it so fast that I had to laugh. She always fast-talked when she was caught.

"But one thing I do know," she recovered, "Mark is too good a man, for you to let him go. I'm serious Kayla."

"I know, Mom," I answered softly.

"Well, look baby, I done spoke my piece. I gotta get your father's dinner on the table so I won't be late for Bingo."

"Alright, Mom," l laughed.

"I love you, baby."

"Love you too, Mom," I responded.

They just didn't understand. I couldn't make a decision like this without talking to Chloe. It's been almost a week and we still hadn't touched base yet. She didn't respond to any of my calls or pages.

On Friday, Mark and I were the guests of honor at a family dinner at my parent's house. His parents were there, also. Although the word 'wedding' wasn't mentioned, the engagement word was bounced around a few times.

"Where's the ring, Kayla?" my mother finally asked after eyeing my bare hand all through dinner.

"Yeah, where is it?" Tony asked, jumping on the family's personal bandwagon. "I know it's got to be at least ten carats," he bellowed, slapping Mark on the back.

"It's in my purse," I said, rolling my eyes at Tony.

"Well, let us see it," both mothers yelled in unison. As I went to get the ring from my purse, I couldn't help but feel ambushed. I was told that this was just going to be a simple dinner with no theme.

"I'm sorry, Kayla," I heard Mark saying, as he followed me into the living room.

"Why are you sorry?"

"When my mom accepted the dinner invitation from your mom; I told her not to mention anything about engagements or rings. I told her that we hadn't made a decision yet."

"You said we hadn't?" I asked, surprised.

"Well, I wasn't going to say that you hadn't. That would make me look bad," he said, half-jokingly. I knew the real reason was so I wouldn't feel pressured about not making a decision, yet. This man was too good to be true. I retrieved the velvet box from my purse and headed back to the dining room with Mark in tow.

"Kayla, come on here, girl," my mom was hollering as I entered the room.

"I'm right here, Mom," I smiled, tightly, as I returned to my seat.

"Well stop all the chin music and open up that little box," she said, sarcastically. Tony and Mrs. Fountaine nodded in agreement. I took a deep breath before I opened

127

the box. What I saw, made me gasp, right along with everybody else.

"Girl, you act like you ain't never seen the thing before," my mom laughed. Truth be known, I hadn't. I vowed to myself that I wouldn't look at the ring until I had made my decision. Sitting in that box, was a huge rock. It looked like something from the 'Flintstones'.

"That's got to be at least ten carats." Tony screeched.

"Actually, it's only eight," Mark said, nonchalantly, trying to appear as if he wasn't bragging.

"That's probably worth more than our house," my dad crowed, breaking his silence.

"Ours too," Mark's dad added.

"It ain't worth more than my house," Mom pouted, defensively.

"Ours either," Mrs. Fountaine chimed in, rolling her eyes at her husband.

"But it sure is a beautiful ring," they both agreed.

"Ask her again, in front of all of us," Tony grinned.

"No, man," Mark protested, embarrassed. Once again, I was mortified.

"Yeah, ask her, son," Mr. Fountaine put in his two cents. Now everybody started jumping on that family bandwagon; it was beginning to buckle under the pressure. Mark looked at me sympathetically. It took all my strength not to get up and haul-ass when I saw Mark rising from his chair. The next moment, he was kneeling on one knee in front of me.

"Kayla, my sunshine, the love of my life, Thomas; will you marry me?" He asked so sincerely; it brought tears to my eyes. Now all eyes were on me, watching expectantly.

"Yes," I answered, breathlessly, caught up in the moment.

"You will?" he asked, surprised.

"She said yes, fool," Tony chimed in. Everybody broke out in a fit of laughter, except Mark and me. I knew he was wondering if I had said yes because I felt pressured, or because I really meant it. I was wondering the same thing. I mean, I knew that I loved Mark, but I couldn't help but think about Chloe. Where is she and what is she doing? Boy, I've really done it now. Mom disappeared into the kitchen and came out with a tray of glasses, filled with champagne.

"This was just in case," she said, innocently, obviously reading the expression on my face.

"Um hmm," I mumbled with poked out lips.

"Why didn't you invite your girlfriend, Tony?" Mr. Fountaine asked, grinning. "Maybe this could've been a double celebration."

"Shooot. Mama didn't raise no fool," Tony said, dripping with sarcasm. "Y'all wasn't gonna bamboozle me into no engagement."

Mark and I just looked at each other; no doubt we were both considering strangling Tony.

"Shut up!" Mom interjected. "Obviously I did raise a fool and you need to hurry up and marry that girl before she realizes how big of a fool you really are."

Now that was something even Mark and I could laugh at, and best believe we did, along with me slapping him upside the head. It was well after midnight when everybody decided to head home. Holding hands, Mark walked me to my car.

"I know you weren't ready to accept my proposal, yet," he said softly.

"Are you reneging?" I asked slyly.

"Hell no," he answered so quickly; it made us both laugh.

"But seriously, Kayla," Mark said, clearing his throat. "We both know what happened in there."

"We folded under the pressure," I finished for him.

"Exactly," he responded, looking straight into my eyes. "If you're not ready, we can wait," he said, somberly.

Here's your chance to get out of it, Kayla! I focused directly on Mark. 'Mark is too good a man for you to let go', my mother's words were echoing in my head.

"Only a fool would hold out on you twice," I said, huskily. "Besides, who would be the one to tell our moms

129

that we've decided to wait?" I asked, teasingly.

"Oh Kayla, I'm going to make you the happiest woman alive," Mark said, pulling me into his arms and kissing me passionately.

"I think you two should have the wedding before you start honeymooning," Mom's voice boomed through the kitchen window.

"Aw Toni, leave them alone," Dad admonished.

"Mind your business," Mom responded as her head disappeared from the window.

"That's what I'm trying to tell you," Dad kept it going.

"Are you sure you know what you're getting yourself into?" I laughed.

"Come to think of it, I'm not so sure," Mark murmured, rubbing his chin as if seriously reconsidering his proposal.

"Alright you," I chuckled, playfully kicking his leg.

"Well, we have one more day to spend together before I have to go back to Chicago," Mark said, somberly.

"Oh no, not another two years," I said sarcastically.

"Not on your life," he laughed. "I'll be back in two weeks. We can start making wedding plans when I get back then."

"That gives me two weeks to plan my getaway," I joked.

"Kayla, are you sure about this?" he asked, placing his hands on my shoulders, obviously taking my comment a little serious.

"Yes Mark, I'm sure," I answered, taking his hands in mine. "Ever since I can remember, this has been my dream."

"Okay Sunshine, go get some rest. I'll call you in the morning," he said as he held my door open. "We'll start with breakfast," he added, closing the door, slowly.

"Okay sweetheart," I responded after starting the engine. As I backed out of the driveway, I was instantly glad that Mark hadn't picked me up for the dinner. Now, while driving alone along the darkened streets, my conscience took a swing. What about Chloe?

"What about her?" I said aloud. "She took it upon herself, to take herself out of the equation."

How do you know what she's doing, my conscience retorted.

That's my point. I don't know and she didn't see any reason to tell me. She just disappeared.

As I had this conversation with myself, a feeling of bitterness overcame me. How could you just leave like that?

"Oh well," I said aloud. "She did what she felt she had to do and so did I." I spent the rest of the ride home trying to convince myself of those words.

Mark and I spent all day, Saturday, together. We went to breakfast, then drove to Baltimore Harbor. We walked along the pier, watching the vendors hawking their goods and a variety of performers showcasing their talents. We visited the aquarium and then ate at Phillips. The food was a delicious smorgasbord of all you-can-eat seafood, steak, chicken and vegetables. When Mark and I left, we both had to unsnap our jeans for the ride home. It was only seven thirty when we got back to Philly, so Mark decided to head towards Penn's Landing.

"Where are we going?" I asked. "Delaware Avenue is all clubs. I'm not dressed to go dancing." I complained.

"Oh, we're not going dancing," he announced with a devilish grin.

"What do you have up your sleeve?" I asked, laughing.

"Nothing up my sleeves, pretty lady," he said, sounding like a carnival barker. "Just a little fun and games."

"Just a little fun and games my behind," I smiled as we pulled in front of Dave and Buster's, a combination restaurant and arcade for children and adults.

"You never got over that booty-beating I gave you on that basketball game, did you," I laughed

"I don't believe I recall such a thing," he said, with mock seriousness.

"I guess I'll just have to refresh your memory," I

131

announced, shooting an imaginary hoop.

Three hours later, we stumbled back to the car. It wasn't from the one drink apiece that we had, but from the rigorous virtual reality games we played. We went at if full force and our bodies let us know about it.

"Two out of three," I teased, referring to the number of times that I beat Mark at the basketball game.

"Aw, I let you win," he said, knowing full well that he was lying.

"Whatever," I laughed, as we climbed into the car and merged into traffic. As we neared my house, we both grew silent. I assumed that making love was on both our minds. I knew it was on mine, but neither of us wanted to broach the subject, first. I had a two-fold reason. Although I wanted him, I knew that I would definitely be closing the door on Chloe if I gave into my desires. Even though Mark and I were engaged, it still didn't seem cemented, and it wouldn't until I talked to Chloe. Luckily, Mark broke the silence, taking the decision out of my hands.

"Well, the future Mrs. Kayla Fountaine," he said grandly. "I guess I'll let you go, so you can take a bath with some Epsom Salt and rest those old, aching bones."

"Speak for yourself, grandpa," I laughed. But I did grimace as I stretched my legs to get out of the car.

"You know that I would help you, but I'm too sore to move," he said, honestly.

"Boy, this is sad," I laughed, as I walked to the driver's side and kissed him goodnight.

"Be careful driving home," I said, waving as I approached my walkway.

"Ouch, ouch, ouch," I said with each step on my way into the house. Once he was sure I was safely inside, Mark honked the horn and drove off. I looked through the curtain that covered the small window of the living room door and watched until his car was out of sight. Easing away from the door, I continued my mantra.

"Ouch, ouch," I said, reaching for the banister. "Now where's that Epsom Salt?"

## Chapter Sixteen

Mom, Dad, Tony, Mark's parents and I, all went to the airport to see Mark off. We hugged and kissed and wished him a safe flight. They left us alone as I walked him to the gate, where his plane was boarding.

"I love you, Kayla. I'm so happy you're going to be my wife," he said huskily, grabbing me in a passionate hug.

"I love you too, Mark," I responded, softly.

"I'll be back in two weeks; then we can make all kinds of wonderful plans," he smiled.

"I can't wait," I purred, honestly.

"Sir, the plane will be leaving shortly," the pretty, Asian airline attendant said gently. As we moved apart, we noticed the waiting area was empty, except for the few who were waiting to see their loved one's plane take off.

"Sorry," Mark grinned sheepishly, then rushed down the boarding tunnel. "I love you," he yelled before disappearing around the corner.

"I love you, too," I whispered after him.

"Don't look so sad. He's coming back," Tony teased, as we all headed to the parking lot.

"Shut up," I growled, defensively.

"How about if we all go to breakfast," Mom piped in.

"Let me call Keilani," Tony said. I'm supposed to meet her for breakfast this morning anyway."

"Oh good," Mom responded.

"I think I'm going to pass," I said, heading toward my car.

"Why Kayla?" Mom asked, disappointed by my decision.

"I'm just not hungry Mom," I answered, half-truthfully.

"It's because she's going to be the only one without a date," Tony joked.

"Is that it?" she asked incredulously, hands on her hips. I couldn't believe that she was actually listening to Tony.

"What does she need a date for? She's engaged," Mom was saying as they headed toward their car.

"Leave her alone, Toni and you too, Tony," I could hear Dad saying, in the background.

'She's engaged'. The words were reverberating in my head. Now that Mark was gone, it was really hitting me, hard. As I pulled into my driveway, I had an overwhelming feeling of emptiness. One minute, I was having such a wonderful time with Mark, and the next minute, it was over. I would usually be with Chloe on Sunday. But now, I don't know where she is or what's going on with her. I felt totally lost and alone.

When I entered the house, the blinking light of the answering machine caught my eye. I had two messages. I was in no rush to listen to them. Mark just left, so it couldn't be him. Chloe was AWOL, and my parents were out having breakfast with Tony, Keilani and Mark's parents. Everyone was accounted for. Probably telemarketers, I sighed while I headed to the kitchen to find something to eat. I had settled on a cup of tea and a bagel, which I took with me to the living room and then I plopped down on the sofa. As I reached for the remote, the answering machine seemed to be beckoning me. Telemarketers don't usually call on Sundays. I decided to go ahead and listen to the messages.

"Oh, no you didn't hang up on me like that, last week, girl," Jackie's high-pitched voice squawked through the speaker. "I know you thought that I forgot, but I was so busy, that I'm just now getting a chance to get with you. Hello, I know you're there, Kayla Thomas."

There was a slight pause, as she waited to see if I was actually home and was going to pick up the phone.

"Alright, I guess I'm going to have to let you slide," she picked up where she left off. "But I'll tell you one thing, if Chloe ain't back in this office by tomorrow," she paused for effect, "I'm gonna want some answers. I'm not playing, Kayla," she said sternly; then ended with a sweet, "Call me."

"Jackie, if you don't leave me alone," I said aloud. The sound of the next voice almost made me drop my teacup.

'Hi Kayla, it's me,' Chloe said, sounding as if we hadn't missed a beat.

'I know you probably have a lot of questions that I'm not sure I have all of the answers to, but you do at least deserve an explanation. Well, I'm not going to get into it over the phone. Why don't you give me a call at your earliest convenience? Talk to you then, bye.'

That was it? Call me at your earliest convenience. I could feel the steam escaping from my ears. She left me high and dry without a clue as to what she was up to, and comes back acting like nothing happened. What nerve! But in spite of my anger, I was still anxious to talk to her. Hearing her voice again made me realize how much I missed her. I wanted to pick up the phone immediately and tell her this. I also wanted to tell her off. But I was apprehensive about doing either one because circumstances had changed, drastically. As I pondered this dilemma, the phone rang. Startled, I picked up the receiver without thinking.

"H-hello."

"Hi Kayla, did you get my message?" Chloe asked. Her voice was a mixture of husky and sexy and I was instantly turned on by it.

'Remember, you're angry, Kayla', the little voice inside reminded me. "Yeah, I got it," I said with as much attitude as I could muster.

"Kayla, I know you're angry about the way I left things," she said, hearing the irritability in my voice. "But I needed to get away."

I understood all too well, and after taking inventory of what I had done, I softened my tone.

"I know Chloe," I sighed, "these last couple of weeks haven't been easy on either of us."

"Well, like I said on the answering machine; I don't want to talk about it over the phone. It is Sunday, you know."

"What does that have to do with anything?" I asked, totally confused.

"Well," she said, slowly, "I have the bacon frying, the coffee brewing and I'm whipping up some pancake batter as we speak." Her tone was more of a chipper and friendly nature, different from the teasing, seductive manner that I had been accustomed to. As I was questioning this in my mind, her voice squawked through the receiver.

"Well, are you coming?" she asked with fake agitation.

"Huh?" I responded, returning to our conversation.

"Earth to Kayla," she continued, teasingly. "I'm cooking breakfast over here. Are you coming or what?"

"Oh, I'm sorry," I said quickly. "I'm outta here."

I quickly threw my bagel in the trash, poured the tea into the sink, grabbed my jacket and headed out the door.

# If Loving Two is Wrong . . .

## Chapter Seventeen

On my way to Chloe's apartment, I felt strange. It was like I hadn't driven that path in years, instead of a week. I also contemplated the way Chloe sounded over the phone. Why was she so giddy? I felt as if I was in the twilight zone. I mean, I had been dealing with Chloe for almost a year, hadn't I? And I did just get engaged to Mark, the love of my life for almost twenty years, didn't I? Well, why at this precise moment did I feel as if none of this had really happened? A song on the radio caught my attention. 'I Want To Go Outside In The Rain' was playing. I had heard that song many times and it never really held any significance for me. But now, it seemed as if the words summed up my entire life. At this moment, I felt as if I wanted to be outside in the pouring rain, drenched, cleansing myself of all emotional confusion and absolving myself of any wrongdoing. I began singing the words to the song as if I had written them, incorporating feeling and emotion. Before I knew it, I was pulling into the parking lot at Chloe's building. Instantly, I began to feel hesitant about going in. I wasn't ready to face her after the decision I had made without any input from her. Her words had come back to haunt me. She said that she felt that decisions would be made that affected her life without her having any say, and she was right. I had assured her that I wouldn't do that to her, but I did. At that precise moment, I felt like a snake. I wanted to slither away, crawl under a rock and die.

"Is that a statue, or is that Kayla Thomas?" Chloe hollered from her balcony.

"It's me," I answered, dumbly.

"Well then, get in here! Breakfast is ready, perfect timing, huh?" Her words stung. She had come back just in time to find out that I was engaged to Mark.

**Kim Beverly**

"Yeah, perfect timing," I mumbled as I headed into the building. As soon as I stepped off the elevator, I could smell the aromas of bacon and coffee wafting from Chloe's apartment. It seemed so familiar, yet distant. I was dreading the upcoming conversation, but I knew it was inevitable. Before I could knock, the door swung open.

"C'mon in stranger," Chloe said, smiling brightly. Little did she know, those words hit very close to home. Standing there face to face, I really did feel like a stranger, not only to her, but to myself as well.

"Where have you been?" I asked upon entering. "I've been trying to get in touch with you all week!"

"Well hello to you too," she said smiling. "How about if we play catch up after we eat. The food's getting cold," she added, just a tad too cheerfully. I got the distinct feeling that she wanted to prolong the inevitable too. But how could she possibly know what I was going to say?

"Earth to Kayla, come in Kayla," Chloe was saying, interrupting my thought process. You looked like you were a million miles away," she said, pouring me a cup of coffee.

"Sorry, it's just that things feel strange," I answered truthfully.

"How so?" she asked with raised eyebrows.

"I know it's only been a week, but for some reason, it feels like months since we've seen each other. I feel like there's an awkwardness between us."

"Yeah," she agreed, somberly. "I feel it too. But it's probably only natural, under the circumstances."

"What circumstances," I asked, although I knew what she meant.

"Look," she said, with a slight edge to her voice. "We both know that we have some tough issues to tackle, there's no getting around it. But how about we try to enjoy this wonderful breakfast I've prepared," she said, softening her tone.

"Deal," I answered. We shook hands and began to eat.

An hour and ten pounds later, we were sitting on the sofa, sipping coffee.

# If Loving Two is Wrong . . .

"Now that wasn't right," I sighed, unsnapping the button on my pants.

"What?" she asked with feigned innocence.

"All that food you made. I'm going straight to Jenny Craig when I leave here."

"Who is she," Chloe asked with fake agitation. "Don't tell me there's yet another person that I have to compete with for you affections." As soon as she said it, I could tell she regretted it. Her jovial bogus frown had turned into genuine sadness. But she had done it. She broached the subject that we had both been avoiding.

"Chloe," I sighed, moving in closer and grabbing her hands. "I need to know where you were, what you did and why you left like you did."

"I know Kayla," she said, quietly. "The last two days before I left, I was a wreck," she confided. "I didn't know what to do. I thought about bombarding you and trying to take up all of your time, so you wouldn't have a chance to spend time with Mark. But then, I figured that would be childish and only a temporary fix. Just because your body would've been with me, didn't mean your mind wouldn't be with him."

"But Chloe," I attempted to interrupt.

"No Kayla," Chloe countered, "let me finish. I also thought about outing you to your family and Mark. But that too would be childish and would probably earn me your contempt. So, as I saw it, I only had two choices. I could sit around and wait to see how our little drama unfolded; or I could get away for a little while and get my head together. Obviously, I chose the latter," she said with a wan smile.

"Well, did you get your head together?" I asked, not knowing what else to say. Somehow, the words 'I accepted Mark's proposal', just wouldn't escape my lips.

"I think I did," she answered thoughtfully. "What about you?"

"What about me?" I stalled.

"Kayla, you know full well what I'm asking. But since you insist that I spell everything out, what have you decided to do about Mark?"

I could feel the tears welling in my eyes as I subconsciously squeezed Chloe's hands harder.

"Chloe," I paused. I couldn't get it out. I began sobbing uncontrollably.

"Ssh, ssh," she hushed softly, pulling my head to her bosom consolingly.

"Kayla, there's something that I need to tell you," she said, as she stroked my hair. "You said that you needed to know where I was, what I did and why I left. You already know why I left. I went to the Bahamas. I figured if I had to suffer, I might as well do it in paradise," she said with a dry chuckle, still stroking my hair. She let out a deep sigh before she continued.

"While I was there," she paused, raising my face with her hands so we were eye to eye. "I met someone."

I felt like I had been hit in the chest with a sledgehammer. I could literally feel the blood rushing throughout my body. Time seemed to be suspended. Hundreds of thoughts were careening through my mind. How could you, you bitch? Well, I guess I got what I deserved! So what? It's okay, I've got Mark! I just want to die. Amazingly, all were valid thoughts, but how should I react? With anger? With remorse? Vengefully? Like a Victim? How? I was totally and utterly discombobulated, caught off guard. Here I was, thinking that I was the one with the hand grenade, and she comes out dropping bombs. The sheer irony of it made me laugh aloud; but inside, I was devastated. I had temporarily lost control of my emotions. I wanted to laugh, no, cry, kill, no, be killed. Finally, I found my voice.

"What!" I cried, half sobbing, half-screeching. "How could you?" I demanded, pulling from her grasp. But deep inside, I knew I had no right to berate her. But fair play had no place in my psyche, now.

"Kayla, I don't know how to explain," she said, anguished.

"Who is she?" I asked, knowing full well that it made no difference. All I knew was that someone else would be receiving the attentions of MY Chloe! As I thought it, it reminded me of when I first saw Mark again. He was My Mark. My mind was racing. I was being selfish, but I couldn't help it. What if I hadn't accepted Mark's proposal, then what?

'But you did', my conscience answered.

'Shut up!' I countered. If I hadn't accepted his proposal, Chloe would've come back and dumped me, then what? I guess I would've still had Mark. But what if I had wanted Chloe? Do I still want Chloe? But that decision is out of my hands, now. Chloe met someone else.

I wondered if this was how Chloe had been feeling. I don't care how she felt; she had left and met someone else without waiting to hear my decision.

"I am really cracking up," I said, half to myself and half out loud as I pondered that last statement. Who was I to think that someone had to wait around while I made a decision about their life? Part of me was glad Chloe did what she did. It absolved me of some of the guilt that I was feeling, but it didn't diminish the pain in my heart.

"Kayla, are you alright?" Chloe's voice was penetrating my emotional fog. As I glanced at the mirror behind the counter, I could see why she was asking. My face was red and blotchy, and my eyes were swollen from crying. In other words, I looked a frightful sight.

"Yeah, I'm okay," I said softly, as I refocused my attention on her. "How did it happen?"

"Kayla, that's not important now," she said, quietly.

"I want to know," I said, forcefully.

"I met her while I was sunning myself on the beach," she answered dully.

"Did you approach her, or did she approach you?" I was dreading the answer. In my mind, if Chloe had initiated the contact, that told me that she had no intention of being with me when she got back.

"She came over to me," Chloe answered. "She asked me how I could be in such a beautiful place and look so sad."

"What a line," I drawled, sarcastically.

"It wasn't a line," Chloe said defensively. "I was very despondent, dwelling on what was going on back here."

"Well you're the one who chose to run away instead of staying and fighting for what you wanted!" I was now screaming at the top of my lungs.

"You mean romance you behind the scenes?" Chloe asked quietly.

"What?" I yelled, indignantly.

"You heard me," Chloe responded, her voice beginning to rise. "Mark could openly express his affections and announce his intentions, but I had to wait until no one was around to put my bid in." Chloe was seething with righteous anger.

"That's not fair," I sobbed.

"No, it wasn't fair," Chloe sighed, attempting to calm down. "It wasn't fair to you, to me or to Mark. But that's what happens when you live your life under a shroud of secrecy."

"You know my reasons," I defended weakly.

"Yes, I do, Kayla," she responded. "But those reasons are why we're at the place we are today," she admonished. "At least with Monica I don't have to hide!"

"Monica," I sneered as if something smelled truly funky.

"Yes. Monica," Chloe sighed. "She has no qualms about showing me affection in public and she's doesn't have to struggle with the idea of wanting me."

I couldn't believe what I was hearing. Chloe was actually comparing and contrasting her relationship between me and this Monica woman, a virtual stranger!

"So you were able to ascertain all of this about her in a week's time?" I yelled in frustration.

"Kayla, I didn't plan for this to happen. It started with me being alone and miserable, then just being happy to have a companion to talk to and hang with. But it didn't take long for me to realize that I wasn't ducking and weaving whenever someone came around and might be able to interpret our laughter or hug as being more than friendly."

# If Loving Two is Wrong . . .

"Hug," I paused. "More than friendly?" I repeated in disbelief. "How long did it take for you two to get that close?"

"Kayla, let's not do this," Chloe said softly.

"It's already done," I huffed. "I mean, how much could I have meant to you if you could be embracing someone new in a week's time of being away from me? That's pretty damn insulting," I ended with a wry chuckle.

"Kayla, it wasn't like that," Chloe said moaned. "I'm simply referring to a pat on the back when we said goodnight."

"Yeah right," I snarled.

"Kayla look," Chloe said with growing impatience. "I met Monica in an innocent way. I wasn't looking for anything to develop, but I couldn't help but notice how good it felt not to always have my guard up because a woman is attracted to me and showing me some attention. There is nothing easy about what's going on, but I can't ignore the fact that I prefer an open relationship over a closeted one."

Her words were punching harder than the young Mike Tyson. I literally felt bruised after each sentence.

"Face it, Kayla, we may never have been able to have an open, committed relationship," she said delicately, grabbing a hold of my hands.

Suddenly the words, 'I met someone', popped back into my head. In my mind, words mixed with thoughts and made instant anger. I wanted to lash out because my heart felt like it was breaking. I didn't care if I was wrong. I abruptly pulled my hands from her grasp.

"Well, I'm just glad that I didn't sit around twiddling my thumbs waiting for you, while you were off on Paradise Island somewhere," I huffed.

"What's that supposed to mean?" Chloe asked, indignantly.

"It means," I said, as I placed my coffee cup on the table and grabbed my purse, "that I have already decided to accept Mark's proposal. I spent a lot of time worrying needlessly about how to tell you; but now I can see what a

143

fool I've been." I made a beeline for the door, then turned to face her in dramatic fashion. "I hope you and your Bahama Mama will be very happy. I know Mark and I will be." The tears were dangerously close to falling, so I turned sharply on my heels and slammed the door. I could hear Chloe calling my name through the closed door. But in my mind, I had also slammed the door forever, literally and symbolically, on the Chloe and Kayla chapter of my life.

# If Loving Two is Wrong . . .

## Chapter Eighteen

Chloe had attempted to contact me for three days after I left her condo in such a huff. She called me at work, paged me, and left messages on my answering machine. She was pleading for me to talk to her so we could mend the rift and at least remain friends. She even commissioned Jackie to intervene as a last resort; but I wasn't budging. Even though it was killing me, I refused to give in. I figured if I relented, it would just throw me into a tailspin of confusion and my heart wouldn't be able to take it.

On the fourth day, she came to my house. I was surprised when I looked out the peephole and saw her standing there looking so nervous and vulnerable; not to mention, as beautiful as ever. I refused to answer the door. After fifteen minutes and three cell phone attempts, I watched her turn dejectedly, stare at my car parked in the driveway and then back at the house, before proceeding to her car. I could see the tears in her eyes as she walked away. I was thankful that she didn't have a key to my house since the majority of our time together was spent at her place. Once she pulled off, I felt bad, but knew that it was for the best.

For ten days I avoided everyone like the plague. I didn't want anyone to see me in such a fragile state. I went from crying to screaming to laughing about everything that had occurred in the last two years. I had already given my two-week notice at work, ensuring there would be no surprise visits.

Finally, it was time for Mark's return and my re-entry into socialization. I threw myself into preparing for a life with Mark. Although I was generally happy about him coming back, I knew I was overcompensating to hide the anguish that I was feeling about Chloe .It was decided that we would get married in the next two months. Mark needed to get back to Chicago and his flourishing business. Our mothers had decided it would be best to let them plan the wedding, while Mark and I went back to Chicago and got our house ready to move into. When Mark and I arrived at the house, Sharleen and Troy greeted us.

"Girl, I'm so glad to finally meet you! Mark has done nothing but speak of you nonstop. To tell you the truth, Kayla, I got sick of it. No offense,' she added quickly, squeezing my arm and watching me with wide eyes.

'None taken,' I had responded, smiling at her admission and quick, knee jerk reaction.

"But was I right?" Mark asked as he grabbed me around the waist, pulling me to him, possessively.

"Yeah, you were right," Troy chimed in, "but that little eighth grade picture you kept shoving under our noses did not do justice to Kayla. She's an absolute freak!"

"Hey," Mark and Sharleen, both responded. Sharleen followed hers up with a playful jab to Troy's ribs. "I've only been in Chicago for a few months," Sharleen said enthusiastically. "But I've searched out the best movie theaters, restaurants malls. Mark and Troy are always so busy with work that we're going to be each other's lifeline."

"Well I'm looking forward to hitting those malls," I readily admitted.

"How about if we check a few of them tomorrow?" Sharleen asked, wiggling with excitement.

"Sounds like a plan," I said, giving her a high five and falling into instant girlfriend mode.

"Uh oh," Mark grimaced. "Hide your wallet, Troy."

"There is no hiding place for a woman determined to shop," Troy informed Mark with a groan.

"Oh quit groaning, you big babies. You had to know there would be a price to pay to land women of our caliber," I sassily as I gave Sharleen a quick ghetto fist pound.

"Ooh, we're going to get along fabulously," Sharleen cooed in response to my comment. Then she wrapped her arm around my shoulders and we headed

# If Loving Two is Wrong . . .

indoors.

The next day Sharleen and I headed out for a day of shopping and exploration for me. As Sharleen chauffeured me around town, I couldn't help but be caught up in her bubbly personality. She was so friendly and unpretentious, not a hint of insincerity in her demeanor.

"Where would you like to go first?" she asked, turning to glance at me.

"Well, I think I'd like to start with some home decorating stores," I responded.

"I know just the place," she smiled, flinging her shoulder-length auburn hair from her face. Sharleen was very attractive. She had gold-flecked eyes, the color of tea with a touch of lemon and cappucino colored skin. I had already determined her to be a perfect size twelve with sporty cute taste. Today she had on a sky blue sweatsuit with the same color sneakers and matching accessories, right down to the sunglasses. We spent the entire day shopping. During lunch, we got better equated over some deep-dish pepperoni pizza.

"How did you and Troy meet?" I asked while grabbing a slice of the steaming pie.

"We were childhood sweethearts," she answered, dropping a hot slice onto her paper plate and blowing on her fingers.

"Wow," I exclaimed, "Mark was my childhood sweetheart, it just took him a longer time to recognize it," I laughed.

"I know," Sharleen giggled. Mark told us all about the puppy love crush you had on him.

"Oh yeah?" I snorted, "Well as you can see, milk did a body good and brought the big dog running to me."

"I hear you girl," Sharleen smirked, pointing a blue and white polished fingernail in my direction. "But you know, Kayla," she said seriously. "We are both very lucky women to have men like Troy and Mark."

"Trust me, I know it. Mark has been my Prince Charming since I was a little girl and nothing has changed

147

over the years. Sometimes I pinch myself to make sure I'm not dreaming," I said, biting into the cheesy pie.

"I'm so glad that Mark has someone like you Kayla. I'm really looking forward to the four of us building a life here," she said softly. She looked almost as if she was on the verge of tears.

"I'm looking forward to it, too," I said gently, puzzled by her display of emotion.

"It's just that I've been really home sick these last few months and it feels really good to have a girlfriend again. All my close friends are in Jersey and although we talk often, it's not the same as having someone to go shopping with and talk to face to face."

"I understand," I said, walking over to give her a hug. "I know we're going to be great friends, Sharleen."

"Well you can start by calling me Shar," she sniffled.

"You got it, Shar," I smiled. "Now come on, we got some more shopping to do."

Things were rolling along fine until I received a call from my mother, asking for Chloe's address. That's when she realized that she hadn't heard from Chloe in weeks and was so sure that I would want her to be a part of the wedding. All of the hurt and frustration came flooding back. It had been a month and a half since that fateful day that I stormed out of Chloe's apartment. I told my mother that Chloe and I had a falling out and weren't speaking.

"Oh Kayla," she moaned. "Chloe's like family. You two were closer than Siamese twins. Do you really want to let a stupid disagreement come between your friendship?" I pondered my mother's question. I no longer felt any of the anger that had fueled our separation so many weeks ago. It had been replaced with feelings of emptiness and deep emotional loss.

"You're right, Mom," I relented, "it is silly."

"I know it is," Mama crowed. "If I had known that this silliness was going on, I would've put a stop to it long ago. Now give me her address."

As I read out the numbers of Chloe's address, I

didn't know how to feel. I longed to see her, but didn't know if I could handle it.

"Who was that, baby?" Mark asked as he entered the newly furnished living room, catching me in deep thought.

"That was your mother-in-law," I said with an exaggerated eye roll.

"Not yet," he joked. "I still have two weeks to change my mind."

"Oh, good one, Mr. Fountaine," I laughed, faking a knockout punch.

"Ouch," he played along, "More wedding preparations?"

"No, just reassuring me that everything is set," I lied, not wanting to discuss Chloe with him. I had traveled home five times in the last month and half for fittings and final approvals, so I was already confident that the wedding was going to be perfect. I had to admit that our mothers were doing an excellent job.

"I know it's set," Mark said, hugging me around the waist. "The only detail I care about is making sure the preacher is there to pronounce us man and wife; everything else is negotiable," he laughed.

"Don't tell our mothers that," I cautioned. "They think that every detail is vital. Gotta love 'em," I laughed.

"Dearly," he concurred.

"Well babe, it's getting late and as much as I hate to do it..."

"No, don't say it," he pleaded, mockingly.

"I have to," I moaned. "Time for you to go," I said as I begrudgingly heaved him towards the door.

Mark and I had agreed that we would not sleep together in our new home until we were married. So, Troy and Sharleen agreed to help us out.

The last two weeks were a blur. Before I knew it, September twenty-first, our wedding day, had arrived. It was a beautiful crisp day. The sun was shining, not a dark cloud in sight. Everything went off without a hitch. Tony, Troy,

Mark, and our dads were so handsome and well behaved; they almost stole the show. Almost, but not quite. The Thomas and Fountaine women were the true showstoppers. My Aunt Pat had put a hurting on some material when she created the eighth and ninth wonders of the world, better known as my wedding and bridesmaid gowns. It was the wedding of my dreams and I marveled at how it was done in such a short time. My only regret was that I didn't see Chloe. My mother assured me that she had sent the invitation and even left phone messages, but never received a reply. It was as if Chloe had dropped off the face of the earth, again. I accepted the news gracefully, but my mother knew that I was deeply hurt.

During the ceremony, nothing but Mark filled my thoughts. It was at the reception that thoughts of Chloe kept gnawing at my conscience. But when Mark took my hand and led me to the floor for our first dance as man and wife, once again, all of my thoughts were concentrated on him. He was the only man to capture my heart, besides my Daddy, and I was so proud to be his wife.

Two hours, two champagne toasts, one garter belt fiasco and one cake in the face later, Mark and I were leaving the reception, heading for the airport and Hawaii for our honeymoon. As I turned and looked out the rear window of the limo for one last glance at the wedding party, I saw her.

Standing across the street from the reception hall, leaning against a large tree, was Chloe. She was dressed in light blue jeans, a turquoise sweater, turquoise leather jacket and white sneakers. Her hair was pulled back into her signature ponytail. She looked as beautiful as ever as she raised her hand and blew me a kiss. With a tear in my eye, I gave her a wink and mouthed a silent thank you. I turned back to face my husband with a full heart. I knew everything was going to be perfect.

# If Loving Two is Wrong . . .

## Chapter Nineteen

The fourteen-hour flight to Hawaii seemed like only a matter of minutes. Mark and I were like Siamese twins joined at the lips. We separated long enough to share a Champagne toast with the rest of the first-class passengers and to hear the captain congratulate us on the intercom, generating a smattering of applause. When we touched down in Honolulu, a line of beautiful Hawaiian ladies was waiting to place colorful leis around our necks. In the background was a group of muscle-bound well-oiled Hawaiian men were playing rhythmic island music that added to the utopian ambiance. We had reservations at the Hakulani Hotel and rode the hotel shuttle along with at least twenty other people, including a group of seven barely twenty-one girls who shrieked at the sight of every tanned male for the entire ride. At least that was the complaint another couple made when we were disembarking from the shuttle, Mark and I had been oblivious to any and everything except each other. The Hakulani was a five and a half-star hotel and it was immediately evident why. Mai, obviously a native with her long, silky black hair and doe eyes, greeted us at the entrance and accompanied Mark and me to one of line of small floral decorated rooms. She offered us a seat on the comfortable chairs in front of a medium-sized wooden desk that held a computer and other necessities. When she found our names in the computer, she burst into a radiating smile.

"I see congratulations are in order. I should've known when you first walked in. Newlyweds seem to a certain glow about them and you two certainly have it," she said, beaming; her nice, white teeth appeared to gleam against her smooth, reddish brown skin and the deep dimples on each cheek further accented her smile.

Although Mark and I were perfectly happy with the luxury suite we had picked from the brochure, Mai insisted on upgrading us to the Presidential Suite.

"It comes complete with a semi-private elevator and baby grand piano," she grinned, obviously pleased to be able to offer us such accommodations. Mark and I immediately turned to each other with pressed lips and arched eyebrows. Then, simultaneously faced Mai and said in unison, "Who are we to argue?"

"I see why you two are soulmates," Mai said, laughing at our unorchestrated, tandem movements. "Excuse me one moment, please," she said, picking up the phone and requesting a bellboy for us. Within seconds, a twenty-something, well-tanned young man appeared in the doorway. Mai rose from the desk and smoothed the front of her floral print dress before coming around to stand beside us.

"Mr. and Mrs. Fountaine, this is Chad," she announced, making a sweeping gesture in the bellboy's direction.

"He will assist you with your luggage and show you to your room. Take good care of the Fountaines, Chad. The newlyweds will being staying in the Presidential Suite."

"Aloha and congratulations," Chad said, bowing at the waist. He looked adorable in his pristine, white Bermuda shorts and Hawaiian shirt.

"It will be my extreme pleasure to escort you to your room. Your luggage has already been loaded onto my cart, so if you'd please follow me..." he trailed off.

"I trust you will enjoy your stay, if you need anything at all, don't hesitate to contact me," Mai said, handing me a cardboard keyholder. The elegantly written name and a picture of the hotel adorned the front of the little cardboard casing. I checked inside to ensure there were two keys before handing them to Mark. In the elevator, Mark was watching me with such an intensity, I knew if it wasn't for Chad, we would have taken full advantage of having this semi-private space, but there would be plenty of time for that.

# If Loving Two is Wrong . . .

When the doors opened, I nearly swooned. What greeted us was a veritable paradise within paradise. We stepped out of the elevator onto a gold- veined, pearly white marble floor. On either side were matching marble columns. A thin gold strip separated the beautiful marble from the aqua blue carpet that seemed to extend outside the sliding glass door and into the majestic, greenish blue waters of the Pacific Ocean. To the far left was a fully stocked wet bar. The living room consisted of a polished, white baby grand piano, a soft turquoise leather sofa with matching love seats and a white entertainment center complete with a forty-two inch colored television, DVD/CD player and electric fireplace. The living room was separated from the fully functional kitchen by a long breakfast bar with cinnamon colored stools. The rest of the space consisted of a den, two bedrooms with their own baths and dressing room and a large, wrap-around lanai

I anxiously waited for Mark to tip the bellboy and watched as he disappeared behind the elevator doors.

"Whoowee, we just hit the jackpot ba-bee," I said, strolling around the room like Huggy Bear on 'Starsky and Hutch'. Mark couldn't help but laugh.

"Girl, you are crazy!" Then his face grew serious.

"But really, Kayla, I knew I hit the jackpot the moment you said yes," he said, huskily. The emotion on his face and in his voice stopped me from making a witty remark. Instead, I got serious, too.

"Mark, I'm the lucky one. Standing here with you on our honeymoon is a dream come true. I've known since I was nine that I was going to marry you, I just had to wait for you to grow up and realize it, too."

Mark started to speak, but I hushed him with a gentle kiss. Next, I grabbed his hand and led him down the hallway to the master suite. Once inside the spacious bedroom, I pushed Mark's five-foot eleven-inch frame onto the bed and straddled his stomach. I was both nervous and bold at the same time. I was not used to being so aggressive in the bedroom, but I wanted Mark badly and I wanted him to know just how much. If he wasn't comfortable with the idea, it didn't show. I placed my hands on either side of his head and leaned into him. I started with a soft kiss that grew more passionate as I reached down and began to slowly pull his white cotton shirt from the confines of his khaki shorts. I paused long enough to pull the shirt over his head and then started on the shorts. Once I unbuckled his belt, freed the single button and pulled down his zipper, I reached inside his cotton briefs to finally feel what I was working with. It was obvious that Mark was turned on by manipulations. Nibbling on his ear, I cooed for him to meet me in the Jacuzzi in five minutes. Mark's eyes were closed as he groaned what I assumed was an okay. After gingerly climbing off Mark, I rushed into the marbled bathroom and started running hot water into the sunken tub. There was an assortment of complimentary amenities on the vanity and I picked up a small bottle of mango-scented bubble bath. I poured a generous amount into the tub, hastily pulled off my peach sundress and panties and kicked them out of my way. Then I grabbed a chilled bottle of complimentary champagne from the small refrigerator by the Jacuzzi. There were two gold-rimmed champagne flutes on the vanity and I placed them on the side of the tub. Satisfied with the amount and temperature of the water, I shut off the spigot, stepped out of my sandals and gently eased into the warm, sudsy pool.

"Mark, baby, I'm waiting for you," I cried out in a singsong voice.

"I'll be there in just one minute, sweetheart," he yelled from the living room.

As I surveyed my surroundings, I couldn't help but take in the beauty of the mauve colored fixtures. I noticed a radio on the vanity so I hopped out and quickly found a jazz station, then dashed back into the Jacuzzi. I had barely settled in, when Mark entered with a tray of passion fruits and chocolates. I wasn't the least bit interested with what was on that tray. It was the first time that I had seen him completely naked and I was in awe of his flawless physique. Mark had the build of a top-notch track and field runner. My attention was first drawn to his hairless muscular chest that was in perfect alignment with his six-pack abs. The pesky silver tray concealed his family jewels, but not his formidable, well-toned thighs. His muscles were cut as if he was flexing, but he was simply standing in a natural pose. I followed the bulging veins from his biceps down to his wrist and hands, which held the tray. My eyes trailed him up and down for a full minute before I finally spoke.

"Leave all that other fruit on the tray and just bring me that banana," I ordered with a smile.

Mark raised his eyebrows in surprise at my crudeness, then rushed to do my bidding.

"Your wish is my command," he bowed at the waist, still holding the tray. I guessed we were both using a little comic relief to hide our nervousness about finally making love. The anxiousness that I was feeling was both exasperating and refreshing. It was crazy; we were acting like a couple of teenagers. Enough was enough.

"C'mon," I said, reaching out to him. He finally set the tray down and joined me in the frothing water. Mark reached past me and grabbed the bottle of champagne. After popping the cork, he filled both flutes and offered one to me.

"To us and the fact that true love does exist," he offered as a toast. We did the ceremonious arm wraparound and sipped the sweet, effervescent liquid, looking into each other's eyes.

For an instant, my mind flashed back to a similar scene with Chloe, but just as quickly, I refocused on Mark's gorgeous brown eyes, refusing to let any guilty feelings or past emotions intercede with the moment at hand. With a renewed sense of purpose, I disentangled our arms and took the long, slim glass from Mark's hand. After placing them on the flat surface around the Jacuzzi, I returned my attentions to him. I needed to prove to myself that I could love Mark wholly; we both deserved that. I leaned over and cupped his face in my hands and just stared at his plump, juicy, brown lips for a moment. Then, without even thinking, I leaned in and ran my wet tongue along their smooth edges. It might

155

have been my imagination, but I could've sworn his lips tasted like sweet, dark cherries; they were so enticing. I found myself nibbling on the fleshy bottom lip, then trailing my tongue beneath the ridge to his succulent chin. I could hear a deep, guttural moan escaping from his throat as I straddled my legs over his muscular thighs. The bubbling water was the only barrier between my womanhood and his aroused manhood. Although I could feel the impatient head probing against my lower lips, I wasn't ready to accept him just yet. Teasingly, I would lower myself just enough for him to feel the promise of pleasure yet to come then would raise out of his reach. Mark allowed me to continue my torment for a few seconds before grabbing my hips and attempting to maneuver his way into my softness. But I was having none of it. This was my seduction and it was going to happen my way and at my pace. I stepped over Mark and motioned for him to move onto the top step.

"Kayla, what are you..." he began as he slid up the steps.

"Ssh," I commanded, sharply, "I got this."

I knew Mark had an idea of what I was about to do and felt uneasy. But I was determined to perform at least one virginal act on our wedding night. I grabbed the champagne bottle and took a mouthful and slowly dripped it down his chest, licking the trail it made. When I finally reached the object I had been craving, I took another sip of bubbly and greedily covered his organ with my mouth. Mark's quick intake of breath was the desired result. Slowly, I bobbed my head back forth on his staff of life, intoxicated by the combination of champagne and him. The groans escaping from his lips served as a catalyst for my hastened actions. I never thought that I would enjoy pleasing a man, orally, but I found myself not wanting to stop. Instinctively, I took hold of Mark's taut derriere and pulled him toward me, attempting to force-feed myself with more of him. His increased moans sent me into a frenzy. I wasn't ready to end the delicious torment for him or me, but I couldn't stop myself from bringing him to a mind-blowing climax. I could feel the muscles tensing in his sexy behind as he involuntarily straightened his powerful legs.

"Kayla, I-I-I'm..." His words were lost as he grabbed my head and inadvertently submerged my face into the tepid liquid. Sputtering, I quickly rose out of the water and lay my head on his chest as we both took a moment to catch our breaths.

"Damn, a sister gives you a good time and you try to drown her," I said, when I could finally talk. Mark wrapped his arms tightly around me and let out a throaty laugh.

"Girl, you are too much, you darn near gave me a heart attack."

"Not bad for a first time, huh?" I was hoping to sound nonchalant, considering I felt a little embarrassed by the feat that I had just performed. Mark gently lifted my head from his chest and looked at me with understanding.

"Baby, that was incredible and if it helps any, that was the first time for me, too."

"Get outta here," I said with a smirk. "You can't tell me that none of those fresh behind girls ever did that back in the day."

"Let's just say that no one has ever made me feel the way you just did," he said, sincerely.

"I just want you to know how much I love you," I said softly. "It really means a lot to me to know that I satisfy you."

"I bet not as much as me returning the favor," he grinned as he traded places with me and prepared me for takeoff.

When we finally emerged from the Jacuzzi, the water had turned cold and we were famished, for food. Since it was almost ten o'clock, we decided to order room service and spend the rest of the evening making tender, passionate love in front of the glowing fireplace.

The next morning, Mark and I woke up in each other's arms; naked atop the blanket we had laid on the plush carpet.

"Good morning, Mrs. Fountaine," he said softly, rubbing his fingers through my hair as I lay on his chest.

"Ooh, baby, that sounds sooo good, say it again," I demanded, sweetly.

"Mrs. Fountaine," he obliged. "What do you feel like doing today?"

"Do you even have to ask," I cooed, grabbing his soldier, which was already saluting. "I see Mark Jr., is already wide-awake," I smiled.

"Naw baby, that's Peter the Pumpkin Eater. Mark Jr. is the name reserved for our son."

"Well, Peter," I laughed, talking to his groin. "Hurry up and say hello to Miss Pumpkin, so we can get to greet Mark Jr."

"You are an insatiable nut," he grinned, positioning himself over me and rubbing his member up and down my already moist center before entering me, gently.

"Only when it comes to you," I purred, sexily, gazing up into his eyes. Using his forearms for support, Mark lowered his head and started nuzzling my neck.

"Oh baby, you know that's my spot," I sighed, becoming caught up in his winding motions.

"And this is my spot," he said, huskily, punctuating his words with a forceful thrust.

"Well don't talk about it baby," I said through clenched teeth, "be about it."

I began matching his accelerating movements, stroke for stroke.

"Kayla, I love you so much," Mark moaned repeatedly. The soft wind that escaped at the end of his whispered admissions tickled my ear. I was about to respond, when suddenly he slid his arms beneath mine, grabbed my shoulders from behind and set forth a full assault. I could feel myself building to a climax and wanted him to join me, simultaneously. Although I knew he was close, I squeezed my lower muscles, gripping him tightly, ensuring that he would meet me in ecstasy. My diminishing squeals and Mark's slow; deep groans were the result of the nuclear reaction that had just taken place. Mark rested his head on my breast and we just lay still, silent except for the soft sounds of our breathing.

Mark was the first to stir, rising slightly and supporting himself on his elbow, chin in hand; he looked down at me.

# If Loving Two is Wrong . . .

"Baby, why don't you go ahead and get in the shower while I order some breakfast? I want to get in a little sightseeing today."

"Okay honey," I groaned, stretching languidly. Mark was just staring at me, licking his lips like L.L.Cool J.

"You better go on, baby, or we might not make it out of here today," he said thickly, running his index finger up and down my spine.

"You're right," I agreed, rising slightly and kissing him softly on the lips.

"There is a lot I want to see on this island, but don't underestimate your drawing power, Papi," I said with a seductive Spanish accent. Not waiting for a response, I hopped up and headed toward the master suite.

"I don't know who that chick was, but I hope I see her later," Mark called toward my back.

"Oh really," I stopped dead in my tracks, feigning annoyance. "You do know that you have a very jealous wife, don't you?" I tossed back over my shoulder.

"She can join us, too," he said matter-of-factly, calling my angry bluff.

"I want a Belgian Waffle, scrambled eggs with cheese and hash browns. Make sure they put some onions in them," I ordered as a way of concession before continuing to the shower.

"Chu got it, Mami," Mark said, laughing. I pretended to bristle once more before disappearing into the bedroom.

Half an hour later, I emerged dressed in white shorts, an off the shoulder pink chiffon blouse and pink sandals.

"Go ahead baby, you can get..." I stopped as I rounded the corner toward the kitchen. Mark was standing at the breakfast bar removing the silver tops from the plates. He was dressed in white shorts and a powder blue short- sleeved shirt. He looked adorable.

"How did you get dressed so quickly," I asked, amazed.

"I knew how long you could be, so I used the other bathroom. Besides, I wanted to make sure I was here when they delivered breakfast. Voila, he made a grand gesture of

159

removing the last lid."

After breakfast, Mark and I picked up some brochures from the hotel lobby and asked Mai her opinion about what not to miss. She suggested that we attend a Luau and perhaps visit the Polynesian Cultural Center, which was Hawaii's Polynesian theme park attraction. In addition, she told us about the different activities, from swimming with dolphins to horseback riding. We thanked her, then headed on out to tour the great island.

After an hour, the furthest we had got, was the hotel beach. We had already missed a few of the tours that we might have been interest in and the others didn't start for at least three more hours. We decided to put on our swimsuits and come back out to the beach, sun ourselves and grab a few drinks from the Tiki bar.

Later that evening, we enjoyed an authentic Luau. The food was a veritable Polynesian feast. An all-you-can-eat buffet, consisting of f roast pig, which was baked for hours in an underground oven called an Imu. There were also many fish and chicken dishes, Island vegetables, fresh tropical fruits and desserts.

After dinner, Mark and I stayed for the show. Islanders dressed in native costumes, enchanted us with their fire-knife dance, drumming and music. We were mesmerized, especially Mark, with the hula dancers. At the end of the long evening, we returned to our room, made love and watched television until we fell asleep.

Each day we tried to do a little something different. Mark was a history buff, so I obliged him and took the Arizona Memorial and City Tour. We boarded a Navy shuttle and rode to the Memorial where the remains of the sunken USS Arizona was housed and examined the engraved wall with over eleven hundred names of sailors and marines that died aboard the battleship on Dec. 7, 1941. It was a touching site and Mark really seemed affected by its significance. Although he had been in the army, Mark felt a kinship with all military personnel.

By the end of the week, we had attended at least four Luaus, three malls and numerous beaches. We spent many hours laying on the powdery white beaches and swimming with the abundant rainbow fish. We followed Mai's advice and visited the Polynesian Cultural Center and learned about the different lifestyles of the various Polynesian cultures, like Samoans, Fijians, New Zealanders, etc. They taught us how to crack coconuts, string Fijian leis and we even enjoyed a relaxing canoe tour. At the end, there was an Extravaganza with over a hundred performers. On our last evening, Mark and I dressed in eveningwear. I had on a flowing, sheer, white chiffon gown and white-laced sandals. My hair was turned up in a chignon and I wore light makeup. Mark was wearing a white tuxedo with soft white leather shoes. He had gotten his haircut that morning and he looked so handsome with his tapered sideburns. As we rode the elevator down to the ground floor, I inhaled his Polo cologne. We dined on cracked lobster, filet mignon, Island vegetables and a wonderful rice and peas dish. We drank champagne and then danced to the wonderful island rhythms being played by the hotel's restaurant band. Afterwards, we walked along the sandy beach, close to the water for one last time. Mark had pulled his pant legs up and was holding my sandals in one hand and clasping my hand in his other. When we thought we were alone, we dropped down in the sand to Christian the beaches of Hawaii before we left. It was a harried, but fulfilling endeavor, considering I was a nervous wreck about being seen. Mark laughed all the way back up to the hotel at the way I was mixing moans of passion with shrieks of paranoia. When we got back to our room, we more than made up for the short rendezvous. We both woke up bright and early. Although we had a wonderful time, I was ready to go home and start my life as Mrs. Mark Fountaine. We had a large breakfast before heading to the airport in the limo that came with the Presidential Suite.

"Well if this ain't the best way to end a honeymoon, I don't know what is," I grinned before planting a kiss on Mark's lips.

"I can think of one better way," Mark smirked.

"Oh no, baby," I laughed, remembering my discomfort at the semi-abandoned beach.

# Chapter Twenty

W hen our plane landed at O'Hare on Saturday afternoon, Troy and Sharleen were waiting for us. There was also a small group of our friends and employees of Mark and Troy's. They had party poppers and a large sign that read, 'Welcome Home Newlyweds'. It was a testament to the family atmosphere Mark and Troy created at their company.

"You guys," Mark, laughed loudly, shaking hands within the crowd of men. I was kissing and hugging all of the females that were a part of the welcome wagon. When we finally got our luggage, a caravan followed us home. Shar, Mark, Troy and I had all rode together in Troy's car. When we pulled into our driveway, Shar and I rushed ahead.

"Kayla, don't move," Mark commanded so strongly, I immediately looked around in alarm.

"What's going on," I asked, panic-stricken. Before I could fathom what was happening, Mark had ran up the driveway, scooped me in his arms and marched toward the door.

"I just know you weren't going walk into that house all by yourself, were you?"

"Boy, you scared me half to death," I howled, locking my arms around his neck and kissing him softly on the lips. By now, we were at the door and Mark was fumbling to place the key in the lock.

"Let me get that," Troy offered, grabbing the key from Mark's outstretched hand. He had been nowhere near the lock. Troy unlocked the door and placed Mark's hand on the knob. Our lips were still locked together when Mark opened the door and stepped over the threshold.

"Hooray," a loud cheer erupted from outside.

After another thirty seconds, Mark finally put me down and we were bombarded once again by the friendly mob. Troy and Sharleen had organized a party for our arrival and for the following eight hours, food, drink, cake and dancing were the order of the evening. By the end of the night, everyone was completely partied out and Mark and I couldn't wait for the few stragglers to leave.

"You two go on upstairs, you look beat," Shar ordered. "We'll straighten up."

"Speak for yourself," Troy huffed.

"Okay," Shar said sassily. "I will speak for myself. If someone doesn't help myself clean up, then myself will be withholding certain things from someone."

"Uh, where does this go," Troy asked, holding up a tray of cookies. We all couldn't help but laugh.

"Thanks guys," I said, hugging them both. "This was a great welcome home greeting."

"Yeah," Mark agreed, "and thanks so much for straightening up because I am exhausted. "We'll talk to you tomorrow, uh, late tomorrow," he emphasized late.

"We hear you," Shar said, "now go on upstairs and get some rest, uh, I do mean rest."

"Don't worry Shar, I can't do nothing else but rest," I assured her.

By Wednesday, things had settled into a natural rhythm. Mark and Troy, did full, ten hour days most of the time, while Shar and I spent our time shopping, doing household chores and ruining errands for our husbands and ourselves. Weekends were family nights and sometimes with did things with the four of us and other times just as a couple. Shar and I would let them men off the hook sometimes to watch or attend sporting events with 'all the guys'. But most times, Mark wanted to be with me. I found myself watching more football, basketball and boxing then a lot of men. The weekend meant no cooking for Shar and me. Mark and Troy loved to barbecue and those were their designated days. Sometimes we would invite a few people over, but mainly, it was just the four of us.

It amazed me how in tune Mark and I were with each other. We hardly ever argued and when we did, he made sure that we didn't go to bed angry.

One evening when I complained about him coming home late and making dinner cold, he apologized profusely, ran me a hot bubble bath and gave me a full-body massage for at least forty-five minutes. And that was after him being at the office for thirteen hours. I knew I was overacting at the time, but I felt like such a heel and spoiled brat when Shar later told me that Mark had to fill in at the last minute for one of his executives whose wife had went into early labor. Not only did he have to make the late presentation, but he also had to research and learn all of the material. In other words, he had been under tremendous pressure and the last thing he needed was for me to complain about some cold meatloaf. When I tried to apologize, he simply pulled me into his arms and said it was still his fault for not calling. One time, I was feeling particularly useless and called him to complain about not having a job. Mark offered to find a position for me in the company and when I whined about not being interested in advertising, he suggested I find a job in a pharmacy.

"Baby, that's why I'm working this hard now, so you won't have to do anything. If you want to work you can, but if you decide that's not what you want, you don't have to," he said so tenderly as if speaking to a discontented child. The whole conversation came to an abrupt halt when Sharleen came over and said there was a huge sale going on at Strawbridges.

"Never mind," I said sweetly, before hanging up.

When he came home that evening, I apologized in front of our new fifty-two inch television.

"That's for when you watch your sports," I offered as a way of apology.

"Thank you, baby," he said, genuinely happy with the new television. Mark never spent much time buying things he wanted or even needed, that was my job and I decided to take it more seriously for now on.

"I'm sorry, baby, I'm just not used to not having to do anything all day everyday. I know most women would love this and truthfully, I do, too. I promise that I'll stop acting like a spoiled brat."

"Kayla, you're my spoiled brat and I wouldn't have it any other way. Besides, the way you make up when you're feeling guilty makes it well worth your occasional need for pampering. Now come on and show me how sorry you are this time," he said throatily.

"Yes, daddy," I said, demurely. As he held my hand and led me upstairs, I looked at his tight behind and knew I had nothing to complain about. My life was perfect.

## Chapter Twenty-One

And for the next six years, everything was perfect. Mark and Troy's business was successful beyond their wildest dreams. After their second year of solid profits, the guys had each brought brand spanking new Mercedes Benz's. Shar and I were a little more practical, not because we had to be, but I was still partial to the black Jetta and she liked the Camry. Not only were our garages expanding, but we also learned that our families were, too. Both Shar and I were three months pregnant. We gave Mark and Troy the evil eye, but they swore that they didn't plan it. Due to a slight miscalculation, Shar had Kendall one month before I had Mark Jr. Troy and Mark were so proud, they began stocking up on bats, balls and little boy toys almost immediately. My life in Chicago was pure bliss for six years. Then it happened.

It was Mark Jr.'s fourth birthday. His dad had bought four tickets to a Chicago Bulls game. Michael Jordan was Mark Jr.'s and Kendall's hero. The boys were so excited; they had a hard time sleeping the night before the game. Only the threat of not going sent them into an agitated dreamland. Shar and I were looking forward to a day of shopping and relaxation.

The next day, Shar and I laughed over the fact that we found it hard to sleep, too. We were anticipating a carefree Saturday morning. We all awoke to a bright sun and chirping birds. It was unusually calm and warm for the historically windy city. We all ate breakfast together and then went our separate ways. The guys were off to the toy store and then to the sports arena for the two o'clock game. Shar and I were off for a day of pampering and shopping. Pedicures were first on our agenda, then manicures, eyebrows, massages and lastly, our favorite thing of all,

# If Loving Two is Wrong . . .

CHARGE IT! We planned to be back by four, so we could set up for the small birthday party for Mark Jr. Just ice cream and cake for a few of the kids from the neighborhood. He was going to be so surprised. He had said that all he wanted for his birthday was to see Michael Jordan.

Shar and I had returned home around four-thirty, later than expected and rushed to get things ready for the party. By five-thirty, the guest had arrived and we were all waiting for the guest of honor. By six-thirty, the children were becoming restless, and Shar and I were beginning to get worried. We called both, Troy and Mark's cell phones, but received no answer. We turned on the television to make sure that the game was over and learned the arena had let out over an hour ago. Even with heavy traffic, they should've been home at least twenty minutes ago. After ten minutes, one of the children came into the kitchen and said someone was coming up the walkway. Shar and I rushed into the living room, settled the children down and reminded them to holler surprise when the door opened. I cursed under my breath when I heard the doorbell ring.

"Why in the world would they ring the bell?" I wondered out loud. As I reached for the doorknob, a chill raced up my spine. When I opened the door, the children sprang up from their hiding spots and screamed, "Surprise!" But Mark, Troy, Mark Jr. nor Kendall, were there. Instead, two men, one black and the other white, were standing in front of me with somber faces.

"What's going on?" Shar was asking as she made her way through the kids to get to the front door. I was intuitively shaking, fearing the answer.

"Are you Mrs. Fountaine?" the black man asked, looking me directly in the eye.

"Yes, I am," I managed to stammer.

"I'm Detective Moore and this is Detective Mills," he continued, indicating the man by his side.

"Ma'am, is there somewhere, quiet, where we can speak?" Without thinking, I closed the door, standing outside with the men, leaving Shar and the children inside.

167

"What is it?' I asked, growing more alarmed with each passing second.

"Mrs. Fountaine, there's been an accident," the black detective continued in that voice that I had heard so many times on television.

"Where's my son and husband?" I asked, passing panicky and speeding toward hysteria.

"Ma'am, your son has been taken to the hospital for observation. He sustained some cuts and bruises, but appears to be okay. There was another little boy."

"Kendall," I interrupted shakily.

"Yes," the man confirmed. "He appears to be fine. He's scared and asking for his parents, but the doctors say that he has no physical impairments."

I still was not fully aware of what had happened, but I began screaming for Shar. She burst through the door like gangbusters.

"What's wrong?" she asked with forebodance.

"These men said there's been an accident," I cried.

"Oh no," Shar wailed. "Where are my boys?" she screamed. Just then, a police cruiser pulled up. Two uniformed officers approached the detectives that were still talking to Shar and me.

"We'll take you to the hospital so you can be given up to date information about your husband," Detective Moore said.

"Is he okay," I asked anxiously, wringing my hands.

"I'd rather wait until we get to the hospital to answer any questions," the detective said gently. If you're ready, we can leave now."

"We- we were sup-supposed to be having a party," I stammered. "The children are still here. We have to make sure they get home safely." Although I could feel myself speaking, I felt numb, as if the words were coming from someone else.

"Don't worry ma'am, we'll make sure the children get home safely," Detective Moore assured me.

I simply shook my head as I watched pretty, young Hispanic officer approach, she didn't look a day over eighteen.

"Anything we can do, detective?" the young, female officer asked.

"We need for you to make sure that the children inside get home safely and lock up the house," the white detective finally spoke.

"Yes sir," the officer responded.

Dazedly, I gathered my purse and keys. The detective stated that we would have to wait until we got to the hospital for any further information. I felt as if my brain was numb, not processing any information. Sharleen and I were ushered to the detective's car, and nervously held hands for the entire ride to the hospital. No one uttered a sound. We were all lost in our own private thoughts. Once at the hospital, Sharleen and I reluctantly allowed ourselves to be led in separate directions.

Detective Moore led me down the long sterile hallway, each step felt as if I was wearing lead shoes. We rode the elevator to the third floor. When the doors opened, the sign seemed to be flashing 'Trauma Unit', like a neon sign. As we rounded the nurses' station, everyone seemed to be watching me. Their faces were masks of pity. I could feel my legs growing weak. Mercifully, we came to a stop in front of room 308. Through a small window, I caught a glimpse of a person lying still in the bed. Detective Moore blocked my view before I could determine who it was. Just as I was about to push him out of the way, a tall, thin black man, with graying temples, approached us. He was wearing a doctor's coat and a somber look.

"Mrs. Fountaine?" he asked. I merely nodded my head.

"I'm Doctor Mason," he announced.

"Your husband was involved in a car accident. When the trauma unit brought him in, he was in very bad shape. We did everything we could, but..." Suddenly everything went black. Next, a pungent smell assaulted my nostrils, delivering me from darkness. I was seated in what appeared to be a waiting room. Detective Moore was leaning

169

against the door and Dr. Mason was waving smelling salts under my nose. I shook the cobwebs off and pushed the offending vial away from my nose. Everything returned with complete clarity. Mark had been in an accident and they couldn't save him. Suddenly, I broke into loud wracking sobs.

"Mrs. Fountaine," Dr. Mason said softly, "your husband is on life support."

"He's alive?" I asked, with a loud whimper.

"Yes, he's alive, but I need you to understand," Dr. Mason continued softly. "We're making him as comfortable as we can. He suffered third degree burns over thirty percent of his body. Both of his lungs have been crushed and he has extensive internal injuries."

"What are you saying?" I asked hysterically.

"He's not going to make it, Mrs. Fountaine. I wish there was something more positive, but at this point, there's nothing else we can do, I'm sorry," he said somberly.

"Can I see him?" I asked, barely above a whisper.

"Of course you can," he answered. "But you should know, he won't be able to speak. He's highly sedated, so he'll probably drift in and out of consciousness."

"Okay," I nodded, as I tried to steel myself for my visit with Mark. "How could this be," I wondered aloud. "We were just together this morning. We were supposed to be celebrating Mark Jr.'s birthday at this very moment." At the thought of Mark Jr., I began to sob anew.

"Where is my son?" I asked frantically.

"He's fine," Dr. Mason assured me. "Would you like the nurse to bring him in?"

"Not yet," I answered, fighting to gather my composure. "Let me see my husband first, please," I managed weakly.

"Of course," Dr. Mason answered, then he and Detective Moore led me back to room 308. I inhaled deeply as I stood at the threshold. Slowly, I pushed the door open, willing myself to remain calm. What I saw made me gasp for air. Although Dr. Mason had warned me, nothing could've prepared me for what I encountered.

# If Loving Two is Wrong . . .

"That's not Mark!" I screeched. I could feel Dr. Mason's hands on my shoulders, attempting to comfort me. "Calm down, Mrs. Fountaine. I know it's a shock, that's why I tried to prepare you for what you would see," he said in soothing tones. The still, lifeless body, covered with bandages and an array of tubes carrying both life sustaining medicines and painkillers, posed a pitiful sight.

"You don't understand," I repeated dully, "that's not my husband."

"I'm sorry Mrs. Fountaine, but I don't understand what you're trying to tell us," Detective Moore intervened. He was watching me as if I had suddenly gone mad.

"That's Troy Waters, my husband's best friend," I said, lacking emotion.

"Are you sure?" he asked, dumbly. I gave him a look that indicated that was exactly how I felt about his question.

"I'm sorry," he recovered. "I just don't understand. The wallet found at the scene contained the identification for Mark Fountaine. Due to his injuries, we couldn't reconcile the victim with the picture on the driver's license."

I heard the detective talking, but I wasn't really listening. My mind was on Mark. Where was he?

"Where's my husband?" I asked abruptly.

"Mrs. Fountaine, I honestly don't know what to say," Detective Moore responded. "This gentleman and the two boys were the only ones at the scene. Oh, and the truck driver."

"Truck driver?" I repeated, confused and bewildered. But before I could question him further, I heard a commotion just outside the door. Dr. Mason had sent a nurse to inform Sharleen about Troy. Now, she was outside the room and I could hear the doctor attempting to calm her before letting her enter the room. Detective Moore went outside to assist. I focused on Troy, reconciling that the awful prognosis was for him. Troy was dying. My heart began to ache anew, but this time for him. Although Mark was very much in the forefront of my mind, I eased him aside momentarily and approached Troy's bedside. Gingerly,

I placed my hand atop his and gently kissed his forehead. His eyes fluttered open. There was no denying that this was definitely Troy. Those startling green eyes were still piercing, as he attempted to focus in on me. I fought to hold back my tears as I tried to reconcile the beautiful man that I knew, with this broken mass before me. He gurgled in an attempt to speak, but I quickly hushed him. I wanted him to save his breaths for Sharleen. I desperately wanted to ask him about Mark, but decided that I would have to get my answers elsewhere. I could hear the door opening and turned in time to see a bleary-eyed Sharleen entering the room. I hugged her fiercely, then, without speaking a word; I left the room to give them privacy. Outside the room, I lost it. I demanded to know where my husband was. Dr. Mason and Detective Moore ushered me into a private office nearby.

"Please calm down, Mrs. Fountaine. I know you want answers. Trust me, so do I. I'm as anxious to get to the bottom of this as you are."

"Well, he couldn't have disappeared into thin air. And how could you mistake Troy for my Mark," I snapped. "Mark has, brown eyes. Beautiful, brown eyes," I yelled. "You said you found his license. Did you look at it? It says brown eyes. Troy has green eyes! How could you mistake Mark for Troy?" I was beyond consolation.

"I'm very sorry Mrs. Fountaine," the detective was adequately contrite. "You're absolutely right. But Mr. Waters was already at the hospital and in surgery by the time we got to the scene. The license and the fact that he was the only adult male there, besides the truck driver, led us to believe that Mr. Waters was indeed your husband. But we should have made sure before we informed you."

The detective was on the verge of babbling. I knew he was sincere. The look on his face was that of a little boy who had been caught by his mother with his 'thing' out.

"Bear with us, Mrs. Fountaine," he continued. "We're still gathering information. Everyone from the accident scene was transported here. We haven't been able to question anyone yet. It appears that the truck driver had a heart attack, but that's all we know. The doctors are still working on him. We have officers questioning potential witnesses at the scene. As soon as we have any word, we'll relay it to you immediately."

Although I wanted to rant and rave, I knew it would be senseless. The detective was only doing his job and he was being very sympathetic and supportive. He could only tell me what he knew, which at this point, wasn't diddly. Still, I needed to vent.

"Well, somebody needs to come up with some answers," I snapped.

"Believe me, we're working on it," he said, humbly.

"Yeah, well," was all I could think to say as I fell into an angry silence.

Dr. Mason excused himself to check on Shar. Minutes later, a nurse peeked into the room and asked if she could be of any assistance.

"Can you bring my son to me?" I asked softly. She looked at the detective, who nodded his approval.

"Right away, Mrs. Fountaine," she said, quickly, then disappeared from sight. A few moments later, the door opened and Mark Jr. came racing in.

"Mommy," he yelled as he sprung into my arms. He was wearing a Chicago Bulls uniform with Jordan sneakers. He wasn't wearing that when Shar and I left them that morning. It must've been another birthday gift. I had to smile at his father's indulgences.

"Mommy," Mark Jr.'s anxious cry pierced my thoughts.

"Yes baby," I said, hugging him fiercely.

"This big truck crashed into Uncle Troy's car. We kept rolling over, then a man helped pull me and Uncle Troy out of the car," he rambled excitedly.

"Where was your dad?" I asked anxiously. This was the first time that I was hearing in-depth details of the accident and it took everything I had to remain calm for Mark Jr.'s sake.

"I don't know," he said breathlessly, "at first he was sitting next to Uncle Troy and then I didn't see him anymore. I was calling for him when the man pulled me out of the car, but I didn't see him and he didn't answer me. Uncle Troy went back and pulled Kendall out of his car seat. Then the car was on fire and made a loud a noise. Uncle Troy had fire on him and he was flying. Kendall was in his arms and they fell down on the ground!" Mark's voice rose to a high pitch and his eyes were opened wide.

"Where was your father?" I pressed, feeling the hysteria beginning to build.

"Wow son, you were very brave," Detective Moore intervened enthusiastically. He could see that I was about to erupt and I was instantly grateful for his interference. Mark turned toward the detective and eyed him quizzically, but was too excited to make any inquiries.

"We were really scared and crying. I was calling for Daddy, but he didn't come. Then the policeman and the fireman came over and gave us some juice. They let us wear their hats and said if we were good, we could be honory, um, hon," he shook his head, exasperated at not being able to say honorary. "Well they said Kendall could be a fireman and I could be a police officer and then they let us ride in the police car. They did the sirens and everything for us! Then they brought us here," he ended with a smile that was three teeth short of a full set.

"Where is Daddy?" he asked. That was the dreaded question that I only wished that I could answer.

"I don't know baby, everybody is looking for him," I answered with a hint of the hope that I desperately wanted to feel.

The next few hours went by at a snail's pace. The truck driver was in the intensive care recovery room. It was determined that he fell asleep while driving. He woke just before the crash and tried to regain control of the tractor-trailer: but it was too late. After pulling Troy and Mark Jr. to safety, he suffered a heart attack. He had no explanation for Mark's disappearance.

By midnight, I was heading home with Mark Jr. and Kendall. Shar stayed with Troy, who was still holding on, barely. The ordeal had taken a toll on the boys and their excitement over the day's events had been replaced with exhaustion. They could not reconcile the events of the day with tragedy. To them it was like one big action adventure, even after explaining that their daddy's weren't coming home. After placing them into bed, I went into my own room to feel closer to Mark. I immediately dropped to my knees and thanked the Lord for keeping the boys safe. Then I said a prayer for Mark's safe return or at least for some sort of closure. I laid my head on Mark's pillow and cried myself into a restless sleep.

I awoke with a start, wishing that yesterday had just been a horrible nightmare; but as I stared at the empty space beside me, I knew it was all too real. I checked on the boys, who were still sleeping soundly, then headed to the kitchen. Party favors and streamers were still strewn about the living room and the cake was still on the dining room table. I quickly cleared the room and contemplated throwing the cake in the trash, but placed it in the refrigerator instead. I started the coffeemaker and then fished Detective Moore's business card out of my purse. He answered after the second ring.

"Good morning, Mrs. Fountaine," he answered, indicating that he had caller ID.

"I was going to call you, I just didn't want to disturb you too early," he said brightly.

"It would've been okay. I didn't sleep well anyway," I sighed sadly, a direct contrast to his chipper disposition.

"Do you have any further information?" I blurted out. I didn't mean to appear rude, but let's face it; this was not a social call.

"As a matter of fact, I do. That's why I wanted to get in touch with you. Is it possible for me to come by?" he asked in a more businesslike tone.

"Can't you just tell me now?" I asked impatiently.

"I would prefer to speak with you in person," he pressed.

"Fine," I said with forebodance. "I'll be expecting you."

"I'm on my way," he responded.

It seemed like hours before the doorbell chimed, but actually, it had only been twenty minutes.

"Good morning Detective, come on in," I greeted him at the door.

"Morning Mrs. Fountaine," he returned upon entering.

"Coffee?" I asked, retreating to the kitchen. Now that he was here, I wasn't so anxious to hear his news. I could just feel that it wasn't going to be good.

"Uh, I take it black, thank you," he responded.

When I returned from the kitchen, Detective Moore was still standing awkwardly at the threshold.

"Have a seat," I offered, handing him the steaming mug.

"Mrs. Fountaine, there's no easy way to say this, so I'm just going to get right to it," he said, settling into the chair.

"Please do," I said, shakily.

"There was no sign of your husband at the scene. The truck driver has no recollection of him. He remembered pulling Mr. Waters and a little boy out, which was your son. He also remembers Mr. Waters returning to the car for someone and the car blowing up, but that's it. Due to his condition, we haven't been able to question Mr. Waters," he said sympathetically.

"How can this be?" I asked, exasperated.

"The accident was on a stretch of road that was pretty secluded. I imagine they were trying to avoid all of the game traffic. Our investigators said that the witnesses didn't arrive on the scene until after the car exploded," he said slowly, looking at me as if he had more to say.

"Go on," I pushed.

"The tanker was filled with combustible materials. All indications are that Mr. Fountaine perished in the explosion," he surmised.

"No," I cried out. Just the thought of my darling Mark dying in such a horrendous way was too much to bear.

"I'm sorry, Mrs. Fountaine," he said awkwardly, not

knowing how to handle my outburst. For the next few moments, silence filled the room. I needed time to process what he had just told me. Finally, I broke the silence.

"Thank you for coming by personally, Detective," I said, dismissing him. I needed time alone before the boys woke up.

"You're welcome," he said, standing. "If there's anything I can do for you, don't hesitate to ask," he said sincerely.

"I will," I promised.

"I'll keep you informed about our investigation," he said, handing me his mug before leaving.

## Chapter Twenty-Two

The next few days were a whirlwind of activity. Although Mark Jr. said he understood that Daddy was an angel in heaven now, he would still ask, 'when is Daddy coming home'? Each time, my heart would break over and over again. Mark's and my parents had arrived the day after the accident. In spite of their grief, his parents, along with mine, were the glue that held me together. Three days after the accident, Troy succumbed to his injuries. He never fully regained consciousness, but Shar was able to convey her love to him during his brief moments of lucidity. She was a wreck, but we managed to keep it together for the sake of the boys. Troy's parents were in town and held up quite well under the circumstances. The funeral for Troy doubled as a memorial service for Mark. We figured it was only fitting, considering the two men were inseparable in life. We hadn't realized how many friends and associates Mark and Troy had. Almost all of the employees attended the services and appeared to be as broken up as the family members. But Theodore Haskins stood out. Everyone called him Teddy and he was one of the accountants that also held a seat on the Executive Board. He was the butt of a lot of jokes around the office because he was so fidgety, but he was an ace at crunching numbers. I couldn't help but smile as he stood in front of me with his combed-over toupee and ill-fitting brown polyester suit, wrinkled blue shirt and brown wing-tipped shoes.

'Um, um, I would just, um, I want to give my condolences on you um,loss. Mark and Troy were good men and will be um, greatly missed," he said, fiddling with his green paisley tie. "If you ever need anything, Mrs. Fountaine, um, you know um, like help with the business," he paused momentarily, glancing furtively around the room, "um, I'd be happy to help."

I stifled the laughter that was begging to come out as I watched his attempt to smile. Those were the most words that I had ever heard Teddy manage to string together since I'd met him. Shar and I would occasionally sit in on board meetings and attended all company picnics and although Teddy would be in attendance, he barely spoke three words.

"Thanks a lot Theodore," I said, touching his hand slightly, causing him to flinch. "I'll remember that and I really appreciate you coming." He simply nodded and headed toward the refreshments. Then, Pamela Henry, Mark's longtime personal assistant had approached me with red-rimmed eyes.

"Please accept my condolences, Kayla. Mark was such a wonderful boss, we're all going to miss him very much," she sniffed, dabbing her nose with a tissue.

"Thank you so much, Pam," I said, sincerely. "You were Mark's lifeline and I really appreciate the way you took care of Mark at the office. You're going to be really important to Sharleen and me now. I'm going to have to depend on you to keep on top of things for us at the office. But now's not the time for this conversation, but I will definitely be speaking to you soon about this, okay?"

"Of course, Kayla," she said, softly, as I embraced her and patted her shoulders.

The outpouring of love and support was overwhelming. It was a true testament of the kind of men they were. Tony was crushed because he couldn't make the trip to Chicago. He was an integral part of a business meeting that had been planned months ahead with an international client that couldn't be rescheduled. But he was relieved to know that another service would be held in Philadelphia.

The Fountaine's remained in Chicago for a week after the funeral for Troy and memorial service for Mark. No one was satisfied with the idea that there was no trace of Mark. We hounded the police daily, asking if any further information had come in.

"I can assure you that we're doing everything possible to find out if there is any other explanation for your husband's disappearance, Mrs. Fountaine," Detective Moore said, wearily. He had been very patient with us and seemed genuinely sorry that he couldn't tell us anything different from the initial report.

"It just doesn't seem feasible that everyone else survived but Mark," Mr. Fountaine said after dinner one evening.

"My poor baby," Mrs. Fountaine began sobbing.

"There has to be something we can do," my Mom said, standing and walking around the table to Sandra.

"I agree Mom," I said, somberly. "Why don't we check the area hospitals and put up missing posters. I mean if there's a chance that Mark survived, I want to make sure we overturn every rock to find him. The police aren't going to do it, they're not emotionally involved enough, shit, um, I mean shoot, if they could mix up their identities, they darn sure could miss some other things." I could feel myself getting riled up at the thought of Mark lying in a hospital bed somewhere, unclaimed. There's no way I could allow my baby to be somebody's John Doe.

"You know Kayla, you're right," Dad pitched in. "If there is any chance that Mark's out there, we should take it upon ourselves to check."

Sandra's sobbing had slowed to a sniffle as a ray of hope glistened on her bronzed face.

"Do you th- think that my baby could still be alive?' she asked, sounding like a small child whose pet gold fish had stopped swimming.

"I don't know, Mother Fountaine, but if he is, we'll find him," I said with resolve.

For the next week, we all visited area hospitals, asking about any John Doe's, any burn victims and any other kind of patient that may have come in that could've been Mark. We posted missing posters with Mark's photo on every tree and in every storefront that we could. We stayed glued to the television set hoping for a story of an unidentified person showing up at a hospital or an amnesia victim. One evening the local news had a late breaking story and everybody just waited with baited breath, silently praying for it to be news about Mark. But unfortunately, it was a tragic story of a horrific storm in the southern part of the country. Thousands of people lost their lives and were displaced. The story was the main topic of the news for several days and although we were all saddened by the events, we still hoped desperately for a breaking story about Mark, but it was to no avail. By the second week, it was time for Mark's parents to return home and we were all exhausted and disheartened.

"Well we tried everything we could," Sandra said before bursting out in tears.

"Yes we did," Mom and Dad agreed as we all gathered in the center of the living room for a group hug.

"But I promise, Mom and Dad," I said, referring to the Fountaines, "I won't give up."

"We know you won't, Kayla," Lawrence said, kissing me on the cheek. The next day, the Fountaines left to go back to Philadelphia. Two days later, Mom, Dad, Mark Jr., Kendall, Shar and I followed.

Mark Jr. and I had been in Philly for two weeks after the memorial service before I decided it was time to return to Chicago. My parents tried to convince me to stay, but I insisted that we needed to go back.

"That was Mark's and my home, I can't just abandon it," I said, full of emotion. "Besides, Sharleen and Kendall will need us."

"What if her parents convince her to move back to Jersey?" Mom asked with a purpose.

"Then we'll come back home, too," I relented.

"See, you said home," Mom said, passionately.

"Philly will always be my true home," I admitted.

It was only during the plane ride back to Chicago that I realized that I hadn't contacted or even thought about Chloe while I was home. I recalled the day I saw her after the wedding. Memories threatened to return, but I quickly pushed them to the rear. Those thoughts evoked bittersweet emotions within me that I didn't want to revisit just yet. I looked at Mark Jr. sitting next to me, he was already drifting off and I decided to follow suit.

Back in Chicago, Shar was still fighting to hold it together. Her parents had just left the day before we returned. For the following three weeks, our numerous friends barraged us with love and support. Sometimes they took the boys, who were coping extremely well under the circumstances, so that Shar and I could have some alone time. Our refrigerators were stocked to capacity and our church provided all the spiritual support we could ever need. But still, Shar and I relied on each other for the emotional support that we both so desperately needed. We had become so close over the years, and our lives were so intertwined; we were like identical twin sisters. We were very in tune with each other's thought processes. As close as we were, I never let her know all the times I had called the police department and hospitals, hoping for some news about Mark. I knew she would be supportive of me, but I wanted to keep that ritual to myself. Besides, I didn't want to be a constant reminder to her of Troy's death. In fact, the constant disappointment of no new developments was really wearing on me, but I couldn't resist checking.

After almost three months, we decided that it was time to take charge of our lives and get back on track. We had a thriving business to attend to and owed it to the memory of Mark and Troy to keep it together. Shar and I were determined to pass Mark Jr. and Kendall a legacy they could be proud of. We attended a boardroom meeting at the company that Mark and Troy founded and now belonged to us. We were majority stockholders and wanted our presence to be felt. We were well acquainted with the board members and managers and trusted them. However, we were also very knowledgeable about the everyday operations and knew how to keep track of things. Mark and Troy had insisted on that. Shar and I decided to leave the reins in the hands of the Board of Directors, but insisted on quarterly reports. Plus, I had already advised Pam to keep an eye on things for me.

# If Loving Two is Wrong . . .

Mark trusted her implicitly and she knew the ins and outs of the business almost as well as Mark and Troy.

Between the business, life insurance policies, stocks and other savings and investments, Shar and I were very financially stable. We had also received a very hefty settlement from the trucking company's insurance. Mr. Williams, the truck driver, had made a full recovery from his heart attack. He was charged and found guilty of reckless vehicular manslaughter for his role in the accident. By the time the trial had occurred, Shar and I had overcome our anger about the circumstances of the accident. We were thankful for the role he had played in the rescue and apprised the judge of our feelings before the sentencing. The sixty-three year old man received a ten-year suspended sentence and three years probation. Mr. Williams had shown a great deal of remorse and Shar and I were satisfied with the verdict. We still had our beautiful sons to remind us of the love we shared with their wonderful fathers.

I kept the promise I had made to the Fountaines and called Detective Moore religiously, checking for any updates. Until I had some tangible proof of Mark's death, it would never be real to me. Mark and Kendall were over Shar's house and I was going to surprise them with some homemade brownies. I was just cracking an egg on the side of the stainless-steel bowl when the phone rang.

"Hello," I answered, still holding the egg in my hand.

"Hello, Mrs. Fountaine."

The voice made my heart stop momentarily.

"Mrs. Fountaine, are you okay," Detective Moore asked, responding to my sharp intake of breath.

"Y-yes," I hesitated. I knew his call could mean one of two things. Either he was going to tell me that they found Mark and he's alive or they've found concrete proof of his death. Either way, I was rapidly turning into a trembling wreck.

"Mrs. Fountaine, I have some information, but I think it would be better if you came down to the station," he said somberly.Just from his tone, I knew it wasn't good news.

"I'd like prefer if you'd tell me now Detective," I answered, steeling myself for his next words.

"Well, I wish I didn't have to tell you this, but a motorist discovered a body in a ditch about a mile from the accident scene involving your husband."

The sound of an eggshell cracking caused me took look at my hand and I noticed the yellow yolk dripping down my wrist. I leaned against the kitchen counter, attempting to steady my legs which were beginning to feel like cooked spaghetti. When I felt comfortable to walk, I eased unsteadily over to the kitchen table and sat down.

"Go on, Detective," a managed in a weak, raspy voice that was almost unrecognizable to me.

"Are you sure you don't want to wait and come to the station for the details," he asked, concern lined his voice.

"Detective, please," I snapped impatiently. "I just need to know what you found."

"Okay, Mrs. Fountaine. The motorist said he pulled over to go to the bathroom. He went into the bush a little and that's where he saw some remains. It was over partially covered by brush beneath an embankment. That's probably why we didn't discover it sooner. The coroner was unable to make a positive identification because the body was severely burned and in an advanced state of decomposition. The only way to identify him would be through dental records. That's why I'm calling, there is nothing on file, so we were wondering if perhaps you could obtain a copy of them," he ended contritely.

I was quiet for a long moment as I took some time to digest what he was saying.

"Mrs. Fountaine," pause, "Mrs. Fountaine," he repeated.

"I'm here Detective Moore," I sighed, dejectedly. "I'll have to call his parents and ask them. I'll get back to you as soon as possible."

"Okay, Mrs. Fountaine, and once again, I'm sorry to I don't have more positive news for you."

"Me too, Detective, me too."

# If Loving Two is Wrong . . .

Once I hung up, I pondered the information over and over before calling Mark's parents with the news. I knew it would be like stabbing them in the heart all over again. It might've been better if the body had never been found; at least there would still be hope. But then again, at least now we would have closure, even if it was going to reopen unhealed wounds. After washing the drying eggyolk off my hand, I called my parents and broke the news to them first.

"Oh, baby, I'm so sorry," my mother wailed.

"Uh, uhh," my father grunted his disbelief on the other line.

"Do you want us to call Sandra and Larry for you, baby?" Mom asked.

"No Mom, this is something that I have to do," I answered, sadly.

"Okay, baby, but call us if you need us and let us know what the next step is."

"Yeah," Daddy added.

"I will and thank you Mom and Daddy," I sighed, wearily.

I knew Sandra was going to take the news bad and I wasn't wrong. I barely got the word body out before I heard the phone drop and the dreadful wailing begin. Moments later, Mr. Fountaine picked up the line and I relayed the information to him that Detective Moore had given me. Larry started weeping, which caused me to run my own little waterworks and I suggested that they give me a call in a few moments after we all had time to compose ourselves. I immediately called Shar and informed her about what had happened.

"Oh Kayla, baby. I am so sorry. I'm shocked. I don't know what to say."

"I know Shar, I'm still in a state of shock. Can you please keep Mark overnight? I don't want him to see me falling apart like this," I broke into sobs.

"Of course, Kayla, is there anything I can do for you?"

"No, honey. I just have to get my bearings together. They need dental records and..." I couldn't finish the sentence as I began to weep uncontrollably into the phone. After a few moments, I was able to continue. "I'm going to wait to hear from Mark's parents and we'll decide what to do from there."

"Okay, Kayla. But if you need anything, I mean anything at all, call me."

"I will darling and thanks."

As soon as I clicked off with Shar, my phone rang. The Fountaines called and said they spoke to their family dentist who said he didn't have any dental records for Mark. Mark had always had perfect teeth and there had never been a need for x-rays. I sagged back into the chair upon hearing the news. Mark's parents decided to fly back out to Chicago the next day to help sort out all of this and my parents came right along with them.

"Why didn't y'all find his body earlier," Sandra demanded of Detective Moore when we visited the police station the same afternoon that they arrived.

"Ma'am, the body was a mile away from the accident scene and was found covered with shrubs in a ditch under an embankment. I solemnly wish that we had found it sooner," he said, patiently.

"Well it's certainly crazy to me how a man stopping to go to the bathroom on the highway can find a body, but a whole police force, dogs and all couldn't sniff it out," my Mom huffed.

"Toni," Dad attempted squash her tirade before it could gain momentum.

"Toni, nothing," Mom raised her voice and eyebrows in Dad's direction. "I mean it, it don't make no sense."

"I understand all of your frustrations," Detective Moore addressed the room, "but we did the best we could under the circumstances."

"Humph," Mom grunted loudly, attempting to start again.

"I understand Detective," Larry said, gruffly, shaking Detective Moore's hand. "Will we be able to take my son so we can bury him?"

"In light of the circumstances, I don't see there being a

problem. I just wish there were some dental records. We contacted military dental department and they didn't have any records on file either," Detective Moore sighed. "I'll make the arrangements so that you can take possession in twenty-four hours."

That night, we decided to bury Mark in Chicago. Mark and Troy had already purchased cemetery plots next to each other, so we honored their wishes. The next day, we contacted the funeral parlor and made the arrangements. It was such a sad affair. We had all decided not to view the charred, unrecognizable remains. It was better to remember him as the beautiful human being that he was, opposed to the mangled mass that lay in the closed coffin. Two days after the service, my parents and the Fountaines returned to Philadelphia with heavy hearts. Grief hung over my head and followed me around like it was my own personal thunder cloud. I wafted in and out of misery, punctuated with bouts of uncontrollable crying. Shar took care of Mark on the days that I just couldn't function.

I woke up on a Saturday, two weeks after the funeral and had decided to get myself together. The night before had been a particularly bad evening for me so Mark Jr. had spent the night at Shar's. I had been looking at Mark's and my photo album and vacillated between laughing and crying. I traced the outline of my life married to Mark with the pictures situated in that album. I gently ran my finger over each photo, taking in every detail and closing my eyes in remembrance. I could visually recreate in my mind each feeling and moment. From the wedding to the honeymoon to the birth of Mark Jr. Each event became a punctuation mark in my mind and by the end of the night, with the help of a prescribed muscle relaxer, I was able to find some sort of closure and drifted into the first peaceful sleep since the funeral. The next day, I woke up still feeling the calmness that I slept with and reached over and turned on the radio on my nightstand. The sweet sound of Frankie Beverly and Maze drifted out of the speakers.

The ones that you care for,give you so much pain, oh,

but it's alright, they're both one in  the same. Joy and pain are like sunshine and rain...

"You are so right, Frankie," I said, reaching for the phone. "Hey, Shar, what do you say to me treating you and the boys to breakfast today?"

I knew I wasn't one hundred percent yet, but I was taking the first steps to get there.

## Chapter Twenty-Three

"**L**et's go out to a club," Sharleen blurted out of the clear blue sky one night.

"What?" I said, looking at her like she had two heads.

"You heard me," she said sassily. "It's been almost a year since the accident and we haven't been out on the town once."

"I know," I sighed wearily. "I just don't know how to be single again. I don't even know if I'm ready."

"Pump your brakes, Kayla," Sharleen laughed.

"I'm not suggesting that we pick up men, just let our hair down a little. I don't know about you, but I'm still a bit of a bomb," she said with a wink.

"A bit of a bomb," I repeated with a snort. "Just saying it like that shows what kind of old cornball you are."

"Whatever, you're just hatin'," she said with a fake attitude. "You just be ready to go at nine o'clock."

"What about the boys?" I sputtered, searching for a way out.

"Got it covered," she said as she headed toward the door. "They're going to spend the night with Kelly." Kelly was one of our friends that had a son, Patrick, who was Mark and Kendall's age.

"Well," I began, desperately trying to think of another excuse.

"La La La," she said, placing her hands over her head as she disappeared out the door.

Kelly picked up the boys at six o'clock, which gave me three hours to get ready. I had already resigned myself to the fact that I was going out to a club, but I began to panic.

I don't know what to wear or how to act and I haven't danced in years. I mean, I danced with Mark when

we went out, but that was married, dancing with your
husband dancing. I don't know what people are doing now.

"I wonder if Soul Train is on," I said aloud as I
headed upstairs to get ready.

At ten minutes to nine, the phone rang. "I'll be
outside your door in ten minutes," Shar's shrill voice came
over the line.

"I, uh, I," I was still trying to think of a way out.

"Just have your raggedy behind out there."

"Shar," I wailed in exasperation.

"Oh c'mon Kayla. I'm about to introduce you to my
friend, Tone," she said pleadingly.

"Oh no, Shar," I whined. "I'm not ready for this,
who's Tone?" But before I even finished the question, I
found out. The loud dial tone was beeping annoyingly in my
ear.

"That hussy," I laughed aloud, then headed outside.

"Tone, huh," I huffed as I got into the car.

"Girl, I saw that on some television show and
couldn't wait to use it," she laughed.

"Well, you better not use it on me again," I said with
phony agitation.

Shar and I chatted it up on the way to the club. We
talked about how we were going to act if a guy approached
us, how we would dance and what to do when the other
women were hatin' on our beauty. But all the talking came to
an abrupt halt when we reached the front of the club.

"You go on ahead," she goaded.

"No, you first," I countered.

"Girl, you act like we're going into a morgue or
something," she said seriously, attempting to hide her
anxiety.

"And what's holding you back?" I asked, just as
serious.

"Not a thing," she answered, grabbing my arm and
propelling me forward. As we crossed the dance floor, Shar
and I looked like Dorothy and the Cowardly Lion going to
meet the Wizard. We were clinging to each other for dear
life. We saw an empty table ahead and raced to it like two

clumsy gazelles. Only after we crashed into our chairs did we take time out to laugh at our foolishness. We looked around the dimly lit club and realized that there was only a sprinkling of people, mostly women. A chill raced up my spine as I recalled being in a similar situation, oh so long ago. Chloe sprung to mind and I let out a little chuckle as I remembered my first time at a gay club.

"What's so funny?" Shar asked.

I wasn't ready to let her in on my private thought, so I simply said; "You sure picked a winner tonight. This club doesn't seem to be happening at all."

"Kayla, it's only nine thirty," she said, exasperated. "We came early because it's ladies' night and we get in free until ten and half price on drinks until eleven. That's what time most of the players come out," she said sassily, obviously schooling me and impressed by her own savviness. "I figured that would give us some time to chill out, have a few drinks and be ready for prime time," she said, snapping her fingers.

"Check you out," I chortled, surprised by Shar's hipness. It was good to see her lively again. Every since Troy's death, she was barely a shell of her former self. Now that she was ready to come out of her shell, she was busting out. I was genuinely happy for her, but I wasn't sure if I was ready for this scene. After an hour and a few Cosmopolitans, I still wasn't feeling any better about the situation. Images of Mark kept springing up in mind and I was beginning to feel guilty. I missed him. He had been the love of my life and for the last six years, he had been my rock, my security. Suddenly, I felt very vulnerable. Tears threatened to surface and I was about to tell Shar that I was ready to leave, but something had changed. It was as if someone had opened the floodgates and throngs of people invaded the club. The atmosphere had definitely changed. The once sparsely covered dance floor had now come alive with gyrating bodies.

"When did all of this happen?" I asked Sharleen, dazedly.

"While you were in outer space," she smiled. "Are you okay?"

"Yeah," I smiled wanly. "I was just thinking about Mark. I don't know if I'm ready to be here yet."

"Kayla, Mark and Troy wouldn't want us moping around forever. It's been months since we've done anything remotely like this. It's time for us to get our feet wet and become card-carrying members of life again. Don't feel guilty. No one could ever take the place of my Troy, but that's not why I'm here," she said seriously, placing her hand atop mine for reassurance.

"I'm here to let my hair down a little and have a little fun. Lord knows we both deserve it."

'She's right', an inner voice said. I had to smile at Shar's growing confidence.

"Okay, I'll try," I relented.

"That's the spirit," she smiled as we watched a waitress place two drinks in front of us.

"We didn't order these," I said slowly.

"They're from the gentlemen over at the bar," the waitress informed us. Shar and I, quickly, with no sophistication or decorum at all, turned to see who she was talking about. Two men, seated at the bar, raised their glasses. Shar and I repeated the gesture and quickly began talking under our breaths.

"Do you see how big he is?" Shar asked, referring to the muscular guy on the left.

"Yeah," I responded through clenched teeth, "and his friend looks like he's barely old enough to be in here."

"That's alright chile. But do you realize that we just received our first free drinks," Shar smirked, reminding me of my old friend, Jackie.

"Hey," we both said in unison, sounding like Kim and Nicky on 'The Parkers'. But our jubilation came to an abrupt halt when we noticed the two men approaching our table.

"Oh Lordy," I mumbled under my breath.

"Pull it together, girl," Shar attempted to say through clenched teeth.

## If Loving Two is Wrong . . .

"What do I do, I'm not ready for this," I mumbled, ventriloquist style.

"Just play it cool," Shar said through the veneer of a smile. She was just too hip for me. I was just about to tell her this, when I noticed the gargantuan standing in front of me.

"Would you ladies care to dance?" the baby-faced one asked, looking straight at Sharleen.

"Sure," she answered simultaneously with my, 'No thank you."

"Looks like we have a split decision," baby face grinned.

"I think I'll sit this one out," I answered, trying to roll my eyes at her, discreetly.

"No worries," muscleman said in a strong deep voice. A jolt went through me. His voice reminded me of Barry Sanders. Danger signs flashed like neon signs in my mind. 'Lightening wouldn't strike the same spot twice,' I rationalized.

"Why don't you two hit the dance floor? I'll keep the lady company," he said with a boyish grin.

"Okay," Shar said, obviously ignoring my subtle negative gestures and wide-eyed stare.

As I watched Sharleen head to the dance floor, I felt like a child whose mother just left them behind on their first day of kindergarten. In spite of myself, I had to smile. His grin made him look like a devilish, insecure little boy, but his physique was that of a full-grown man. He was well over six feet and more than two hundred pounds. He had a shiny, bald, head and humongous hands, which he was extending in my direction.

"I'm sorry, we haven't been properly introduced," Mr. Muscles said, engulfing my small hand with his. "My name is John, John Redding.

"Kayla Fountaine," I returned, instantly remembering Mark. I couldn't help but compare and contrast the differences between Mark and this gargantuan standing before me. Mark had been five foot eleven with a smooth

193

chestnut brown complexion. He had a track star's athletic build that I found extremely sexy. He also had a naturally smooth approach that instantly put you at ease. Mr. Redding was an extremely imposing figure. But in all fairness, he did seem gentle, despite his hugeness.

"Are you okay?" he asked, noticing my sudden, contemplative silence.

"Sorry, I was just thinking about my husband," I answered honestly.

"Husband?" he sputtered with arched eyebrows and jumping back as if someone had just jabbed him with a hot poker.

"Yes, my Mark. I'm a widow," I sighed as I invited him to sit down. I proceeded to tell him the whole sad story about Mark and Troy. He listened politely and expressed a sincere amount of sympathy. I surprised myself by opening up so much to this stranger. But he was so easy to talk to that I found myself actually enjoying our conversation. I felt so at ease that I didn't even flinch when he placed his hand atop mine for reassurance. Time was flying. Two songs and two drinks later, Shar and baby face, whose real name, Charles told me was James, still hadn't come off the dance floor. By the time they were returning, I had loosened up enough to go out for a spin.

"What," Sharleen howled as we headed toward her and James.

"You go, girl," she said, giving me a low five as we passed. I was amazed at how easily I flowed with the rhythm of the music. But then again, I had always been a good dancer, I reminded myself. The next song was a slow one and as I headed back to the table, John gently grabbed my hand and pulled me in close. At first, I was apprehensive. Those mental demons were telling me that I was betraying Mark. But at the same time, John's strong arms were making me feel secure, like everything was alright. My confusion gave way to acquiescence. As we swayed to the music, the drinks, combined with the sultry lyrics of 'Reasons' by 'Earth, Wind and Fire', made me feel giddy. When it was over, I literally floated to my seat. Sharleen was watching me with amusement in her eyes.

"Earth to Kayla. Do you need help coming down from cloud nine?" she laughed.

"Oh, shut up," I snapped, jokingly. We ordered another round of drinks and engaged in a lively conversation. Before we knew it, we had closed down the club. John and I exchanged numbers.

The next day, Shar and I were sitting at my kitchen table having coffee and corn muffins. She told me that she didn't give her number to James, but took his.

"This way, I have the power," she explained.

"Why didn't you tell me that?" I asked, exasperated.

"It doesn't matter," she said. "You seemed to like John, anyway."

"He was alright," I said sheepishly. I was embarrassed to admit that I did find him charming.

"Alright?" she crowed, "you looked like you were in seventh heaven out there on that dance floor."

"I did not," I said defensively. Once again, I was filled with feelings of betrayal. I needed a way to retaliate and get the heat off of me. "Well, what about you and that baby-faced boy?" I asked grouchily.

"Kayla please," Shar snorted. "You said it yourself. James looks like he should be drinking Similac, not Hennessey. I wanted to smack his hand every time he reached for his drink."

In spite of myself, I lost it. We both doubled over with laughter.

"Kayla," Shar said, growing serious. "I know you have a fierce loyalty to Mark's memory. I feel the same way about Troy, but they're gone. We have to learn to move on without them. I'm not saying you're ready to get married, but it's okay to date, to enjoy a man's company."

"But I can't help but feel guilty," I admitted.

"Well it's only natural," she said soothingly "But just know that no one else is judging you. In this case, you're your worst enemy. When you learn to forgive yourself for being human, just know that the world will forgive you, too."

"I'm not worried about the world, just Mark," I answered somberly.

"He of all people would understand," she said seriously.

"I know," I sighed. "It's just hard to think about moving on with somebody else."

"I know, baby," she replied, hugging me.

It had been almost a week since we had gone to that club. Although I had thought about John and looked at his number at least a dozen times, I refused to call him. I was old school and that meant that the girls didn't call the boys. Or, in my case, women didn't initiate the first move with a man. But by today's standards, I imagined anything went and in that case, I would be alone for a long time. Just as I was conveying my philosophy to Sharleen, who was old school too, my other line beeped.

"Hold on a sec, it's my other line," I informed her before clicking over.

"Hello," I answered.

"Hi, may I speak to Kayla?" a deep voice replied. I knew it was John, instantly. There was no mistaking his voice.

"Hold on a moment," I said before returning to Sharleen.

"Girl, it's him," I said breathlessly.

"John," she asked knowingly.

"Yeah," I responded.

"Say no more," she laughed. "Just call me back later with an update."

"Will do," I said and then clicked back over to John.

"I'm back," I announced, not knowing what else to say.

"How you been?" he asked.

"Pretty good," I answered. "And you?"

"I've been pretty anxious to talk to you, but I didn't want to appear desperate," he said honestly.

"Oh, come on," was all I could respond with. I was embarrassed by his admission.

# If Loving Two is Wrong . . .

"Seriously," he said. "It's not easy to put your pride on the line and chance getting shot down."

"Well, if I was going to do that, I wouldn't have given you my number. At least not the correct number," I laughed, warming to our conversation.

"That's true," he conceded. "Do you think I could take you out to breakfast?"

"When?" I asked quickly, caught off guard by his invitation.

"This morning," he answered. "Breakfast is the most important meal of the day and I just want to make sure you start today off right"

"Well," I stalled, "I don't know. This is such short notice."

"Spontaneity is good sometimes," he informed me. I looked at the clock; it was only eight-thirty. Mark Jr. had already left on the school bus.

"What time?" I asked slowly.

"About ten," he responded.

"Okay," I answered decisively. "Where should I meet you?" Once again, thoughts of Barry Sanders entered my mind. Although it seemed like forever since I'd had to follow my old rule, I still stood by it. I wasn't giving out my address until I was comfortable with someone, especially now that I had Mark Jr. to consider.

"Um," he mumbled sheepishly. "I could meet you or you could pick me up." There was a silent pause as we were both contemplating what he had just said.

'What the hell?! He doesn't have a car?' my mind screamed.

"My car is in the shop," he said quickly, as if reading my thoughts.

"Oh, okay," I said with growing confidence, "where am I going?"

He gave me the address and I called Shar as soon as we hung up.

"Go on girl! You have a good time," she gushed after hearing the news.

"It's only breakfast," I groaned.

"I know," she responded, "but I still want you to enjoy it."

"Thanks, sweetie. I'll call you when I get back."

"Do you want to set up an emergency call?" she asked.

"Emergency call?" I repeated, dumbfounded.

"You know, just in case things aren't going well and you need to be rescued," she said seriously.

I laughed, but decided to take her up on her offer.

"I'm picking him up at ten."

"Picking him up?" she squawked.

Yeah, his car is in the shop," I explained.

"Oh, I was about to say," she scoffed.

"I reacted the same way," I laughed.

"I'll just call at eleven," she said and then hung up.

I rushed to get ready. I was actually excited at the prospect of seeing John again. I pushed any guilty emanations aside, grabbed my keys and headed out the door. Breakfast went extremely well. We discussed our life philosophies, expectations and even a little sports and politics. The conversation was light and easy going over eggs, pancakes, bacon and coffee. I was so engrossed with the rapport that we were developing that I ignored the vibrations of my cell phone on my hip. A few moments later, I excused myself and headed to the ladies room to call Sharleen and fill her in.

"I'm glad you called," she said, answering on the second ring. "I didn't know if things were going that good or so bad that you couldn't call. Girl, you know me and my imagination," she laughed.

And boy did she have one. Once, she called for a rescue squad because she had cut her finger while slicing onions and was scared that she had nicked an artery and either she would bleed to death or gangrene was going to set in. She got mad at Troy, Tony and me when we laughed so hard when the rescue squad left after applying antiseptic, a bandage and advising her that a two hundred and fifty dollar bill would be arriving in the mail.

## If Loving Two is Wrong . . .

"Yes, I'm well aware of your imagination," I responded.

"But things are going great. Our conversation is flowing and he's cuter than I remembered. Oh, and did I mention his body?" I joked.

"That part I remember on my own," Sharleen chuckled.

"Well girl, I came in the bathroom to call you, I'd better get back before he thinks I fell in."

"Well don't worry about Mark Jr. He can come over after school if you don't make it back in time," she said coyly.

"I should be back in time, but thanks anyway, smartyass."

Before returning to the table, I fluffed my hair, applied a fresh coat of lipstick and checked my cleavage. I felt like a nervous schoolgirl as I approached my seat. John didn't rise to seat me, I noticed. That was a definite difference between him and Mark. But Mark was an exception, I reasoned as I pushed any negative thoughts from my mind. After breakfast, we caught a matinee movie, then John suggested a businessman's special at Wrigley's Stadium. I had never been to a baseball game and I bristled at the notion of attending a sporting event. It always brought Mark's accident to mind. But Shar's words rushed to the forefront; it was time to grab life by the horns and move forward. Two hours later, John and I were leaving the stadium, full on popcorn, hot dogs and soda. We were engrossed in a lively conversation.

"I told you my Phillies would win," I teased, displaying my loyalty to my original hometown team.

"If Abreu hadn't hit that two run homer at the bottom of the ninth, it would've been curtains for your team," he announced.

"Blah, blah, blah. If ifs were fifths, we'd be drunk right now," I joked. "Just pay me what you owe me."

"Alright, alright," he sighed resignedly. "You sure drive a hard bargain," he said, plucking a dollar bill from his

199

wallet and placing it in the palm of my open hand.

I used the ride to his apartment to find out more about him. He said that he was a general contractor and worked for himself. He'd never been married, had no kids and was estranged from his family because he refused to give handouts to a boatload of beggars, as he called them.

His conversation was peppered with a few curse words that caught me by surprise, but I just chalked it up to the fact that he was passionate about what he was saying and I was a little out of touch with reality. Mark rarely said a curse word in my presence and when he did, it was nothing worse than damn. I reasoned that I was spoiled by Mark and needed to re-evaluate my expectations and standards.

John was chatting away, but I was only half listening. I was contemplating the possibilities of him and me. Before I knew it, I was pulling up in front of his apartment building. The sun seemed to be spotlighting the structure that appeared dilapidated, now that I was paying attention to details. The paint was old and chipped, the sign that held the name of building was faded and a few of the letters were missing. In addition, the grounds surrounding the building resembled a small safari. I peered closely for a glimpse of a tiger or some other jungle creature to emerge.

"Would you like to come in?" he asked, disrupting my search.

"Oh no, I can't. I need to get back. Mark Jr. should be home by now," I said, half in truth. I knew Shar had Mark; I just didn't want to go anywhere near that uninhabitable looking structure.

"How old is he again?" John asked with a hint of agitation.

"Almost five," I said proudly, choosing to ignore his tone and the gnawing ache in the pit of my stomach.

"Five," he repeated incredulously. "He's still a damn baby."

"Excuse me," I said defensively.

"I was just thinking about all the things I could teach a young boy," he responded, cleaning up his act, quickly. "You know, fishing, sports, things like that."

## If Loving Two is Wrong . . .

"Mmm hmm," I mumbled, eyeing him suspiciously.

"Well, I better get going."

"I'll call you later," he said before disappearing into the building.

"He didn't even wait for me to drive off," I said to aloud. All the way home, I replayed the last moments of our date. Although my female intuition told me to steer clear of Mr. Redding, an inner voice said to give him a chance. But deep inside, I knew he wasn't the kind of guy for me. When I walked through the door, Kendall and Mark Jr. were in the yard playing and Sharleen was poised to pounce.

"Oh, I'll probably be back before Mark Jr. arrives," she said, mimicking me. "You must've had a great time, rolling in here at seven-thirty," she said, glancing at the kitchen wall clock.

She seemed so genuinely happy for me, I decided not to tell her my doubts just yet. I wanted to be sure that I wasn't being overly sensitive before I confided those thoughts to her.

Over the next three months, John and I were seeing quite a lot of each other. I had never told Shar about those initial conversations and actions that had disturbed me, but she seemed to pick up on some things on her own.

"I don't know Kay," she warned. "He seems like he has a bit of a temper and I noticed he likes to drink a lot."

"Oh Shar, he's just passionate," I defended weakly. "And so what if he likes to drink a few beers with his friends. The important thing is that he gets along well with Mark Jr."

"Kendall told me that Mark isn't that fond of him," she said with raised eyebrows.

"He's never said anything like that to me," I countered.

"Kayla, I love you and Mark Jr. I'm just trying to look out for your best interest," she said, feeling the tension in the air.

"I know Shar, I'm sorry. I guess I've just gotten accustomed to John being around. And it feels good to have a man to do

201

things with and make me feel secure," I reasoned. Even as I said the words, I knew I was settling. But John had been so persistent lately. I found myself just riding his waves. Truthfully, I didn't feel like myself. I had never been the type of woman to let a man steamroll over me, but for some reason; I was content to let John take control. It was never an issue between Mark and me because we seemed to be in sync. We flowed naturally and seemed to be on the same page about almost everything. Things that we did disagree about, we found a way to compromise, peacefully. Because Mark was such a good man, in the end I was always willing to let him be the main decision-maker. We followed the golden rule; never go to bed angry. With John it was different. Mentally, I was tired, tired of keeping on my toes, tired of making all of the decisions, tired of crying nightly about Mark and being angry at him for leaving me without a husband and Mark Jr. without a father. The bottom line was…I was just plain tired! So when John proposed to me after just three months, I accepted.

## Chapter Twenty-Four

"Kayla, are you crazy?!" That was Sharleen's response. We were in my living room, having a glass of Peach wine. The boys were asleep in Mark's room.

"Thanks for being happy for me," I said tersely.

"If I thought it was a good thing, I would be happy for you. I'd be ecstatic; you know that Kay," she assured me.

"But Shar, he gives me a sense of security," I whined. Then I ran down my list of things that I was tired of.

"I understand that; you know I do," she commiserated. "But you're vulnerable now and he's taking advantage of that."

"Shar, please don't do this," I pleaded. "John loves me."

"He would be crazy not to, but do you love him?" she questioned.

"I'm fond of him," I answered honestly.

"It's only been three months that you've known him, don't you think you're rushing it? I know you're lonely Kay. Lord knows I am too, but you need more time. Besides, John has too many hang-ups."

"Like what?" I asked with attitude. As soon as the words left my lips, I instantly regretted it. I didn't mean to respond so harshly to Shar's concerns, but I didn't want to hear a litany of John's flaws. Partly because I knew they were true.

"Well," she said, taking a deep breath, "he's supposed to be a contractor, but he can never keep a client. I don't know if it's because of his work or his temper. He blames his family for all his failures and says black women are gold diggers that always have their hands in a black man's pocket; as if that's the reason he doesn't have any money. And he never did get that imaginary car out of the shop!"

"Shar, don't you think you're being a little hard on him?" I interrupted.

"Hell no," she screeched. "If anything, I'm not being hard enough. How about when your pipe burst and he suggested that you call a plumber?" she snorted. "I mean, isn't that supposed to be the kind of thing he does?" she ended with an eye roll.

"Well Shar, it was a lot of work. Besides, I could more than afford to pay for it," I reasoned.

"That's not the point," she said, incredulously.

"You shouldn't have had to pay for that," she said, pointing toward the kitchen sink. "You pay for everything else as it is."

"But he is good with Mark Jr. Mark needs a male role model," I said softly, casting my eyes toward the floor. Sharleen pounced immediately.

"Role model," she huffed. "John is hardly the type of man that Mark Jr. should pattern his life after!"

"Shar, that's enough," I said wearily. I knew she was right, but I had already resigned myself to marrying John. I wanted a family again. I wanted to feel whole again. And even though deep down I knew John was not the man of my dreams, I didn't see him as quite the nightmare that Sharleen was describing.

"I'm marrying John and that's that," I said with a total lack of enthusiasm. Hearing my resolve, Shar decided to change tactics.

"Okay Kayla. If that's what you're determined to do, I'll support you. But I couldn't let you marry him without voicing my concerns."

"I know Shar. You're a good friend and I appreciate your concerns, but I'm just going to trust that John loves me and things will turn out for the best." I was exhausted by our exchange. After Shar left, I called Detective Moore. There was nothing new to report.

"I don't mean to sound insensitive Mrs. Fountaine, but the police consider this case closed and aren't investigating any further. However, if something should arise, I will be the first to let you know."

"I understand Detective, but I can't help but wonder, especially after the way he..." I halted, fearing I was going to break into tears.

"I understand Mrs. Fountaine. If you should anything, and I mean anything that you think can lead us in another direction, call me. I'd be more than happy to help."

"Thank you Detective," I said wearily. After hanging up, I went straight to bed.

If I thought Sharleen had been tough, it was nothing compared to the nuclear eruption of Mount Saint Toni. My mother went ballistic upon hearing about my wedding plans over the phone. Shar had wasted no time in calling her and informing her about John's character flaws. Although I had mentioned John to my family, I hadn't made it sound like it was that serious. Mom insisted that I was making a big mistake that I would regret later. Dad, who was listening in, was his usual quiet self, allowing Mom to be the enforcer. But his grunts conveyed his disapproval.

"Don't just sit there like a bump on a log. Say something Gerald," Mom demanded.

"I think you're jumping the gun, baby girl. But if you're determined, I'll support you. He just better not do anything to hurt you or my grandbaby," Dad huffed over the crackling of the speakerphone.

"Well thanks a lot," Mom said sarcastically. "I'm trying to dissuade her and you're up here giving her your blessings."

"Aw Toni. She's grown," Dad sighed. "She has to make her own decisions, good or bad," he said, emphasizing the word bad. It hurt me to hear my dad speak so negatively about my wedding plans, but I decided not to comment. In my mind, it was already a do, done deal.

## Chapter Twenty-Five

My parents arrived two weeks after our phone call for the small ceremony in front of the Justice of the Peace. Tony had said that he couldn't make it, but I could tell by his tone that he didn't support my decision. The Fountaine's politely declined their invitation, but offered wan congratulations. The hurt, which I understood, was evident in their voices, but I pretended not to notice. Mom and Dad were cordial to John, but it was obvious that they weren't pleased.

"I'm going to be a good husband to your daughter, Mr. Thomas," John said excitedly as he shook my father's limp hand.

"I'm counting on that, "Dad said sternly. "And you better take good care of my grandson."

"Oh, Mark and I get along just fine," John answered, quickly. "I'm going to be a good father to him."

"He already has a father," Mom snapped, still loyal to Mark's memory. "You just keep him happy," she ended with her hands on her hips.

"Yes ma'am," John said solemnly. He looked like a little boy whose hand had just been smacked. I felt sorry for him. I had never seen my family respond this way to anyone. That gnawing feeling in the pit of my stomach returned. A ball of doubt was churning inside of me, but once again, I pushed them aside as I had done so many times before. I decided to put the onus on my family. They couldn't accept John because he wasn't Mark. Mark had been a yardstick and everyone else would always be a twelve-inch ruler in comparison.

"Your parents hate me," John sulked as he followed me into the kitchen.

"No they don't," I sighed.

"Yes they do," he said, growing angry. "First they

make me sign a prenuptial agreement and now they're talking to me as if I'm some kind of monster. This is supposed to be a wedding, damn it!"

"John, calm down," I soothed, although I could understand his pain. My parents insisted that the only way they would attend the ceremony was if John signed a prenuptial agreement. John had balked at the idea, but I stood firm. I needed my parents at my wedding and if a prenuptial agreement was the condition, so be it. Besides, I was lucid enough to know that it was in my best interest.

"Is everything okay in there?" Mom asked upon hearing our raised voices.

"Everything is fine," I covered, re-entering the room with a tray of champagne glasses.

"I'll make the toast," John said enthusiastically. He desperately wanted to gain their approval. I didn't think it was possible, but I smiled at his attempt.

"Everyone raise your glasses," he urged. With all glasses in the air, including Kendall and Mark Jr.'s sparkling grape juice, John forged ahead.

"To my lovely, beautiful wife. I will do everything possible to be the best husband and stepfather," he said, glancing at my mother for her approval. After observing her nod, he continued, "and to the two people who made this all possible. Mr. and Mrs. Thomas, if it wasn't for you two, none of this could have taken place," he ended, grinning proudly.

"Come again," Mom interjected rudely, arm raised in mid-air.

"I just meant that if you two didn't have Kayla, I would never have been able to marry her," he explained wide-eyed. Telltale beads of sweat were beginning to form on his chocolate head. It was such a trip watching this big hulk of a man, fidgeting in front of my little ole mom and dad.

"I told you to wear protection," Mom said with fake anger as she playfully punched Dad on the arm. Dad appeared embarrassed by the whole subject, as his face was

207

quickly turning a brilliant red.

"I'm just joking," Mom covered with a phony smile.

"Yeah, joking with the truth," I murmured to Shar, who had been quiet throughout the whole ceremony. She attempted a half-hearted smile, but I knew that she was still bothered by the whole ordeal.

## Chapter Twenty-Six

Mom and Dad stayed in Chicago with Mark, Jr. while John and I went to the Bahamas for our honeymoon. By the third day, I was ready to go home. The first night, John got totally intoxicated. He pawed and groped me to the point that I was ready to hit him over the head with the complimentary bottle of champagne supplied by the hotel. Luckily, he passed out before he could get his clothes off. On the second day, he was nearly arrested. One of the friendly natives had called me a beautiful lady and John shoved and threatened him for what he considered a lack of respect. John towered over most of the police officers, who didn't carry guns, and outweighed them by almost two to one. I was thankful that they let him go with a warning when they discovered that we were on our honeymoon.

By four o'clock on the third day, John had successfully gambled away the remainder of the money budgeted for the rest of the week. He had returned from the Princess Casino Hotel on Paradise Island, staggering and sloshed. He immediately fell asleep on the couch in our living room suite. As I watched him with disgust, my mind transported me back to a severely contrasting moment in time.

When Mark and I honeymooned in Hawaii, the sparks flew and the romance flourished from the minute the plane touched down in Honolulu until the day he died. Mark had been so attentive and loving. We spent our days walking along the sandy beaches holding hands, exploring the islands, sometimes alone and sometimes with sightseeing groups. Our nights were filled with romantic dinners, exciting nightlife, strolls beneath the starry moonlit sky and earth shattering lovemaking.

Suddenly, a loud snore dragged me back to reality. Tears sprung to my eyes as I looked at John and woefully wondered what the future held. I exhaled sharply as I plopped back in the soft recliner and focused unseeingly on the television.

An hour later, I realized that I must've drifted into a fitful sleep because I awoke just in time to see John stirring. As soon as he opened his eyes, I let him have it.

"I want to go home tomorrow," I announced.

"What?" he asked groggily. "I'm having a great time. Why do you want to go home?"

"Why?" I exploded. "Yeah, sure you're having a great time!" Then I ran down his daily list of activities. By the time I finished, I had screamed him sober.

"I'm sorry, baby," he said somberly. "It's just that I've been under a lot of pressure."

"What kind of pressure?" I screeched.

"Baby, you know your parents don't like me. Mark Jr. is struggling to accept me because he's still grieving for his father and Sharleen acts like she can't stand me," he said ruefully.

"But you didn't marry Sharleen or my parents. You married me. Mark Jr. and I are the ones you have to worry about pleasing," I responded.

"You don't understand how it is to feel like you're living under a microscope. Your parents and your best friend don't like me; that can only cause problems. And you and your son make me feel inadequate," he said passionately.

"Oh, you're just grasping for straws now," I said, waving my hand dismissively.

"No I'm not Kayla. I feel like I'm fighting a ghost or something."

"A ghost?" I screamed. "What are you talking about?" I asked, leery of where the conversation was heading.

"Everywhere I turn, I'm reminded of what a great man Mark was. It's all I ever hear and I just can't compete with a memory," he sobbed, placing his hands on both sides of his head. He was actually crying.

"I know you don't think I hear you when you cry for him. I've even heard you call the police station and hospitals to see if there were any unidentified patients."

I was genuinely shocked by that admission because I had always tried to be careful when making those calls. But there were times when I couldn't help the urge to call when John was home, but thought I was discreet. Obviously I wasn't discreet enough, but he had never mentioned it before.

As I listened to his explanation, my anger began to subside. I had never looked from his point of view. Yeah, it had to be difficult to hear how wonderful Mark had been all the time. Although I knew that John could never compete with Mark, memory or otherwise, I didn't mean to make him feel like he couldn't.

"I'm sorry," I sighed. "I didn't know that I was making you feel that way. But that's no excuse for your behavior these last few days. This is supposed to be our honeymoon and you've turned it into a personal, private party."

"You're right," he said apologetically, sniffing intermittently. "I promise that for now on, I will be on my best behavior. Scout's honor," he ended with a mock salute, reminiscent of Benny Hill. He looked so silly; I couldn't help but laugh.

"Were you ever a Boy Scout?" I asked, raising my eyebrows.

"Nope," he grinned sheepishly, but all my friends were and they initiated me. My parents couldn't afford the dues or the uniforms," he ended with a hint of sadness in his voice.

Now that I was looking at John through new eyes, I decided to wipe the slate clean. I would give him another chance. For the remainder of our honeymoon, John was fantastic! He opened doors, pulled out chairs and insisted that we participate in a variety of activities. The booze cruise was my favorite. Couples and singles were all packed aboard a party boat filled with food, booze and a deejay. At first, everyone tended to mingle among themselves in their own little private cliques. But when the boat hit the open sea and the booze had been freely flowing for more than an hour, it was on! Everybody was shaking a tail feather with everybody else. By the time we docked in the late evening, a few new couples had been formed and everybody was hugging goodbye as if we were long lost friends. The last song of the evening had been a romantic slow tune tinged with seductive island rhythms. John had pulled me in close and we swayed gently to the sexy music. It reminded me of the way I felt when we danced the first night that I met him at the club with Sharleen. It had been a long time since I felt that way about John. But truthfully, I think the ambiance was more responsible for my amorous mood than John. It could've been Frankenstein holding me tightly and I don't think it would've made a bit of difference. John and I made love over and over that night. It was more animalistic than romantic. I had been under a lot of stress lately and my body was screaming for a much-needed release. Subconsciously, I couldn't help but compare John with Mark. Mark had always been so tender and compassionate; John was rough and unorthodox. Once I realized that I was comparing, I immediately pushed the thoughts from my mind.

As we prepared to leave the next morning, I looked long and hard at John as he piled clothes into his suitcase. He had behaved so wonderfully the last half of our trip that I decided not to confide to anyone about how the honeymoon began or his admission about feeling inadequate to Mark's memory. But as the familiar tightening began in my stomach, I had a feeling that I had received a glimpse of the true John. I also had a feeling that that John would surface again. And I wasn't wrong.

## Chapter Twenty-Seven

**M** **"** ark, baby, can you go to the den and ask John if he would like to order a pizza?"

"Sure, mom. Can we get pepperonis please?" he begged, clasping his hands together and jumping up and down.

"We can get whatever you want on it, sweetheart," I said, laughing at his silly antics. I just shook my head as I watched him skip towards the den. From the kitchen I could hear John having a conversation on the phone, although I couldn't make out the words, I could hear his loud laughter. I knew Mark Jr. would be privy to every word.

'Marriage is pretty good man,' John was saying. 'A beautiful woman, home-cooking almost every night and regular sex, what more can a man ask for? But her son, man, that's another subject. That's the only problem. He's like a little bug, always in the way. And she dotes on him like he's a fucking baby. But I'm gonna put a stop to that shit, and soon man.'

He went on to talk about other things; but the damage had already been done.

"What did John say about the pizza, baby?" I asked over my shoulder when Mark returned to the kitchen. He was just standing in the archway drawing imaginary lines with the toe of his sneaker and looking at the floor.

"What's the matter, sweetheart," I asked, noticing the drastic change in his demeanor.

"Why doesn't John like me," he asked,

dejectedly, skipping my question.

"Why do you say that?"

"He was telling someone that on the phone," he mumbled, close to tears.

"I'm sure he didn't mean it," was all I could manage. How else could I explain it? Mark was far from dumb.

"Yes, he did. He called me a little bug and said you baby me and I get on his nerves," he said in a sad voice.

"What else did he say?" I asked. I wanted to be fully armed when I confronted John.

"He said you were beautiful and the sex is good and he was going to stop it."

I was flabbergasted by the mention of sex and knew by the content of Mark's sentence, that Mark wasn't grasping that part of the conversation. I decided not to question him any further.

"Go to your room and watch one of your videos, honey. I'll call you when the pizza gets here and I'll make sure they put lots and lots of pepperoni on it, okay?"

"Okay," he said, brightening just a little at the thought of pizza with extra pepperoni.

When I was sure he had gone upstairs, I marched straight to the den. John was still on the phone as I stood in front of the television with my arms folded over my chest. He just continued talking, ignoring my presence.

"John, I need to talk to you," I said calmly after waiting for over two minutes. He just cut his eyes at me and continued talking on the phone.

"Now," I said, sharply.

"Look man, I'm gonna call you back, Kayla's over here tripping." He paused a minute with raised eyebrows, then let out a snicker before hanging up.

"Now what's your problem," he asked, leering at me and taking a swig of the beer in his hand.

## If Loving Two is Wrong . . .

"Mark asked me why you don't like him," I said evenly, trying to hide some of the angst I was feeling.

"What are you talking about?" he asked, lowering the beer can and glaring at me.

"Mark said he heard you telling someone you don't like him and not only that, why were you discussing our sex life with your friends?"

"Why was he even listening to my conversation?" John snapped, attempting to take the focus off of him.

"He wasn't eavesdropping," I said defensively, I sent him to ask if you wanted to order a pizza and he overheard you talking."

"Yeah, well, I didn't say that," he said, waving me off with his beer free hand.

"Well what did you say?" I had demanded, hands on my hips.

"I don't remember my exact words," he hedged, defensively.

"Paraphrase, then," I snapped, complete with dramatic head movements.

"C'mon Kayla, you know Mark doesn't like me. I might've said some things in anger, but I didn't say all that stuff he said I did," he huffed, his voice rising.

"John," I sighed, unconvinced by his admission, "you need to have more patience with Mark."

"I need to have patience," he sputtered.

"That's all I hear. Have patience with Mark, he misses his father, have patience with me," he said, placing both hands on his chest and talking in a raspy falsetto that I assumed was a very poor imitation of my voice. "I'm still grieving my deceased husband. Have patience with Sharleen; she's not used to me being married to you. Have patience with my parents; they're still not convinced you're good enough for me. Well what about me, Kayla?" He had returned to his normal tone, albeit, a little louder than usual.

"Who the hell is having any patience with me?" His

215

temper had risen out of control; veins were bulging in his neck and forehead. It kind of scared me, so I decided to drop the subject for the moment and just monitor his interactions with Mark very closely. He reminded me of the same John I had encountered on our honeymoon, the one that had promised to never come back again. BANG!! The first warning shot had been fired.

Now as I watched my son approach, I was filled with incredible emotions. But before my mind could send me on a sentimental journey, Mark Jr. was roughly wrapping his arms around my neck.

"Mom, can I spend the night over Kendall's house?" he asked energetically. His dark chocolate eyes were as wide as saucers and filled with hope. His enchanting smile was just like his dad's, his real dad; except Mark Jr. was missing two front teeth.

"Isn't John taking you fishing tomorrow?" I asked, returning his hug.

"Yes," Mark Jr. sulked, "but I don't want to go."

"Mark," I sighed, "John is trying really hard to be a good stepfather, at least give him a chance."

"He's not my father," Mark said quietly, then ran to his bedroom.

I followed him up the stairs and watched from the doorway while he cried into his Spiderman pillowcase. My eyes wandered around his room, which was filled with sports paraphernalia and posters of his favorite basketball players, including an autographed photo of Michael Jordan. A wave of sadness washed over me. I flashbacked to when Mark Sr. found out that he was having a son. He proudly went shopping for any and everything a little boy could want.

When I returned my gaze to Mark Jr., I wanted to put my face next to his on that pillow and let out a good cry too, but I couldn't. I had to be strong for my son, for me. Mark Jr. had been through more in the last two years than any six-year-old deserved. I lay atop his matching bedspread, complete with jeans, t-shirt and slippers and cradled my baby in my arms. I hummed quietly as Mark's

# If Loving Two is Wrong . . .

heaving shoulders slowed to a halt, along with his sniffling sobs.

"How about if I ask John if Kendall can go along with you?" I asked, careful not to say 'your father' again. "Do you think he'll say yes?" Mark asked, a ray of hope glistening on his tear stained face. "I'll see baby," I said, kissing him on the forehead. Then I slid from his bed and left the room. I glanced at the mirror in the hall and did a double take.

"I look a wreck," I said aloud as I noticed the bags under my eyes. The dark rings really stood out against my skin, which was the color of coffee with one and a half creams. The accident and my marriage to John seemed to age me beyond my thirty-five years. I put my hand to my face and noticed my raggedy nails. Not long ago, I used to have a standing appointment at my favorite nail salon, I thought, wistfully.

"Hairdresser too," I mumbled as I grabbed a handful of my shoulder-length black hair and checked for split ends.

"I have to get myself together," I sighed and headed downstairs to start dinner.

I heard John's car pull into the driveway around five-thirty. The pungent scent of the garlic bread could be detected over the aroma of basil, tomato and oregano. While I searched the refrigerator for the Kraft's Parmesan cheese, I heard the front door open.

"Hi babe," John said when he entered the kitchen, a two thousand watt smile plastered on his simple face. He's usually in a good mood after spending a Saturday afternoon drinking beer and watching sports with his friends, I thought disdainfully.

"Perfect timing," I smiled, attempting to lighten my mood, "dinner's ready." I reached up and started taking plates from the cabinet

"Mmm, spaghetti, my favorite," he said, sniffing the air and encircling my waist from behind. He planted a kiss on the side of my face and rubbed his stubbled cheek against my smooth one. He reeked of beer, but I was just glad that he was in a good mood. I figured this would be as good a time as any to ask him about Kendall.

"John, sweetheart," I began, immediately going for the butter up. "Do you think that Kendall can go fishing with you and Mark tomorrow?"

"Fishing? Oh, I completely forgot," he shrugged dismissively as he opened the refrigerator and pulled out a beer. John always made sure to keep a supply of Private Stock on hand. I grimaced. I hated when he smelled of beer and hated the way he acted after a few of them even more.

"I promised the guys that I would meet them at Jerry's tomorrow for a few beers and watch the game."

Jerry's was a local sports bar that John and his friends frequented. I was sure they owned stock in the place; at least they should have. Recalling Mark's earlier reaction to going fishing with John, I decided not to push the issue about the importance of keeping a promise to a little boy. I was about to call Mark for dinner when the phone rang.

"Hello," I answered.

"Hi Kayla, how's everything?"

"Good Shar, how about you?"

"I could complain, but I won't. Listen, Kendall's been begging me to call and ask if Mark can spend the night. Please say yes before I have to tar and feather this little boy."

"Hey, it's fine with me," I laughed. "I'll send him down after dinner."

"He can eat here if he wants. Tell him I'm making his favorite, at Kendall's request."

"Oooh, you don't play fair, girl, trying to sabotage my son. You know he can't resist fried chicken."

"And you know that's right. But all's fair in love and sanity." Shar chuckled.

"Come again."

"Well, you know I love Mark, and having him over is the only way I'll be able to keep my sanity. Otherwise, Kendall will drive me nuts with his questions. 'Why can't Mark come over, Mommy? What happened? Did Aunt Kayla say no? Why'd she say no, Mommy'."

# If Loving Two is Wrong . . .

Sharleen was doing her best Kendall imitation. I could understand her pain. I had often been interrogated about why someone couldn't spend the night; it was nothing pretty. "Okay," I surrendered, "let me pack him a bag and I'll send him down, but I think that we've been had."

"What do you mean?" Shar asked.

"Both of them asking us if Mark can stay over, Kendall requesting Mark's favorite for dinner; those two monsters put their little heads together to play us," I laughed.

"You know what? I think you're right," Shar laughingly agreed. "Just call when he leaves so I can look out for him."

She only lived across the street and seven houses down. It was an easy commute, but we were both very protective of our boys. When I approached Mark's room, I could hear him moving around.

"Have a good nap?" I asked upon entering.

"I think so, "he yawned, wiping sleep from his eyes. "I must have been hungry."

"Why do you say that?" I asked, pushing a strand of hair from my forehead.

"Because I kept dreaming about spaghetti," he laughed.

"That's what we're having for dinner. You probably smelled mommy's terrific spaghetti in your sleep," I smiled.

"Oh," he said quickly. "Did you ask Aunt Shar if Kendall could go with us tomorrow," he continued, dismissing my spaghetti plug.

"Well, I have some bad news," I said, seriously.

"He can't go?" Mark asked, sadly.

"No, he can't go," I continued my masochistic act.

"Why," he sighed. "Did John say no."

"Actually, John can't make it tomorrow," I answered, ending my playful torment.

"Really?" he asked, his eyes wide. He was torn between being remorseful or elated.

219

"Really," I answered. "By the way, Aunt Shar called and wanted to know if you wanted to spend the night. But I told her no way."

"Why Mom?" he groaned.

"Because I knew you wouldn't want to miss a spaghetti dinner with me and John," I joked.

"How about if I eat spaghetti with you and John and then go over to Kendall's?" I smiled at Mark's attempt to be diplomatic.

"Oh, you're so sweet, giving up Aunt Shar's fried chicken for my spaghetti." I teased.

"Fried chicken," he said in awe."

I decided I had played enough with his emotions and let him off the hook.

"How about if you go over Kendall's tonight and you can have some of my spaghetti when you come home."

"Thanks Mom," he grinned and gave me a big hug.

I packed Mark's bag while he picked out tapes and video games to take with him. When we entered the kitchen, John was stuffing a forkful of spaghetti into his already red-stained mouth.

"Hi, John," Mark said meekly, looking at the floor and tracing the outline around one of the mosaic tiles with his sneaker. I hated that Mark was so introverted around John. He was usually such a happy go lucky child. I had suggested counseling a few months ago, but John had balked at the idea. I knew something was going to have to give soon.

"What's up, l'il bug," John answered and then took a swig of beer. I noticed the two empty bottles on the table. Mark hated when he called him l'il bug, especially because he knew the reason behind it.

"Going somewhere," he asked, eyeing the overnight bag in Mark's hand.

I knew John had heard my conversation with Sharleen on the phone a few moments ago, so I just answered his question.

# If Loving Two is Wrong . . .

"Mark's going over Sharleen's house to spend the night."

"I asked li'l bug," he said sarcastically.

"I'm going to spend the night over Kendall's house," Mark said quietly.

"Did anybody ask me?" John sneered, looking up at the ceiling as if an answer was going to fall from there. He had that familiar look in his eyes. The one that preceded an alcohol induced mood change. I attempted to tread softly.

"I didn't think you'd mind," I said brightly, attempting to lighten the mood.

"Since you don't get paid to think, you damn sure shouldn't do it for free," he said nastily and took another swig of beer. I bristled. I had been letting John get away with making smart comments and doing a lot of things that I disapproved of during our marriage. Things like: frequent intoxicated binges, constantly losing contracting jobs because 'somebody was disrespectin' him or trying to cheat him', and constantly complaining that I spent too much time with Sharleen and not enough with him. I never would have tolerated these things before it happened. I never had to. Mark Sr. had spoiled me.

John's behavior was like some horror movie that had to end at some point. But that night, something inside me snapped. Not wanting Mark Jr. to be subjected to the storm that was brewing, I told him to head on over to Sharleen's house. As I picked up the phone to let her know Mark was on his way, John shot up out of his chair, knocking it to the floor. He kicked it out of the way and strode purposefully to the kitchen door, blocking Mark's exit. His baldhead was glistening with sweat. He reminded me of an angry, chocolate Mr. Clean, right down to the pierced ear.

"PUT THE GOT DAMN PHONE DOWN, KAYLA," he screamed, pointing at me menacingly. Shocked, but feeling defiant, I continued dialing Shai's number. Before I knew what was happening, John had snatched the phone from me with his right hand, grabbed me by the throat with his left and shoved me violently against the wall. I looked in Mark's eyes and saw sheer determination. I wasn't sure if he was scared of John or mortified by what he was witnessing, but I could tell he was preparing to take action. I wanted to scream at him, 'no, just run and tell Aunt Shar to call the police', but the words were stuck in my throat, bulging just below the tight grip John maintained on my larynx. In a flash, Mark was kicking and pummeling John's arm, back and legs, screaming, "get off my mommy," over and over again. John's eyes were bloodshot red and registered pure hatred as he dropped the phone and backhanded Mark with the full-strength of his right hand. Mark went sailing, knocking over a kitchen chair and landing with a thud as his head crashed into the cabinet beneath the sink. BANG!! Shot number two. Mustering all the strength I had, I pushed John away from me. The force was enough to make him lose his balance for a moment. As he struggled for control, I grabbed a butcher knife from the strainer by the sink and bent down to check on Mark.

"Are you alright, baby?" I asked, noticing a bright red handprint on the right side of his face.

"Yes, I'm okay," he sniffled, trying to be tough. John took a step toward us, and paused when he noticed the glistening steel in my hand.

"Oh, you're gonna cut me bitch! Well you better kill me. And the next time your little punk ass son puts his hands on me, I'm gonna snap his puny neck."

BANG!!! Shot number three. And true to the credo, three strikes and he was out! I went 'Color Purple' on his ass.

"Listen to me, you bullying son of a bitch," I said through clenched teeth while pointing the knife at him.

"If you ever threaten, let alone touch my son again, I'll filet your trifling, stinking ass."

"Fuck you and your son," he yelled as he headed toward the door, making sure to keep an eye on the knife and me. He didn't get far. As he opened the door, I could see the flashing lights of a patrol car.

"Oh, shit," John sighed and slumped against the

# If Loving Two is Wrong . . .

doorframe in resignation. A short, stocky, black female officer entered the open door, while her thin white male partner questioned John outside.

"Ma'am, I need you to put the knife down on the table for me, okay," the officer said with a calm, yet authoritative voice. Suddenly conscious of still having the knife in my hand, I released my white knuckled grip and placed it on the table.

"I'm Officer Mitchell. Can you tell me what happened," she asked softly, her eyes taking in the scene. I related the incident to her and in spite of my efforts, found myself wiping away tears.

"Are you okay, sweetie," she asked Mark, noticing the handprint on his cherub-like face.

"Yes, ma'am," Mark answered, barely above a whisper.

"How did you get that mark on your face?" the officer asked.

"John hit me," he said, looking down at his hands as he twiddled his fingers.

"That's quite a bruise on your neck, ma'am. Are you sure you're okay?" Officer Mitchell asked, turning her attention to me and writing something on her notepad.

"I'm okay," I answered, clearing my throat, which felt a bit scratchy.

"How about your son?" she asked.

I rubbed Mark's head for any signs of lumps; there were none. But he grimaced when I touched the back of his head.

"He did hit his head kind of hard. He seems okay, but I'd like to get him checked out," I reasoned.

"That's no problem, Mrs. Redding. But I need to know, are you willing to press charges?"

I didn't answer her right away. Misled by my hesitation, she continued.

"If you don't want to, based on what I've witnessed, meaning you and your son's bruises and the disarray of the area, the police department can press charges."

When she initially asked me the question, I had replayed the scenario with John in my mind. That was the reason for my slow response.

"Oh, yes, I'm more than willing to press charges," I answered, decisively. The vision of Mark sailing in the air and crashing to the ground, would more than sustain my burning desire to see justice served to John, ice-cold. A male voice interrupted my thoughts.

"What's going on Willa?" her partner asked from the threshold. John wasn't visible through the doorway. Not wanting to alert him of their plans, Officer Mitchell criss-crossed her hands and bumped her wrists together, silently telling her partner to handcuff John. Seconds later, there was yelling.

"Aw, this is bullshit!"

"Just relax, Mr. Redding," the male officer responded.

"Fuck you," John yelled.

We heard a scuffle ensuing and Officer Mitchell rushed to her partner's aid. I told Mark to stay put and I went to the door to see what was happening. John was releasing the full brunt of his rage on the officers, who were much smaller than he was. John was 6'3 and 280lbs of pure muscle. The two officers looked as if their combined weight barely equaled his. Just as I thought about dialing 911 for reinforcements, a second squad car and a paddy wagon pulled up. By the time the officers handcuffed John, he had some well-deserved lumps, bumps and bruises.

After John was placed in the wagon and they pulled off, Officer Mitchell asked if I wanted them to take us to the hospital or if I wanted to drive myself. I chose the latter. She said a detective would meet us there to take my statement and pictures of our bruises. By that time, the whole neighborhood was watching and those not bold enough to come outside, peeked through their shades. I couldn't believe that I was the focus of such attention. In my wildest dreams, I would've never imagined anything like this happening to me.

Sharleen insisted that she drive us to the hospital.

# If Loving Two is Wrong . . .

Before we left, I stopped to make sure the side entrance to the kitchen was locked. All the lights were on and I decided to go in and turn them off real quick. When I entered, the sight made me gasp. Overturned chairs and the butcher knife I had pulled on John seemed to be flashing like beacons for my attention. The lid for the spaghetti was on the counter so I quickly placed on the pot and put it in the refrigerator. Before I could take any further inventory, Sharleen was outside honking the horn. Hastily, I cut off the light switch, rechecked the lock and rushed toward Sharleen's car. She and Kendall sat by Mark's and my side as I gave my statement to Detective Robinson, an attractive woman with chin-length black hair, who appeared to be in her mid-forties and was sharply dressed in a dark gray pantsuit. She had already taken several pictures of my neck before we were summoned to an examining room. When we emerged with the doctor, he informed the detective that Mark had a slight concussion, but should be okay. She had already taken pictures of Mark's face and now took notes on the doctor's diagnosis. She informed me that John would be detained at least until Monday because judges didn't work on weekends. She also advised me to obtain an emergency protection order with eviction that night so John couldn't come back to the house if he was granted bail and released on Monday. I thanked her for her time and advice and we left the hospital. We piled into Shar's mint green Camry and without saying a word, she headed straight to the Cook County Circuit Court on California Avenue. I looked over at Sharleen, who was in complete disarray. Her usual neatly coifed hair was a discombobulated pile atop her head. She had on blue sweatpants bottoms and a brown sweater. I looked down at her feet and saw a pair of pink fuzzy slippers with no socks. I realized that she must have dropped everything when she noticed the commotion at my house. What a true friend. I returned my gaze to the windshield and stared straight ahead until we pulled in front of the courthouse.

Half an hour later, with paperwork in hand, we headed to the police station. I wanted John to be served while he was locked up. That way, he already had the paperwork that was supposed to keep him away from Mark, my house and me, for at least sixty days. It was almost nine-thirty when we pulled up in front of Sharleen's house.

"I think you and Mark should stay the night," Shar said as she put the car in park.

"That's not necessary Shar," I said, wearily.

"I know it's not necessary, but I want you to stay. It will give me peace of mind and besides, I did promise Mark some fried chicken," she murmured the last part.

"I want fried chicken," Mark hollered out.

"So much for whispering," I smirked.

"Then I guess it's decided, we'll all stay at my house tonight."

"Yay," Mark and Kendall yelled in unison.

"I know when I'm licked," I surrendered, holding my hands up.

Once inside, Shar went straight to the kitchen and started frying chicken, while the boys went Kendall's room to play video games. Shar made some coffee and we discussed the day's events. After dinner, the boys watched a few videos and played a couple of games before they were put to bed. Sharleen and I popped some popcorn, made some margaritas and watched How Stella Got Her Groove Back and Waiting to Exhale. Two women empowering movies that gave me ideas about what I needed to do.

Early Sunday morning, Shar's snoring woke me up. I had to smile as I watched her splayed out on the makeshift bed we made on the living room floor. I scribbled a note asking her to watch Mark for a few hours while I handled some things at home. I promised to call her later. Before I left, I looked around Shar's comfortable living room. It was decorated in tranquil earthtones, lots of brown and tan. We had pushed the large, soft, tan leather couch that usually dominated the center of the living room, to the rear wall. In its place, we had made homemade pallets on the plush chocolate chip colored carpet. Family portraits decorated the cream colored walls and a large breakfront showcased trophies, knickknacks and precious memories. There was a

## If Loving Two is Wrong . . .

tan Steinway, which Shar still swore that she was going to learn to play, against the wall that led to a spiral staircase. A large portrait of Troy, Shar and Kendall that seemed to stare at you from all angles sat on the piano. I took another look at Shar. She had added a little whistle to her snoring ensemble. We had been through so many things together: good, bad and terrible. Our friendship had endured it all. I'm going to miss you.

## Chapter Twenty-Eight

I unlocked the kitchen door and stepped in. Everything was exactly as I had left it. I inhaled deeply. The sight of overturned chairs and the dangling phone transported me back to the day before. It was as clear as if it were happening right at that moment. The sound of a passing car broke me out of my reverie. I was on a mission and after replacing the phone on the hook; I set on it with a vengeance. By one o'clock, I had packed the most important things in crates, boxes and bags. I filled a few suitcases for Mark and me and set them near the living room door. I called Shar and told her to come over with the boys for lunch. There was plenty of left over spaghetti from yesterday.

When they arrived, they were shocked to see the array of boxes and crates.

"Are we going somewhere Mommy?" Mark asked apprehensively.

"Yeah, are we going somewhere, Mommy?" Shar followed up dazedly. I hadn't let her in on my idea last night because I wasn't completely sure if I was going to follow through with it.

"Yes we are," I answered with a cheeriness I really didn't feel. "We're going to Philadelphia."

"Yay!" Mark screamed and began jumping up and down with youthful exuberance. "We're going to see Grandma and Grandpa and Uncle Tony," he said to Kendall.

"Hey Mom," he continued excitedly, as if a brilliant idea had just popped into his head.

"Yes, baby," I answered, watching him in the mirror that covered the entire length of one living room wall.

"Can Kendall go visiting with us?"

The question took me by surprise.

"We'll see baby," I said slowly. I didn't have the heart to tell him that it was going to be more than a visit.

## If Loving Two is Wrong . . .

After lunch, the boys were in the backyard playing basketball on the miniature court that Mark's father had put up when Mark was just two years old. Shar and I were sitting at the kitchen table, talking over coffee and Danish.

"Wow, this is really taking me by surprise," Shar said, her hazel eyes getting misty.

"I know girl, but I think it's for the best." I said, sipping my vanilla flavored coffee.

"But this is so sudden, what are your plans?" she asked, rising from her chair and checking on the boys. A slight frown adorned her face.

"I haven't sorted it all out yet, but I do have a few ideas," I said.

"Care to let me in on them," she asked, turning to face me with her hands on her trim waist.

"Well, for starters, I have to call my parents and tell them what's happened," I sighed. I was dreading that. They warned me not to marry John in the first place. But in the end, they stood by my decision and were supportive for Mark's and my sake.

"Then, first thing Monday morning, I'm putting John's few things in storage, which ain't much," I sneered

"Next, I'm going to call my realtor and have her list the house for sale."

"Kayla, no," Shar wailed, her auburn, shoulder-length ponytail flung side to side as she took in the meaning of my last sentence. The finality of the situation was just sinking in.

"Shar, except for you and Kendall, I have nothing left to keep me in Chicago. I need to make this move for Mark's sake. This house hasn't held any happiness for me or him since…" I paused, fighting the choking emotions that were welling up inside of me.

"I know baby," Shar said softly, coming over to give me a hug. She knew all too well the pain that I was feeling because she felt it too.

"Hey, I have an idea," I said, brightening at the very

thought of it.

"What's that?" Shar asked, wiping tears from her eyes.

"Why don't you and Kendall come to Philly with us, my treat," I followed up on Mark Jr.'s idea.

"Oh Kayla, I don't know," she answered slowly. "It hadn't crossed my mind."

"I think it's a great idea," I gushed, warming to it even more. "It's summer vacation, so Kendall's not in school. And you can visit your family in Jersey." I was really pouring it on.

"Well, when are you leaving?" she asked, rubbing her chin, considering my proposal.

"Tuesday, if everything goes smoothly. Wednesday, at the latest," I said, biting into a cheese danish.

"Wow, so soon?" she gasped.

"Why wait? I figure, the sooner, the better. I don't know what kind of mindset John's going to be in if and when he gets out, and I don't want to be here to find out."

"Sheeit," Shar snarled. "We both need to be right here waiting for that fool with baseball bats and steel-toed boots."

"He ain't worth it, girl," I snickered. "I'm just ready to get away."

"I guess you're right," Shar drawled. "It's just that everything seems to be happening so fast."

"I know, but the more I think about it, the more I know it's the right thing to do. And the more I know that it's right, the quicker I want to get started."

"I hate to say it," Shar laughed, "but that actually made sense."

"Well, what do you say?" I asked, returning to my invitation.

"Uh, you did say it was your treat, right?" she asked with raised eyebrows.

"You would remember that," I laughed and playfully punched her on the arm. "Yes, I did say it was my treat."

"In that case, count us in," she said, clapping her hands in excitement.

# If Loving Two is Wrong . . .

"Yay," I yelled, jumping up and down, imitating Mark's earlier moves.

"You're so silly," Shar smiled. "Well, I'm going home to pack. I think I'll hold off on calling my parents. I'll wait and surprise them. You can send Kendall home when you're ready. Mark's welcome, too, if you want to send him."

"Okay," I said as I watched her open the kitchen door to leave. "Oh, and Shar," I said, softly.

"Yes," she answered, spinning around to face me.

"I just wanted to say, thank you, and..." I paused momentarily. "I love you."

"Right back at you," she said with a wink. "Right back at you," she repeated softly as she closed the kitchen door. I poured myself another cup of coffee and made a mental list of things to do the next day.

I woke up early on Monday, anxious to start tying up loose ends. As I checked my list, I crossed off plane tickets. The night before I had charged four first class tickets to my Visa; two with an open return because I wasn't sure how long Sharleen was going to stay. I had also called my parents and informed them about what was going on. I wasn't surprised that they didn't go into the well deserved, I told you so's. That wasn't their style. Instead, they responded with outrage toward John and concern for Mark's and my safety. Then, Mom insisted on coming to Chicago and giving John a piece of her mind.

"I'm gonna give him more than that," I could hear Dad in the background. "Nobody messes with my baby and grandbaby," he huffed. I had to laugh. The thought of my father going after John created a cartoon image in my mind.

"Mom, tell Gerald 'The Tiger' Thomas, that won't be necessary. Actually, I'm calling because Mark and I are coming to Philly. I was hoping you and Dad could meet us at the airport."

"Oh, baby," Mom said in a voice that made it difficult to tell if it was good news or bad.

"What's the matter?" Dad asked anxiously.

"Oooh, I can't believe it," Mom wailed with happiness. Her reaction reminded me of the mother character in the "Klumps", when she would clap her hands, saying, 'Hercules, Hercules'.

"Toni, what's going on," my dad asked, irritated that he wasn't privy to our conversation. I could almost see him trying to press his ear to the receiver, next to Mom's.

"Gerald, give me room to breathe, please."
I could imagine Mom waving him off as if shooing away a pesky gnat.

"Well, tell me what's going on," Dad pleaded.

"It's good news, Gee," Mom snapped, using her little nickname for Dad. "Kayla and Mark are coming home on Wednesday. Sharleen and Kendall are coming with them."

"Good," Dad said, excitedly. "Tell her we'll be there to pick them up. Find out what time their plane is coming in. Ask her what airline they're using," Dad was barking out orders.

"Gee, will you calm down and be quiet. I'm going to get all the information," Mom hissed, exasperated.

I couldn't help but laugh at their comical exchange. It reminded me of when I was younger and had to hear their mini arguments all the time. But no matter how heated they got, they're anger never lasted for more than five minutes after the last word. I attributed this round to their being excited about our return. I hadn't seen my parents since John and I got married almost a year ago.

"Girl, whatever time you get here, it better be in plenty of time for me to get back home, spoil my grandson and go to Bingo," Mom laughed. But I knew she was joking with the truth. Bingo had been like a second job to my mother for over thirty years and she hated to miss a night.

Mom verified the information three times after she wrote it down, then we said our good-byes. As I was lowering the receiver from my ear, I could hear Dad in the background.

## If Loving Two is Wrong . . .

"Aw, Toni, I wanted to talk to her," he groaned.

"She hung up already, you'll see her on Wednesday," Mom responded.

"What am I getting myself into?" I laughed as I replaced the receiver.

Getting back to my list of things to do, next was call my realtor. We set up the terms for the sale of the house and she assured me that she would handle everything in my absence. I called Detective Robinson to find out if there was any information on John. She said she hadn't heard anything, but she would check and call me back within the hour. I knew I'd be leaving out soon, so I gave her my cell number. My next order of business was to call my lawyer. I informed him of the exigent circumstances and he told me to come right in. Then, I called Hertz to arrange for a rental car to be dropped off to me on Wednesday morning. I needed to handle the rest of things on the list in person, so I let out a stress-induced shriek and headed for the shower.

Mark Jr. had spent the night at Shar's house, so I called to make sure everything was okay.

"I have a few errands to run, Shar, can you keep Mark a little longer?"

"I'll bust you in the mouth, girl, asking me that silly question," she laughed. "Sometimes it's easier to have two kids than one. That way they occupy each other and leave me alone."

"I hear you," I chuckled. "I should only be a couple of hours. I'll bring lunch back. Any suggestions?"

"I think this would be a good pizza day. One pepperoni and one extra cheese should do the trick."

"Okay," I answered. "If I'm running late, I'll call."

"Alright," Shar said. "Anything I can do to help?"

"You're already doing it, sweetheart," I answered and we hung up. Half an hour later, armed with my 'to do' list; I set out on my mission.

## Chapter Twenty-Nine

I loved my lawyer. Don Fleming was so efficient. He was sixty-five, about 5'7and always wore impeccably tailored suits. He had a full head of black hair, thanks to a well-maintained toupee. But the gray eyebrows were a telltale sign that something didn't quite add up. Don's legal mind was sharp as a tack and I trusted him implicitly. I had given him a brief synopsis of events when I talked to him earlier that morning. When I arrived at the offices of Fleming, Lewis and Pearl at nine-thirty, he already had the divorce papers drawn up. As I looked around his distinguished office, I realized that I had only visited it twice. Once when Mark Sr. and I drew up our wills and again when John and I signed the prenuptial agreement. Any other meetings, business or social were held at either Mark and my house or Troy and Sharleen's.

Don used to handle all of Mark and Troy's legal issues. He and his wife, Barbara, had been like members of the family when Mark and I were married, but after I married John, we hardly saw each other. Don sympathetically held my arm and led me to the cherry wood chair in front of his desk. I sat down on the hard leather cushion and shifted, uncomfortably. I was embarrassed that I hadn't kept in touch since marrying John and now I was in his office asking for help to end this fiasco of a marriage. Don and Barbara had tried to dissuade me from marrying John when I had told them of my plans, but I politely declined their advice.

"Kayla, it's good to see you, I'm just sorry that it's under these circumstances," Don said, soothingly as he settled into his high-backed maroon leather chair.

"I know Don," I whispered, lowering my eyes. I didn't want to look at him over the heavy oak desk that separated us. "I feel like such a fool," I added sadly.

# If Loving Two is Wrong . . .

"Well, the most important thing when you've made a mistake is to recognize it, accept it and then find a way to correct it. That's what you're doing now. I'm just glad that you had the foresight to safeguard yourself," he smiled, leaning forward and placing his well manicured, dark chocolate hands on the desk. I couldn't help but smile as I listened to Don talk. Mark used to say that he dispatched advice like the father on the Brady Bunch and this time was no exception. I still wasn't ready to look him in the eye, so I gazed behind him, out the large picture window at the Chicago skyline.

We discussed my plans and went over the ironclad prenuptial agreement that prevented John from making any claims against assets that I had prior to our marriage. He had no claim to the house, or the 2000 Mercedes, which was in Mark Sr.'s and my name. The only thing that John was entitled to was half of the money in our joint account; most of which I had contributed. But truthfully, I didn't care about that. Money had never been an issue for me since my marriage to Mark. The marketing and consulting business that he and Troy owned was very successful.

While at the lawyer's, my cell phone rang. It was Detective Robinson. John hadn't gone before the judge yet. His charges included one count each of aggravated assault against Mark and me, as well as against the first two officers at the scene, and one count of vandalism. The idiot had kicked and shattered one of the squad car windows while they were escorting him to the wagon that night.

The detective couldn't say with any degree of certainty when John would be granted bail. But she felt that he could be released in a few days if he could pay his bail. After we hung up, Don and I continued discussing the best way to handle the divorce. By the end of our meeting, the old familiarity had set in. I felt comfortable when he came from behind his desk and embraced me before I left his office and headed to the bank.

"Come on into my office, Mrs. Redding," Mr. Cummings, the bank manager beckoned.

"Thanks, Charles," I smiled as we made our way through the crowded bank towards the offices in the rear. Charles, a forty-seven year old, handsome man with mocha colored skin, had been a regular houseguest of Mark Sr.'s and mine for years. That too, had changed when John entered the picture. A lot of Mark and my old friends had stopped coming around and calling during the past year. I shook my head with remorse at the thought of it.

"What can I do for you, Kayla?" he asked, converting to the first name basis we'd shared for years. I told him about my situation with John and he responded with sincere concern.

"Whatever I can do, Kayla, just let me know."

Since my name was on our account, Charles informed me that I was well within my rights to empty it out, which I did immediately. I didn't want John to have access to the money in case he was granted bail. He needed to use any and all of the time given to him to think about what he did and to contemplate his future. Once I got things settled to the point where I felt comfortable, I would release funds back into the account and remove my name. I'd leave enough for him to find an apartment for at least a year and have some spending money. I was also leaving the Benz for him. Before leaving the bank, I had called Detective Robinson. John's bail hearing still hadn't taken place yet. She said I could bring a copy of the divorce papers to her and she would see to it that he was served. I gave her a list of phone numbers and the address where I could be reached in Philly; I had already done the same for Don and Charles. I checked my watch and it was a quarter to twelve. It felt as if I had done a million things in a short amount of time, probably, because I had. I called Shar on my cell phone and told her to order the pizzas and I would pick them up. I stopped at the storage place, which was two blocks from the pizza parlor and leased space for six months. Finally completing my list, I picked up the two large pies and headed to Shar's.

## Chapter Thirty

"You're all heart, Kay," she said with disbelief as she cleared the paper plates from the kitchen table. "You don't owe that bastard anything but the measly twenty five hundred bucks that he contributed to your joint account. I can't believe you're going to leave him that much money. And the Benz...," she shook her head in disbelief.

"I know Shar," I responded wearily. "But I don't want him to be able to blame me for his failures. You know he's always saying that a black woman can sure tear a black man down. I left him with far more than he came with and I'm leaving with a clear conscience. Besides, that car has been nothing but a grim reminder of that tragic day."

"I hear you, girl, but I still say you're doing more than he deserves. Who really gives a rat's ass about his philosophy on the black woman? Look at him! He's lazy, he's shiftless, I mean, all of his unaccomplishments speak for itself," she huffed.

"I can't argue with you, Shar. We both know that John wasn't the ideal man, but he had never put his hands on me until that night. I never told you before, but he's always had an inferiority complex."

"What," Shar smirked.

"Yeah, he always felt like he was in competition with Mark's ghost."

"Reee-dic-u-lous," Shar scoffed. "There's no way he could compete with Mark, ghost or otherwise."

"I know, but right or wrong, I feel sorry for him. Besides, you know what they say. The Lord takes care of babies and fools. And John qualifies for both," I said sarcastically.

"Girl, you ain't never lied," Shar agreed and we

both shared a wry laugh.

Once again, we spent the night at Shar's. We all found it hard to sleep that night, each tossing and turning and I assumed, thinking of tomorrow. Mark and Kendall were probably excited about catching a plane. It was the second time for both of them. The first was a trip to Disney World when they were just two years old. I pictured Mark Sr., Mark Jr. and I, along with Shar, Troy and Kendall walking through the park and seeing the boys' faces as they rode the rides. I laughed aloud as I envisioned the boys as they stared with a degree of awe and fright at the seven-foot characters. We had a ball; but those were during happier times. Achingly, I pushed the memory from my mind.

In the past, my parents had been the ones to travel to Chicago, so there hadn't been much need to fly. Mark Sr. and I had some exciting trips planned for the future, but once again, I forced myself to close the door to my mental closet. I assumed that Shar was excited about surprising her parents with her visit. She had already called a few friends and made plans to get together with them. My mind was a potpourri of thoughts. I vacillated between excitement about returning home, anger over the cause of all this turmoil and nervous anticipation of starting all over again in Philly. The thought of renewing some old acquaintances really caused a stir in the pit of my stomach. One name in particular kept rising to the surface, Chloe Lane.

---

On Wednesday morning, we got off to an early start. The rental agent dropped off the car at eight o'clock and we were off by eight forty-five. I left two keys at Don's office; one was for the Mercedes and the other was to the storage locker where I had left John's belongings. I'd already told a few of my closest neighbors to keep an eye on the house. I also informed them that John was not supposed to be on the premises, and if they saw him, they should call the police. They were all more than happy to oblige me, considering none of them were fond of John.

After breakfast at IHOP, we headed to the airport.

## If Loving Two is Wrong . . .

We dropped off the rental car and caught the shuttle to our terminal. Since we still had about forty-five minutes before our plane boarded, I asked Shar to take the boys to the gift shop for some snacks and reading materials. While they were gone, I decided to call Detective Robinson for an update. John's bail had been set at fifty thousand dollars. He would need ten percent to walk. I knew the few family members that still spoke to him didn't have access to that kind of money. She said he was enraged by the restraining order and yelled that he was the one that needed protection.

"Wait until he gets the divorce papers," I commented. Then, I told her about how I had taken the money out of our joint account so he couldn't make bail.

"I wish I could be a fly on the wall when he finds out about the bank account," I chuckled.

"Wow," she laughed. "When he does get out, you're going to have one angry man on your hands."

"Too damn bad," I snapped, irritably. "He's lucky that I'm leaving him with anything. He needs to stew in a cell for awhile. He's so damn pathetic, I feel sorry for him. By the time he gets out, I will have restored his money, and then some, to the bank account. Plus, I'm leaving him the car. He should have more than enough for a new start and soothed feelings," I sighed, growing weary talking about John.

"Well, from my experience, Mrs. Redding, for men like John, it's more than a matter of money. They tend to think of their wives as property. And you leaving him hits him where it hurts, his pride and his ego."

"I'll just have to cross that bridge when I come to it." I frowned. I didn't want to talk about John and the future. I wanted to concentrate on leaving all thoughts of him and Chicago far behind.

"Well, I'm hoping you won't have to, Mrs. Redding, I really am."

"I'm sorry, what were you saying?" I asked, temporarily caught up in my own thoughts.

"I was saying that I hope that you won't ever have to

cross that bridge," she repeated.

"Me too, Detective. I want to thank you for all of your help," I said, sincerely.

"That's what I'm here for, Mrs. Redding. Good luck with your plans and I'll keep you updated with what's happening on this end."

"Thanks again," I said, before we hung up.

Just as the boarding call came out, my gang arrived with their hands full of bags.

"Wow, it's only a two hour flight," I laughed.

"They had so much good stuff, it was hard to decide," Mark said, his mouth already stuffed with Hershey's Chocolate Kisses. Sharleen and Kendall obviously agreed; remnants of chocolate bars surrounded the corners of their mouths, too.

"C'mon here, three Musketeers," I said as I pushed them toward the plane.

Fifteen minutes later we taxied down the runway.

"Ooh, look how fast we're going!" The boys screamed with delight as the plane sped up, preparing to take off. As we climbed into the air, their eyes widened and they both pressed their faces against the window. I leaned past Mark and watched as we headed farther and farther from the place I had called home for almost eight years. I said my silent good-byes to Chicago. There was nothing to go back for, and no one to go back to.

After twenty-five minutes, the boys had grown accustomed to flying. They had settled down and were engrossed in their self-imposed required reading, the latest X-Men comics. Sharleen couldn't decide if she wanted to sleep or read. I couldn't help but laugh as I looked behind me and watched her nod hard enough to wake herself up, then look at the book in her hand. It had held the same page for the last fifteen minutes. I decided to relax and catch a few winks, myself. Hopefully, when I woke up we would be landing. I removed the complimentary earphones from the rear pouch of the seat in front of me and placed them on my ears. I found an easy listening station and sat back, prepared to be lulled to sleep. Just as I was drifting into peaceful

## If Loving Two is Wrong . . .

oblivion, a song came on that caused me to bolt upright in my seat. My heart was racing at a thousand beats per minute as I realized that I was incorporating the music into a dream sequence. Breathing heavily, I scanned the plane to see if anyone had noticed my sudden reaction, apparently not. Shar had finally chosen sleep over her book. The boys weren't far off; they were struggling to read their comics. Their eyelids were fighting a losing battle, drooping as if they weighed a ton. As I caught my breath, I motioned to the stewardess for a cocktail, which I gulped half of immediately. Then I settled back into my chair. Only this time, I was more prepared for the song that had sent me into such a tizzy. This wasn't the first time that Prince's "Adore" had had that effect on me. I realized that I'd been dreaming about that fateful night at Chloe's apartment, when we had first made love. My mind drifted into as I replayed that scene, vividly, in my mind.

## Chapter Thirty-One

"Ladies and gentlemen, we are beginning our descent into the Philadelphia International Airport," the pilot's crackling voice came over the intercom, returning me to the present.

As we headed up the walkway from the plane, I could see my mother's head bobbing in the sea of faces anxious to greet their loved ones.

"Kayla, Mark Jr., here we are," she bellowed. In spite of my embarrassment, I had to laugh as everyone turned to see who the loud woman was screaming at. I just nodded my head in acceptance of my instant celebrity.

Tony and Keilani had come to the airport with my parents, and we all began to talk, excitedly, at once. There was at least ten minutes of hugging, kissing and talking, before we began to stroll to the baggage claim. I was lagging behind, caught up in the reality that I was back in Philadelphia for good. It felt wonderful to be home.

"Come on Kayla, get the lead out," Mom urged.

"Why are you in such a rush, Mom? Our luggage probably hasn't even been unloaded yet," I said, wrinkling my nose at her impatience.

"Well what if it is? You don't want anyone to steal it, or take the wrong bags, do you," she asked, almost galloping to the escalator.

"What's up with her?" I asked Tony.

"She's just excited that y'all are here," he responded, looking like the cat that just ate the canary. Keilani had a big ole lopsided grin on her face, too. Finally, I turned to my father.

"What's going on here, Dad?" I asked, hoping for some kind of alliance.

"Aw, you know your mother," was all he said,

# If Loving Two is Wrong . . .

giving away nothing. As we stepped off the escalator, there was a throng of people from our flight anxiously waiting at an empty baggage carousel.

"See, I told you that our luggage wasn't..."
Standing by a bank of pay phones, was a sight for sore eyes. Chloe looked the same as the day we met. I almost burst into tears as I watched her saunter over in my direction and engulf me in a tight embrace.

"You guys," I squealed in delight as we ended our hug. I hadn't seen Chloe since that chance spotting after Mark and my wedding. And I had talked to her only once since that fateful day when I stormed out of her apartment. There was so much that I wanted to say to her, but knew that it wasn't the time or place. I introduced her to Mark Jr., Sharleen and Kendall. The rumbling of the baggage carousel interrupted our reunion and we all concentrated on retrieving the correct bags. Once we were satisfied that all of the suitcases were accounted for, we piled into the three vehicles and headed to my parent's house, where a full scale welcome home party commenced immediately. The Fountaines had even stopped by. Although the strain of Mark's death still showed on their faces, I could tell that they were genuinely relieved that I had left John and came home with their grandson.

Sharleen and Kendall stayed with us for two days before heading home to New Jersey. During that time, Shar, Chloe and I spent a lot of time together. Shar and Chloe got acquainted, while Chloe and I got reacquainted. I was amazed at how we all bonded, as if we were all long, lost friends.

"Chloe is so nice," Shar had commented after the gathering on our first night home. "Is she married?"

"I don't think so," I answered, warily. Although I was being cautious, I realized that I really didn't know the answer to that question. I had been out of touch with Chloe for almost seven years. We exchanged the occasional Christmas card, but had agreed, over an intense phone conversation, that it was best not to continue a close relationship.

"Well, she sure is gorgeous. And nice, too," Shar repeated, oblivious to my faraway look. "I'm sure she's making some guy a very happy man," she said, refocusing her attention on me.

"Earth to Kayla, come in Kayla," she laughed, snapping her fingers to get my attention.

"Huh, what did you say," I asked, returning to our conversation. I had momentarily revisited my wedding day, seven years ago.

"Forget about what I was saying, where were you just now?" she asked, wide-eyed, searching for gossip.

"I was just thinking about how close Chloe and I used to be before I moved to Chicago," I lamented.

"Well, what happened? How come she never came out to visit? You hardly ever mentioned her, maybe once or twice," Shar said, striking a nerve.

"I guess we just lost touch with each other," I answered, trying to sound cavalier.

"Yeah, but if you two were as close as you say," Shar started, but I interrupted her.

"Shit happens," I snapped, immediately regretting my tone. I didn't mean to take out my pent-up frustration on her, but she was trying to travel down a road that I wasn't ready to travel just yet, at least not with her. Sharleen and I had experienced the most tragic event to ever happen in our lives, together. We were as close as stink on doo doo, and you know that's pretty damn close, but I wasn't ready to confide in her about Chloe and me. Not because I was ashamed, but I was still very protective about what Chloe and I had shared and I still felt a degree of guilt over how things ended.

I had called Chloe when Mark and I returned to Chicago after the honeymoon. After seeing her that day, I knew I had to talk to her. What she told me branded a permanent mark on my heart. Her divulgence convinced me that I couldn't keep in close contact with her. Not, if I wanted Mark and me to be happy. Sensing that I was uncomfortable with the subject, Shar decided to change it.

# If Loving Two is Wrong . . .

"So, how does it feel to be home?" she asked brightly. I understood what she was doing and was grateful to have such a dynamic friend. But I still knew that she didn't deserve my harsh tone.

"I'm sorry, Shar," I apologized. "I didn't mean to bite your head off. It's just that..." I paused, not knowing where to go from there.

"No worries," she said sympathetically. "If there's more to the story that you want me to know, you'll tell me when you're ready."

I grabbed her hands and squeezed.

"Thank you."

"For what?" she asked, perplexed.

"For being the best friend a girl could have," I said, close to tears.

"Aw, shut up girl before you make me cry," she said, smacking my hands away and embracing me. Although Shar never broached the subject again for the remainder of her stay, she kept a close eye on any interaction between Chloe and me. Before she left, she couldn't take it anymore. She vowed to get to the bottom of the situation, one day.

"Whatever you say, girlfriend," I said sweetly, as I tapped the roof of her rental car.

"Ooh, you're wicked," she laughed as she and Kendall drove off, waving, heading to Jersey.

Not long after Shar and Kendall left, Chloe pulled up and asked if Mark Jr. and I wanted to go for a ride. I asked him, even though I knew it was a moot point. Mark had developed a huge crush on Chloe, almost from the very beginning.

"Like mother like son," Chloe had joked when she first found out.

"Aren't you lucky?" I responded with a light punch on the arm. "If it was like father like son, Mark Jr. would be keeping as far away from you as possible," I smiled, reminiscing about the tension-filled first meeting between Mark Sr. and Chloe.

"Yeah, well that was a long time ago," Chloe sighed. "And under very intense circumstances."

Not wanting to get into it at that moment, I was relieved when Mark Jr. came bounding out the door and jumped off the porch.

"Where are we going, Miss Chloe?" he asked excitedly.

"It's a surprise," she answered, reluctantly taking her eyes off me and smiling at Mark. We ended up at the amusement park in Allentown, Pa and Mark yelled with excitement as he eyed the roller coaster looming up ahead.

"Yay!" I playfully joined Mark's excitement.

"Dorney Park. I used to come here with my family every year when I was a kid," I explained, elatedly.

"I remember you telling me that," Chloe said softly. A look passed between us, but I quickly turned away.

Inside the park, Mark kept us busy. When we couldn't all ride together, we alternated riding with him. I graciously allowed Chloe to be the one to take on the roller coasters and anything else that had to do with loop de loops, high speeds and spinning. During a cool down period, while Mark was on the merry-go-round, Chloe and I had a chance to talk, seriously. We both admitted to missing each other terribly over the seven years since I left.

"When I called you that day and you told me that you had never really met anyone in the Bahamas, that you just told me that to free me, I was flabbergasted. You could've knocked me over with a feather. But I knew that if we continued to communicate, it would wreak havoc on my marriage."

"I know," she nodded in agreement. "In retrospect, I guess I shouldn't have told you then, but I needed you to know that I didn't just cast you aside like you thought. I saw the pain you were in trying to juggle your emotions and thought it would be easier for you if I took the choice out of your hands."

My eyes began to glaze over as I thought about the sacrifice she had made.

"Well, the important thing is that you're here now,"

246

she smiled, attempting to bring some levity to the situation.

"Yeah, but look at the road I traveled to get here," I sighed. Just then, Mark Jr. screamed from the carousel. "Can I go around again, Mommy?"

"Yes baby," I laughed. Luckily, the park wasn't crowded, so we were able to ride many times without having to get back in line. After I watched to see where he was situated, I returned my attention to Chloe. Although Shar and I had recounted Mark and Troy's accident to Chloe, I repeated it again. Then I ran down the sordid details of my brief marriage to John.

"How did you even allow yourself to get entangled with that loser?" she asked, grabbing my hands and peering into my eyes.

"Good question," I responded. "I was weak. I knew I was vulnerable, but it just seemed easier to surrender than to struggle to keep it together," I surmised.

"I'm sorry you had to go through all of that by yourself," she said softly.

"I had Shar," I announced brightly, determined not to turn this into a pity party.

"Yeah, she seems like a great person," Chloe smiled.

"She is," I agreed. "She's also pretty observant. She sensed something about you and me," I laughed.

"What?" Chloe said, incredulously. "What did you tell her," a mischievous grin was plastered on her face.

"Nothing," I shrugged. "She sensed I didn't want to talk about it and changed the subject."

"Lucky you," Chloe laughed.

"Yeah," I chuckled, "but before she left, she vowed to get to the bottom of the situation. And if I know Shar, she won't rest until she gets answers."

"Come to think of it, I did feel as if she was scrutinizing me more closely after that first night," she said, rubbing her chin thoughtfully.

"Well Columbo," I laughed, "you and Kojak can have fun trying to figure each other out."

"Is there anything to figure out," Chloe asked,

eyeing me questioningly. Just then, Mark Jr. came running over to where we were sitting.

"You're not off the hook," Chloe mouthed, as Mark grabbed our hands and pulled us toward the pirate ride, again. By the time we left the park, it was dark and Mark was exhausted. A loud snore from the back seat assured us that he was asleep. Chloe pounced.

"Back to the question I asked earlier in the park," she smiled nervously.

"In a minute," I responded, stalling. "We've talked about me ad nauseam, what have you been doing over the last few years?"

"Ah, your stalling tactics," she smiled. "I remember them well. But I will indulge you. When you first left, I was very distraught. Some might even say despondent," she said, smiling wanly. "I decided to throw myself into my work."

"How sad," I said softly.

"Yeah, sad for me, but great for my clients. I was rolling over whoever got in my way in the courtroom. Companies were begging to settle rather than face me in litigation," she laughed in retrospect.

"Then what happened?" I asked curiously.

"Then I met Alyssa," she said as if in a trance.

"Alyssa," I repeated, complete with attitude and a frown.

"Yeah," she responded, ignoring my reaction.

"I had met Alyssa at that same club I took you to that time, remember?" she asked, not really expecting an answer.

"Um hmm," I grunted, anyway.

"She was so nice. At first, I kept her at arms length because I wasn't over you. But she understood and was very patient. As time went on, we became close."

"How close," I asked with a tinge of jealousy.
Chloe threw a quick look at me, as if to say she knew I couldn't possibly be jealous. I knew I had no right to be, but when had that ever stopped a jealous streak?

"Anyway," Chloe sighed wistfully, "it was good for almost two years."

## If Loving Two is Wrong . . .

"Then what happened," I asked, extremely interested. My heart was pounding.

"She decided to move to Atlanta," she said sadly.

"What?" I crowed. "Just out of the blue?" I asked, recalling her reaction when Mark had left me and went to Chicago.

"No, her mother was sick, so she wanted to be close to her. She asked me to come, but I wasn't prepared to make that kind of move. I often wonder how far things would've went if she hadn't left." A melancholy look briefly swept across her pretty face.

'I'm glad she did', I thought devilishly, but kept that to myself. Instead, I said, "Oh, I'm so sorry."

"Save it," Chloe said, laughing at my fake sincerity.

"You got me," I admitted. "Selfish as it may seem, I must admit that I'm happy you're not involved with anyone."

"Did I say I wasn't?" she asked coyly.

"Well are you?" I demanded, not up for a guessing game.

"What's with the 'tude?" she asked, smiling, undaunted by my tone.

"I just want to know," I responded, softening my voice.

"Would it make a difference?" she asked, determined to return to where we left off at the park.

"Smooth segue," I admitted, growing serious.

"Well, would it?" she urged.

"Chloe, I have been through more in the past two years than I could've ever imagined in a lifetime. Being in your presence again is like a gift from heaven, but honestly, I don't know how I want to proceed with the rest of my life. Not right at this moment."

I looked over at Chloe, who was gripping the steering wheel so hard that her knuckles were turning pale. She was staring straight ahead at the road, but I could tell that she was listening intently.

"I have to think about Mark Jr. and what's best for

him." I said, looking at the road.

"Are you implying that I couldn't be good for him," she asked stoically.

"Not at all," I said quickly. "Mark is already in love with you, but I don't know how that would translate if things were to become more between us," I answered honestly.

"I couldn't be any worse than that moron, John," she pouted defensively.

"You're right about that," I adamantly agreed.

"But I'm just not ready to make any life altering decisions just yet. I have too many variables to consider."

"Like what?" she inquired.

"Well," I began, "for starters, John and I aren't even divorced, yet. I just served him a few days ago. Secondly, I have to decide where I want to live. I sold my house, here, when Mark and I got married. And even though I love my parents dearly, Mark Jr. and I need our own space. Plus, " I said, surprising myself with my growing list, "I will have to go back to Chicago to tie up loose ends."

"What loose ends," she asked, trying to hide her disappointment about the flow of the conversation. Although I knew these weren't the words she wanted to hear, I felt I had to be honest. I was in such a tailspin right now. I didn't want to remind Chloe about the shroud of secrecy that we had lived in before I married Mark. I didn't want to chance hurting her again. I picked up the conversation where I left off.

"I still have to finalize the sale of the house and establish my position with the board of directors at the company. And lastly," I said, rolling my eyes, "I have to re-establish John's bank account."

"What?" Chloe screeched.

I relayed the whole sordid tale about the way I hastily wrapped things up before leaving Chicago.

"Wow, you did have some spunk left in you after all, huh?" she smiled in amazement.

## Chapter Thirty-Two

C hloe and I were growing closer and closer by the day, but we still didn't blur the lines of our friendship. After a month, things began to get hectic. There was a buyer for the house in Chicago, there were rumors floating around about a member of the board plotting a takeover and lastly, John was still stewing in jail, unable to raise the bail money.

Pam Henry, Mark Sr.'s longtime secretary had called and advised me that Teddy was trying to drum up support to oust Shar and me as co-CEOs. Chloe offered to accompany me back to Chicago while Mark Jr. stayed with my parents. I graciously accepted. I contacted Shar, who was still in Jersey and contemplating relocating, and told her I would handle the company business and check on her house. She readily accepted my offer. Although she was proud of the company because her husband helped build it, she wasn't interested in the details. Plus, as she put it, she was more than sure that Chloe and I would sock it to them good.

"Are you ready to disclose any information about you and Chloe?" she asked solicitously.

"Bye Shar," I laughed. "Give Kendall a kiss for me. As a matter of fact, bring him up to visit Mark."

"Okay," she promised. "But I still…" she was trying one last time, but I cut her off.

"I'll fill you in when I get back." I paused for a moment to let my words sink in.

"About the meeting, that is," I blurted out before I hung up laughing. I counted to three and sure enough, the phone was ringing. I knew it was Shar, my parents had caller ID.

"Yes Shar," I answered after the second ring.

"You stinking hussy," she said laughing. "You know

251

I thought you meant you would clue me in on the goods with you and Chloe, that's why I didn't push."

"I know," I giggled. "That's why I said it like that. I knew you couldn't resist the bait."

"C'mon Kayla, now you've really got me curious," she sulked.

"You're not curious," I corrected her, "you're nosy."

"Kayla," she whined.

"Look who's here," I said, interrupting her appeal.

"Who?" she asked coyly, "Chloe?"

"No," I answered sassily, "you know my brother Tone, right?"

"Yeah," she began. "I met him…"

I never heard the end of her sentence because I banged on her. I had never gotten over that time she did that to me when we were in Chicago. I vowed I would get her back and I just got the opportunity. After I finished having a good laugh, I realized she hadn't called back. I didn't want her to be mad at me, so I called her back.

"Kayla," she answered on the first ring, "the whole concept of that gag is to hang up because you don't want to talk anymore, not to call the person back and apologize," she said sarcastically.

"Oh," I said, dumbly. "Well since you already know Tone, you won't mind getting reacquainted," I said and hung up again. I waited ten seconds, no call back. 'I hope she's not angry;' I mused as I headed upstairs to bed.

A week later, Chloe and I headed to Chicago. I quickly realized how fortuitous it was that she came with me. Although Don was a great lawyer, Chloe was a pitbull. Her preparation and work ethic was well known in the courtroom and her reputation often preceded her. Prior to my presenting her to the board, Chloe had thoroughly researched the company. She knew everything about the investors, board members, holdings, percentages, assets, etc. By our second day in Chicago, Chloe had zeroed in on the renegade board member. When she told me that Theodore "Teddy" Haskins was the culprit, I was floored. Teddy was so unassuming, the consummate nerdy board member who knew nothing except crunching numbers.

"Yeah, they're the ones you have to watch closely," Chloe informed me. "They're experts with numbers, seem harmless and can be easily overlooked while they gather pertinent information. Then they look for weaknesses and wait for the right moment to pounce."

When I suggested that we talk to him privately, Chloe balked.

"Are you kidding me? I know you're soft hearted, Kayla, but this is business, big business. You have to handle this decisively and make an example of him to avoid situations like this in the future."

"I still can't believe it's Teddy," I sighed. "He had always been so polite and nervous acting, always twitching. And to think I used to feel sorry for him." The more I thought about his betrayal, the angrier I got.

"Do what you have to do Chloe, teach that sucker and any other ones that think they can get over on a couple of soft-hearted widows, a lesson."

The word widow instantly triggered thoughts of Mark. Chloe must've realized what I was thinking because she immediately embraced me and kissed me softly on the forehead. I returned her hug, then straightened up before a tear could fall.

"So what's your plan, counselor?" I asked, brightly, trying to change my demeanor.

"Do you trust me, Kayla?"

"Oh no, where had I heard that before," I chuckled.

"Shut up and answer the question," she smirked.

"Implicitly," I responded.

"Then watch me work."

I couldn't help but smile as I watched her grin turn serious, almost instantaneously. She smoothed the lapels on her gray pinstriped, tailor-made pantsuit, moved the streamlined black-rimmed glasses from her atop her forehead, to her nose and walked to the mirror on the wall. Chloe checked her flawless face in the mirror, placed a well manicured hand to head, making sure her austere bun was in place. Satisfied that there was not a rebel hair in sight, she turned to me.

"Let's go kick some corporate ass!" She winked and strode out the door.

Out of nowhere, I thought I heard the Partridge Family singing, 'I think I love you'. I shook my head to clear my mind then quickly joined Chloe.

When we entered the oak wood-paneled boardroom, everyone was seated around the oblong conference table. Ironically, Haskins, wearing an ill-fitting brown suit and striped blue shirt, had occupied one of the end seats that should've been reserved for either Sharleen or me. I attributed that to the informal meetings we used to have, where Shar and I had never bothered with seating etiquette. The voting board consisted of five men and three women besides Shar and me. Most had no idea why I had called this emergency meeting. Confusion was rampant among the furrowed eyebrows, but the worried look on Haskins's face was priceless.

Chloe's no-nonsense demeanor had set the tone. Everyone was wondering who she was and when they looked at me, I had on my poker face. I gave no indication of being the friendly, silent owner that they were accustomed to dealing with.

"Ladies and gentleman," Chloe dove right in, "my name is Chloe Lane and I am acting counsel on behalf of both Mrs. Redding and Mrs. Waters. It has come to their attention that at least one of you is no longer satisfied with your position in this company and believes that you can do a better job of running Water-Fountaine Advertising."

She paused for a moment allowing time for the sharp intakes of breaths and looks of utter disbelief. I zeroed in on Haskins. His nervous tics had kicked into high gear. He was performing a 'Lords of the Dance' beneath the table with his brown wing-tipped shoes and he was doing a drum solo atop the polished black chrome table.

"I'm not one for dramatics," Chloe deadpanned, a lie that almost cracked my serious visage. All eyes were on Chloe, enraptured.

## If Loving Two is Wrong . . .

"So," she continued, "I will come straight to the point. Mr. Haskins," she called his name sharply and then paused. I could almost hear the 'dah dah dum' that usually accompanied dramatic moments on television and in the movies. Everyone's focus immediately turned to Haskins.

"It has come to our attention that you have been trying to undermine the integrity of this company by falsifying account records to shareholders. You've also been sending memos to companies whose accounts are managed by Water-Fountaine Advertising, misrepresenting yourself as acting on behalf of Mrs. Redding and Mrs. Waters.

It was like watching a tennis match as all heads swiveled back and forth from Chloe to Haskins. Teddy cleared his throat as if preparing to comment on Chloe's accusations. His eyes were blinking in rapid succession and beads of perspiration had formed on his balding forehead just above his thinning, salt and pepper comb-over. The sweat served as a true testament to his guilty conscience, considering many were wearing sweaters and suit jackets in the cool meeting room. .

"Before you make any attempts to deny these accusations," Chloe continued, thwarting any chances of Haskins getting a word in, "I have copies of a few of the correspondences that you've sent."

She walked over to him and placed one of a few crisp, dark blue folders she held in her hands on the table in front of him.

"I've made copies for everyone, but before distributing them, I will give Mr. Haskins a chance to address the issue before him."

Even in the midst of such a serious moment, I was thinking of how proud I was of Chloe and how lucky I was to have her in my life, yet again.

Haskins slowly opened the folder and quickly perused the information inside. His expression was that of a deer caught in headlights. When he found his voice, it was shaky, but tinged with a hint of defiance.

"I don't know how you came up with these documents,

but I am not admitting to any wrong doing. I'm going to have my lawyer check into these allegations and this situation will be addressed accordingly."

By the time he finished his sentence, he was standing, clutching the rumpled folder in his hand. Haskins made a grand gesture of raising his head high and taking forceful strides to the door. After nervously fumbling with the knob for a moment, he swung the door wide and stepped through, allowing it to close on its own. I couldn't believe it. Was that fumbling Don Knotts act just a clever veneer for a cold, calculating menace? Chloe's voice brought me back to the matter at hand.

"Ladies and gentlemen, I deeply regret that a situation of this magnitude had to be brought into this boardroom today. But as you must understand by now, actions such as this cannot and will not be tolerated. Mrs. Redding and Mrs. Waters have always regarded the members of this board, as well as employees of this company as family. However, even families have rogue members that must be dealt with and that is what we were faced with today. I cannot stress enough that this is in no way a reflection on any of you," Chloe paused, giving each board member a personal glance, "but unfortunately, when an action like this occurs, we all must take extra caution to ensure it doesn't get to this point again."

Although she made sure to include them as being needed in the policing of business matters, it was clear that Chloe was putting everyone on notice that things would be watched much more closely from now on.

"Thank you for your time. I am sure that this ugly incident will not be repeated and Water-Fountaine Advertising can continue to share the camaraderie that it has always enjoyed in the past."

Chloe graced them with a warm, scintillating smile, removing a great deal of the chill that she had brought in with her. I allowed her to make a grand exit while I stuck around for a few minutes to put everyone at ease. We had already agreed not to meet up directly after the meeting. Chloe thought it best for her to come in suddenly and disappear just as quickly. 'Keep 'em off guard,' she had said. 'They'll never know if and when I may come again.' I had chuckled when she first said that, but when I finally left the office, I could see the wisdom of what had she said and could feel the impact her visit had on everyone in the office. It wasn't all bad. A lot of people, both women and men, were commenting on the beautiful bombshell that came in like a lion and went out like a... well, a beautiful lion.

Back at the hotel, where Chloe and I shared a nice two-bedroom suite, we had a giant laugh over the whole scenario. We had no doubt that everyone felt on notice and we literally picked apart every facial and body movement of everyone involved.

"But seriously, Chloe, you were unbelievable today. I felt so proud of you. I literally had to concentrate to pay attention to the matter at hand instead of you. You were mesmerizing."

"Oh, really," Chloe said with a sly smirk. "How mesmerizing was I," she asked, teasingly.

"Enough that I thought to get you this." I reached into my purse and got out a gift certificate for a massage and spa treatment at the hotel.

"Thank you, Kayla," she said, slowly, reading the information on the card. She had a half smile on her face and her eyebrows were raised as if in resignation. I wasn't sure, but her reaction left me wondering if she was hoping for something else.

"I could really use a nice massage. You're coming with me, aren't you?" She raised her eyes to me. I knew Chloe well enough to know that she was forcing the extra bright smile that was plastered on her face.

"You better know it," I laughed, uneasily. I knew and felt the opening to revisit the place that we had shared so many years ago. But I was not ready for that kind of emotion just yet.

"C'mon, it's only one o'clock, we can get in on the one thirty session," I said, pulling her toward the door.

The next morning, I was at the office by eight

o'clock. Chloe arrived half an hour later, just fifteen minutes before Haskins and his attorney. Haskins had decided not to take things any further, considering the criminal element related to his actions. Begrudgingly, he took his lawyer's advice and resigned, taking the meager package offered to him. When we left the office that day, I was more than sure that I wouldn't have to address anything like that again. Chloe had already spoken to, as well as sent out the necessary memorandum to the shareholders and companies that were affected by Haskins's manipulations.

Next, we tackled the John debacle. Chloe found a way to fast track the divorce, restored money to John's account and made a provision that it couldn't be accessed until we notified the bank that we were back in Philadelphia. John also had to sign a document stating that he wouldn't attempt to contact me in any form or fashion once he was released. That was also a condition before he could touch any money, another one of Chloe's initiatives. Lastly, we finalized the sale of the house. That was such a weight off my shoulders and Chloe was wonderful. She handled the whole transaction. I hadn't realized the toll it was going to take on me to be back in Chicago and to let go of the house where Mark and I had spent so many happy times and celebrated the birth of Mark Jr. The trip had been completely successful, thanks to Chloe, but very exhausting. And on the fourth day, we rested and enjoyed all of the luxuries our hotel had to offer.

It started with a hearty breakfast, consisting of all the things Chloe used to make on Sundays so many years ago. Then we half-heartedly worked out, laughing at each other most of the time. Later, we sat around the indoor heated pool, reading the latest magazines and drinking cocktails. Next, it was off to the sauna, followed by a manicure and pedicure. After a brief nap, we ordered room service and dined in on lobster, New York strip steak, salad, string beans almandine, baked potatoes, rolls and a bottle of White Zinfandel. We struggled to eat the huge slices of chocolate cake and passed out halfway through. When we woke up four hours later, we were still stuffed. Chloe rented

## If Loving Two is Wrong . . .

a movie from the hotel's list and we finished the bottle of wine. At some point, we both drifted to sleep and were awakened by the shrill sound of the telephone.

"Good thing you ordered that wake-up call," I said as Chloe hung up.

"I know that's right," she answered groggily. "But I still have a few more hogs to call."

"Well call them on the plane," I laughed, throwing my pillow at her and heading to the shower.

An hour and a half later, we were taxiing down the runway. Neither of us exhibited any signs of the hangover we were both harboring.

"Can I offer you ladies a drink?" the friendly male flight attendant offered, once we were comfortably in the air.

"Bloody Mary, please," Chloe and I said in unison.

"I see," the flight attendant smiled as he prepared the mixture. After receiving our drinks, we settled back into our seats. I was grateful for all the space that first class offered as I stretched my legs out in front of me. I peeked over at Chloe. She was sipping her drink, sunglasses firmly in place, shielding her eyes from the offending sun.

"What is it Kayla?" she asked, obviously catching me with her peripheral vision or just feeling my vibe.

"I was just thinking how lucky I am to have you in my life," I answered, half-truthfully.

"Yes you are," she responded casually. "We're both lucky," she compromised," now get some rest."

I reached past her and pulled the window shade down. Then, I settled comfortably into the soft leather chair. As I closed my eyes, preparing to drift off, my mind was filled with thoughts of Mark and Chloe. The same thoughts I was pondering a few moments ago when Chloe felt me looking at her. Can my heart stand another chance at love?

## Chapter Thirty-Three

While Chloe and I waited at the baggage claim, I called my parent's house.

"Hi Mom, Chloe and I are at the airport. We're waiting for our luggage."

"Hey baby, I'm glad you two made it back safely," Mom crowed into the phone. "How'd things go?"

"Everything went really well. I'll tell you all about it when I see you. How's Mark?"

"How's Mark? How do you think he is? I managed to raise you and your brother without killing the two of you, didn't I?" she snapped.

Home, sweet home.

"I didn't mean it like that, Mom," I sighed.

"I know, baby. I'm just joking with you. Now you know who you get your funny side from. But seriously, Mark is with Tony and Keilani. They went to Wildwood and picked up Kendall on the way."

"Oh, that's nice. I'm glad Tony and Keilani enjoy spending time with Mark like that."

"Enjoy it," Mom said, incredulously, "shoot, you better watch it, they've been acting like 'The Hand That Rocks The Cradle' around here. Me and your father barely get a chance to see the boy. Every time I turn around, they're picking him up and taking him somewhere. Well, anyway," she said with an exaggerated sigh, "what time will you two be coming here?"

"I'm not sure, Mom. I think we're going to stop at Chloe's place first. I'll probably be there for awhile."

Chloe heard that comment and looked at me questioningly. It was an impulsive statement, but I knew we needed to resolve some things.

"Well if y'all ain't here before six o'clock, you won't see me until I get home from Bingo. And how come y'all didn't call and let someone know you was getting in today?"

"We wanted to surprise you," another spontaneous statement.

"Well aren't you burnt," she chuckled. "The surprise is on you, cause ain't nobody gonna be here to greet you. Tony, Keilani and Mark are at the shore, I'm going to bingo and your father's going up the street to watch the fight. I bet you'll think twice next time before you call yourself sneaking into town and surprising somebody."

"Mom, I can barely hear you, you're breaking up," I lied, making crackling noises into my cell phone.

"I'll break you up," she laughed. "I know you're making that noise with your mouth. Anyway, tell my baby, Chloe I said hi and I'll see y'all later."

"Okay, Mom."

"Was everyone surprised to here we're back?" Chloe asked.

"Yeah, they were surprised alright. So surprised that nobody's going to be home," I laughed.

"Whaaat,"Chloe gawked in amazement.

I gave her a complete rundown of the conversation with my mother. When I finished, the baggage carousel had begun making its rounds. Chloe and I grabbed our bags and went outside to hail cab.

We were both quiet for the half-hour that it took to reach Chloe's condo. I reflected on the past few days that we had spent together and was contemplating the conversation that I planned to have with her. When I occasionally looked at her, Chloe wore a pensive expression. She'd alternate between staring straight ahead and out her side window.

What am I going to do?

When we arrived in front of Chloe's building, she paid the cab driver and waited for me. I hesitated, lost in a déjà vu moment. This was the first time since being back in Philly that I had been to Chloe's apartment. The unfamiliar doorman greeted us with a smile as he held the door wide.

"I'll have your bags brought up, Ms. Lane," he said, tipping his hat.

"Thank you, Randy. By the way, this is Ms. Redding. If she ever comes by herself, it's okay to let her in."

"Yes, ma'am," he answered, "pleasure to meet you, Ms. Redding."

"Nice to meet you, also, Randy. But you can call me Kayla," I smiled, trying to level the playing field.

"Yes ma'am," he grinned sheepishly as we passed him by.

"You know he won't," Chloe said, tipping her head in my direction. "I've already tried that."

"Yeah, I know, but it just seemed awkward to have someone so young looking call me Ms. Redding. For anyone to call me Ms. Redding," I frowned at the mention of my married name. "I'm going to have to change that," I sniffed in repulsion. "Anyway, what happened to Mr. Williams," I asked, fearing the worst.

"Oh, he retired about four years ago. He was almost seventy when you left," she informed me. "We've had one other doorman before Randy came. Everyone seems to like him."

"Well how old is he?"

"I don't know, exactly, Kayla. But I think he's in his early thirties. Why, are you interested?" she asked, watching me with elevated eyebrows.

"Nooo," I answered, sucking my teeth. "He's just such a contrast to Mr. Williams, who I remembered." I was trying to make sure Chloe knew that I wasn't interested in the doorman.

"Cool it," Chloe, said. "I was just joking."

"I can't tell," I teased. I figured she was just heating up for the verbal sparring match that she assumed was about to occur behind closed doors. Her demeanor had become increasingly subdued since the cab ride. But what she didn't know was that I didn't have much fight left in me. When I heard her tell the new doorman to give me full access to her apartment, I knew she was making a statement and it felt good. It felt right. I felt as though I belonged someplace, again. I realized that being with Chloe felt like home.

I was watching her intensely as she walked ahead of me

toward the elevator. With each step I was closing the gap, not only physically, but emotionally as well. Once on the elevator, I faced Chloe and grabbed her hands. She cocked her head and looked at me with furrowed brows.

"What's going on, Kayla?"

"I don't know," I answered, honestly. "I'm just doing what my mind and heart are telling me." Just then, the elevator doors opened and a short, light-skinned elderly woman with bluish gray hair was standing there. She was wearing a light blue polyester pant set, with white, open-toed Dr. Scholls and a look of suspicion. I was acutely aware that I was still holding Chloe's hands, but I didn't release them. This was definitely a defining moment for me. The older woman's expression had changed to stone, indecipherable as she said, "Sorry, I hit the wrong button." As the doors closed, I thought I saw a slight scowl on her face. I couldn't quite tell, but then again, I didn't really care.

Once again, Chloe looked at me quizzically.

"What's going on here, Kayla?"

Before I could answer, the elevator came to a halt again.

"This is our stop," she announced, gently disengaging one of her hands from my grasp. When the doors opened, she gave a slight tug with her other hand, which I still held firmly in mine, leading me to her door. She pulled the key from her right jacket pocket and placed it into the lock. As she turned the knob, she faced me.

"Home sweet home," she said with a wry smile.

Once we entered the condo, I pulled the door secure and then pulled Chloe towards me. I took hold of her other hand again, securing them both gingerly within mine. I wanted to regain some of the momentum that I had in the elevator before I lost my nerve.

"I had wanted to take hold of your hand in the taxi, but I didn't for fear of what the driver might think," I said softly.

"I was wondering why you were looking so pensive," Chloe interrupted.

"Yeah," I continued. "I was thinking about how wonderful you've been these last few weeks, last few years, actually. From the day we met, you've been having a big impact on my life."

"Hmmph, tell me about it," she said with a lopsided grin.

I was determined not to be sidetracked, so I ignored her sarcasm.

"Chloe," I said, looking deeply into her eyes, "You've been my rock, my conscious, my best friend and even a martyr, at great expense to your own happiness."

I could see tears forming in her beautiful hazel eyes and I lifted my hand to wipe them away, before continuing.

"When I think back to all you've sacrificed and the way I've acted, I'm embarrassed."

"Kayla don't," Chloe began with a half sob."

"No Chloe, it's true. See, you're trying to do it again. You've always tried to protect me. Now it's time to let me care about your heart and your feelings. I can't say that I've figured everything out, yet, but I do know that I can't deny my feelings for you."

"Oh Kayla," Chloe said, almost choking with emotion. "I've waited so long to hear you say those words. As long as I know that I have your heart, fully, the details don't matter so much."

I knew what she was saying and had to smile. Once again she was letting me off the hook. I decided to leave it at that because I wasn't sure how I would tell my family. But I did know with Mark gone, there would be no one else to divide my heart. We sealed our admissions with a soul-searching kiss, which was interrupted by a sharp rap on the door. As we parted, I almost laughed aloud at the glassy look on Chloe's face.

"I don't know what you find so funny," she said, looking down her nose at me. "You've got that lovin' feelin' look on your face, too," she grinned, so in tune with my thoughts.

"Just get the luggage," I growled, playfully pushing her toward the tapping sound.

At five thirty, I called my mother and told her I would be over in the morning since she and Dad wouldn't be home until late and Mark Jr. wasn't due back until tomorrow evening.

"Yeah, yeah, fine," she said, attempting to rush me off the phone. "Dorothy's outside honking the horn like she's crazy. I never honk like that when I'm the one driving to Bingo."

"Oh, Mom," I said, slowly, emphasizing each syllable. "You know Aunt Dorothy means well, she just…"

"Oh, Kayla, I don't have time for your slow talking foolishness. I'm running late, bye." The next sound I heard was her hanging up. I just stood there looking at the receiver.

"Hurricane Toni late for Bingo?" Chloe asked, chuckling at my reaction.

"You know it," I responded with a head nod.

"Well, seeing that we have the rest of the evening to ourselves, what say we get a few videos, a bottle of wine, some take out and relax," Chloe said, eyeing me for approval.

"Sounds like a plan to me."

When we returned from getting all of the necessary ingredients for our evening, Chloe went into the kitchen for plates and glasses. I took a moment to look around. I was amazed at how natural it felt to be back here. I walked past the kitchen to my old room in the back. I was surprised to see the color scheme had changed. The once pale pink bedroom was now peach. Shock was quickly replaced with jealousy.

"Was this Alyssa's favorite color," I wondered aloud.

"As a matter of fact, it wasn't," Chloe whispered from behind. "I changed the color the day I saw you disappear in that limo and knew I had truly lost you. I couldn't bear returning to my place and seeing that room day after day. Knowing that you used occupy that room and how much you loved the décor. I had to change it or it would drive me nuts" she said, sadly.

"I understand," I commiserated, feeling guilty for my childish jealousy.

"C'mon Gloomy Glenda, let's go eat before the noodles

gets cold." Chloe nudged.

Upstairs in Chloe's room, we were nestled on the bed, feeling quite full after our Chinese smorgasbord. Chloe poured us both a glass of wine and we sat back, prepared to watch the movies that she had chosen.

"These had better be some good flicks," I warned her, teasingly.

"You know me," she laughed as she pressed the start button for the DVD player. What I saw on the screen made me roar with laughter.

"Oh, no you didn't," I said, snorting.

"Oh, yes I did, "she replied, giggling. And we both settled down, determined to give our undivided attention to 'Beloved'.

# If Loving Two is Wrong . . .

## Chapter Thirty-Six

Chloe and I had spent the night peacefully in each other's arms. When I awoke, I was surprised to be alone. But as soon as I smelled the coffee and bacon, I knew what was going on. It was Sunday, after all. I rushed downstairs to find Chloe performing the Sunday ritual that I had grown accustomed to so many years ago.

"Hungry, babe?"

"I like the sound of that," I said, feeling a little frisky.

"What? Hungry?"

"Don't be smart," I said, reaching by her to get a strip of crispy bacon.

"I know what you mean, baby," she laughed.

Suddenly I giggled at my own private thought.

"What's so funny?" she inquired.

I found myself relating the story about the time I was at the family barbecue and felt butterflies every time she called me 'baby' over the phone.

"What?!" Chloe screeched as if I had just said the most ridiculous thing in the world.

"Yeah," I defended. "You have to remember, everything was so new to me."

"Yeah, I guess you're right. I can see you feeling like that, considering I ain't nothing to sneeze at," she said with a sly smirk on her face.

"Alright, Miss Conceited," I laughed. "Can we eat before your head gets any bigger and bumps me completely out of the kitchen?"

"Whatever you say, babe," she laughed, heartily.

"But seriously," I interrupted her comedic moment. "You're going to have to stop cooking like this. We're not getting any younger and we can't eat like we used to."

"Speak for yourself, honey. I've been the same size

eight for the last fifteen years. Now shut up and pass me the jelly."

When we finally went to my parent's house, it was like a big celebration. Everyone was there: Mom, Dad, Tony, Keilani, Mark Jr., Sharleen, Kendall, Chloe and I were all gathered around the dinner table. I was relating the story of how Chloe had handled the Haskins fiasco for the third time. All of the adults were fascinated with her business acumen and the kids liked all the faces and motions I made while mimicking the board members, especially Teddy. But for some reason, I kept feeling like I was the focus of someone's extreme attention, besides Chloe.

"That Teddy Haskins, or whatever his name is sounds like a pure 'D' nut to me," Mom crowed, ending with a clucking sound. "Shoot, that outfit alone should've gotten him fired," she scoffed, dead serious.

Just as I was throwing my head back in laughter, I caught her. Shar was watching me with narrowed eyes, which made me cut my horselaugh short. Lowering my head and closing my gaping mouth, I tried to mirror the look on Shar's face as I followed her gaze from me to Chloe. All I could do was smile and shake my head. Sharleen was determined to get to the bottom of this and I decided that I would need an ally in my relationship with Chloe until I was ready to tell my family. Although I knew it was inevitable that I would hook up with Jackie again, I didn't want to discuss Chloe and my relationship with her until it was in the open. Jackie had a way of letting things slip out of her mouth without thinking sometimes and I didn't want to leave anything to chance. Besides, Chloe had already informed me that Jackie had wrecked her last nerve trying to find out the "real deal" about her and me, but Chloe hadn't budged.

'I can't wait for that initial meeting', I thought, wryly.

After desert, the boys were in the living room playing video games and the adults were in the den having coffee and conversation. The sound of the doorbell, brought everyone's talking to a halt, momentarily.

"I'll get it," I offered, anxious to get away from Shar's annoying stare.

# If Loving Two is Wrong . . .

The Fountaines were at the door and after hugging and kissing each of them; I directed them to the living room to see Mark Jr. and advised them that the adults were in the den. I barely had the door closed, before Shar accosted me.

"I'm not going anywhere until you tell me what's going on between you and Chloe," she said in a low growl, poking me playfully in the ribs.

"Girl, you are one stone cold nut," I laughed. "You must be part bloodhound the way you stick with a scent."

"When I'm onto something, I can be relentless," she admitted. "Besides, there's something palpable emanating from you two."

"Really," I asked in a conspiratorial tone. "C'mon here," I said, opening the door and pulling her outside.

"What do you mean something palpable," I asked with nervous tension.

"Aww girl, I just thought that sounded good. I figured it would push you over the edge," she cackled.

"Shut up, Shar. That's not funny," I said in a hushed tone.

"Damn, ain't nobody out here, Kayla. Why are you acting so paranoid? I'm onto something ain't I," she asked, narrowing her eyes in anticipated triumph.

"Yeah, you're onto something," I sighed.

"Hot dam, I knew it," she crowed, slapping her thigh.

"Look Shar, this isn't easy for me," I said, my tone pleading for understanding.

"I'm sorry, sweetheart," she responded, her whole demeanor changing to nothing but concern. "It's just that from the moment I saw you and Chloe interact, I felt there was something going on there, something deeper than just friends. She always looks at you adoringly and you look at her like an admiring fan. I know I was picking, but we've grown so close, it bothered me to think that you would hold something that you're feeling back from me. I just wanted to find out, but I'm sorry if I took it too far," she said, sincerely.

"No, you were right," I plunged in, deciding it was now

269

or never. "Before Mark and I got back together, I had been involved in a relationship with Chloe. It was after he had left for that long period of time to start the business. I was waiting for him, but when I didn't hear from him for so long," I paused in reflection.

"Sssh, Kayla," Shar said, wrapping her arms around me. "You don't have to explain. I know how deeply and fully you loved Mark. And I know if you had something with Chloe, it must've been very special."

Stepping back from Sharleen, I was looking at her with a renewed sense of adoration and a hint of surprise.

"Oh girl, please. I am from New Jersey, not East Jablip. But you will have to fill me in on the details," she drawled.

"I will," I promised. I just felt so relieved to tell someone and was especially glad that it was Sharleen. I didn't know how she would react, but was I pleasantly surprised by her response. Suddenly, the front door opened and Chloe came out to join us.

"Speak of the devil," Shar said with a smirk.
Chloe was caught off guard and raised her brow at Shar's remark.

"I told her about us," I informed Chloe, who immediately turned back to Shar.

"It's all good, girlfriend. "Your secret is safe with me," she said, embracing Chloe.

"Hey, watch it," I said, jokingly.

"Don't start, Kayla," Shar grinned, rolling her eyes. When we were about to step into the house, a familiar sound was coming from a light blue Cadillac rolling down the street. It was a convertible and the hood was down. The light skinned woman was bobbing her head to the music. She looked happy and carefree. As she passed the house I could hear the distinct sound of Frankie Beverly, singing, "Joy and pain are like sunshine and rain". A smile crossed my lips. I had a feeling that there would be nothing but rainbows in my future.

# PREY FOR LOVE – Leyton Wint

*All he needs in this life of sin, is his gun and his girlfriend.*

Not only does Alex "Lex" Walker kill people for a living, but he's good at what he does. Skills and discipline has Lex at the top of his game and the gig in Miami seems to be just another step towards retiring rich. That is, right up until he crosses paths with Chaine, a mysterious sensually daring beauty who's got all the right moves and the curves to match. Love isn't on his agenda, but Lex soon finds himself caught up. Distracted by an intense love affair, Lex is unable to see that the girl of his dreams just might be his worst nightmare. As the lines between business and personal get blurred he finds himself on a wild ride fueled by sex, exotic locations, and gunplay.

In the world of murder-for-hire hitting your mark means the difference between survival and starvation, and falling in love is a liability that could cost everything. The game that once showed him love threatens to take Lex under. It's a fight for his freedom, fortune, and his very life; as the predator becomes the prey.

www.myspace.com/preyforlove
www.preyforlove.com

# _Raw_

## _Money make me cum – money, money make me cum . . ._

Chastity Jones is the real thing. She's beautiful, she's classy, and she's got money to spend. Other people's money. As long as there are men around, 19-year-old Chastity will be rolling in their dough.

It wasn't always like that – her father was sent to prison when she was 16, and after being placed in a foster home, she was brutally raped.

She runs away, and starts stripping at a men's club, and there she catches the eye of Legend, a mysterious and handsome 6-4 hunk with straight black hair that hangs over his shoulders. His brownstone parties are famous – attended by celebrities, ballers, and hustlers alike. But the real parties are in his basement; sex parties that include girl-on-girl action, and even kinkier fare. His parties are so successful he easily clears $25,000 to $40,000 a weekend.

For Chastity it's love at first sight, but try as she might Legend only treats her like a little sister –and under his tutelage Chastity is soon hanging with the big dawgs. They buy her cars, pay the rent on her condo, buy her expensive jewelry and take her on shopping sprees. But the man she wants most shows her no romantic interest; and that's Legend.

And then she meets Hunter – he's a drug kingpin with millions of dollars, and also Legend's cousin – and he falls for Chastity in a big way. Suddenly Chastity is caught up in a whirlwind of money, sex, drugs and danger – and the only way out lies in death.

_www.myspace.com/rawnovel_
_www.rawnovel.com_

# Harlem Godfather: The Rap on My Husband, Ellsworth "Bumpy" Johnson

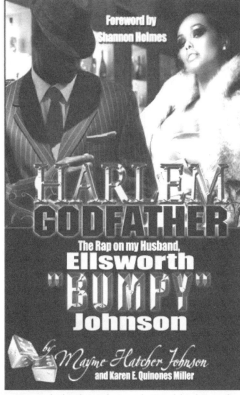

Forget Nicky Barnes and Frank Lucas, when it came to Harlem the undisputed king of the underworld was, Ellsworth "Bumpy" Johnson.

He was called an old-fashioned gentleman. He was called a pimp. A philanthropist and a thief. A scholar and a thug. A man who told children to stay in school, and a man whom some say introduced heroin into Harlem. Bumpy used his fists and his guns to get what he wanted, but he also used his money to help those in need. To this day – forty years after his death – people still sing his praises.

And no one more than his 94-year-old widow, Mayme Hatcher Johnson, author of *Harlem Godfather: The Rap on My Husband, Ellsworth "Bumpy" Johnson.*

Read the real story of the larger than life Bumpy Johnson, who was portrayed in the blockbuster movies *Cotton Club, Hoodlum*, and *American Gangster.*

Find out Bumpy's *real* relationship with Frank Lucas. And learn the story of a real man -- who never snitched – and loved as hard as he fought.

www.harlemgodfather.com

# THE GUIDE TO BECOMING THE SENSUOUS BLACK WOMAN (AND DRIVE YOUR MAN WILD IN AND OUT OF BED!)

*The Guide To Becoming The SENSUOUS Black Woman And Drive Your Man Wild In And Out Of Bed! by "Miss T."*

EDITED BY KAREN E. QUINONES MILLER

*LADIES . . . DON'T LET YOUR HUSBAND OR BOYFRIEND READ THIS BOOK! SOME SECRETS NEED TO BE KEPT TO OURSELVES!*

Ever wonder why some women seem to get all the men? Even the ones who are no where near as good looking as you? Wondering what it is they've got that you don't? They're tuned into their SENSUAL-ITY! These are The Sensuous Black Women, and you can join their number by reading **The Guide To Becoming The Sensuous Black Woman (And Drive Your Man Wild In And Out Of Bed!)**

Sensuality/Sexuality Tips Include:
- How to Attract a Man From Across The Room
- Been Bad While He's Away? Learn exercises and remedies that will ensure he'll never know.
- Find out how Lifesavers™ can make more than just your "breath" tasty!

**Oshun**
PUBLISHING

www.oshunpub.com

Oshun Publishing Company, Inc., 7715 Crittenden Street, #377, Philadelphia, PA 19118
**(Please Print!)**

Name:

_____

Address:

_____


_____

City:_____ State:___ Zip Code:_____

**If Loving Two is Wrong**   Quantity: ___ ($12 plus $3.00 for shipping & handling for each book.)

**Raw: An Erotic Street Tale**   Quantity: ___ ($12 plus $3.00 for shipping & handling for each book.)

**Prey For Love**   Quantity: ___ ($12 plus $3.00 for shipping & handling for each book.)

**Harlem Godfather**   Quantity: ___ ($12 plus $3.00 for shipping & handling for each book.)

**The Guide to Becoming The Sensuous Black Woman**
Quantity: ___ ($12 plus $3.00 for shipping & handling/each book.)

**All books are also available in bookstores nationwide!**